The Spen

A Tale of the Third

Harry Leon Wilson

Alpha Editions

This edition published in 2024

ISBN : 9789361471766

Design and Setting By
Alpha Editions
www.alphaedis.com
Email - info@alphaedis.com

Contents

FOREWORD

The wanderers of earth turned to her—outcast
of the older lands—
With a promise and hope in their pleading,
and she reached them pitying hands;
And she cried to the Old-World cities that
drowse by the Eastern main:
"Send me your weary, house-worn broods and
I'll send you Men again!
Lo, here in my wind-swept reaches, by my
marshalled peaks of snow,
Is room for a larger reaping than your
o'ertilled fields can grow.
Seed of the Main Seed springing to stature and
strength in my sun,
Free with a limitless freedom no battles of
men have won,"
For men, like the grain of the corn fields, grow
small in the huddled crowd,
And weak for the breath of spaces where a
soul may speak aloud;
For hills, like stairways to heaven, shaming the
level track,
And sick with the clang of pavements and the
marts of the trafficking pack.
Greatness is born of greatness, and breadth of
a breadth profound;
The old Antaean fable of strength renewed
from the ground
Was a human truth for the ages; since the hour
of the Edenbirth
That man among men was strongest who
stood with his feet on the earth!

SHARLOT MABRIDTH HALL.

CHAPTER I.

The Second Generation is Removed

When Daniel J. Bines died of apoplexy in his private car at Kaslo Junction no one knew just where to reach either his old father or his young son with the news of his death. Somewhere up the eastern slope of the Sierras the old man would be leading, as he had long chosen to lead each summer, the lonely life of a prospector. The young man, two years out of Harvard, and but recently back from an extended European tour, was at some point on the North Atlantic coast, beginning the season's pursuit of happiness as he listed.

Only in a land so young that almost the present dwellers therein have made it might we find individualities which so decisively failed to blend. So little congruous was the family of Bines in root, branch, and blossom, that it might, indeed, be taken to picture an epic of Western life as the romancer would tell it. First of the line stands the figure of Peter Bines, the pioneer, contemporary with the stirring days of Frémont, of Kit Carson, of Harney, and Bridger; the fearless strivers toward an ever-receding West, fascinating for its untried dangers as for its fabled wealth,—the sturdy, grave men who fought and toiled and hoped, and realised in varying measure, but who led in sober truth a life such as the colours of no taleteller shall ever be high enough to reproduce.

Next came Daniel J. Bines, a type of the builder and organiser who followed the trail blazed by the earlier pioneer; the genius who, finding the magic realm opened, forthwith became its exploiter to its vast renown and his own large profit, coining its wealth of minerals, lumber, cattle, and grain, and adventurously building the railroads that must always be had to drain a new land of savagery.

Nor would there be wanting a third—a figure of this present day, containing, in potency at least, the stanch qualities of his two rugged forbears,—the venturesome spirit that set his restless grandsire to roving westward, the power to group and coordinate, to "think three moves ahead" which had made his father a man of affairs; and, further, he had something modern of his own that neither of the others possessed, and yet which came as the just fruit of the parent vine: a disposition perhaps a bit less strenuous, turning back to the risen rather than forward to the setting sun; a tendency to rest a little from the toil and tumult; to cultivate some graces subtler than those of adventure and commercialism; to make the most of what had been done rather than strain to the doing of needless more; to live, in short, like a philosopher and a gentleman who has more golden dollars a year than either philosophers or gentlemen are wont to enjoy.

And now the central figure had gone suddenly at the age of fifty-two, after the way of certain men who are quick, ardent, and generous in their living. From his luxurious private car, lying on the side-track at the dreary little station, Toler, private secretary to the millionaire, had telegraphed to the headquarters of one important railway company the death of its president, and to various mining, milling, and lumbering companies the death of their president, vice-president, or managing director as the case might be. For the widow and only daughter word of the calamity had gone to a mountain resort not far from the family home at Montana City.

There promised to be delay in reaching the other two. The son would early read the news, Toler decided, unless perchance he were off at sea, since the death of a figure like Bines would be told by every daily newspaper in the country. He telegraphed, however, to the young man's New York apartments and to a Newport address, on the chance of finding him.

Locating old Peter Bines at this season of the year was a feat never lightly to be undertaken, nor for any trivial end. It being now the 10th of June, it could be known with certainty only that in one of four States he was prowling through some wooded canon, toiling over a windy pass, or scaling a mountain sheerly, in his ancient and best loved sport of prospecting. Knowing his habits, the rashest guesser would not have attempted to say more definitely where the old man might be.

The most promising plan Toler could devise was to wire the superintendent of the "One Girl" Mine at Skiplap. The elder Bines, he knew, had passed through Skiplap about June 1st, and had left, perhaps, some inkling of his proposed route; if it chanced, indeed, that he had taken the trouble to propose one.

Pangburn, the mine superintendent, on receipt of the news, despatched five men on the search in as many different directions. The old man was now seventy-four, and Pangburn had noted when last they met that he appeared to be somewhat less agile and vigorous than he had been twenty years before; from which it was fair to reason that he might be playing his solitary game at a leisurely pace, and would have tramped no great distance in the ten days he had been gone. The searchers, therefore, were directed to beat up the near-by country. To Billy Brue was allotted the easiest as being the most probable route. He was to follow up Paddle Creek to Four Forks, thence over the Bitter Root trail to Eden, on to Oro Fino, and up over

Little Pass to Hellandgone. He was to proceed slowly, to be alert for signs along the way, and to make inquiries of all he met.

"You're likely to get track of Uncle Peter," said Pangburn, "over along the west side of Horseback Ridge, just beyond Eden. When he pulled out he was talking about some likely float-rock he'd picked up over that way last summer. You'd ought to make that by to-morrow, seeing you've got a good horse and the trail's been mended this spring. Now you spread yourself out, Billy, and when you get on to the Ridge make a special look all around there."

Besides these directions and the telegram from Toler, Billy Brue took with him a copy of the Skiplap *Weekly Ledge*, damp from the press and containing the death notice of Daniel J. Bines, a notice sent out by the News Association, which Billy Brue read with interest as he started up the trail. The item concluded thus:

"The young and beautiful Mrs. Bines, who had been accompanying her husband on his trip of inspection over the Sierra Northern, is prostrated with grief at the shock of his sudden death."

Billy Brue mastered this piece of intelligence after six readings, but he refrained from comment, beyond thanking God, in thought, that he could mind his own business under excessive provocation to do otherwise. He considered it no meddling, however, to remember that Mrs. Daniel J. Bines, widow of his late employer, could appear neither young nor beautiful to the most sanguine of newsgatherers; nor to remember that he happened to know she had not accompanied her husband on his last trip of inspection over the Kaslo Division of the Sierra Northern Railway.

CHAPTER II.

How the First Generation Once Righted Itself

By some philosophers unhappiness is believed—rather than coming from deprivation or infliction—to result from the individual's failure to select from a number of possible occupations one that would afford him entire satisfaction with life and himself. To this perverse blindness they attribute the dissatisfaction with great wealth traditional of men who have it. The fault, they contend, is not with wealth inherently. The most they will admit against money is that the possession of much of it tends to destroy that judicial calm necessary to a wise choice of recreations; to incline the possessor, perhaps, toward those that are unsalutary.

Concerning the old man that Billy Brue now sought with his news of death, a philosopher of this school would unhesitatingly declare that he had sounded the last note of human wisdom. Far up in some mountain solitude old Peter Bines, multimillionaire, with a lone pack-mule to bear his meagre outfit, picked up float-rock, tapped and scanned ledges, and chipped at boulders with the same ardour that had fired him in his penniless youth.

Back in 1850, a young man of twenty-four, he had joined the rush to California, working his passage as deck-hand on a vessel that doubled the Horn. Landing without capital at San Francisco, the little seaport settlement among the shifting yellow sand-dunes, he had worked six weeks along the docks as roustabout for money to take him back into the hills whence came the big fortunes and the bigger tales of fortunes. For six years he worked over the gravelly benches of the California creeks for vagrant particles of gold. Then, in the late fifties, he joined a mad stampede to the Frazer River gold-fields in British Columbia, still wild over its first knowledge of silver sulphurets, he was drawn back by the wonder-tales of the Comstock lode.

Joining the bedraggled caravan over the Carson trail, he continued his course of bitter hardship in the Washoe Valley. From a patch of barren sun-baked rock and earth, three miles long and a third of a mile wide, high up on the eastern slope of Mount Davidson, he beheld more millions taken out than the wildest enthusiast had ever before ventured to dream of. But Peter Bines was a luckless unit of the majority that had perforce to live on the hope produced by others' findings. The time for his strike had not come.

For ten years more, half-clad in flannel shirt and overalls, he lived in flimsy tents, tattered canvas houses, and sometimes holes in the ground. One abode of luxury, long cherished in memory, was a ten-by-twelve redwood shanty on Feather River. It not only boasted a window, but there was a round hole in the "shake" roof, fastidiously cut to fit a stove-pipe. That he never possessed a stove-pipe had made this feature of the architecture not less sumptuous and engaging. He lived chiefly on salt pork and beans, cooked over smoky camp-fires.

Through it all he was the determined, eager, confident prospector, never for an instant prey to even the suggestion of a doubt that he would not shortly be rich. Whether he washed the golden specks from the sand of a sage-brush plain, or sought the mother-ledge of some wandering golden child, or dug with his pick to follow a promising surface lead, he knew it to be only the matter of time when his day should dawn. He was of the make that wears unbending hope as its birthright.

Some day the inexhaustible placer would be found; or, on a mountainside where the porphyry was stained, he would carelessly chip off a fragment of rock, turn it up to the sun, and behold it rich in ruby silver; or, some day, the vein instead of pinching out would widen; there would be pay ore almost from the grass-roots—rich, yellow, free-milling gold, so that he could put up a little arastra, beat out enough in a week to buy a small stamp-mill, and then, in six months—ten years more of this fruitless but nourishing certainty were his,—ten years of the awful solitudes, shared sometimes by his hardy and equally confident wife, and, at the last, by his boy, who had become old enough to endure with his father the snow and ice of the mountain tops and the withering heat of the alkali wastes.

Footsore, hungry most of the time, alternately burned and frozen, he lived the life cheerfully and tirelessly, with an enthusiasm that never faltered.

When his day came it brought no surprise, so freshly certain had he kept of its coming through the twenty years of search.

At his feet, one July morning in 1870, he noticed a piece of dark-stained rock in a mass of driftstones. So small was it that to have gone a few feet to either side would have been to miss it. He picked it up and examined it leisurely. It was rich in silver.

Somewhere, then, between him and the mountain top was the parent stock from which this precious fragment had been broken. The sun beat hotly upon him as it had on other days through all the hard years when certainty, after all, was nothing more than a temperamental faith. All day he climbed and searched methodically, stopping at noon to eat with an appetite unaffected by his prospect.

At sunset he would have stopped for the day, camping on the spot. He looked above to estimate the ground he could cover on the morrow.

Almost in front of him, a few yards up the mountainside, he looked squarely at the mother of his float: a huge boulder of projecting silicate. It was there.

During the following week he ascertained the dimensions of his vein of silver ore, and located two claims. He named them "The Stars and Stripes" and "The American Boy," paying thereby what he considered tributes, equally deserved, to his native land and to his only son, Daniel, in whom were centred his fondest hopes.

A year of European travel had followed for the family, a year of spending the new money lavishly for strange, long-dreamed-of luxuries—a year in which the money was joyously proved to be real. Then came a year of tentative residence in the East. That year was less satisfactory. The novelty of being sufficiently fed, clad, and sheltered was losing its fine edge.

Penniless and constrained to a life of privation, Peter Bines had been strangely happy. Rich and of consequence in a community where the ways were all of pleasantness and peace, Peter Bines became restless, discontented, and, at last, unmistakably miserable.

"It can't be because I'm rich," he argued; "it's a sure thing my money can't keep me from doin' jest what I want to do."

Then a suspicion pricked him; for he had, in his years of solitude, formed the habit of considering, in a leisurely and hospitable manner, even the reverse sides of propositions that are commonly accepted by men without question.

"The money *can't* prevent me from doin' what I jest want to—certain—but, maybe, *don't* it? If I didn't have it I'd fur sure be back in the hills and happy, and so would Evalina, that ain't had hardly what you could call a good day since we made the strike."

On this line of reasoning it took Peter Bines no long time to conclude that he ought now to enjoy as a luxury what he had once been constrained to as a necessity.

"Even when I was poor and had to hit the trail I jest loved them hills, so why ain't it crafty to pike back to 'em now when I don't have to?"

His triumphant finale was:

"When you come to think about it, a rich man ain't really got any more excuse fur bein' mis'able than a poor man has!"

Back to the big hills that called him had he gone; away from the cities where people lived "too close together and too far apart;" back to the green, rough earth where the air was free and quick and a man could see a hundred miles, and the people lived far enough apart to be neighbourly.

There content had blessed him again; content not slothful but inciting; a content that embraced his own beloved West, fashioning first in fancy and then by deed, its own proud future. He had never ceased to plan and stimulate its growth. He not only became one with its manifold interests, but proudly dedicated the young Daniel to its further making. He became an ardent and bigoted Westerner, with a scorn for the East so profound that no Easterner's scorn for the West hath ever by any chance equalled it.

Prospecting with the simple outfit of old became his relaxation, his sport, and, as he aged, his hobby. It was said that he had exalted prospecting to the dignity of an art, and no longer hunted gold as a pot-hunter. He was even reputed to have valuable deposits "covered," and certain it is that after Creede made his rich find on Mammoth Mountain in 1890, Peter Bines met him in Denver and gave him particulars about the vein which as yet Creede had divulged to no one. Questioned later concerning this, Peter Bines evaded answering directly, but suggested that a man who already had plenty of money might have done wisely to cover up the find and be still about it; that Nat Creede himself proved as much by going crazy over his wealth and blowing out his brains.

To a tamely prosperous Easterner who, some years after his return to the West, made the conventional remark, "And isn't it amazing that you were happy through those hard years of toil when you were so poor?" Peter Bines had replied, to his questioner's hopeless bewilderment: "No. But it *is* surprisin' that I kept happy after I got rich—after I got what I wanted.

"I reckon you'll find," he added, by way of explaining, "that the proportion of happy rich to unhappy rich is a mighty sight smaller than the proportion of happy poor to the unhappy poor. I'm one of the former minority, all right,—but, by cripes! it's because I know how to be rich and still enjoy all the little comforts of poverty!"

CHAPTER III.

Billy Brue Finds His Man

Each spring the old man grew restive and raw like an unbroken colt. And when the distant mountain peaks began to swim in their summer haze, and the little rushing rivers sang to him, pleading that he come once more to follow them up, he became uncontrollable. Every year at this time he alleged, with a show of irritation, that his health was being sapped by the pernicious indulgence of sleeping on a bed inside a house. He alleged, further, that stocks and bonds were but shadows of wealth, that the old mines might any day become exhausted, and that security for the future lay only in having one member of the family, at least, looking up new pay-rock against the ever possible time of adversity.

"They ain't got to makin' calendars yet with the rainy day marked on 'em," he would say. "A'most any one of them innocent lookin' Mondays or Tuesdays or Wednesdays is liable to be *it* when you get right up on to it. I'll have to start my old bones out again, I see that. Things are beginnin' to green up a'ready." When he did go it was always understood to be positively for not more than two weeks. A list of his reasons for extending the time each year to three or four months would constitute the ideal monograph on human duplicity. When hard-pushed on his return, he had once or twice been even brazen enough to assert that he had lost his way in the mountain fastnesses. But, for all his protestations, no one when he left in June expected to see him again before September at the earliest. In these solitary tours he was busy and happy, working and playing. "Work," he would say, "is something you want to get done; play is something you jest like to be doin'. Snoopin' up these gulches is both of 'em to me."

And so he loitered through the mountains, resting here, climbing there, making always a shrewd, close reading of the rocks.

It was thus Billy Brue found him at the end of his second day's search. A little off the trail, at the entrance to a pocket of the cañon, he towered erect to peer down when he heard the noise of the messenger's ascent. Standing beside a boulder of grey granite, before a background of the gnarled dwarf-cedars, his hat off, his blue shirt open at the neck, his bare forearms brown, hairy, and muscular, a hammer in his right hand, his left resting lightly on his hip, he might have been the Titan that had forged the boulder at his side, pausing now for breath before another mighty task. Well over six feet tall, still straight as any of the pines before him, his head and broad shoulders in the easy poise of power, there was about him from a little distance no sign of age. His lines were gracefully full, his bearing had still the alertness of youth. One must have come as near as Billy Brue now came to detect the marks of time in his face. Not of age—merely of time; for here was no senility, no quavering or fretful lines. The grey eyes shone bright and clear from far under the heavy, unbroken line of brow, and the mouth was still straight and firmly held, a mouth under sure control from corner to corner. A little had the years brought out the rugged squareness of the chin and the deadly set of the jaws; a little had they pressed in the cheeks to throw the high bones into broad relief. But these were the utmost of their devastations. Otherwise Peter Bines showed his seventy-four years only by the marks of a well-ordered maturity. His eyes, it is true, had that look of *knowing* which to the young seems always to betoken the futility of, and to warn against the folly of, struggle against what must be; yet they were kind eyes, and humourous, with many of the small lines of laughter at their corners. Reading the eyes and mouth together one perceived gentleness and sternness to be well matched, working to any given end in amiable and effective compromise. "Uncle Peter" he had long been called by the public that knew him, and his own grandchildren had come to call him by the same term, finding him too young to meet their ideal of a grandfather. Billy Brue, riding up the trail, halted, nodded, and was silent. The old man returned his salutation as briefly. These things by men who stay much alone come to be managed with verbal economy. They would talk presently, but greetings were awkward.

Billy Brue took one foot from its stirrup and turned in his saddle, pulling the leg up to a restful position. Then he spat, musingly, and looked back down the cañon aimlessly, throwing his eyes from side to side where the grey granite ledges showed through the tall spruce and pine trees.

But the old man knew he had been sent for.

"Well, Billy Brue,—what's doin'?"

Billy Brue squirmed in the saddle, spat again, as with sudden resolve, and said:

"Why,—uh—Dan'l J.—*he's* dead."

The old man repeated the words, dazedly.

"Dan'l J.—*he's* dead;—why, who else is dead, too?"

Billy Brue's emphasis, cunningly contrived by him to avoid giving prominence to the word "dead," had suggested this inquiry in the first moment of stupefaction.

"Nobody else dead—jest Dan'l J.—*he's* dead."

"Jest Dan'l J.—my boy—my boy Dan'l dead!"

His mighty shape was stricken with a curious rigidity, erected there as if it were a part of the mountain, flung up of old from the earth's inner tragedy, confounded, desolate, ancient.

Billy Brue turned from the stony interrogation of his eyes and took a few steps away, waiting. A little wind sprang up among the higher trees, the moments passed, and still the great figure stood transfixed in its curious silence. The leathers creaked as the horse turned. The messenger, with an air of surveying the canon, stole an anxious glance at the old face. The sorrowful old eyes were fixed on things that were not; they looked vaguely as if in search.

"Dan'l!" he said.

It was not a cry; there was nothing plaintive in it. It was only the old man calling his son: David calling upon Absalom. Then there was a change. He came sternly forward.

"Who killed my boy?"

"Nobody, Uncle Peter; 'twas a stroke. He was goin' over the line and they'd laid out at Kaslo fer a day so's Dan'l J. could see about a spur the 'Lucky Cuss' people wanted—and maybe it was the climbin' brought it on."

The old man looked his years. As he came nearer Billy Brue saw tears tremble in his eyes and roll unnoted down his cheeks. Yet his voice was unbroken and he was, indeed, unconscious of the tears.

"I was afraid of that. He lived too high. He et too much and he drank too much and was too soft—was Dan'l.—too soft—"

The old voice trembled a bit and he stopped to look aside into the little pocket he had been exploring. Billy Brue looked back down the canon, where the swift stream brawled itself into white foam far below.

"He wouldn't use his legs; I prodded him about it constant—"

He stopped again to brace himself against the shock. Billy Brue still looked away.

"I told him high altitudes and high livin' would do any man—" Again he was silent.

"But all he'd ever say was that times had changed since my day, and I wasn't to mind him." He had himself better in hand now.

"Why, I nursed that boy when he was a dear, funny little red baby with big round eyes rollin' around to take notice; he took notice awful quick—fur a baby. Oh, my! Oh, dear! Dan'l!"

Again he stopped.

"And it don't seem more'n yesterday that I was a-teachin' him to throw the diamond hitch; he could throw the diamond hitch with his eyes shut —I reckon by the time he was nine or ten. He had his faults, but they didn't hurt him none; Dan'l J. was a man, now—" He halted once more.

"The dead millionaire," began Billy Brue, reading from the obituary in the Skiplap *Weekly Ledge*, "was in his fifty-second year. Genial, generous to a fault, quick to resent a wrong, but unfailing in his loyalty to a friend, a man of large ideas, with a genius for large operations, he was the type of indefatigable enterprise that has builded this Western empire in a wilderness and given rich sustenance and luxurious homes to millions of prosperous, happy American citizens. Peace to his ashes! And a safe trip to his immortal soul over the one-way trail!"

"Yes, yes—it's Dan'l J. fur sure—they got my boy Dan'l that time. Is that all it says, Billy? Any one with him?"

"Why, this here despatch is signed by young Toler—that's his confidential man."

"Nobody else?"

The old man was peering at him sharply from under the grey protruding brows.

"Well, if you must know, Uncle Peter, this is what the notice says that come by wire to the *Ledge* office," and he read doggedly:

"The young and beautiful Mrs. Bines, who had been accompanying her husband on his trip of inspection over the Sierra Northern, is prostrated by the shock of his sudden death."

The old man became for the first time conscious of the tears in his eyes, and, pulling down one of the blue woollen shirt sleeves, wiped his wet cheeks. The slow, painful blush of age crept up across the iron strength of his face, and passed. He looked away as he spoke.

"I knew it; I knew that. My Dan'l was like all that Frisco bunch. They get tangled with women sooner or later. I taxed Dan'l with it. I spleened against it and let him know it. But he was a man and his own master—if you can rightly call a man his own master that does them things. Do you know what-fur woman this one was, Billy?"

"Well, last time Dan'l J. was up to Skiplap, there was a swell party on the car—kind of a coppery-lookin' blonde. Allie Ash, the brakeman on No. 4, he tells me she used to be in Spokane, and now she'd got her hooks on to some minin' property up in the Coeur d'Alene. Course, this mightn't be the one."

The old man had ceased to listen. He was aroused to the need for action.

"Get movin', Billy! We can get down to Eden to-night; we'll have the moon fur two hours on the trail soon's the sun's gone. I can get 'em to drive me over to Skiplap first thing to-morrow, and I can have 'em make me up a train there fur Montana City. Was he—"

"Dan'l J. has been took home—the noozepaper says."

They turned back down the trail, the old man astride Billy Brue's horse, followed by his pack-mule and preceded by Billy.

Already, such was his buoyance and habit of quick recovery and readjustment under reverses, his thoughts were turning to his grandson. Daniel's boy—there was the grandson of his grandfather—the son of his father—fresh from college, and the instructions of European travel, knowing many things his father had not known, ready to take up the work of his father, and capable, perhaps, of giving it a better finish. His beloved West had lost one of its valued builders, but another should take his place. His boy should come to him and finish the tasks of his father; and, in the years to come, make other mighty tasks of empire-building for himself and the children of his children.

It did not occur to him that he and the boy might be as far apart in sympathies and aims as at that moment they were in circumstance. For, while the old man in the garb of a penniless prospector, toiled down the steep mountain trail on a cheap horse, his grandson was reading the first news of his father's death in one of the luxurious staterooms of a large steam yacht that had just let down her anchor in Newport Harbour. And each—but for the death—had been where most he wished to be—one with his coarse fare and out-of-doors life, roughened and seamed by the winds and browned by the sun to mahogany tints; aged but playing with boyish zest at his primitive sport; the other, a strong-limbed, well-marrowed, full-breathing youth of twenty-five, with appetites all alert and sharpened, pink and pampered, loving luxury, and prizing above all things else the atmosphere of wealth and its refinements.

CHAPTER IV.

The West Against the East

Two months later a sectional war was raging in the Bines home at Montana City. The West and the East were met in conflict,—the old and the new, the stale and the fresh. And, if the bitterness was dissembled by the combatants, not less keenly was it felt, nor less determined was either faction to be relentless.

A glance about the "sitting-room" in which the opposing forces were lined up, and into the parlour through the opened folding-doors, may help us to a better understanding of the issue involved. Both rooms were large and furnished in a style that had been supremely luxurious in 1878. The house, built in that year, of Oregon pine, had been quite the most pretentious piece of architecture in that section of the West. It had been erected in the first days of Montana City as a convincing testimonial from the owner to his faith in the town's future. The plush-upholstered sofas and chairs, with their backs and legs of carved black walnut, had come direct from New York. For pictures there were early art-chromos, among them the once-prized companion pieces, "Wide Awake" and "Fast Asleep." Lithography was represented by "The Fisherman's Pride" and "The Soldier's Dream of Home." In the handicrafts there were a photographic reproduction of the Lord's Prayer, illustrated originally by a penman with uncommon genius for scroll-work; a group of water-lilies in wax, floating on a mirror-lake and protected by a glass globe; a full-rigged schooner, built cunningly inside a bottle by a matricide serving a life-sentence in the penitentiary at San Quinten; and a mechanical canarybird in a gilded cage, acquired at the Philadelphia Centennial,—a bird that had carolled its death—lay in the early winter of 1877 when it was wound up too hard and its little insides snapped. In the parlour a few ornamental books were grouped with rare precision on the centre-table with its oval top of white marble. On the walls of the "sitting-room" were a steel engraving of Abraham Lincoln striking the shackles from a kneeling slave, and a framed cardboard rebus worked in red zephyr, the reading of which was "No Cross, No Crown."

Thus far nothing helpful has been found.

Let us examine, then, the what-not in the "sitting-room" and the choice Empire cabinet that faces it from the opposite wall of the parlour.

The what-not as an American institution is obsolete. Indeed, it has been rather long since writers referred to it even in terms of opprobrious sarcasm. The what-not, once the cherished shrine of the American home, sheltered the smaller household gods for which no other resting-place could be found. The Empire cabinet, with its rounding front of glass, its painted Watteau scenes, and its mirrored back, has come to supplant the humbler creation in the fulfilment of all its tender or mysterious offices.

Here, perchance, may be found a clue in symbol to the family strife.

The Bines what-not in the sitting-room was grimly orthodox in its equipment. Here was an ancient box covered with shell-work, with a wavy little mirror in its back; a tender motto worked with the hair of the dead; a "Rock of Ages" in a glass case, with a garland of pink chenille around the base; two dried pine cones brightly varnished; an old daguerreotype in an ornamental case of hard rubber; a small old album; two small China vases of the kind that came always in pairs, standing on mats of crocheted worsted; three sea-shells; and the cup and saucer that belonged to grandma, which no one must touch because they'd been broken and were held together but weakly, owing to the imperfections of home-made cement.

The new cabinet, haughty in its varnished elegance, with its Watteau dames and courtiers, and perhaps the knowledge that it enjoys widespread approval among the elect,—this is a different matter. In every American home that is a home, to-day, it demands attention. The visitor, after eyeing it with cautious side-glances, goes jauntily up to it, affecting to have been stirred by the mere impulse of elegant idleness. Under the affectedly careless scrutiny of the hostess he falls dramatically into an attitude of awed entrancement. Reverently he gazes upon the priceless bibelots within: the mother-of-pearl fan, half open; the tiny cup and saucer of Sèvres on their brass easel; the miniature Cupid and Psyche in marble; the Japanese wrestlers carved in ivory; the ballet-dancer in bisque; the coral necklace; the souvenir spoon from the Paris Exposition; the jade bracelet; and the silver snuff-box that grandfather carried to the day of his death. If the gazing visitor be a person of abandoned character he makes humourous pretence that the householder has done wisely to turn a key upon these treasures, against the ravishings of the overwhelmed and frenzied connoisseur. He wears the look of one who is gnawed with envy, and he heaves the sigh of despair.

But when he notes presently that he has ceased to be observed he sneaks cheerfully to another part of the room.

The what-not is obsolete. The Empire cabinet is regnant. Yet, though one is the lineal descendant of the other—its sophisticated grandchild—they are hostile and irreconcilable.

Twenty years hence the cabinet will be proscribed and its contents catalogued in those same terms of disparagement that the what-not became long since too dead to incur. Both will then have attained the state of honourable extinction now enjoyed by the dodo.

The what-not had curiously survived in the Bines home—survived unto the coming of the princely cabinet—survived to give battle if it might.

Here, perhaps, may be found the symbolic clue to the strife's cause.

The sole non-combatant was Mrs. Bines, the widow. A neutral was this good woman, and a well-wisher to each faction.

"I tell you it's all the same to me," she declared, "Montana City or Fifth Avenue in New York. I guess I can do well enough in either place so long as the rest of you are satisfied."

It had been all the same to Mrs. Bines for as many years as a woman of fifty can remember. It was the lot of wives in her day and environment early to learn the supreme wisdom of abolishing preferences. Riches and poverty, ease and hardship, mountain and plain, town and wilderness, they followed in no ascertainable sequence, and a superiority of indifference to each was the only protection against hurts from the unexpected.

This trained neutrality of Mrs. Bines served her finely now. She had no leading to ally herself against her children in their wish to go East, nor against Uncle Peter Bines in his stubborn effort to keep them West. She folded her hands to wait on the others.

And the battle raged.

The old man, sole defender of the virtuous and stalwart West against an East that he alleged to be effete and depraved, had now resorted to sarcasm,—a thing that Mr. Carlyle thought was as good as the language of the devil.

"And here, now, how about this dog-luncheon?" he continued, glancing at a New York newspaper clutched accusingly in his hand. "It was give, I see, by one of your Newport cronies. Now, that's healthy doin's fur a two-fisted Christian, ain't it? I want to know. Shappyronging a select company of lady and gentlemen dogs from soup to coffee; pressing a little more of the dog-biscuit on this one, and seein' that the other don't misplay its finger-bowl no way. How I would love to read of a Bines standin' up, all in purty velvet pants, most likely, to receive at one of them bow-wow functions;—functions, I believe, is the name of it?" he ended in polite inquiry.

"There, there, Uncle Peter!" the young man broke in, soothingly; "you mustn't take those Sunday newspapers as gospel truth; those stories are printed for just such rampant old tenderfoots as you are; and even if there is one foolish freak, he doesn't represent all society in the better sense of the term."

"Yes, and *you*!" Uncle Peter broke out again, reminded of another grievance. "You know well enough your true name is Peter—Pete and Petie when you was a baby and Peter when you left for college. And you're ashamed of what you've done, too, for you tried to hide them callin'-cards from me the other day, only you wa'n't quick enough. Bring 'em out! I'm bound your mother and Pish shall see 'em. Out with 'em!"

The young man, not without embarrassment, drew forth a Russia leather card-case which the old man took from him as one having authority.

"Here you are, Marthy Bines!" he exclaimed, handing her a card; "here you are! read it! Mr. P. Percival Bines.' *Now* don't you feel proud of havin' stuck out for Percival when you see it in cold print? You know mighty well his pa and me agreed to Percival only fur a middle name, jest to please you—and he wa'n't to be called by it;—only jest Peter or 'Peter P.' at most; and now look at the way he's gone and garbled his good name."

Mr. P. Percival Bines blushed furiously here, but rejoined, nevertheless, with quiet dignity, that a man's name was something about which he should have the ruling voice, especially where it was possible for him to rectify or conceal the unhappy choice of his parents.

"And while we're on names," he continued, "do try to remember in case you ever get among people, that Sis's name is Psyche and not Pish."

The blond and complacent Miss Bines here moved uneasily in her patent blue plush rocker and spoke for the first time, with a grateful glance at her brother.

"Yes, Uncle Peter, for mercy's sake, *do* try! Don't make us a laughing-stock!" "But your name is Pish. A person's name is what their folks name 'em, ain't it? Your ma comes acrost a name in a book that she likes the looks of, and she takes it to spell Pish, and she ups and names you Pish, and we all calls you Pish and Pishy, and then when you toddle off to public school and let 'em know how you spell it they tell you it's something else— an outlandish name if spellin' means anything. If it comes to that you ought to change the spellin' instead of the name that your poor pa loved."

Yet the old man had come to know that he was fighting a lost fight,—lost before it had ever begun.

"It will be a good chance," ventured Mrs. Bines, timidly, "for Pishy—I mean Sike—Sicky—to meet the right sort of people."

"Yes, I should *say*—and the wrong sort. The ingagin' host of them lady and gentlemen dogs, fur instance."

"But Uncle Peter," broke in the young man, "you shouldn't expect a girl of Psyche's beauty and fortune to vegetate in Montana City all her life. Why, any sort of brilliant marriage is possible to her if she goes among the right people. Don't you want the family to amount to something socially? Is our money to do us no good? And do you think I'm going to stay here and be a moss-back and raise chin whiskers and work myself to death the way my father did?"

"No, no," replied the old man, with a glance at the mother; "not *jest* the way your pa did; you might do some different and some better; but all the same, you won't do any better'n he did any way you'll learn to live in New York. Unless you was to go broke there," he added, thoughtfully; "in that case you got the stuff in you and it'd come out; but you got too much money to go broke."

"And you'll see that I lead a decent enough life. Times have changed since my father was a young man."

"Yes; that's what your pa told me,—times had changed since I was a young man; but I could 'a' done him good if he'd 'a' listened."

"Well, we'll try it. The tide is setting that way from all over the country. Here, listen to this editorial in the *Sun*." And he read from his own paper:

"A GOOD PLACE TO MOVE TO.

"One of the most interesting evidences of the growth of New York is the news that Mr. Anson Ledrick of the Consolidated Copper Company has purchased an extensive building site on Riverside Drive and will presently improve it with a costly residence. Mr. Ledrick's decision to move his household effects to Manhattan Island is in accordance with a very marked tendency of successful Americans.

"There are those who are fond of depreciating New York; of assailing it with all sorts of cheap and sensational vituperation; of picturing it as the one great canker spot of the Western hemisphere, as irretrievably sunk in wickedness and shame. The fact remains, however, that the city, as never before, is the great national centre of wealth, culture, and distinction of every kind, and that here the citizen, successful in art, literature, or practical achievement, instinctively seeks his abiding-place.

"The restlessness of the average American millionaire while he remains outside the city limits is frequently remarked upon. And even the mighty overlords of Chicago, falling in with the prevailing fashion, have forsaken the shores of the great inland sea and pitched their tents with us; not to speak of the copper kings of Montana. Why is it that these interesting men, after acquiring fortune and fame elsewhere, are not content to remain upon the scene of their early triumphs? Why is it that they immediately pack their carpet-bags, take the first through train to our gates, and startle the investing public by the manner in which they bull the price of New York building lots?"

The old man listened absently.

"And probably some day I'll read of you in that same centre of culture and distinction as P. Percival Bines, a young man of obscure fam'ly, that rose by his own efforts to be the dashin' young cotillion leader and the well-known club-man, and that his pink teas fur dogs is barked about by every fashionable canine on the island."

The young man continued to read: "These men are not vain fools; they are shrewd, successful men of the world. They have surveyed New York City from a distance and have discovered that, in spite of Tammany and in spite of yellow journals, New York is a town of unequalled attractiveness. And so they come; and their coming shows us what we are. Not only millionaires; but also painters and novelists and men and women of varied distinction. The city palpitates with life and ambition and hope and promise; it attracts the great and the successful, and those who admire greatness and success. The force of natural selection is at work here as everywhere; and it is rapidly concentrating in our small island whatever is finest, most progressive, and best in the American character."

"Well, now do me a last favour before you pike off East," pleaded the old man. "Make a trip with me over the properties. See 'em once anyway, and see a little more of this country and these people. Mebbe they're better'n you think. Give me about three weeks or a month, and then, by Crimini, you can go off if you're set on it and be 'whatever is finest and best in the American character' as that feller puts it. But some day, son, you'll find out there's a whole lot of difference between a great man of wealth and a man of great wealth. Them last is gettin' terrible common."

CHAPTER V.

Over the Hills

So the old man and the young man made the round of the Bines properties. The former nursed a forlorn little hope of exciting an interest in the concerns most vital to him; to the latter the leisurely tour in the private car was a sportive prelude to the serious business of life, as it should be lived, in the East. Considering it as such he endured it amiably, and indeed the long August days and the sharply cool nights were not without real enjoyment for him.

To feel impartially a multitude of strong, fresh wants—the imperative need to live life in all its fulness, this of itself makes the heart to sing. And, above the full complement of wants, to have been dowered by Heaven with a stanch disbelief in the unattainable,—this is a fortune rather to be chosen than a good name or great riches; since the name and riches and all things desired must come to the call of it.

Our Western-born youth of twenty-five had the wants and the sense of power inherited from a line of men eager of initiative, the product of an environment where only such could survive. Doubtless in him was the soul and body hunger of his grandfather, cramping and denying through hardship year after year, yet sustained by dreaming in the hardest times of the soft material luxuries that should some day be his. Doubtless marked in his character, too, was the slightly relaxed tension of his father; the disposition to feast as well as the capacity to fast; to take all, feel all, do all, with an avidity greater by reason of the grinding abstinence and the later indulgence of his forbears. A sage versed in the lore of heredity as modified by environment may some day trace for us the progress across this continent of an austere Puritan, showing how the strain emerges from the wilderness at the Western ocean with a character so widely differing from the one with which he began the adventurous journey,—regarding, especially, a tolerance of the so-called good and many of the bad things of life. Until this is done we may, perhaps, consider the change to be without valid cause.

Young Bines, at all events, was the flower of a pioneer stock, and him the gods of life cherished, so that all the forces of the young land about him were as his own. Yet, though his pulses rhymed to theirs he did not perceive his relation to them: neither he nor the land was yet become introspective. So informed was he with the impetuous spirit of youth that the least manifestation of life found its answering thrill in him. And it was sufficient to feel this. There was no time barren enough of sensation to reason about it. Uncle Peter's plan for an inspection of the Bines properties had at first won him by touching his sense of duty. He anticipated no interest or pleasure in the trip. Yet from the beginning he enjoyed it to the full. Being what he was, the constant movement pleased him, the out-of-doors life, the occasional sorties from the railroad by horse to some remote mining camp, or to a stock ranch or lumber-camp. He had been away for six years, and it pleased him to note that he was treated by the people he met with a genuine respect and liking as the son of his father. In the East he had been accustomed to a certain deference from very uncertain people because he was the son of a rich man. Here he had prestige because he was the son of Daniel Bines, organiser and man of affairs. He felt sometimes that the men at mine, mill, or ranch looked him over with misgiving, and had their cautious liking compelled only by the assurance that he was indeed the son of Daniel. They left him at these times with the suspicion that this bare fact meant enough with them to carry a man of infelicitous exterior.

He was pleased, moreover, to feel a new respect for Uncle Peter. He observed that men of all degrees looked up to him, sought and relied upon his judgment; the investing capitalist whom they met less than the mine foreman; the made man and the labourer. In the drawing-room at home he had felt so agreeably superior to the old man; now he felt his own inferiority in a new element, and began to view him with more respect. He saw him to be the shrewd man of affairs, with a thorough grasp of detail in every branch of their interests; and a deep man, as well; a little narrow, perhaps, from his manner of life, but of unfailing kindness, and with rather a young man's radicalism than an old man's conservatism; one who, in an emergency, might be relied upon to take the unexpected but effective course.

For his own part, old Peter Bines learned in the course of the trip to understand and like his grandson better. At bottom he decided the young man to be sound after all, and he began to make allowance for his geographical heresies. The boy had been sent to an Eastern college; that was clearly a mistake, putting him out of sympathy with the West; and he had never been made to work, which was another and a graver mistake, "but he'd do more'n his father ever did if 'twa'n't fur his father's money," the old man concluded. For he saw in their talks that the very Eastern experience which he derided had given the young fellow a poise and a certain readiness to grasp details in the large that his father had been a lifetime in acquiring.

For a month they loitered over the surrounding territory in the private car, gliding through fertile valleys, over bleak passes, steaming up narrow little canons along the down-rushing streams with their cool shallow murmurs.

They would learn one day that a cross-cut was to be started on the Last Chance, or that the concentrates of the True Grit would thereafter be shipped to the Careless Creek smelter. Next they would learn that a new herd of Galloways had done finely last season on the Bitter Root ranch; that a big lot of ore was sacked at the Irish Boy, that an eighteen-inch vein had been struck in the Old Crow; that a concentrator was needed at Hellandgone, and that rich gold-bearing copper and sand bearing free gold had been found over on Horseback Ridge.

Another day they would drive far into a forest of spruce and hemlock to a camp where thousands of ties were being cut and floated down to the line of the new railway.

Sometimes they spent a night in one of the smaller mining camps off the railroad, whereof facetious notes would appear in the nearest weekly paper, such as:

"The Hon. Peter Bines and his grandson, who is a chip of the old block, spent Tuesday night at Rock Rip. Young Bines played the deal from soda card to hock at Lem Tully's Turf Exchange, and showed Lem's dealer good and plenty that there's no piker strain in him."

Or, it might be:

"Poker stacks continue to have a downward tendency. They were sold last week as low as eighty chips for a dollar; It is sad to see this noble game dragging along in the lower levels of prosperity, and we take as a favourable omen the appearance of Uncle Peter Bines and his grandson the other night. The prices went to par in a minute. Young Bines gave signs of becoming as delicately intuitional in the matter of concealed values as his father, the lamented Daniel J."

Again it was:

"Uncle Peter Bines reports from over Kettle Creek way that the sagebrush whiskey they take a man's two bits for there would gnaw holes in limestone. Peter is likelier to find a ledge of dollar bills than he is good whiskey this far off the main trail. The late Daniel J. could have told him as much, and Daniel J.'s boy, who accompanies Uncle Peter, will know it hereafter."

The young man felt wholesomely insignificant at these and other signs that he was taken on sufferance as a son and a grandson.

He was content that it should be so. Indeed there was little wherewith he was not content. That he was habitually preoccupied, even when there was most movement about them, early became apparent to Uncle Peter. That he was constantly cheerful proved the matter of his musings to be pleasant. That he was proner than most youths to serious meditation Uncle Peter did not believe. Therefore he attributed the moods of abstraction to some matter probably connected with his project of removing the family East. It was not permitted Uncle Peter to know, nor was his own youth recent enough for him to suspect, the truth. And the mystery stayed inviolate until a day came and went that laid it bare even to the old man's eyes.

They awoke one morning to find the car on a siding at the One Girl mine. Coupled to it was another car from an Eastern road that their train had taken on sometime in the night. Percival noted the car with interest as he paced beside the track in the cool clear air before breakfast. The curtains were drawn, and the only signs of life to be observed were at the kitchen end, where the white-clad cook could be seen astir. Grant, porter on the Bines car, told him the other car had been taken on at Kaslo Junction, and that it belonged to Rulon Shepler, the New York financier, who was aboard with a party of friends.

As Percival and Uncle Peter left their car for the shaft-house after breakfast, the occupants of the other car were bestirring themselves.

From one of the open windows a low but impassioned voice was exhausting the current idioms of damnation in sweeping dispraise of all land-areas north and west of Fifty-ninth Street, New York.

Uncle Peter smiled grimly. Percival flushed, for the hidden protestant had uttered what were his own sentiments a month before.

Reaching the shaft-house they chatted with Pangburn, the superintendent, and then went to the store-room to don blouses and overalls for a descent into the mine.

For an hour they stayed underground, traversing the various levels and drifts, while Pangburn explained the later developments of the vein and showed them where the new stoping had been begun.

CHAPTER VI.

A Meeting and a Clashing

As they stepped from the cage at the surface Percival became aware of a group of strangers between him and the open door of the shaft-house,—people displaying in dress and manner the unmistakable stamp of New York. For part of a minute, while the pupils of his eyes were contracting to the light, he saw them but vaguely. Then, as his sight cleared, he beheld foremost in the group, beaming upon him with an expression of pleased and surprised recognition, the girl whose face and voice had for nearly half a year peopled his lover's solitude with fair visions and made its silence to be all melody.

Had the encounter been anticipated his composure would perhaps have failed him. Not a few of his waking dreams had sketched this, their second meeting, and any one of the ways it had pleased him to plan it would assuredly have found him nervously embarrassed. But so wildly improbable was this reality that not the daringest of his imagined happenings had approached it. His thoughts for the moment had been not of her; then, all at once, she stood before him in the flesh, and he was cool, almost unmoved. He suspected at once that her father was the trim, fastidiously dressed man who looked as if he had been abducted from a morning stroll down the avenue to his club; that the plump, ruddy, high-bred woman, surveying the West disapprovingly through a lorgnon, would be her mother. Shepler he knew by sight, with his big head, massive shoulders, and curiously short, tapering body. Some other men and a woman were scanning the hoisting machinery with superior looks.

The girl, before starting toward him, had waited hardly longer than it took him to eye the group. And then came an awkward two seconds upon her whose tact in avoiding the awkward was reputed to be more than common.

With her hand extended she had uttered, "Why, Mr.—" before it flashed upon her that she did not know the name of the young man she was greeting.

The "Mister" was threatening to prolong itself into an "r" of excruciating length and disgraceful finality, an "r" that is terminated neatly by no one but hardened hotel-clerks. Then a miner saved the day. "Mr. Bines," he said, coming up hurriedly behind Percival with several specimens of ore, "you forgot these."

"-r-r-r. Bines, how *do* you do!" concluded the girl with an eye-flash of gratitude at the humble instrument that had prevented an undue hiatus in her salutation. They were apart from the others and for the moment unnoticed.

The young man took the hand so cordially offered, and because of all the things he wished and had so long waited to say, he said nothing.

"Isn't it jolly! I am Miss Milbrey," she added in a lower tone, and then, raising her voice, "Mamma, Mr. Bines—and papa," and there followed a hurried and but half-acknowledged introduction to the other members of the party. And, behold! in that moment the young man had schemed the edifice of all his formless dreams. For six months he had known the unsurpassable luxury of wanting and of knowing what he wanted. Now, all at once, he saw this to be a world in which dreams come more than true.

Shepler and the party were to go through the mine as a matter of sight-seeing. They were putting on outer clothes from the store-room to protect them from the dirt and damp.

Presently Percival found himself again at the bottom of the shaft. During the descent of twelve hundred feet he had reflected upon the curious and interesting fact that her name should be Milbrey. He felt dimly that this circumstance should be ranked among the most interesting of natural phenomena,—that she should have a name, as the run of mortals, and that it should be one name more than another. When he discovered further that her Christian name was Avice the phenomenon became stupendously bewildering. They two were in the last of the party to descend. On reaching bottom he separated her with promptness and guile from two solemn young men, copies of each other, and they were presently alone. In the distance they could see the others following ghostly lamps. From far off mysterious recesses came the muffled musical clink of the sledges on the drills. An employee who had come down with them started to be their guide. Percival sent him back.

"I've just been through; I can find my way again."

"Ver' well," said the man, "with the exception that it don't happen something,—yes?" And he stayed where he was.

Down one of the cross-cuts they started, stepping aside to let a car of ore be pushed along to the shaft.

"Do you know," began the girl, "I am so glad to be able to thank you for what you did that night."

"I'm glad you *are* able. I was beginning to think I should always have those thanks owing to me."

"I might have paid them at the time, but it was all so unexpected and so sudden,—it rattled me, quite."

"I thought you were horribly cool-headed."

"I wasn't."

"Your manner reduced me to a groom who opened your carriage door."

"But grooms don't often pick strange ladies up bodily and bear them out of a pandemonium of waltzing cab-horses. I'd never noticed before that cab-horses are so frivolous and hysterical."

"And grooms know where to look for their pay."

They were interrupting nervously, and bestowing furtive side-looks upon each other.

"If I'd not seen you," said the girl, "glanced at you—before—that evening, I shouldn't have remembered so well; doubtless I'd not have recognised you to-day."

"I didn't know you did glance at me, and yet I watched you every moment of the evening. You didn't know that, did you?"

She laughed.

"Of course I knew it. A woman has to note such things without letting it be seen that she sees."

"And I'd have sworn you never once so much as looked my way."

"Don't we do it well, though?"

"And in spite of all the time I gave to a study of your face I lost the detail of it. I could keep only the effect of its expression and the few tones of your voice I heard. You know I took those on a record so I could make 'em play over any time I wanted to listen. Do you know, that has all been very sweet to me, my helping you and the memory of it,—so vague and sweet."

"Aren't you afraid we're losing the others?"

She halted and looked back.

"No; I'm afraid we won't lose them; come on; you can't turn back now. And you don't want to hear anything about mines; it wouldn't be at all good for you, I'm sure. Quick, down this way, or you'll hear Pangburn telling some one what a stope is, and think what a thing that would be to carry in your head."

"Really, a stope sounds like something that would 'get you' in the night! I'm afraid!"

Half in his spirit she fled with him down a dimly lighted incline where men were working at the rocky wall with sledge and drill. There was that in his manner which compelled her quite as literally as when at their first meeting he had picked her up in his arms.

As they walked single-file through the narrowing of a drift, she wondered about him. He was Western, plainly. An employee in the mine, probably a manager or director or whatever it was they called those in authority in mines. Plainly, too, he was a man of action and a man who engaged all her instinctive liking. Something in him at once coerced her friendliest confidence. These were the admissions she made to herself. She divined him, moreover, to be a blend of boldness and timidity. He was bold to the point of telling her things unconventionally, of beguiling her into remote underground passages away from the party; yet she understood; she knew at once that he was a determined but unspoiled gentleman; that under no provocation could he make a mistake. In any situation of loneliness she would have felt safe with him—"as with a brother"—she thought. Then, feeling her cheeks burn, she turned back and said:

"I must tell you he was my brother—that man—that night."

He was sorry and glad all at once. The sorrow being the lesser and more conventional emotion, he started upon an awkward expression of it, which she interrupted.

"Never mind saying that, thank you. Tell me something about yourself, now. I really would like to know you. What do you see and hear and do in this strange life?"

"There's not much variety," he answered, with a convincing droop of depression. "For six months I've been seeing you and hearing you—seeing you and hearing you; not much variety in that—nothing worth telling you about."

Despite her natural caution, intensified by training, she felt herself thrill to the very evident sincerity of his tones, so that she had to affect mirth to seem at ease.

"Dear, dear, what painful monotony; and how many men have said it since these rocks were made; and now you say it,—well, I admit—"

"But there's nothing new under the sun, you know."

"No; not even a new excuse for plagiarism, is there?"

"Well, you see as long as the same old thing keeps true the same old way of telling it will be more or less depended upon. After a few hundred years of experiment, you know, they hit on the fewest words that tell the most, and everybody uses them because no one can improve them. Maybe the prehistoric cave-gentleman, who proposed to his loved one with a war club just back of her left ear, had some variation of the formula suiting his simple needs, after he'd gotten her home and brought her to and she said it was 'all so sudden;' and a man can work in little variations of his own to-day. For example—"

"I'm sure we'd best be returning."

"For example, I could say, you know, that for keeping the mind active and the heart working overtime the memory of you surpasses any tonic advertised in the backs of the magazines. Or, that—"

"I think that's enough; I see you *could* vary the formula, in case—"

"—*have* varied it—but don't forget I prefer the original unvaried. After all, there are certain things that you can't tell in too few words. Now, you—"

"You stubborn person. Really, I know all about myself. I asked you to tell me about yourself."

"And I began at once to tell you everything about myself—everything of interest—which is yourself."

"I see your sense of values is gone, poor man. I shall question you. Now you are a miner, and I like men of action, men who do things; I've often wondered about you, and seriously, I'm glad to find you here doing something. I remembered you kindly, with real gratitude, indeed. You didn't seem like a New York man either, and I decided you weren't. Honestly, I am glad to find you here at your work in your miner's clothes. You mustn't think we forget how to value men that work."

On the point of saying thoughtlessly, "But I'm not working here—I own the mine," he checked himself. Instead he began a defence of the man who doesn't work, but who could if he had to. "For example," he continued, "here we are at a place that you must be carried over; otherwise you'd have to wade through a foot of water or go around that long way we've come. I've rubber boots on, and so I pick you up this way—" He held her lightly on his arm and she steadied herself with a hand between his shoulders.

"And staggering painfully under my burden, I wade out to the middle of this subterranean lake." He stopped.

"You see, I've learned to do things. I could pick you from that slippery street and put you in your carriage, and I can pick you up now without wasting words about it—"

"But you're wasting time—hurry, please—and, anyway, you're a miner and used to such things."

He remained standing.

"But I'm *not* wasting time, and I'm not a miner in the sense you mean. I own this mine, and I suppose for the most part I'm the sort of man you seem to have gotten tired of; the man who doesn't have to do anything. Even now I'm this close to work only because my grandfather wanted me to look over the properties my father left."

"But, hurry, please, and set me down."

"Not until I warn you that I'm just as apt to do things as the kind of man you thought I was. This is twice I've picked you up now. Look out for me;—next time I may not put you down at all."

She gave a low little laugh, denoting unruffled serenity. She was glorying secretly in his strength, and she knew his boldness and timidity were still justly balanced. And there was the rather astonishing bit of news he had just given her. That needed a lot of consideration.

With slow, sure-footed steps he reached the farther side of the water and put her on her feet.

"There, I thought I'd reveal the distressing truth about myself while I had you at my mercy."

"I might have suspected, but I gave the name no thought. Bines, to be sure. You are the son of the Bines who died some months ago. I heard Mr. Shepler and my father talking about some of your mining properties. Mr. Shepler thought the 'One Girl' was such a funny name for your father to give a mine."

Now they neared the foot of the shaft where the rest of the party seemed to await them. As they came up Percival felt himself raked by a broadside from the maternal lorgnon that left him all but disabled. The father glowered at him and asked questions in the high key we are apt to adopt in addressing foreigners, in the instinctive fallacy that any language can be understood by any one if it be spoken loudly enough. The mother's manner was a crushing rebuke to the young man for his audacity. The father's manner was meant to intimate that natives of the region in which they were then adventuring were not worthy of rebuke, save such general rebukes as may be conveyed by displaying one's natural superiority of manner. The other members of the party, excepting Shepler, who talked with Pangburn at a little distance, took cue from the Milbreys and aggressively ignored the abductor of an only daughter. They talked over, around, and through him, as only may those mortals whom it hath pleased heaven to have born within certain areas on Manhattan Island.

The young man felt like a social outcast until he caught a glance from Miss Milbrey. That young woman was still friendly, which he could understand, and highly amused, which he could not understand. While the temperature was at its lowest the first load ascended, including Miss Milbrey and her parents, a chatty blonde, and an uncomfortable little man who, despite his being twelve hundred feet toward the centre thereof, had three times referred bitterly to the fact that he was "out of the world." "I shall see you soon above ground, shall I not?" Miss Milbrey had asked, at which her mother shot Percival a parting volley from her rapid-fire lorgnon, while her father turned upon him a back whose sidelines were really admirable, considering his age and feeding habits. The behaviour of these people appeared to intensify the amusement of their child. The two solemn young men who remained continued to chat before Percival as they would have chatted before the valet of either. He began to sound the spiritual anguish of a pariah. Also to feel truculent and, in his own phrase, "Westy." With him "Westy" meant that you were as good as any one else "and a shade better than a whole lot if it came to a show-down." He was not a little mortified to find how easy it was for him to fall back upon that old cushion of provincial arrogance. It was all right for Uncle Peter, but for himself,— well, it proved that he was less finely Eastern than he had imagined.

As the cage came down for another ascent, he let the two solemn young men go up with Shepler and Pangburn, and went to search for Uncle Peter.

"There, thank God, is a man!" he reflected.

CHAPTER VII.

The Rapid-fire Lorgnon Is Spiked

He found Uncle Peter in the cross-cut, studying a bit of ore through a glass, and they went back to ascend.

"Them folks," said the old man, "must be the kind that newspaper meant, that had done something in practical achievement. I bet that girl's mother will achieve something practical with you fur cuttin' the girl out of the bunch; she was awful tormented; talked two or three times about the people in the humbler walks of life bein' strangely something or other. You ain't such a humble walker now, are you, son? But say, that yellow-haired woman, she ain't a bit diffident, is she? She's a very hearty lady, I *must* say!"

"But did you see Miss Milbrey?"

"Oh, that's her name is it, the one that her mother was so worried about and you? Yes, I saw her. Peart and cunnin', but a heap too wise fur you, son; take my steer on that. Say, she'd have your pelt nailed to the barn while you was wonderin' which way you'd jump."

"Oh, I know I'm only a tender, teething infant," the young man answered, with masterly satire. "Well, now, as long's you got that bank roll you jest look out fur cupboard love—the kind the old cat has when she comes rubbin' up against your leg and purrin' like you was the whole thing."

The young man smiled, as they went up, with youth's godlike faith in its own sufficiency, albeit he smarted from the slights put upon him.

At the surface a pleasant shock was in store for him. There stood the formidable Mrs. Milbrey beaming upon him. Behind her was Mr. Milbrey, the pleasing model of all a city's refinements, awaiting the boon of a hand-clasp. Behind these were the uncomfortable little man, the chatty blonde, and the two solemn young men who had lately exhibited more manner than manners. Percival felt they were all regarding him now with affectionate concern. They pressed forward effusively.

"So good of you, Mr. Bines, to take an interest in us—my daughter has been so anxious to see one of these fascinating mines." "Awfully obliged, Mr. Bines." "Charmed, old man; deuced pally of you to stay by us down in that hole, you know." "So clever of you to know where to find the gold—"

He lost track of the speakers. Their speeches became one concerted effusion of affability that was music to his ears.

Miss Milbrey was apart from the group. Having doffed the waterproofs, she was now pluming herself with those fussy-looking but mysteriously potent little pats which restore the attire and mind of women to their normal perfection and serenity. Upon her face was still the amused look Percival had noted below.

"And, Mr. Bines, do come in with that quaint old grandfather of yours and lunch with us," urged Mrs. Milbrey, who had, as it were, spiked her lorgnon. "Here's Mr. Shepler to second the invitation—and then we shall chat about this very interesting West."

Miss Milbrey nodded encouragement, seeming to chuckle inwardly.

In the spacious dining compartment of the Shepler car the party was presently at lunch.

"You seem so little like a Western man," Mrs. Milbrey confided graciously to Percival on her right.

"We cal'late he'll fetch out all straight, though, in a year or so," put in Uncle Peter, from over his chop, with guileless intent to defend his grandson from what he believed to be an attack. "Of course a young man's bound to get some foolishness into him in an Eastern college like this boy went to."

Percival had flushed at the compliment to himself; also at the old man's failure to identify it as such.

Mr. Milbrey caressed his glass of claret with ardent eyes and took the situation in hand with the easy confidence of a master.

"The West," said he, affably, "has sent us some magnificent men. In truth, it's amazing to take count of the Western men among us in all the professions. They are notable, perhaps I should say, less for deliberate niceties of style than for a certain rough directness, but so adaptable is the American character that one frequently does not suspect their—er—humble origin."

"Meaning their Western origin?" inquired Shepler, blandly, with secret intent to brew strife.

"Well—er—to be sure, my dear fellow, not necessarily humble,—of course—perhaps I should have said—"

"Of course, not necessarily disgraceful, as you say, Milbrey," interrupted Shepler, "and they often do conceal it. Why, I know a chap in New York who was positively never east of Kansas City until he was twenty-five or so, and yet that fellow to-day"—he lowered his voice to the pitch of impressiveness—"has over eighty pairs of trousers and complains of the hardship every time he has to go to Boston."

"Fancy, now!" exclaimed Mrs. Drelmer, the blonde. Mr. Milbrey looked slightly puzzled and Uncle Peter chuckled, affirming mentally that Rulon Shepler must be like one of those tug-boats, with most of his lines under the surface.

"But, I say, you know, Shepler," protested one of the solemn young men, "he must still talk like a banjo."

"And gargle all his 'r's,'" added the other, very earnestly. "They never get over that, you know."

"Instead of losin' 'em entirely," put in Uncle Peter, who found himself feeling what his grandson called "Westy." "Of course, he calls it 'Ne' Yawk,' and prob'ly he don't like it in Boston because they always call 'em 'rawroystahs.'"

"Good for the old boy!" thought Percival, and then, aloud: "It *is* hard for the West and the East to forgive each other's dialects. The inflated 'r' and the smothered 'r' never quite harmonise."

"Western money talks good straight New York talk," ventured Miss Milbrey, with the air of one who had observed in her time.

Shepler grinned, and the parents of the young woman resisted with indifferent success their twin impulses to frown.

"But the service is so wretched in the West," suggested Oldaker, the carefully dressed little man with the tired, troubled eyes, whom the world had been deprived of. "I fancy, now, there's not a good waiter this side of New York."

"An American," said Percival, "never *can* make a good waiter or a good valet. It takes a Latin, or, still better, a Briton, to feel the servility required for good service of that sort. An American, now, always fails at it because he knows he is as good as you are, and he knows that you know it, and you know that he knows you know it, and there you are, two mirrors of American equality face to face and reflecting each other endlessly, and neither is comfortable. The American is as uncomfortable at having certain services performed for him by another American as the other is in performing them. Give him a Frenchman or an Italian or a fellow born within the sound of Bow Bells to clean his boots and lay out his things and serve his dinner and he's all right enough."

"Hear, hear!" cried Uncle Peter.

"Fancy, now," said Mrs. Drelmer, "a creature in a waiter's jacket having emotions of that sort!"

"Our excellent country," said Mr. Milbrey, "is perhaps not yet what it will be; there is undeniably a most distressing rawness where we might expect finish. Now in Chicago," he continued in a tone suitably hushed for the relation of occult phenomena, "we dined with a person who served champagne with the oysters, soup, fish, and *entrée*, and for the remainder of the dinner—you may credit me or not—he proffered a claret of 1875—. I need hardly remind you, the most delicate vintage of the latter half of the century—and it was served *frappé*." There was genuine emotion in the speaker's voice.

"And papa nearly swooned when our host put cracked ice and two lumps of sugar into his own glass—"

"*Avice, dear!*" remonstrated the father in a tone implying that some things positively must not be mentioned at table.

"Well, you shouldn't expect too much of those self-made men in Chicago," said Shepler.

"If they'd only make themselves as well as they make their sausages and things," sighed Mr. Milbrey.

"And the self-made man *will* talk shop," suggested Oldaker. "He thinks you're dying to hear how he made the first thousand of himself."

"Still, those Chicago chaps learn quickly enough when they settle in New York," ventured one of the young men.

"I knew a Chicago chap who lived East two years and went back not a half bad sort," said the other. "God help him now, though; his father made him go back to work in a butcher shop or something of the sort."

"Best thing I ever heard about Chicago," said Uncle Peter, "a man from your town told me once he had to stay in Chicago a year, and, says he, 'I went out there a New Yorker, and I went home an American,' he says." The old man completed this anecdote in tones that were slightly inflamed.

"How extremely typical!" said Mrs. Milbrey. "Truly the West is the place of unspoiled Americanism and the great unspent forces; you are quite right, Mr. Bines."

"Think of all the unspent forces back in that silver mine," remarked Miss Milbrey, with a patent effort to be significant.

"My perverse child delights to pose as a sordid young woman," the fond mother explained to Percival, "yet no one can be less so, and you, Mr. Bines, I am sure, would be the last to suspect her of it. I saw in you at once those sterling qualities—"

"Isn't it dreadfully dark down in that sterling silver mine?" observed Miss Milbrey, apropos of nothing, apparently, while her mother attacked a second chop that she had meant not to touch.

"Here's hoping we'll soon be back in God's own country," said Oldaker, raising his glass.

"Hear, hear!" cried Uncle Peter, and drained his glass eagerly as they drank the toast. Whereat they all laughed and Mrs. Drelmer said, "What a dear, lively wit, for an old gentleman."

"Oldaker," said Shepler, "has really been the worst sufferer. This is his first trip West."

"Beg pardon, Shepler! I was West as far as Buffalo—let me see—in 1878 or '79."

"Dear me! is that so?" queried Uncle Peter. "I got East as fur as Cheyenne that same year. We nearly run into each other, didn't we?"

Shepler grinned again.

"Oldaker found a man from New York on the train the other day, up in one of the emigrant cars. He was a truck driver, and he looked it and talked it, but Oldaker stuck by him all the afternoon."

"Well, he'd left the old town three weeks after I had, and he'd been born there the same year I was—in the Ninth ward—and he remembered as well as I did the day Barnum's museum burned at Broadway and Ann. I liked to hear him talk. Why, it was a treat just to hear him say Broadway and Twenty-third Street, or Madison Square or City Hall Park. The poor devil had consumption, too, and probably he'll never see them again. I don't know if I shall ever have it, but I'd never leave the old town as he was doing."

"That's like Billy Brue," said Uncle Peter. "Billy loves faro bank jest as this gentleman loves New York. When he gets a roll he *has* to play. One time he landed in Pocatello when there wa'n't but one game in town. Billy found it and started in. A friend saw him there and called him out. 'Billy,' says he, 'cash in and come out; that's a brace game.' 'Sure?' says Billy. 'Sure,' says the feller. 'All right,' says Billy, 'much obliged fur puttin' me on.' And he started out lookin' fur another game. About two hours later the feller saw Billy comin' out of the same place and Billy owned up he'd gone back there and blowed in every cent. 'Why, you geezer,' says his friend, 'didn't I put you on that they was dealin' brace there?' 'Sure,' says Billy, 'sure you did. But what could I do? It was the only game in town!'"

"That New York mania is the same sort," said Shepler, laughing, while Mrs. Drelmer requested everybody to fancy immediately.

"Your grandfather is so dear and quaint," said Mrs. Milbrey; "you must certainly bring him to New York with you, for of course a young man of your capacity and graces will never be satisfied out of New York."

"Young men like yourself are assuredly needed there," remarked Mr. Milbrey, warmly.

"Surely they are," agreed Miss Milbrey, and yet with a manner that seemed almost to annoy both parents. They were sparing no opportunity to make the young man conscious of his real oneness with those about him, and yet subtly to intimate that people of just the Milbreys' perception were required to divine it at present. "These Westerners fancy you one of themselves, I dare say," Mrs. Milbrey had said, and the young man purred under the strokings. His fever for the East was back upon him. His weeks with Uncle Peter going over the fields where his father had prevailed had made him convalescent, but these New Yorkers—the very manner and atmosphere of them—undid the work. He envied them their easier speech, their matter-of-fact air of omniscience, the elaborate and cultivated simplicity of their dress, their sureness and sufficiency in all that they thought and said and did. He was homesick again for the life he had glimpsed. The West was rude, desolate, and depressing. Even Uncle Peter, whom he had come warmly to admire, jarred upon him with his crudity and his Western assertiveness.

And there was the woman of the East, whose presence had made the day to seem dream-like; and she was kind, which was more than he would have dared to hope, and her people, after their first curious chill of indifference, seemed actually to be courting him. She, the fleeting and impalpable dream-love, whom the thought of seeing ever again had been wildly absurd, was now a human creature with a local habitation, the most beautiful name in the world, and two parents whose complaisance was obvious even through the lover's timidity.

CHAPTER VIII.

Up Skiplap Canon

The meal was ending in smoke, the women, excepting Miss Milbrey, having lighted cigarettes with the men. The talk had grown less truculently

Mr. Milbrey described with minute and loving particularity the preparation of *oeufs de Faisan, avec beurre au champagne.*

Mrs. Milbrey related an anecdote of New York society, not much in itself, but which permitted the disclosure that she habitually addressed by their first names three of the foremost society leaders, and that each of these personages adopted a like familiarity toward her.

Mrs. Drelmer declared that she meant to have Uncle Peter Bines at one of her evenings the very first time he should come to New York, and that, if he didn't let her know of his coming, she would be offended. Oldaker related an incident of the ball given to the Prince of Wales, travelling as Baron Renfrew, on the evening of October 12, 1860, in which his father had figured briefly before the royal guest to the abiding credit of American tact and gentility.

Shepler was amused until he became sleepy, whereupon he extended the freedom of his castle to his guests, and retired to his stateroom.

Uncle Peter took a final shot at Oldaker. He was observed to be laughing, and inquiry brought this:

"I jest couldn't help snickerin' over his idee of God's own country. He thinks God's own country is a little strip of an island with a row of well-fed folks up and down the middle, and a lot of hungry folks on each side. Mebbe he's right. I'll be bound, it needs the love of God. But if it is His own country, it don't make Him any connysoor of countries with me. I'll tell you that."

Oldaker smiled at this assault, the well-bred, tolerant smile that loyal New Yorkers reserve for all such barbaric belittling of their empire. Then he politely asked Uncle Peter to show Mrs. Drelmer and himself through the stamp mill.

At Percival's suggestion of a walk, Miss Milbrey was delighted.

After an inspection of the Bines car, in which Oldaker declared he would be willing to live for ever, if it could be anchored firmly in Madison Square, the party separated. Out into the clear air, already cooling under the slanting rays of the sun, the young man and the girl went together. Behind them lay the one street of the little mining camp, with its wooden shanties on either side of the railroad track. Down this street Uncle Peter had gone, leading his charges toward the busy ant-hill on the mountainside. Ahead the track wound up the canon, cunningly following the tortuous course of the little river to be sure of practicable grades. On the farther side of the river a mountain road paralleled the railway. Up this road the two went, followed by a playful admonition from Mrs. Milbrey: "Remember, Mr. Bines, I place my child in your keeping."

Percival waxed conscientious about his charge and insisted at once upon being assured that Miss Milbrey would be warm enough with the scarlet golf-cape about her shoulders; that she was used to walking long distances; that her boots were stoutly soled; and that she didn't mind the sun in their faces. The girl laughed at him.

Looking up the canon with its wooded sides, cool and green, they could see a grey, dim mountain, with patches of snow near its top, in the far distance, and ranges of lesser eminences stepping up to it. "It's a hundred miles away," he told her.

Down the canon the little river flickered toward them, like a billowy silver ribbon "trimmed with white chiffon around the rocks," declared the girl. In the blue depths of the sky, an immense height above, lolled an eagle, lazy of wing, in lordly indolence. The suggestions to the eye were all of spacious distances and large masses—of the room and stuff for unbounded action.

"Your West is the breathingest place," she said, as they crossed a foot-bridge over the noisy little stream and turned up the road. "I don't believe I ever drew a full breath until I came to these altitudes."

"One *has* to breathe more air here—there's less oxygen in it, and you must breathe more to get your share, and so after awhile one becomes robust. Your cheeks are already glowing, and we've hardly started. There, now, there are your colours, see—"

Along the edge of the green pines and spruce were lavender asters. A little way in the woods they could see the blue columbines and the mountain phlox, pink and red.

"There are your eyes and your cheeks."

"What a dangerous character you'd be if you were sent to match silks!"

On the dry barren slopes of gravel across the river, full in the sun's glare, grew the Spanish bayonet, with its spikes of creamy white flowers.

"There I am, more nearly," she pointed to them; "they're ever so much nearer my disposition. But about this thin air; it must make men work harder for what comes easier back in our country, so that they may become able to do more—more capable. I am thinking of your grandfather. You don't know how much I admire him. He is so stanch and strong and fresh. There's more fire in him now than in my father or Launton Oldaker, and I dare say he's a score of years older than either of them. I don't think you quite appreciate what a great old fellow he is."

"I admire Uncle Peter much more, I'm sure, than he admires me. He's afraid I'm not strong enough to admire that Eastern climate of yours—social and moral."

"I suppose it's natural for you to wish to go. You'd be bored here, would you not? You couldn't stay in these mountains and be such a man as your grandfather. And yet there ought to be so much to do here; it's all so fresh and roomy and jolly. Really I've grown enthusiastic about it."

"Ah, but think of what there is in the East—and you are there. To think that for six months I've treasured every little memory of you—such a funny little lot as they were—to think that this morning I awoke thinking of you, yet hardly hoping ever to see you, and to think that for half the night we had ridden so near each other in sleep, and there was no sign or signal or good omen. And then to think you should burst upon me like some new sunrise that the stupid astronomers hadn't predicted.

"You see," he went on, after a moment, "I don't ask what you think of me. You couldn't think anything much as yet, but there's something about this whole affair, our meeting and all, that makes me think it's going to be symmetrical in the end. I know it won't end here. I'll tell you one way Western men learn. They learn not to be afraid to want things out of their reach, and they believe devoutly—because they've proved it so often—that if you want a thing hard enough and keep wanting it, nothing can keep it away from you."

A bell had been tinkling nearer and nearer on the road ahead. Now a heavy wagon, filled with sacks of ore, came into view, drawn by four mules. As they stood aside to let it pass he scanned her face for any sign it might show, but he could see no more than a look of interest for the brawny driver of the wagon, shouting musically to his straining team.

"You are rather inscrutable," he said, as they resumed the road.

She turned and smiled into his eyes with utter frankness.

"At least you must be sure that I like you; that I am very friendly; that I want to know you better, and want you to know me better. You don't know me at all, you know. You Westerners have another way, of accepting people too readily. It may work no harm among yourselves, but perhaps Easterners are a bit more perilous. Sometimes, now, a *very* Eastern person doesn't even accept herself—himself—very trustingly; she—he—finds it so hard to get acquainted with himself."

The young man provided one of those silences of which a few discerning men are instinctively capable and for which women thank them.

"This road," she said, after a little time of rapid walking, "leads right up to the end of the world, doesn't it? See, it ends squarely in the sun." They stopped where the turn had opened to the west a long vista of grey and purple hills far and high. They stood on a ridge of broken quartz and gneiss, thrown up in a bygone age. To their left a few dwarf Scotch firs threw shadows back toward the town. The ball of red fire in the west was half below the rim of the distant peak.

"Stand so,"—she spoke in a slightly hushed tone that moved him a step nearer almost to touch her arm,—"and feel the round little earth turning with us. We always think the sun drops down away from us, but it stays still. Now remember your astronomy and feel the earth turn. See—you can actually *see* it move—whirling along like a child's ball because it can't help itself, and then there's the other motion around the sun, and the other, the rushing of everything through space, and who knows how many others, and yet we plan our futures and think we shall do finely this way or that, and always forget that we're taken along in spite of ourselves. Sometimes I think I shall give up trying; and then I see later that even that feeling was one of the unknown motions that I couldn't control. The only thing we know is that we are moved in spite of ourselves, so what is the use of bothering about how many ways, or where they shall fetch us?"

"Ah, Miss Khayyam, I've often read your father's verses."

"No relation whatever; we're the same person—he was I."

"But don't forget you can see the earth moving by a rising as well as by a setting star, by watching a sun rise—"

"A rising star if you wish," she said, smiling once more with perfect candour and friendliness.

They turned to go back in the quick-coming mountain dusk.

As they started downward she sang from the "Persian Garden," and he blended his voice with hers:

"Myself when young did eagerly frequent

Doctor and Saint and heard great argument

About it and about: but evermore

Came out by the same door where in I went."

"With them the seed of Wisdom did I sow,

And with my own hand wrought to make it grow;

And this was all the Harvest that I reaped—'

I came like Water and like Wind I go.'"

"I shall look forward to seeing you—and your mother and sister?—in New York," she said, when they parted, "and I am sure I shall have more to say when we're better known to each other."

"If you were the one woman before, if the thought of you was more than the substance of any other to me,—you must know how it will be now, when the dream has come true. It's no small thing for your best dream to come true."

"Dear me! haven't we been sentimental and philosophic? I'm never like this at home, I assure you. I've really been thoughtful."

From up the cañon came the sound of a puffing locomotive that presently steamed by them with its three dingy little coaches, and, after a stop for water and the throwing of a switch, pushed back to connect with the Shepler car.

The others of the party crowded out on to the rear platform as Percival helped Miss Milbrey up the steps. Uncle Peter had evidently been chatting with Shepler, for as they came out the old man was saying, "'Get action' is my motto. Do things. Don't fritter. Be something and be it good and hard. Get action early and often."

Shepler nodded. "But men like us are apt to be unreasonable with the young. We expect them to have their own vigour and our wisdom, and the infirmities of neither."

The good-byes were hastily said, and the little train rattled down the cañon. Miss Milbrey stood in the door of the car, and Percival watched her while the glistening rails that seemed to be pushing her away narrowed in perspective. She stood motionless and inscrutable to the last, but still looking steadily toward him—almost wistfully, it seemed to him once.

"Well," he said cheerfully to Uncle Peter.

"You know, son, I don't like to cuss, but except one or two of them folks I'd sooner live in the middle kittle of hell than in the place that turns 'em out. They rile me—that talk about 'people in the humbler walks of life.' Of course I *am* humble, but then, son, if you come right down to it, as the feller said, I ain't so *damned* humble!"

CHAPTER IX.

Three Letters, Private and Confidential

From Mr. Percival Bines to Miss Psyche Bines, Montana City.

On car at Skiplap, Tuesday Night.

Dear Sis:—When you kept nagging me about "Who is the girl?" and I said you could search me, you wouldn't have it that way. But, honestly, until this morning I didn't know her myself. Now that I can put you next, here goes.

One night last March, after I'd come back from the other side, I happened into a little theatre on Broadway where a burlesque was running. It's a rowdy little place—a music hall—but nice people go there because, though it's stuffy, it's kept decent.

She was in a box with two men—one old and one young—and an older woman. As soon as I saw her she had me lashed to the mast in a high sea, with the great salt waves dashing over me. I never took much stock in the tales about its happening at first sight, but they're as matter-of-fact as market reports. Soon as I looked at her it seemed to me I'd known her always. I was sure we knew each other better than any two people between the Battery and Yonkers, and that I wasn't acting sociable to sit down there away from her and pretend we were Strangers Yet. Actually, it rattled me so I had to take the full count. If I hadn't been wedged in between a couple of people that filled all the space, and then some, it isn't any twenty to one that I wouldn't have gone right up to her and asked her what she meant by cutting me. I was udgy enough for it. But I kept looking and after awhile I was able to sit up and ask what hit me.

She was dressed in something black and kind of shiny and wore a big black hat fussed up with little red roses, and her face did more things to me in a minute than all the rest I've ever seen. It was *full* of little kissy places. Her lips were very red and her teeth were very white, and I couldn't tell about her eyes. But she was bred up to the last notch, I could see that.

Well, I watched her through the tobacco smoke until the last curtain fell. They were putting on wraps for a minute or so, and I noticed that the young fellow in the party, who'd been drinking all through the show, wasn't a bit too steady to do an act on the high-wire. They left the box and came down the stairs and I bunched into the crowd and let myself ooze out with them, wondering if I'd ever see her again.

I fetched up at an exit on the side street, and there they were directly in front of me. I just naturally drifted to one side and continued my little private corner in crude rubber. It was drizzling in a beastly way, the street was full of carriages, numbers were being called, cab-drivers were insulting each other hoarsely, people dashing out to see if their carriages weren't coming—everything in a whirl of drizzle and dark and yells, with the horses' hoofs on the pavement sounding like castanets. The two older people got into a carriage and were driven off, while she and the young fellow waited for theirs. I could see then that he was good and soused. He was the same lad they throw on the screen when the "Old Homestead" Quartet sings "Where Is My Wandering Boy To-night?" I could see she was annoyed and a little worried, because he was past taking notice.

The man kept yelling the number of their carriage from time to time, while the others he'd called were driving up—it was 249 if any one ever tries to worm it out of you—and then I saw from her face that 249 had wriggled pretty near to the curb, but was still kept away by another carriage. She said something to the drunken cub and started to reach the carriage by going out into the street behind the one in its way. At the same time their carriage started forward, and the inebriate, instead of going with her, started the other way to meet it, and so, there she was alone on the slippery pavement in this muddle of prancing horses and yelling terriers. If you can get any bets that I was more than two seconds getting out there to her, take them all, and give better than track odds if necessary. Then I guess she got rattled, for when I would have led her back to the curb she made a dash the other way and all but slipped under a team of bays that were just aching to claw the roses off her hat. I saw she was helpless and "turned around," so I just naturally grabbed her and she was so frightened by this time that she grabbed me, and the result was that I carried her to the sidewalk and set her down. Their carriage still stood there with little Georgie Rumlets screaming to the driver to go on. I had her inside in a jiffy, and they were off. Not a word about "My Preserver!" though, of course, with the fright and noise and her mortification, that was natural.

After that, you can believe it or not, she was the girl. And I never dreamed of seeing her any place but New York again.

Well, this morning when I came up from below at the mine *she* was standing there as if she had been waiting for me. She is Miss Avice Milbrey, of New York. Her father and mother—fine people, the real thing, I judge—were with her, members of a party Rulon Shepler has with him on his car. They've been here all day; went through the mine; had lunch with them, and later a walk with *her*, they leaving at 5.30 for the East. We got on fairly well, considering. She is a wonder, if anybody cross-examines you. She is about your height, I should judge, about five feet four, though not so plump as you; still her look of slenderness is deceptive. She's one of the build that aren't so big as they look, nor yet so small as they look. Thoroughbred is the word for her, style and action, as the horse people say, perfect. The poise of her head, her mettlesome manner, her walk, show that she's been bred up like a Derby winner. Her face is the one all the aristocrats are copied from, finely cut nose, chin firm but dainty, lips just delicately full and the reddest ever, and her colour when she has any a rose-pink. I don't know that I can give you her eyes. You only see first that they're deep and clear, but as near as anything they are the warm slatish lavender blue you see in the little fall asters. She has so much hair it makes her head look small, a sort of light chestnut, with warmish streaks in it. Transparent is another word for her. You can look right through her—eyes and skin are so clear. Her nature too is the frank, open kind, "step in and examine our stock; no trouble to show goods" and all that, and she is so beautifully unconscious of her beauty that it goes double. At times she gave me a queer little impression of being older at the game than I am, though she can't be a day over twenty, but I guess that's because she's been around in society so much. Probably she'd be called the typical New York girl, if you wanted to talk talky talk.

Now I've told you everything, except that the people all asked kindly after you, especially her mother and a Mrs. Drelmer, who's a four-horse team all by herself. Oh, yes! No, I can't remember very well; some kind of a brown walking skirt, short, and high boots and one of those blue striped shirt-waists, the squeezy looking kind, and when we went to walk, a red plaid golf cape; and for general all-around dearness—say, the other entries would all turn green and have to be withdrawn. If any one thinks this thing is going to end here you make a book on it right away; take all you can get. Little Willie Lushlets was her brother—a lovely boy if you get to talking reckless. With love to Lady Abercrombie, and trusting, my dear Countess, to have the pleasure of meeting you at Henley a fortnight hence, I remain,

Most cordially yours,

E. MALVERN DEVYR ST. TREVORS,

Bart. & Notary Public.

From Mrs. Joseph Drelmer to the Hon. Cecil G. H. Mauburn, New York.

EN ROUTE, August 28th.

MY DEAR MAUBURN:—Ever hear of the tribe of Bines? If not, you need to. The father, immensely wealthy, died a bit ago, leaving a widow and two children, one of the latter being a marriageable daughter in more than the merely technical sense. There is also a grandfather, now a little descended into the vale of years, who, they tell me, has almost as many dollars as you or I would know what to do with, a queer old chap who lounges about the mountains and looks as if he might have anything but money. We met the son and the old man at one of their mines yesterday. They have a private car as large as Shepler's and even more sybaritic, and they'd been making a tour of inspection over their properties. They lunched with us. Knowing the Milbreys, you will divine the warmth of their behaviour toward the son. It was too funny at first. Avice was the only one to suspect at once that he was the very considerable personage he is, and so she promptly sequestered him, with a skill born of her long practice, in the depths of the earth, somewhere near China, I fancy. Her dear parents were furious. Dressed as one of the miners they took him to be an employee. The whole party, taking the cue from outraged parenthood, treated him icily when he emerged from one of those subterranean galleries with that tender sprig of girlishness. That is, we were icy until, on the way up, he remaining in the depths, Avice's dear mother began to rebuke the thoughtless minx for her indiscretion of strolling through the earth with a working person. Then Avice, sweet chatterbox, with joyful malice revealed that the young man, whose name none of us had caught, was Bines, and that he owned the mine we were in, and she didn't know how many others, nor did she believe he knew himself. You should have felt the temperature rise. It went up faster than we were going.

By the time we reached the surface the two Milbreys wore looks that would have made the angel of peace and good-will look full of hatred and distrust. Nothing would satisfy them but that we wait to thank the young Croesus for his courtesy. I waited because I remembered the daughter, and Oldaker and the Angstead twins waited out of decency. And when the genius of the mine appeared from out his golden catacombs we fell upon him in desperate kindness.

Later in the day I learned from him that he expects to bring his mother and sister to New York this fall, and that they mean to make their home there hereafter. Of course that means that the girl has notions of marriage. What made me think so quickly of her is that in San Francisco, at a theatre last winter, she was pointed out to me, and while I do you not the injustice of supposing it would make the least difference to you, she is rather a beauty, you'll find; figure fullish, yellow hair, and a good-natured, well-featured, pleasing sort of face; a bit rococo in manner, I suspect; a little too San Francisco, as so many of these Western beauties are, but you'd not mind that, and a year in New York will tone her down anyway.

Now if your dear uncle will only confer a lasting benefit upon the world and his title upon you, by paying the only debt he is ever liable to pay, I am persuaded you could be the man here. I know nothing of how the fortune was left, nor of its extent, except that it's said to be stiffish, and out here that means a big, round sum. The reason I write promptly is that you may not go out of the country just now. That sweet little Milbrey chit—really, Avice is far too old now for ingenue parts—has not only grappled the son with hooks of steel, but from remarks the good mother dropped concerning the fine qualities of her son, she means to convert the daughter's *dot* into Milbrey prestige, also. What a glorious double stroke it would be, after all their years of trying. However, with your title, even in prospective, Fred Milbrey is no rival for you to fear, providing you are on the ground as soon as he, which is why I wish you to stay in New York.

I am indeed gratified that you have broken off whatever affair there may have been between you and that music-hall person. Really, you know, though they talk so about us, a young man can't mess about with that sort of thing in New York as he can in London. So I'm glad she's gone back, and as she is in no position to harm you I should pay no attention to her threats. What under heaven did the creature expect? Why *should* she have wanted to marry you?

I shall see you probably in another fortnight.

You know that Milbrey girl must get her effrontery direct from where they make it. She pretended that at first she took young Bines for what we all took him, an employee of the mine. You can almost catch them winking at each other, when she tells it, and dear mamma with such beautiful resignation, says, "My Avice is *so* impulsively democratic." Dear Avice, you know, is really quite as impulsive as the steel bridge our train has just rattled over. Sincerely,

JOSEPHINE PRESTON DRELMER.

From Miss Avice Milbrey to Mrs. Cornelia Van Geist, New York.

Mütterchen, dearest, I feel like that green hunter you had to sell last spring—the one that would go at a fence with the most perfect display of serious intentions, and then balk and bolt when it came to jumping. Can it be that I, who have been trained from the cradle to the idea of marrying for money, will bolt the gate after all the expense and pains lavished upon my education to this end; after the years spent in learning how to enchant, subdue, and exploit the most useful of all animals, and the most agreeable, barring a few? And yet, right when I'm the fittest—twenty-four years old, knowing all my good points and just how to coerce the most admiration for each, able nicely to calculate the exact disturbing effect of the *ensemble* upon any poor male, and feeling confident of my excessively eligible *parti* when I decide for him—in this situation, striven for so earnestly, I feel like bolting the bars. How my trainer and jockey would weep tears of rage and despair if they guessed it!

There, there—I know your shrewd grey eyes are crackling with curiosity and, you want to know what it's all about, whether to scold me or mother me, and will I please omit the *entrées* and get to the roast mutton. But you dear, dear old aunt, you, there is more vagueness than detail, and I know I'll strain your patience before I've done. But, to relieve your mind, nothing at all has really happened. After all, it's mostly a *troublesome state of mind*, that I shall doubtless find gone when we reach Jersey City,—and in two ways this Western trip is responsible for it. Do you know the journey itself has been fascinating. Too bad so many of us cross the ocean twenty times before we know anything of this country. We loiter in Paris, do the stupid German watering-places, the Norway fjords, down to Italy for the museums, see the *chateaux* of the Loire, or do the English race-tracks, thinking we're 'mused; and all the time out here where the sun goes down is an intensely interesting and beautiful country of our own that we overlook. You know I'd never before been even as far as Chicago. Now for the first time I can appreciate lots of those things in Whitman, that—

"I think heroic deeds were all conceived in the open air, and free poems, also. Now I see the secret of making the best persons: It is to grow in the open air and to eat and sleep with the earth."

I mayn't have quoted correctly, but you know the sort of thing I mean, that sounds so *breezy* and *stimulating*. And they've helped me understand the immensity of the landscapes and the ideas out here, the big, throbbing, rough young life, and under it all, as Whitman says, "a meaning— Democracy, *American* Democracy." Really it's been interesting, *the jolliest time of my life,* and it's got me all unsettled. More than once in watching some scene typical of the region, the plain, busy, earnest people, I've actually thrilled to think that this was *my country*—felt that queer little tickling tingle that locates your spine for you. I'm sure there's no *ennui* here. Some one said the other day, "*Ennui* is a disease that comes from living on other people's money." I said no, that I'd often had as fine an attack as if I'd been left a billion, that *ennui* is when you don't know what to do next and wouldn't do it if you did. Well, here they always *do* know what to do next, and as one of them told me, "*We always get up early the day before to do it.*"

Auntie, dear, the trip has made me *more restless and dissatisfied* than ever. It makes me want to *do* something—to *risk* something, to want to *want* something more than I've ever learned to want.

That's one reason I'm acting badly. The other will interest you more.

It's no less a reason than *the athletic young Bayard* who cheated those cab-horses of their prey that night Fred didn't drink all the Scotch whiskey in New York. Our meeting, and the mater's treatment of him before she discovered who he was, are too delicious to write. I must wait to tell you.

It is enough to say that now I heard his name it recalled nothing to me, and I took him from his dress to be a *workingman* in the mine we visiting, though from his speech and manner of a gentleman, someone in authority. Dear, he was *so* dear and so Westernly breezy and progressive and enterprising and so *appallingly candid*. I've been the "one woman", the "unknown but remembered ideal" since that encounter. Of course, that was to be said, but strangely enough he meant it. He was actually and unaffectedly making love to me. He's not so large or tall, but quick and springy, and muscled like a panther. He's not beautiful either but pleasant to look at, one of those broad high-cheeked faces one sees so much in the West, with the funniest quick yellowish grey eyes and the most disreputable moustache I ever saw, yellow and ragged, If he must eat it, I wish he would *eat it off even* clear across. And he's likely to talk the most execrable slang, or to quote Browning. But he was making real love, and you know I'm not used to that. I'm accustomed to go my pace before sharply calculating eyes, to show if I'm worth the *asking price*. But here was real love being made off down in the earth (we'd run away from the others because I *liked him at once*). I don't mind telling you he moved me, partly because I had wondered about him from that night, and partly because of all I had come to feel about this new place and the new people, and because he seemed such a fine, active specimen of Western manhood. I won't tell you all the wild, lawless thoughts that scurried and *sneaked* through my mind—they don't matter now—for all at once it came out that he was the only son of that wealthy Bines who died awhile ago—you remember the name was mentioned that night at your house when they were discussing the exodus of Western millionaires to New York; some one named the father as one who liked coming to New York to dissipate occasionally, but who was still rooted in the soil where his millions grew.

There was the son before me, just *an ordinary man of millions*, after all—and my little toy balloon of romance that I'd been floating so gaily on a string of sentiment was pricked to nothing in an instant. I felt my nostrils expand with the excitement of the chase, and thereafter I was my *coldly professional self*. If that young man has not now a high estimate of my charms of person and mind, then have my ways forgot their cunning and I be no longer the daughter of Margaret Milbrey, *née* van Schoule.

But, Mütterchen, now comes the disgraceful part. I'm afraid of myself, even in spite of our affairs being so bad. Dad has doubtless told you something must be done very soon, and I seem to be the only one to do it. And yet I am shying at the gate. This trip has unsettled me, I tell you, letting me, among other things, see my old self. Before I always rather liked the idea of marriage, that is, after I'd been out a couple of years—not too well, but well enough—and now some way I rebel, not from scruples, but from pure selfishness. I'm beginning to find that I want to *enjoy myself* and to find, further, that I'm not indisposed to *take chances*—as they say out here. Will you understand, I wonder? And do women who sell themselves ever find any real pleasure in the bargain? The most eloquent examples, the ones that sell themselves to *many men,* lead wretched lives. But does the woman who sells herself to *but one* enjoy life any more? She's surely as bad, from any standpoint of morals, and I imagine sometimes she is less happy. At any rate, she has less *freedom* and more *obligations* under her contract. You see I am philosophising pretty coldly. Now be *horrified* if you will.

I am selfish by good right, though. "Haven't we spent all our surplus in keeping you up for a good marriage?" says the mater, meaning by a good marriage that I shall bring enough money into the family to *"keep up its traditions."* I am, in other words, an investment from which they expect large returns. I told her I hoped she could trace her selfishness to its source as clearly as I could mine, and as for the family traditions, Fred was preserving those in an excellent medium. Which was very ugly in me, and I cried afterwards and told her how sorry I was.

Are you shocked by my cold calculations? Well, I am trying to let you understand me, and I--

"...have no time to waste In patching fig-leaves for the naked truth."

I am cursed not only with consistent feminine longings and desires, but, in spite of my training and the examples around me, with a disinclination to be wholly vicious. Awhile ago marriage meant only more luxury and less worry about money. I never gave any thought to the husband, certainly never concerned myself with any notions of duty or obligation toward him. The girls I know are taught painstakingly how to get a husband, but nothing of how to be a wife. The husband in my case was to be an inconvenience, but doubtless an amusing one. For all his oppression, if there were that, and even for *the mere offence of his existence,* I should wreak my spite merrily on his vulgar dollars.

But you are saying that I like the present eligible. That's the trouble. I like him so well I haven't the heart to marry him. When I was twenty I could have loved him devotedly, I believe. Now something seems to be gone, some freshness or fondness. I can still love—I know it only too well night and day—but it must be a different kind of man. He is so very young and reverent and tender, and in a way so unsophisticated. He is so afraid of me, for all his pretence of boldness.

Is it because I must be taken by sheer force? I'll not be surprised if it is. Do we not in our secret soul of souls nourish this beatitude: "Blessed is the man who *destroys all barriers"?* Florence Akemit said as much one day, and

Florence, poor soul, knows something of the matter. Do we not sit defiantly behind the barriers, insolently challenging—threatening capital punishment for any assault, relaxing not one severity, yet falling meek and submissive and glad, to the man who brutally and honestly beats them down, and *destroys them utterly?* So many fail by merely beating them down. Of course if an *untidy litter* is left we make a row. We reconstruct the barrier and that particular assailant is thenceforth deprived of a combatant's rights. What a dear you are that I can say these things to you! Were girls so frank in your time?

Well, my knight of the "golden cross" (*joke; laughter and loud applause, and cries of "Go on!"*) has a little, much indeed, of the impetuous in him, but, alas! not enough. He has a pretty talent for it, but no genius. If I were married to him to-morrow, as surely as I am a woman I should be made to inflict pain upon him the next day, with an insane stress to show him, perhaps, I was not the ideal woman he had thought me—perhaps out of a jealousy of that very ideal I had inspired—rational creatures, aren't we?—beg pardon—not we, then, but I. Now he, being a real likable man of a man, can I do that—for money? Do I want the money *badly enough?* Would I not even rather be penniless with the man who coerced every great passion and littlest impulse, body and soul—*perhaps with a very hateful insolence of power over me?* Do you know, I suspect sometimes that I've trained down too fine, as to my nerves, I mean. I doubt if it's safe to pamper and trim and stimulate and refine a woman in that hothouse atmosphere—at least *if she's a healthy woman.* She's too apt sometime to break her gait, get the bit of tradition between her teeth, and then let her impulses run away with her.

Oh, Mütterchen, I am so sick and sore, and yet filled with a strange new zest for this old puzzle of life. Will I ever be the same again? This man is going to ask me to marry him the moment I am ready for him to. Shall I be kind enough to tell him no, or shall I steel myself to go in and hurt him—*make him writhe?*

And yet do you know what he gave me while I was with him? I wonder if women feel it commonly? It was a desire for *motherhood*—a curiously vivid and very definite longing—entirely irrespective of him, you understand, although he inspired it. Without loving him or being at all moved toward him, he made me sheerly *want* to be a mother! Or is it only that men we don't love make us feel motherly?

Am I wholly irrational and selfish and bad, or what am I? I know you'll love me, whatever it is, and I wish now I could snuggle on that soft, cushiony shoulder of yours and go to sleep.

Can anything be more pitiful than "a fine old family" afflicted with *dry-rot* like ours? I'm always amused when I read about the suffering in the tenements. The real anguish is up in the homes like ours. We have *to do without so very many more things*, and mere hunger and cold are easy compared to the suffering we feel.

Perhaps when I'm back to that struggle for appearances, I'll relent and "barter my charms" as the old novels used to say, sanely and decently like a well brought-up New York girl—*with certain reservations*, to a man who can support the family in the style to which it wants to become accustomed. Yet there may be a way out. There is a Bines daughter, for example, and mamma, who never does one half where she can as well do two, will marry her to Fred if she can. On the other hand, Joe Drelmer was putting in words for young Mauburn, who will be Lord Casselthorpe when his disreputable old uncle dies.

She hasn't yet spent what she got for introducing the Canovass prince to that oldest Elarton girl, so if she secures this prize for Mauburn, she'll be comfortable for a couple of more years. Perhaps I could turn my hand to something like that. I know the ropes as well as she does.

There, it *is* a punishment of a letter, isn't it, dear? But I've known *every bad place in it*, and I've religiously put in your "Come, come, child!" every time it belonged, so you've not still to scold me, for which be comforted a little; and give me only a few words of cheerful approval if your conscience will let you. I need that, after all, more than advice. Look for us in a week. With a bear-hug for you,

AVICE.

P.S. Is it true that Ned Ristine and his wife have fixed it up and are together again since his return? Not that I'm interested especially, but I chanced to hear it gossiped the other day here on the car. Indeed, I hope you know *how thoroughly I detest that man*!

CHAPTER X.

The Price of Averting a Scandal

As the train resumed speed after stopping at a station, Grant, the porter, came back to the observation room of the Bines car with a telegram for Uncle Peter. The old man read it and for a time mused himself into seeming oblivion. Across the car, near by, Percival lounged in a wicker arm-chair and stared cheerfully out into the gathering night. He, too, was musing, his thoughts keeping pleasantly in time with the rhythmic click of the wheels over the rail-joints. After a day in the open air he was growing sleepy.

Uncle Peter aroused him by making his way back to the desk, the roll-top of which he lifted with a sudden rattle. He called to Percival. Sitting down at the desk he read the telegram again and handed it to the young man, who read:

"Party will try to make good; no bluff. Won't compromise inside limit set. Have seen paper and wish another interview before following original instructions. Party will wait forty-eight hours before acting. Where can you be seen? Wire office to-night.

"TAFE & COPLEN."

The young man looked up with mild interest. Uncle Peter was writing on a telegraph blank.

"TAFE & COPLEN, Butte, Montana.

"Due Butte 7.30 A.M. to-morrow. Join me on car nought sixteen, go to Montana City.

"PETER BINES.

"D.H.F. 742."

To the porter who answered his ring he handed the message to be put off at the first stop.

"But what's it all about?" asked Percival, seeing by Uncle Peter's manner that he was expected to show concern.

Uncle Peter closed the desk, lighted one of his best cigars, and dropped into a capacious chair. The young man seated himself opposite.

"Well, son, it's a matter I cal'lated first off to handle myself, but it looks now as if you better be in on it. I don't know just how much you knew about your pa's ways, but, anyhow, you wouldn't play him to grade much higher above standard than the run of 'em out here that has had things comin' too easy for 'em. He was all right, Dan'l J. was. God knows I ain't discountin' the comfort I've always took in him. He'd stand acid all right, at any stage of the game. Don't forget that about your pa."

The young man reflected.

"The worst story I ever heard of pa was about the time he wanted to draw twenty thousand dollars from the bank in Tacoma. They telegraphed the Butte National to wire his description, and the answer was 'tall and drunk.'"

"Well, son, his periodicals wa'n't all. Seems as if this crowd has a way fur women, and they generally get the gaff because they're so blamed easy. You don't hear of them Eastern big men gettin' it so often, but I've seen enough of 'em to know it ain't because they're any straighter. They're jest a little keener on business propositions. They draw a fine sight when it comes to splittin' pennies, while men out here like your pa is lavish and careless. You know about lots of the others.

"There's Sooley Pentz, good-hearted a man as ever sacked ore, and plenty long-headed enough for the place he's bought in the Senate, but Sooley is restless until he's bought up one end of every town he goes into, from Eden plumb over to Washington, D. C.,—and 'tain't ever the Sunday-school end Sooley buys either. If he was makin' two million a month instead of one Sooley'd grieve himself to death because they don't make that five-dollar kind of wine fast enough.

"Then there was Seth Larby. We're jest gettin' to the details of Seth's expense account after he found the Lucky Cuss. I see the courts have decided against the widow and children, and so they'll have to worry off about five or six millions for the poor lady he duped so outrageously—with a checker on the chips.

"As fur old Nate Kranil, a lawyer from Cheyenne was tellin' me his numerous widows by courtesy was goin' to form an association and share his leavin's pro raty. Said they'd all got kind of acquainted and made up their minds they was such a reg'lar band of wolves that none of 'em was able to do any of the others in the long run, so they'd divide even.

"Then there was Dave Kisber, and—"

"Never mind any more—" Percival broke in. "Do you mean that my father was mixed up like those old Indians?"

"Looks now as if he was. That telegram from Coplen is concernin' of a lady—a party that was with him when he died. The press report sent out that the young and beautiful Mrs. Bines was with her husband, and was prostrated with grief. Your ma and Pishy was up to Steamin' Springs at the time, and I kep' it from them all right."

"But *how* was he entangled?—to what extent?"

"That's what we'll get more light on in the morning. She made a play right after the will was filed fur probate, and I told Coplen to see jest what grounds she had, and I'd settle myself if she really had any and wa'n't unreasonable."

"It's just a question of blackmail, isn't it? What did you offer?"

"Well, she has a slew of letters—gettin' them is a matter of sentiment and keepin' the thing quiet. Then she claims to have a will made last December and duly witnessed, givin' her the One Girl outright, and a million cash. So you can see she ain't anything ordinary. I told Coplen to offer her a million cash for everything rather'n have any fuss. I was goin' to fix it up myself and keep quiet about it."

"And this telegram looks as if she wanted to fight."

"Well, mebbe that and mebbe it means that she knows we *don't* want to fight considerable more than a million dollars' worth."

"How much do you think she'll hold out for?"

"Can't tell; you don't know how big pills she's been smokin'."

"But, damn it all, that's robbery!"

"Yes—but it's her deal. You remember when Billy Brue was playin' seven-up with a stranger in the Two-Hump saloon over to Eden, and Chiddie Fogle the bartender called him up front and whispered that he'd jest seen the feller turn a jack from the bottom. 'Well,' says Billie, looking kind of reprovin' at Chiddie, 'it was *his deal*, wa'n't it?' Now it's sure this blond party's deal, and we better reckon ahead a mite before we start any roughhouse with her. You're due to find out if you hadn't better let her turn her jack and trust to gettin' even on your deal. You got a claim staked out in New York, and a scandal like this might handicap you in workin' it. And 'tain't as if hushin' her up was something we couldn't well afford. And think of how it would torment your ma to know of them doin's, and how 'twould shame Pish in company. Of course, rob'ry is rob'ry, but mebbe it's our play to be sporty like Billy Brue was."

"Pretty bad, isn't it? I never suspected pa was in anything of this sort."

"Well, I knew Dan'l J. purty well, and I spleened against some of his ways, but that's done fur. Now the folks out in this part of the country have come to expect it from a man like him. They don't mind so much. But them New York folks—well, I thought mebbe you'd like to take a clean bill of health when you settle in that centre of culture and enlightenment,—and remember your ma and Pish."

"Of course the exposure would mean a lot of cheap notoriety—"

"Well, and not so all-fired cheap at that, even if we beat. I've heard that lawyers are threatenin' to stop this thing of workin' entirely fur their health. There's that to weigh up."

"But I hate to be done."

"Well, wouldn't you be worse done if you let a matter of money, when you're reekin' with it, keep you from protectin' your pa's name? Do you want folks to snicker when they read that 'lovin' husband and father' business on his gravestone? My! I guess that young woman and her folks we met the other day'd be tickled to death to think they knew you after they'd read one of them Sunday newspaper stories with pictures of us all, and an extry fine one of the millionaire's dupe, basely enticed from her poor but honest millinery business in Spokane."

Percival shuddered.

"Well, let's see what Coplen has to say in the morning. If it can be settled within reason I suppose we better give up."

"That's my view now, and the estate bein' left as simply as it was, we can make in the payments unbeknownst to the folks."

They said good-night, and Percival went off to dream that a cab-horse of mammoth size was threatening to eat Miss Milbrey unless he drove it to Spokane Falls and bought two million millinery shops.

When he was jolted to consciousness they were in the switching yard at Butte, and the car was being coupled to the rear of the train made up for Montana City. He took advantage of the stop to shave. By the time he was dressed they were under way again, steaming out past the big smelters that palled the sky with heavy black smoke.

At the breakfast-table he found Uncle Peter and Coplen.

"I'm inclined," said the lawyer, as Percival peeled a peach, "to agree with your grandfather. This woman—if I may use the term—is one of the nerviest leg-pullers you're ever likely to strike."

"Lord! I should hope so," said Percival, with hearty emphasis.

"She studied your father and she knew him better than any of us, I judge. She certainly knew he was liable to go at any time, in exactly the way he did go. Why, she even had a doctor down from 'Frisco to Monterey when they were there about a year ago—introduced him as an old friend and had him stay around three days—just to give her a private professional opinion on his chances. As to this will, the signature is undoubtedly genuine, but my judgment is she procured it in some way on a blank sheet of paper and had the will written above on sheets like it. As it conforms to the real will word for word, excepting the bequests to her, she must have had access to that before having this one written. Of course that helps to make it look as if the testator had changed his mind only as to the one legatee—makes it look plausible and genuine. The witnesses were of course parties to the fraud, but I seriously question our ability to prove there was fraud. We think they procured a copy of the will we kept in our safe at Butte through the clerk that Tafe fired awhile back because of his drinking habits and because he was generally suspicious of him. Of course that's only surmise."

"But can't we fight it?" demanded Percival, hungrily attacking the crisp, brown little trout.

"Well, if we allowed it to come to a contest, we might expose the whole thing, and then again we might not. I tell you she's clever. She's shown it at every step. Now then, if you do fight," and the lawyer bristled, as if his fighting spirit were not too far under the control of his experience-born caution, "why, you have litigation that's bound to last for years, and it would be pretty expensive. I admit the case is tempting to a lawyer, but in the end you don't know what you'll get, especially with this woman. Why, do you know she's already, we've found, made up to two different judges that might be interested in any litigation she'd have, and she's cultivating others. The role of Joseph," he continued, "has never, to the best of my belief, been gracefully played in the world's history, and you may have noticed that the members of the Montana judiciary seem to be particularly awkward in their essays at it. In the end, then, you'll be out a lot of money even if you win. On the other hand, you have a chance to settle it for good and all, getting back everything—excepting the will, which, of course, we couldn't touch or even concede the existence of, but which would, if such an instrument *were* extant, be destroyed in the presence of a witness whose integrity I could rely upon—well—as upon my own. The letters which she has, and which I have seen, are also such as would tend to substantiate her claims and make the large bequests to her seem plausible—and they're also such letters as—I should infer—the family would rather wish not to be made public, as they would be if it came to trial."

"Jest what I told him," remarked Uncle Peter.

"What she'll hold out for I don't know, but I'd suggest this, that I meet her attorney and put the case exactly as I've found it out as to the will, letting them suspect, perhaps, that we have admissions of some sort from Hornby, the clerk, that might damage them. Then I can put it that, while we have no doubt of our ability to dispose of the will, we do wish to avoid the scandal that would ensue upon a publication of the letters they hold and the exposure of her relations with the testator, and that upon this purely sentimental ground we are willing to be bled to a reasonable extent. The One Girl is a valuable mine, but my opinion is she'll be glad to get two million if we seem reluctant to pay that much."

With that gusto of breakfast-appetite which arouses the envy of persons whose alimentation is not what it used to be, Percival had devoured ruddy peaches and purple grapes, trout that had breasted their swift native currents that very morning, crisp little curls of bacon, muffins that were mere flecks of golden foam, honey with the sweetness of a thousand fragrant blossoms, and coffee that was oily with richness. For a time he had seemed to make no headway against his hill-born appetite. The lawyer, who had broken his fast with a strip of dry toast and a cup of weak tea, had watched him with unfeigned and reminiscent interest. Grant, who stood watchful to replenish his plate, and whose pleasure it was to see him eat, regarded him with eyes fairly dewy from sympathy. To A. L. Jackson, the cook, on a trip for hot muffins, he observed, "He eats jes' like th' ole man. I suttin'y do love t' see that boy behave when he got his fresh moral appetite on him. He suttin'y do ca'y hisse'f mighty handsome."

With Coplen's final recommendation to settle Percival concluded his meal, and after surveying with fondly pleasant regret the devastation he had wrought, he leaned back in his chair and lighted a cigar. He was no longer in a mood to counsel fight, even though he disliked to submit.

"You know," he reminded Uncle Peter, "what that editorial in the Rock Rip *Champion* said about me when we were over there: 'We opine that the Junior Bines will become a warm piece of human force if he isn't ground-sluiced too early in the game.' Well—and here I'm ground-sluiced the first rattle out of the box."

But the lawyer went over the case again point by point, and Percival finally authorised him to make the best settlement possible. He cared as little for the money as Uncle Peter did, large sum though it was. And then his mother and sister would be spared a great humiliation, and his own standing where most he prized it would not be jeopardised.

"Settle the best you can," was his final direction to Coplen. The lawyer left them at the next station to wait for a train back to Butte.

CHAPTER XI.

How Uncle Peter Bines Once Cut Loose

As the train moved on after leaving Coplen, Percival fell to thinking of the type of man his father had been.

"Uncle Peter," he said, suddenly, "they don't *all* cut loose, do they? Now *you* never did?"

"Yes, I did, son. I yanked away from all the hitchin' straps of decency when I first struck it, jest like all the rest of 'em. Oh, I was an Indian in my time—a reg'ler measly hop-pickin' Siwash at that.

"You don't know, of course, what livin' out in the open on bacon and beans does fur a healthy man's cravin's. He gets so he has visions day and night of high-livin'—nice broiled steaks with plenty of fat on 'em, and 'specially cake and preserves and pies like mother used to make—fat, juicy mince pies that would assay at least eight hundred dollars a ton in raisins alone, say nothing of the baser metals. He sees the crimp around the edges made with a fork, and the picture of a leaf pricked in the middle to vent the steam, and he gets to smellin' 'em when they're pulled smokin' hot out of the oven. And frosted cake, the layer kind—about five layers, with stratas of jelly and custard and figs and raisins and whatever it might be. I saw 'em fur years, with a big cuttin' out to show the cross-section.

"But a man that has to work by the day fur enough to take him through the prospectin' season can't blow any of his dust on frivolous things like pie. The hard-workin' plain food is the kind he has to tote, and I never heard of pie bein' in anybody's grub-stake either.

"Well, fur two or three years at a time the nearest I'd ever get to them dainties would be a piece of sour-dough bread baked on a stove-lid. But whenever I was in the big camps I'd always go look into the bake-shop windows and just gloat.—'rubber' they call it now'days. My! but they would be beautiful. Son, if I could 'a' been guaranteed that kind of a heaven, some of them times, I'd 'a' become the hottest kind of a Christian zealot, I'll tell you that. That spell of gloatin' was what I always looked forward to when I was lyin' out nights.

"Well, the time before I made the strike I outfitted in Grand Bar. The bake-joint there was jest a mortal aggravation. Sakes! but it did torment a body so! It was kep' by a Chink, and the star play in the window was a kind of two-story cake with frostin' all over the place—on top and down the sides, and on the bottom fur all I knew, it looked that rich. And it had cocoanut mixed in with it. Say, now, that concrete looked fit to pave the streets of the New Jerusalem with—and a hunk was cut out, jest like I'd always dream of so much—showin' a cross-section of rich yellow cake and a fruity-lookin' fillin' that jest made a man want to give up.

"I was there three days, and every day I'd stop in front of that window and jest naturally hone fur a slice of that vision. The Chink was standin' in the door the first day.

"'Six doll's,' he says, kind of encin' me.

"He might as well 'a' said six thousand. I shook my head.

"Next day I was there again, yearnin'. The Chink see me and come out.

"'One doll' li'l piece", he says.

"I says, 'No, you slant-eyed heathen,' or some such name as that. But when you're looking fur tests of character, son, don't let that one hide away from you. I'd play that fur the heftiest moral courage *I've* ever showed, anyway.

"The third day it was gone and a lemon pie was there, all with nice kind of brownish snow on top. I was on my way out then, pushin' the mule. I took one lingerin' last look and felt proud of myself when I saw the hump in the pack made by my bag of beans.

"'That-like flummery food's no kind of diet to be trackin' up pay-rock on,' I says to kind of cheer myself.

"Four weeks later I struck it. And six weeks after that I had things in shape so't I was able to leave. I was nearer to other places 'twas bigger, but I made fur Grand Bar, lettin' on't I wanted to see about a claim there. I'd 'a' felt foolish to have anyone know jest why I was makin' the trip.

"On the way I got to havin' night-mares, 'fear that Chink would be gone. I knew if he was I'd go down to my grave with something comin' to me because I'd never found jest that identical cake I'd been famishin' fur.

"When I got up front of the window, you can believe it or not, but that Chink was jest settin' down another like it. Now you know how that Monte Cristo carried on after he'd proved up. Well, I got into his class, all right. I walked in past a counter where the Chink had crullers and gingerbread and a lot of low-grade stuff like that, and I set down to a little table with this here marble oil-cloth on it.

"'Bring her back,' I says, kind of tremblin', and pointin' to the window.

"The Chink pattered up and come back with a little slab of it on a tin plate. I jest let it set there.

"'Bring it all,' I says; 'I want the hull ball of wax.'

"'Six doll's,' he says, kind of cautious.

"I pulled out my buckskin pouch. 'Bring her back and take it out of that,' I says—'when I get through,' I says.

"He grinned and hurried back with it. Well, son, nothing had ever tasted so good to me, and I ain't say'n' that wa'n't the biggest worth of all my money't I ever got. I'd been trainin' fur that cake fur twenty odd year, and proddin' my imagination up fur the last ten weeks.

"I et that all, and I et another one with jelly, and a bunch of little round ones with frostin' and raisins, and a bottle of brandied peaches, and about a dozen cream puffs, and half a lemon pie with frostin' on top, and four or five Charlotte rushes. The Chink had learned to make 'em all in 'Frisco.

"That meal set me back $34.75. When I went out I noticed the plain sponge cakes and fruit cakes and dried-apple pies—things that had been out of my reach fur twenty years, and—My! but they did look common and unappetisin'. I kind of shivered at the sight of 'em.

"I ordered another one of the big cakes and two more lemon pies fur the next day.

"Fur four days I led a life of what they call 'unbridled licentiousness' while that Chink pandered to me. I never was any hand fur drink, but I cut loose in that fancy-food joint, now I tell you.

"The fifth day I begun to taper off. I begun to have a suspicion the stuff was made of sawdust with plasty of Paris fur frostin'. The sixth day I was sure it was sawdust, and my shameful debauch comes to an end right there. I remembered the story about the feller that cal'lated his chickens wouldn't tell any different, so he fed 'em sawdust instead of corn-meal, and by-and-bye a settin' of eggs hatched out—twelve of the chickens had wooden legs and the thirteenth was a woodpecker. Say, I felt so much like two cords of four-foot stove wood that it made me plumb nervous to ketch sight of a saw-buck.

"It took jest three weeks fur me to get right inside again. My, but meat victuals and all like that did taste mighty scrumptious when I could handle 'em again.

"After that when I'd been out in the hills fur a season I'd get that hankerin' back, and when I come in I'd have a little frosted-cake orgy now and then. But I kep' myself purty well in hand. I never overdone it like that again, fur you see I'd learned something. First off, there was the appetite. I soon see the gist of my fun had been the *wantin'* the stuff, the appetite fur it, and if you nursed an appetite along and deluded it with promises it would stay by you like one of them meachin' yellow dogs. But as soon as you tried to do the good-fairy act by it, and give it all it hankered fur, you killed it off, and then you wouldn't be entertained by it no more, and kep' stirred up and busy.

"And so I layed out to nurse my appetite, and aggravate it by never givin' it quite all it wanted. When I was in the hills after a day's tramp I'd let it have its fling on such delicacies as I could turn out of the fryin'-pan myself, but when I got in again I'd begin to act bossy with it. It's *wantin'* reasonably that keeps folks alive, I reckon. The mis-a-blest folks I've ever saw was them that had killed all their wants by overfeedin' 'em.

"Then again, son, in this world of human failin's there ain't anything ever *can* be as pure and blameless and satisfyin' as the stuff in a bake-shop window looks like it is. Don't ever furget that. It's jest too good to be true. And in the next place—pastry's good in its way, but the best you can ever get is what's made fur you at home—I'm talkin' about a lot of things now that you don't probably know any too much about. Sometimes the boys out in the hills spends their time dreamin' fur other things besides pies and cakes, but that system of mine holds good all through the deal—you can play it from soda to hock and not lose out. And that's why I'm outlastin' a lot of the boys and still gettin' my fun out of the game.

"It's a good system fur you, son, while you're learnin' to use your head. Your pa played it at first, then he cut loose. And you need it worse'n ever he did, if I got you sized up right. He touched me on one side, and touched you on the other. But you can last longer if you jest keep the system in mind a little. Remember what I say about the window stuff."

Percival had listened to the old man's story with proper amusement, and to the didactics with that feeling inevitable to youth which says secretly, as it affects to listen to one whom it does not wish to wound, "Yes, yes, I know, but you were living in another day, long ago, and you are not *me!*"

He went over to the desk and began to scribble a name on the pad of paper.

"If a man really loves one woman he'll behave all right," he observed to Uncle Peter.

"Oh, I ain't preachin' like some do. Havin' a good time is all right; it's the only thing, I reckon, sometimes, that justifies the misery of livin'. But cuttin' loose is bad jedgment. A man wakes up to find that his natural promptin's has cold-decked him. If I smoked the best see-gars now all the time, purty soon I'd get so't I wouldn't appreciate 'em. That's why I always keep some of these out-door free-burners on hand. One of them now and then makes the others taste better."

The young man had become deaf to the musical old voice.

He was writing:

"MY DEAR MISS MILBREY:—I send you the first and only poem I ever wrote. I may of course be a prejudiced critic, but it seems to me to possess in abundance those graces of metre, rhyme, high thought in poetic form, and perfection of finish which the critics unite in demanding. To be honest with you—and why should I conceal that conceit which every artist is said secretly to feel in his own production?—I have encountered no other poem in our noble tongue which has so moved and captivated me.

"It is but fair to warn you that this is only the first of a volume of similar poems which I contemplate writing. And as the theme appears now to be inexhaustible, I am not sure that I can see any limit to the number of volumes I shall be compelled to issue. Pray accept this author's copy with his best and hopefullest wishes. One other copy has been sent to the book reviewer of the Arcady *Lyre,* in the hope that he, at least, will have the wit to perceive in it that ultimate and ideal perfection for which the humbler bards have hitherto striven in vain.

"Sincerely and seriously yours,

"P. PERCIVAL BINES"

Thus ran the exalted poem on a sheet of note-paper:

"AVICE MILBREY.

Avice Milbrey, Avice Milbrey, Avice Milbrey,

Avice Milbrey, Avice Milbrey, Avice Milbrey,

Avice Milbrey, Avice Milbrey,

Avice Milbrey, Avice Milbrey,

Avice Milbrey, Avice Milbrey, Avice Milbrey.

And ninety-eight thousand other verses quite like it."

CHAPTER XII.

Plans for the Journey East

Until late in the afternoon they rode through a land that was bleak and barren of all grace or cheer. The dull browns and greys of the landscape were unrelieved by any green or freshness save close by the banks of an occasional stream. The vivid blue of a cloudless sky served only to light up its desolation to greater disadvantage. It was a grim unsmiling land, hard to like.

"This may be God's own country," said Percival once, looking out over a stretch of grey sage-brush to a mass of red sandstone jutting up, high, sharp, and ragged, in the distance—"but it looks to me as if He got tired of it Himself and gave up before it was half finished."

"A man has to work here a few years to love it," said Uncle Peter, shortly.

As they left the car at Montana City in the early dusk, that thriving metropolis had never seemed so unattractive to Percival; so rough, new, garish, and wanting so many of the softening charms of the East. Through the wide, unpaved streets, lined with their low wooden buildings, they drove to the Bines mansion, a landmark in the oldest and most fashionable part of the town. For such distinctions are made in Western towns as soon as the first two shanties are built. The Bines house had been a monument to new wealth from the earliest days of the town, which was a fairly decent antiquity for the region. But the house and the town grated harshly now upon the young man. He burned with a fever of haste to be off toward the East—over the far rim of hills, and the farther higher mountain range, to a land that had warmed genially under three hundred years of civilised occupancy—where people had lived and fraternised long enough to create the atmosphere he craved so ardently.

While Chinese Wung lighted the hall gas and busied himself with their hats and bags, Psyche Bines came down the stairs to greet them. Never had her youthful freshness so appealed to her brother. The black gown she wore emphasised her blond beauty. As to give her the aspect of mourning one might have tried as reasonably to hide the radiance of the earth in springtime with that trifling pall.

Her brother kissed her with more than his usual warmth. Here was one to feel what he felt, to sympathise warmly with all those new yearnings that were to take him out of the crude West. She wanted, for his own reasons, all that he wanted. She understood him; and she was his ally against the aged and narrow man who would have held them to life in that physical and social desert.

"Well, sis, here we are!" he began. "How fine you're looking! And how is Mrs. Throckmorton? Give her my love and ask her if she can be ready to start for the effete East in twenty minutes."

It was his habit to affect that he constantly forgot his mother's name. He had discovered years before that he was sometimes able thus to puzzle her momentarily.

"Why, Percival!" exclaimed this excellent lady, coming hurriedly from the kitchen regions, "I haven't a thing packed. Twenty minutes! Goodness! I do declare!"

It was an infirmity of Mrs. Bines that she was unable to take otherwise than literally whatever might be said to her; an infirmity known and played upon relentlessly by her son.

"Oh, well!" he exclaimed, with a show of irritation. "I suppose we'll be delayed then. That's like a woman. Never ready on time. Probably we can't start now till after dinner. Now hurry! You know that boat leaves the dock for Tonsilitis at 8.23—I hope you won't be seasick."

"Boat—dock—" Mrs. Bines stopped to convince herself beyond a certainty that no dock nor boat could be within many hundred miles of her by any possible chance.

"Never mind," said Psyche; "give ma half an hour's notice and she can start for any old place."

"Can't she though!" and Percival, seizing his astounded mother, waltzed with her down the hall, leaving her at the far end with profusely polite assurances that he would bring her immediately a lemon-ice, an ice-pick, and a cold roast turkey with pink stockings on.

"Never mind, Mrs. Cartwright," he called back to her—"oh, beg pardon— Bines? yes, yes, to be sure—well, never mind, Mrs. Brennings. We'll give you time to put your gloves and a bottle of horse-radish and a nail-file and hammer into that neat travelling-bag of yours.

"Now let me go up and get clean again. That lovely alkali dust has worked clear into my bearings so I'm liable to have a hot box just as we get the line open ninety miles ahead."

At dinner and afterwards the new West and the old aligned themselves into hostile camps, as of yore. The young people chatted with lively interest of the coming change, of the New York people who had visited the mine, of the attractions and advantages of life in New York.

Uncle Peter, though he had long since recognised his cause as lost, remained doggedly inimical to the migration. The home was being broken up and he was depressed.

"Anyhow, you'll soon be back," he warned them. "You won't like it a mite. I tried it myself thirty years ago. I'll jest camp here until you do come back. My! but you'll be glad to get here again."

"Why not have Billy Brue come stay with you," suggested Mrs. Bines, who was hurting herself with pictures of the old man's loneliness, "in case you should want a plaster on your back or some nutmeg tea brewed, or anything? That Wung is so trifling."

"Maybe I might," replied the old man, "but Billy Brue ain't exactly broke to a shack like this. I know just what he'd do all his spare time; he'd set down to that new-fangled horseless piano and play it to death."

Uncle Peter meant the new automatic piano in the parlour. As far as the new cabinet was from the what-not this modern bit of mechanism was from the old cottage organ—the latter with its "Casket of Household Melodies" and the former with its perforated paper repertoire of "The World's Best Music," ranging without prejudice from Beethoven's Fifth Symphony to "I Never Did Like a Nigger Nohow," by a composer who shall be unnamed on this page.

"And Uncle Peter won't have any one to bother him when he makes a litter with all those old plans and estimates and maps of his," said Psyche; "you'll be able to do a lot more work, Uncle Peter, this winter."

"Yes, only I ain't got any more work to do than I ever had, and I always managed to do that, no matter how you did clean up after me and mix up my papers. I'm like old Nigger Pomeroy. He was doin' a job of whitewashin' one day, and he had an old whitewash brush with most of the hair gone out of it. I says to him, 'Pomeroy, why don't you get you a new brush? you could do twice as much work.' And Pomeroy says, 'That's right, Mr. Bines, but the trouble is I ain't got twice as much work to do.' So don't you folks get out on *my* account," he concluded, politely.

"And you know we shall be in mourning," said Psyche to her brother.

"I've thought of that. We can't do any entertaining, except of the most informal kind, and we can't go out, except very informally; but, then, you know, there aren't many people that have us on their lists, and while we're keeping quiet we shall have a chance to get acquainted a little."

"I hear they do have dreadful times with help in New York," said Mrs. Bines.

"Don't let that bother you, ma," her son reassured her. "We'll go to the Hightower Hotel, first. You remember you and pa were there when it first opened. It's twice as large now, and we'll take a suite, have our meals served privately, our own servants provided by the hotel, and you won't have a thing to worry you. We'll be snug there for the winter. Then for the summer we'll go to Newport, and when we come back from there we'll take a house. Meantime, after we've looked around a bit, we'll build, maybe up on one of those fine corners east of the Park."

"I almost dread it," his mother rejoined. "I never *did* see how they kept track of all the help in that hotel, and if it's twice as monstrous now, however *do* they do it—and have the beds all made every day and the meals always on time?"

"And you can *get* meals there," said Percival.

"I've been needing a broiled lobster all summer—and now the oysters will be due—fine fat Buzzard's Bays—and oyster crabs."

"He ain't been able to touch a morsel out here," observed Uncle Peter, with a palpably false air of concern. "I got all worried up about him, barely peckin' at a crumb or two."

"I never could learn to eat those oysters out of their shells," Mrs. Bines confessed. "They taste so much better out of the can. Once we had them raw and on two of mine were those horrid little green crabs, actually squirming. I was going to send them back, but your pa laughed and ate them himself—ate them alive and kicking."

"And terrapin!" exclaimed Percival, with anticipatory relish.

"That terrapin stew does taste kind of good," his mother admitted, "but, land's sakes! it has so many little bits of bones in it I always get nervous eating it. It makes me feel as if all my teeth was coming out."

"You'll soon learn all those things, ma," said her daughter—"and not to talk to the waiters, and everything like that. She always asks them how much they earn, and if they have a family, and how many children, and if any of them are sick, you know," she explained to Percival.

"And I s'pose you ain't much of a hand fur smokin' cigarettes, are you, ma?" inquired Uncle Peter, casually.

"Me!" exclaimed Mrs. Bines, in horror; "I never smoked one of the nasty little things in my life."

"Son," said the old man to Percival, reproachfully, "is that any way to treat your own mother? Here she's had all this summer to learn cigarette smokin', and you ain't put her at it—all that time wasted, when you *know* she's got to learn. Get her one now so she can light up."

"Why, Uncle Peter Bines, how absurd!" exclaimed his granddaughter.

"Well, them ladies smoked the other day, and they was some of the reg'ler original van Vanvans. You don't want your poor ma kep' out of the game, do you? Goin' to let her set around and toy with the coppers, or maybe keep cases now and then, are you? Or, you goin' to get her a stack of every colour and let her play with you? Pish, now, havin' been to a 'Frisco seminary—she can pick it up, prob'ly in no time; but ma ought to have practice here at home, so she can find out what brand she likes best. Now, Marthy, them Turkish cigarettes, in a nice silver box with some naked ladies painted on the outside, and your own monogram 'M.B.' in gold letters on every cigarette—"

"Don't let him scare you, ma," Percival interrupted. "You'll get into the game all right, and I'll see that you have a good time."

"Only I hope the First M.E. Church of Montana City never hears of her outrageous cuttin's-up," said Uncle Peter, as if to himself. "They'd have her up and church her, sure—smokin' cigarettes with her gold monogram on, at *her* age!" "And of course we must go to the Episcopal church there," said Psyche. "I think those Episcopal ministers are just the smartest looking men ever. So swell looking, and anyway it's the only church the right sort of people go to. We must be awfully high church, too. It's the very best way to know nice people."

"I s'pose if every day'd be Sunday by-and-bye, like the old song says, it'd be easier fur you, wouldn't it?" asked the old man. "You and Petie would be 401 and 402 in jest no time at all."

Uncle Peter continued to be perversely frivolous about the most exclusive metropolitan society in the world. But Uncle Peter was a crabbed old man, lingering past his generation, and the young people made generous allowance for his infirmities.

"Only there's one thing," said his sister to Percival, when later they were alone, "we must be careful about ma; she *will* persist in making such dreadful breaks, in spite of everything I can do. In San Francisco last June, just before we went to Steaming Springs, there was one hot day, and of course everybody was complaining. Mrs. Beale remarked that it wasn't the heat that bothered us so, but the humidity. It was so damp, you know. Ma spoke right up so everybody could hear her, and said, 'Yes; isn't the humidity dreadful? Why, it's just running off me from every pore!'"

CHAPTER XIII.

The Argonauts Return to the Rising Sun

It was mid-October. The two saddle-horses and a team for carriage use had been shipped ahead. In the private car the little party was beginning its own journey Eastward. From the rear platform they had watched the tall figure of Uncle Peter Bines standing in the bright autumn sun, aloof from the band of kerchief-waving friends, the droop of his head and shoulders showing the dejection he felt at seeing them go. He had resisted all entreaties to accompany them.

His last injunction to Percival had been to marry early.

"I know your stock and I know *you*" he said; "and you got no call to be rangin' them pastures without a brand. You never was meant fur a maverick. Only don't let the first woman that comes ridin' herd get her iron on you. No man knows much about the critters, of course, but I've noticed a few things in my time. You pick one that's full-chested, that's got a fairish-sized nose, and that likes cats. The full chest means she's healthy, the nose means she ain't finicky, and likin' cats means she's kind and honest and unselfish. Ever notice some women when a cat's around? They pretend to like 'em and say 'Nice kitty!' but you can see they're viewin' 'em with bitter hate and suspicion. If they have to stroke 'em they do it plenty gingerly and you can see 'em shudderin' inside like. It means they're catty themselves. But when one grabs a cat up as if she was goin' to eat it and cuddles it in her neck and talks baby-talk to it, you play her fur bein' sound and true. Pass up the others, son.

"And speakin' of the fair sex," he added, as he and Percival were alone for a moment, "that enterprisin' lady we settled with is goin' to do one thing you'll approve of.

"She's goin'," he continued, in answer to Percival's look of inquiry, "to take her bank-roll to New York. She says it's the only place fur folks with money, jest like you say. She tells Coplen that there wa'n't any fit society out here at all,—no advantages fur a lady of capacity and ambitions. I reckon she's goin' to be 403 all right."

"Seems to me she did pretty well here; I don't see any kicks due her."

"Yes, but she's like all the rest. The West was good enough to make her money in, but the East gets her when spendin' time comes."

As the train started he swung himself off with a sad little "Be good to yourself!"

"Thank the Lord we're under way at last!" cried Percival, fervently, when the group at the station had been shut from view. "Isn't it just heavenly!" exclaimed his sister.

"Think of having all of New York you want—being at home there—and not having to look forward to this desolation of a place."

Mrs. Bines was neither depressed nor elated. She was maintaining that calm level of submission to fate which had been her lifelong habit. The journey and the new life were to be undertaken because they formed for her the line of least resistance along which all energy must flow. Had her children elected to camp for the remainder of their days in the centre of the desert of Gobi, she would have faced that life with as little sense of personal concern and with no more misgivings.

Down out of the maze of hills the train wound; and then by easy grades after two days of travel down off the great plateau to where the plains of Nebraska lay away to a far horizon in brown billows of withered grass.

Then came the crossing of the sullen, sluggish Missouri, that highway of an earlier day to the great Northwest; and after that the better wooded and better settled lands of Iowa and Illinois.

"Now we're getting where Christians live," said Percival, with warm appreciation.

"Why, Percival," exclaimed his mother, reprovingly, "do you mean to say there aren't any Christians in Montana City? How you talk! There are lots of good Christian people there, though I must say I have my doubts about that new Christian Science church they started last spring." "The term, Mrs. Thorndike, was used in its social rather than its theological significance," replied her son, urbanely. "Far be it from me to impugn the religion of that community of which we are ceasing to be integers at the pleasing rate of sixty miles an hour. God knows they need their faith in a different kind of land hereafter!"

And even Mrs. Bines was not without a sense of quiet and rest induced by the gentler contours of the landscape through which they now sped.

"The country here does seem a lot cosier," she admitted.

The hills rolled away amiably and reassuringly; the wooded slopes in their gay colouring of autumn invited confidence. Here were no forbidding stretches of the grey alkali desert, no grim bare mountains, no solitude of desolation. It was a kind land, fat with riches. The shorn yellow fields, the capacious red barns, the well-conditioned homes, all told eloquently of peace and plenty. So, too, did the villages—those lively little clearing-houses for immense farming districts. To the adventurer from New York they seem always new and crude. To our travellers from a newer, cruder region they were actually aesthetic in their suggestions of an old and well-established civilisation.

In due time they were rattling over a tangled maze of switches, dodging interminable processions of freight-cars, barely missing crowded passenger trains whose bells struck clear and then flatted as the trains flew by; defiling by narrow water-ways, crowded with small shipping; winding through streets lined with high, gloomy warehouses, amid the clang and clatter, the strangely-sounding bells and whistles of a thousand industries, each sending up its just contribution of black smoke to the pall that lay always spread above; and steaming at last into a great roomy shed where all was system, and where the big engine trembled and panted as if in relief at having run in safety a gantlet so hazardous.

"Anyway, I'd rather live in Montana City than Chicago," ventured Mrs. Bines.

"Whatever pride you may feel in your discernment, Mrs. Cadwallader, is amply justified," replied her son, performing before the amazed lady a bow that indicated the lowest depths of slavish deference.

"I am now," he continued, "going out to pace the floor of this locomotive-boudoir for a few exhilarating breaths of smoke, and pretend to myself that I've got to live in Chicago for ever. A little discipline like that is salutary to keep one from forgetting the great blessing which a merciful Providence has conferred upon one."

"I'll walk a bit with you," said his sister, donning her jacket and a cap.

"Lest my remarks have seemed indeterminate, madam," sternly continued Percival at the door of the car, "permit me to add that if Chicago were heaven I should at once enter upon a life of crime. Do not affect to misunderstand me, I beg of you. I should leave no avenue of salvation open to my precious soul. I should incur no risk of being numbered among the saved. I should be b-a-d, and I should sit up nights to invent new ways of evil. If I had any leisure left from being as wicked as I could be, I should devote it to teaching those I loved how to become abandoned. I should doubtless issue a pamphlet, 'How to Merit Perdition Without a Master. Learn to be Wicked in your Own Home in Ten Lessons. Instructions Sent Securely Sealed from Observation. Thousands of Testimonials from the Most Accomplished Reprobates of the Day.' I trust Mrs. Llewellen Leffingwell-Thompson, that you will never again so far forget yourself as to utter that word 'Chicago' in my presence. If you feel that you must give way to the evil impulse, go off by yourself and utter the name behind the protection of closed doors—where this innocent girl cannot hear you. Come, sister. Otherwise I may behave in a manner to be regretted in my calmer moments. Let us leave the woman alone, now. Besides, I've got to go out and help the hands make up that New York train. You never can tell. Some horrible accident might happen to delay us here thirty minutes. Cheer up, ma; it's always darkest just before leaving Chicago, you know."

Thus flippantly do some of the younger sons of men blaspheme this metropolis of the mid-West—a city the creation of which is, by many persons of discrimination, held to be the chief romance and abiding miracle of the nineteenth century. Let us rejoice that one such partisan was now at hand to stem the torrent of abuse. As Percival held back the door for his sister to pass out, a stout little ruddy-faced man with trim grey sidewhiskers came quickly up the steps and barred their way with cheery aggressiveness.

"Ah! Mr. Higbee—well, well!" exclaimed Percival, cordially.

"Thought it might be some of you folks when I saw the car," said Higbee, shaking hands all around.

"And Mrs. Bines, too! and the girl, looking like a Delaware peach when the crop's 'failed.' How's everybody, and how long you going to be in the good old town?"

"Ah! we were just speaking of Chicago as you came in," said Percival, blandly. "*Isn't* she a great old town, though—a wonder!"

"My boy," said Higbee, in low, solemn tones that came straight from his heart, "she gets greater every day you live. You can see her at it, fairly. How long since you been here?"

"I came through last June, you know, after I left your yacht at Newport."

"Yes, yes; to be sure; so you did—poor Daniel J.—but say, you wouldn't know the town now if you haven't seen it since then. Why, I run over from New York every thirty days or so and she grows out of my ken every time, like a five-year-old boy. Say, I've got Mrs. Higbee up in the New York sleeper, but if you're going to be here a spell we'll stop a few days longer and I'll drive you around—what say?—packing houses—Lake Shore Drive—Lincoln Park—"

He waited, glowing confidently, as one submitting irresistible temptations.

Percival beamed upon him with moist eyes.

"By Jove, Mr. Higbee! that's clever of you—it's royal! Sis and I would like nothing better—but you see my poor mother here is almost down with nervous prostration and we've got to hurry her to New York without an hour's delay to consult a specialist. We're afraid"—he glanced anxiously at the astounded Mrs. Bines, and lowered his voice—"we're afraid she may not be with us long."

"Why, Percival," began Mrs. Bines, dazedly, "you was just saying—"

"Now don't fly all to pieces, ma!—take it easy—you're with friends, be sure of that. You needn't beg us to go on. You know we wouldn't think of stopping when it may mean life or death to you. You see just the way she is," he continued to the sympathetic Higbee—"we're afraid she may collapse any moment. So we must wait for another time; but I'll tell you what you do; go get Mrs. Higbee and your traps and come let us put you up to New York. We've got lots of room—run along now—and we'll have some of that ham, 'the kind you have always bought,' for lunch. A.L. Jackson is a miserable cook, too, if I don't know the truth." Gently urging Higbee through the door, he stifled a systematic inquiry into the details of Mrs. Bines's affliction.

"Come along quick! I'll go help you and we'll have Mrs. Higbee back before the train starts."

"Do you know," Mrs. Bines thoughtfully observed to her daughter, "I sometimes mistrust Percival ain't just right in his head; you remember he did have a bad fall on it when he was two years and five months old—two years, five months, and eighteen days. The way he carries on right before folks' faces! That time I went through the asylum at Butte there was a young man kept going on with the same outlandish rigmarole just like Percival. The idea of Percival telling me to eat a lemon-ice with an ice-pick, and 'Oh, why don't the flesh-brushes wear nice, proper clothes-brushes!' and be sure and hammer my nails good and hard after I get them manicured. And back home he was always wanting to know where the meat-augers were, saying he'd just bought nine hundred new ones and he'd have to order a ton more if they were all lost. I don't believe there is such a thing as a meat-auger. I don't know what on earth a body could do with one. And that other young man," she concluded, significantly, "they had him in a little bit of a room with an iron-barred door to it like a prison-cell."

CHAPTER XIV.

Mr. Higbee Communicates Some Valuable Information

The Higbees were presently at home in the Bines car. Mrs. Higbee was a pleasant, bustling, plump little woman, sparkling-eyed and sprightly. Prominent in her manner was a helpless little confession of inadequacy to her ambitions that made her personality engaging. To be energetic and friendly, and deeply absorbed in people who were bold and confident, was her attitude.

She began bubbling at once to Mrs. Bines and Psyche of the latest fashions for mourners. Crepe was more swagger than ever before, both as trimming and for entire costumes.

"House gowns, my dear, and dinner gowns, made entirely of crepe in the Princesse style, will exactly suit your daughter—and on the dinner gowns she can wear a trimming of that dull jet passementerie."

From gowns she went naturally to the difficulty of knowing whom to meet in a city like New York—and how to meet them—and the watchfulness required to keep daughter Millie from becoming entangled with leading theatrical gentlemen. Amid Percival's lamentations that he must so soon leave Chicago, the train moved slowly out of the big shed to search in the interwoven puzzle of tracks for one that led to the East.

As they left the centre of the city Higbee drew Percival to one of the broad side windows.

"Pull up your chair and sit here a minute," he said, with a mysterious little air of importance. "There's a thing this train's going to pass right along here that I want you to look at. Maybe you've seen better ones, of course—and then again—"

It proved to be a sign some twenty feet high and a whole block long. Emblazoned upon its broad surface was "Higbee's Hams." At one end and towering another ten feet or so above the mammoth letters was a white-capped and aproned chef abandoning his mercurial French temperament to an utter frenzy of delight over a "Higbee's Ham" which had apparently just been vouchsafed to him by an invisible benefactor.

"There, now!" exclaimed Higbee; "what do you call that—I want to know—hey?"

"Great! Magnificent!" cried Percival, with the automatic and ready hypocrisy of a sympathetic nature. "That certainly is great."

"Notice the size of it?" queried Higbee, when they had flitted by.

"*Did* I!" exclaimed the young man, reproachfully.

"We went by pretty fast—you couldn't see it well. I tell you the way they're allowed to run trains so fast right here in this crowded city is an outrage. I'm blamed if I don't have my lawyer take it up with the Board of Aldermen—slaughtering people on their tracks right and left—you'd think these railroad companies owned the earth—But that sign, now. Did you notice you could read every letter in the label on that ham? You wouldn't think it was a hundred yards back from the track, would you? Why, that label by actual measure is six feet, four inches across—and yet it looks as small—and everything all in the right proportion, it's wonderful. It's what I call art," he concluded, in a slightly dogmatic tone.

"Of course it's art," Percival agreed; "er—all—hand-painted, I suppose?"

"Sure! that painting alone, letters and all, cost four hundred and fifty dollars. I've just had it put up. I've been after that place for years, but it was held on a long lease by Max, the Square Tailor—you know. You probably remember the sign he had there—'Peerless Pants Worn by Chicago's Best Dressers' with a man in his shirt sleeves looking at a new pair. Well, finally, I got a chance to buy those two back lots, and that give me the site, and there she is, all finished and up. That's partly what I come on this time to see about. How'd you like the wording of that sign?"

"Fine—simple and effective," replied Percival.

"That's it—simple and effective. It goes right to the point and it don't slop over beyond any, after it gets there. We studied a good deal over that sign. The other man, the tailor, had too many words for the board space. My advertisin' man wanted it to be, first, 'Higbee's Hams, That's All.' But, I don't know—for so big a space that seemed to me kind of—well—kind of flippant and undignified. Then I got it down to 'Eat Higbee's Hams.' That seemed short enough—but after studying it, I says, What's the use of saying 'eat'? No one would think, I says, that a ham is to paper the walls with or to stuff sofa-cushions with—so off comes 'eat' as being superfluous, and leaving it simple and dignified—'Higbee's Hams.'"

"By the way," said Percival, when they were sitting together again, later in the day, "where is Henry, now?"

Higbee chuckled.

"That's the other thing took me back this time—the new sign and getting Hank started. Henry is now working ten hours a day out to the packinghouse. After a year of that, he'll be taken into the office and his hours will be cut down to eight. Eight hours a day will seem like sinful idleness to Henry by that time."

Percival whistled in amazement.

"I thought you'd be surprised. But the short of it is, Henry found himself facing work or starvation. He didn't want to starve a little bit, and he finally concluded he'd rather work for his dad than any one else.

"You see Henry was doing the Rake's Progress act there in New York— being a gilded youth and such like. Now being a gilded youth and 'a well-known man about town' is something that wants to be done in moderation, and Henry didn't seem to know the meaning of the word. I put up something like a hundred and eighty thousand dollars for Hank's gilding last year. Not that I grudged him the money, but it wasn't doing him any good. He was making a monkey of himself with it, Henry was. A good bit of that hundred and eighty went into a comic opera company that was one of the worst I ever *did* see. Henry had no judgment. He was *too* easy. Well, along this summer he was on the point of making a break that would— well, I says to him, says I, 'Hank, I'm no penny-squeezer; I like good stretchy legs myself,' I says; 'I like to see them elastic so they'll give a plenty when they're pulled; but,' I says, 'if you take that step,' I says, 'if you declare yourself, then the rubber in your legs,' I says, 'will just naturally snap; you'll find you've overplayed the tension,' I says, 'and there won't be any more stretch left in them.'

"The secret is, Hank was being chased by a whole family of wolves—that's the gist of it—fortune-hunters—with tushes like the ravening lion in Afric's gloomy jungle. They were not only cold, stone broke, mind you, but hyenas into the bargain—the father and the mother and the girl, too.

"They'd got their minds made up to marry the girl to a good wad of money—and they'll do it, too, sooner or later, because she's a corker for looks, all right—and they'd all made a dead set for Hank; so, quick as I saw how it was, I says, 'Here,' I says, 'is where I save my son and heir from a passel of butchers,' I says, 'before they have him scalded and dressed and hung up outside the shop for the holiday trade,' I says, 'with the red paper rosettes stuck in Henry's chest,' I says."

"Are the New York girls so designing?" asked Percival.

"Is Higbee's ham good to eat?" replied Higbee, oracularly.

"So," he continued, "when I made up my mind to put my foot down I just casually mentioned to the old lady—say, she's got an eye that would make liquid air shiver—that cold blue like an army overcoat—well, I mentioned to her that Henry was a spendthrift and that he wasn't ever going to get another cent from me that he didn't earn just the same as if he wasn't any relation of mine. I made it plain, you bet; she found just where little Henry-boy stood with his kind-hearted, liberal old father.

"Say, maybe Henry wasn't in cold storage with the whole family from that moment. I see those fellows in the laboratories are puttering around just now trying to get the absolute zero of temperature—say, Henry got it, and he don't know a thing about chemistry.

"Then I jounced Hank. I proceeded to let him know he was up against it—right close up against it, so you couldn't see daylight between 'em. 'You're twenty-five,' I says, 'and you play the best game of pool, I'm told, of any of the chappies in that Father-Made-the-Money club you got into,' I says; 'but I've looked it up,' I says, 'and there ain't really what you could call any great future for a pool champion,' I says, 'and if you're ever going to learn anything else, it's time you was at it,' I says. 'Now you go back home and tell the manager to set you to work,' I says, 'and your wages won't be big enough to make you interesting to any skirt-dancer, either,' I says. 'And you make a study of the hog from the ground up. Exhaust his possibilities just like your father done, and make a man of yourself, and then sometime,' I says, 'you'll be able to give good medicine to a cub of your own when he needs it.'"

"And how did poor Henry take all that?"

"Well, Hank squealed at first like he was getting the knife; but finally when he see he was up against it, and especially when he see how this girl and her family throwed him down the elevator-shaft from the tenth story, why, he come around beautifully. He's really got sense, though he doesn't look it—Henry has—though Lord knows I didn't pull him up a bit too quick. But he come out and went to work like I told him. It's the greatest thing ever happened to him. He ain't so fat-headed as he was, already. Henry'll be a man before his dad's through with him."

"But weren't the young people disappointed?" asked Percival; "weren't they in love with each other?"

"In *love?*" In an effort to express scorn adequately Mr. Higbee came perilously near to snorting. "What do you suppose a girl like that cares for love? She was dead in love with the nice long yellow-backs that I've piled up because the public knows good ham when they taste it. As for being in love with Henry or with any man—say, young fellow, you've got something to learn about those New York girls. And this one, especially. Why, it's been known for the three years we've been there that she's simply hunting night and day for a rich husband. She tries for 'em all as fast as they get in line."

"Henry was unlucky in finding that kind. They're not all like that—those New York girls are not," and he had the air of being able if he chose to name one or two luminous exceptions.

"Silas," called Mrs. Higbee, "are you telling Mr. Bines about our Henry and that Milbrey girl?"

"Yep," answered Higbee, "I told him."

"About what girl?—what was her name?" asked Percival, in a lower tone.

"Milbrey's that family's name—Horace Milbrey—"

"Why," Percival interrupted, somewhat awkwardly, "I know the family—the young lady—we met the family out in Montana a few weeks ago."

"Sure enough—they were in Chicago and had dinner with us on their way out." "I remember Mr. Milbrey spoke of what fine claret you gave him."

"Yes, and I wasn't stingy with ice, either, the way those New York people always are. Why, at that fellow's house he gives you that claret wine as warm as soup.

"But as for that girl," he added, "say, she'd marry me in a minute if I wasn't tied up with the little lady over there. Of course she'd rather marry a sub-treasury; she's got about that much heart in her—cold-blooded as a German carp. She'd marry me—she'd marry *you*, if you was the best thing in sight. But say, if you was broke, she'd have about as much use for you as Chicago's got for St. Louis."

CHAPTER XV.

Some Light With a Few Side-lights

The real spring in New York comes when blundering nature has painted the outer wilderness for autumn. What is called "spring" in the city by unreflecting users of the word is a tame, insipid season yawning into not more than half-wakefulness at best. The trees in the gas-poisoned soil are slow in their greening, the grass has but a pallid city vitality, and the rows of gaudy tulips set out primly about the fountains in the squares are palpably forced and alien.

For the sumptuous blending and flaunt of colour, the spontaneous awakening of warm, throbbing new life, and all those inspiring miracles of regeneration which are performed elsewhere in April and May, the city-pent must wait until mid-October.

This is the spring of the city's year. There be those to hint captiously that they find it an affair of false seeming; that the gorgeous colouring is a mere trick of shop-window cunning; that the time is juiceless and devoid of all but the specious delights of surface. Yet these, perhaps, are unduly imaginative for a world where any satisfaction is held by a tenure precarious at best. And even these carpers, be they never so analytical, can at least find no lack of springtime fervour in the eager throngs that pass entranced before the window show. They, the free-swinging, quick-moving men and women—the best dressed of all throngs in this young world—sun-browned, sun-enlivened, recreated to a fine mettle for enjoyment by their months of mountain or ocean sport—these are, indeed, the ones for whom this afterspring is made to bloom. And, since they find it to be a shifting miracle of perfections, how are they to be quarrelled with?

In the big polished windows waxen effigies of fine ladies, gracefully patient, display the latest dinner-gown from Paris, or the creamiest of be-ribboned tea-gowns. Or they pose in attitudes of polite adieux and greeting, all but smothered in a king's ransom of sable and ermine. Or, to the other extreme, they complacently permit themselves to be observed in the intimate revelations of Parisian lingerie, with its misty froth of embroideries, its fine-spun webs of foamy lace.

In another window, behold a sprightly and enlivening ballet of shapely silken hosiery, fitting its sculptured models to perfection, ranging in tints from the first tender green of spring foliage to the rose-pink of the spring sun's after-glow.

A few steps beyond we may study a window where the waxen ladies have been dismembered. Yet a second glance shows the retained portions to be all that woman herself considers important when she tries on the bird-toque or the picture hat, or the gauze confection for afternoons. The satisfied smiles of these waxen counterfeits show them to have been amply recompensed, with the headgear, for their physical incompleteness.

But if these terraces of colour and grace that line the sides of this narrow spring valley be said to contain only the dry husks of adornment, surely there may be found others more technically springlike.

Here in this broad window, foregathered in a congress of colours designed to appetise, are the ripe fruits of every clime and every season: the Southern pomegranate beside the hardy Northern apple, scarlet and yellow; the early strawberry and the late ruddy peach; figs from the Orient and pines from the Antilles; dates from Tunis and tawny persimmons from Japan; misty sea-green grapes and those from the hothouse—tasteless, it is true, but so lordly in their girth, and royal purple; portly golden oranges and fat plums; pears of mellow blondness and pink-skinned apricots. Here at least is the veritable stuff and essence of spring with all its attending aromas—of more integrity, perhaps, than the same colourings simulated by the confectioner's craft, in the near-by window-display of impossible sweets.

And still more of this belated spring will gladden the eye in the florist's window. In June the florist's shop is a poor place, sedulously to be shunned. Nothing of note blooms there then. The florist himself is patently ashamed of himself. The burden of sustaining his traditions he puts upon a few dejected shrubs called "hardy perennials" that have to labour the year around. All summer it is as if the place feared to compete with nature when colour and grace flower so cheaply on every southern hillside. But now its glories bloom anew, and its superiority over nature becomes again manifest. Now it assembles the blossoms of a whole long year to bewilder and allure. Its windows are shaded glens, vine-embowered, where spring, summer, and autumn blend in all their regal and diverse abundance; and the closing door of the shop fans out odours as from a thousand Persian gardens.

But spring is not all of life, nor what at once chiefly concerns us. There are people to be noted: a little series of more or less related phenomena to be observed.

One of the people, a young man, stands conveniently before this same florist's window, at that hour when the sun briefly flushes this narrow canon of Broadway from wall to wall.

He had loitered along the lively highway an hour or more, his nerves tingling responsively to all its stimuli. And now he mused as he stared at the tangled tracery of ferns against the high bank of wine-red autumn foliage, the royal cluster of white chrysanthemums and the big jar of American Beauties.

He had looked forward to this moment, too—when he should enter that same door and order at least an armful of those same haughty roses sent to an address his memory cherished. Yet now, the time having come, the zest for the feat was gone. It would be done; it were ungraceful not to do it, after certain expressions; but it would be done with no heart because of the certain knowledge that no one—at least no one to be desired—could possibly care for him, or consider him even with interest for anything but his money—the same kind of money Higbee made by purveying hams— "and she wouldn't care in the least whether it was mine or Higbee's, so there was a lot of it."

Yet he stepped in and ordered the roses, nor did the florist once suspect that so lavish a buyer of flowers could be a prey to emotions of corroding cynicism toward the person for whom they were meant.

From the florist's he returned directly to the hotel to find his mother and Psyche making homelike the suite to which they had been assigned. A maid was unpacking trunks under his sister's supervision. Mrs. Bines was in converse with a person of authoritative manner regarding the service to be supplied them. Two maids would be required, and madame would of course wish a butler—

Mrs. Bines looked helplessly at her son who had just entered.

"I think—we've—we've always did our own buttling," she faltered.

The person was politely interested.

"I'll attend to these things, ma," said Percival, rather suddenly. "Yes, we'll want a butler and the two maids, and see that the butler knows his business, please, and—here—take this, and see that we're properly looked after, will you?"

As the bill bore a large "C" on its face, and the person was rather a gentleman anyway, this unfortunate essay at irregular conjugation never fell into a certain class of anecdotes which Mrs. Bines's best friends could now and then bring themselves to relate of her.

But other matters are forward. We may next overtake two people who loiter on this bracing October day down a leaf-strewn aisle in Central Park.

"You," said the girl of the pair, "least of all men can accuse me of lacking heart."

"You are cold to me now."

"But look, think—what did I offer—you've had my trust,—everything I could bring myself to give you. Look what I would have sacrificed at your call. Think how I waited and longed for that call."

"You know how helpless I was."

"Yes, if you wanted more than my bare self. I should have been helpless, too, if I had wanted more than—than you."

"It would have been folly—madness—that way."

"Folly—madness? Do you remember the 'Sonnet of Revolt' you sent me? Sit on this bench; I wish to say it over to you, very slowly; I want you to hear it while you keep your later attitude in mind.

"Life—what is life? To do without avail The decent ordered tasks of every day: Talk with the sober: join the solemn play: Tell for the hundredth time the self-same tale Told by our grandsires in the self-same vale Where the sun sets with even, level ray, And nights, eternally the same, make way For hueless dawns, intolerably pale—'"

"But I know the verse."

"No; hear it out;—hear what you sent me:

"'And this is life? Nay, I would rather see

The man who sells his soul in some wild cause:

The fool who spurns, for momentary bliss,

All that he was and all he thought to be:

The rebel stark against his country's laws:

God's own mad lover, dying on a kiss.'"

She had completed the verse with the hint of a sneer in her tones.

"Yes, truly, I remember it; but some day you'll thank me for saving you; of course it would have been regular in a way, but people here never really forget those things—and we'd have been helpless—some day you'll thank me for thinking for you."

"Why do you believe I'm not thanking you already?"

"Hang it all! that's what you made me think yesterday when I met you."
"And so you called me heartless? Now tell me just what you expect a

woman in my position to do. I offered to go to you when you were ready. Surely that showed my spirit—and you haven't known me these years without knowing it would have to be that or nothing."

"Well, hang it, it wasn't like the last time, and you know it; you're not kind any longer. You can be kind, can't you?"

Her lip showed faintly the curl of scorn.

"No, I can't be kind any longer. Oh, I see you've known your own mind so little; there's been so little depth to it all; you couldn't dare. It was foolish to think I could show you my mind."

"But you still care for me?"

"No; no, I don't. You should have no reason to think so if I did. When I heard you'd made it up I hated you, and I think I hate you now. Let us go back. No, no, please don't touch me—ever again."

Farther down-town in the cosy drawing-room of a house in a side street east of the Avenue, two other persons were talking. A florid and profusely freckled young Englishman spoke protestingly from the hearth-rug to a woman who had the air of knowing emphatically better.

"But, my dear Mrs. Drelmer, you know, really, I can't take a curate with me, you know, and send up word won't she be good enough to come downstairs and marry me directly—not when I've not seen her, you know!" "Nonsense!" replied the lady, unimpressed. "You can do it nearly that way, if you'll listen to me. Those Westerners perform quite in that manner, I assure you. They call it 'hustling.'"

"*Dear* me!"

"Yes, indeed, 'dear you.' And another thing, I want you to forestall that Milbrey youth, and you may be sure he's no farther away than Tuxedo or Meadowbrook. Now, they arrived yesterday; they'll be unpacking to-day and settling to-morrow; I'll call the day after, and you shall be with me."

"And you forget that—that devil—suppose she's as good as her threat?"

"Absurd! how could she be?"

"You don't know her, you know, nor the old beggar either, by Jove!"

"All the more reason for haste. We'll call to-morrow. Wait. Better still, perhaps I can enlist the Gwilt-Athelston; I'm to meet her to-morrow. I'll let you know. Now I must get into my teaharness, so run along."

We are next constrained to glance at a strong man bowed in the hurt of a great grief. Horace Milbrey sits alone in his gloomy, high-ceilinged library.

His attire is immaculate. His slender, delicate hands are beautifully white. The sensitive lines of his fine face tell of the strain under which he labours. What dire tragedies are those we must face wholly alone—where we must hide the wound, perforce, because no comprehending sympathy flows out to us; because instinct warns that no help may come save from the soul's own well of divine fortitude. Some hope, tenderly, almost fearfully, held and guarded, had perished on the day that should have seen its triumphant fruition. He raised his handsome head from the antique, claw-footed desk, sat up in his chair, and stared tensely before him. His emotion was not to be suppressed. Do tears tremble in the eyes of the strong man? Let us not inquire too curiously. If they tremble down the fine-skinned cheek, let us avert our gaze. For grief in men is no thing to make a show of.

A servant passed the open door bearing an immense pasteboard box with one end cut out to accommodate the long stems of many roses.

"Jarvis!"

"Yes, sir!"

"What is it?"

"Flowers, sir, for Miss Avice."

"Let me see—and the card?"

He took the card from the florist's envelope and glanced at the name.

"Take them away."

The stricken man was once more alone; yet now it was as if the tender beauty of the flowers had balmed his hurt—taught him to hope anew. Let us in all sympathy and hope retire.

For cheerfuller sights we might observe Launton Oldaker in a musty curio-shop, delighted over a pair of silver candlesticks with square bases and fluted columns, fabricated in the reign of that fortuitous monarch, Charles the Second; or we might glance in upon the Higbees in their section of a French chateau, reproduced up on the stately Riverside Drive, where they complete the details of a dinner to be given on the morrow.

Or perhaps it were better to be concerned with a matter more weighty than dinners and antique candlesticks. The search need never be vain, even in this world of persistent frivolity. As, for example:

"Tell Mrs. Van Geist if she can't come down, I'll run up to her."

"Yes, Miss Milbrey."

Mrs. Van Geist entered a moment later.

"Why, Avice, child, you're glowing, aren't you?"

"I must be, I suppose—I've just walked down from 59th Street, and before that I walked in the Park. Feel how cold my cheeks are,—Mütterchen."

"It's good for you. Now we shall have some tea, and talk."

"Yes—I'm hungry for both, and some of those funny little cakes."

"Come back where the fire is, dear; the tea has just been brought. There, take the big chair."

"It always feels like you—like your arms, Mütterchen—and I am tired."

"And throw off that coat. There's the lemon, if you're afraid of cream."

"I wish I weren't afraid of anything but cream."

"You told me you weren't afraid of that—that cad—any more."

"I'm not—I just told him so. But I'm afraid of it all; I'm tired trying not to drift—tired trying not to try, and tired trying to try—Oh, dear—sounds like a nonsense verse, doesn't it? Have you any one to-night? No? I think I must stay with you till morning. Send some one home to say I'll be here. I can always think so much better here—and you, dear old thing, to mother me!"

"Do, child; I'll send Sandon directly."

"He will go to the house of mourning."

"What's the latest?"

"Papa was on the verge of collapse this morning, and yet he was striving so bravely and nobly to bear up. No one knows what that man suffers; it makes him gloomy all the time about everything. Just before I left, he was saying that, when one considers the number of American homes in which a green salad is never served, one must be appalled. Are you appalled, auntie? But that isn't it."

"Nothing has happened?"

"Well, there'll be no sensation about it in the papers to-morrow, but a very dreadful thing has happened. Papa has suffered one of the cruellest blows of his life. I fancy he didn't sleep at all last night, and he looked thoroughly bowled over this morning."

"But what is it?"

"Well—oh, it's awful!—first of all there were six dozen of early-bottled, 1875 Château Lafitte—that was the bitterest—but he had to see the rest go, too—Château Margeaux of '80—some terribly ancient port and Madeira—

the dryest kind of sherry—a lot of fine, full clarets of '77 and '78—oh, you can't know how agonising it was to him—I've heard them so often I know them all myself."

"But what on earth about them?"

"Nothing, only the Cosmopolitan Club's wine cellar—auctioned off, you know. For over a year papa has looked forward to it. He knew every bottle of wine in it. He could recite the list without looking at it. Sometimes he sounded like a French lesson—and he's been under a fearful strain ever since the announcement was made. Well, the great day came yesterday, and poor pater simply couldn't bid in a single drop. It needed ready money, you know. And he had hoped so cheerfully all the time to do something. It broke his heart, I'm sure, to see that Château Lafitte go—and only imagine, it was bid in by the butler of that odious Higbee. You should have heard papa rail about the vulgar *nouveaux riches* when he came home—he talked quite like an anarchist. But by to-night he'll be blaming me for his misfortunes. That's why I chose to stay here with you."

"Poor Horace. Whatever are you going to do?"

"Well, dearie, as for me, it doesn't look as if I could do anything but one thing. And here is my ardent young Croesus coming out of the West."

"You called him your 'athletic Bayard' once."

"The other's more to the point at present. And what else can I do? Oh, if some one would just be brave enough to live the raw, quivering life with me, I could do it, I give you my word. I could let everything go by the board—but I am so alone and so helpless and no man is equal to it, nowadays. All of us here seem to be content to order a 'half portion' of life."

"Child, those dreams are beautiful, but they're like those flying-machines that are constantly being tested by the credulous inventors. A wheel or a pinion goes wrong and down the silly things come tumbling."

"Very well; then I shall be wise—I suppose I shall be—and I'll do it quickly. This fortune of good gold shall propose marriage to me at once, and be accepted—so that I shall be able to look my dear old father in the face again—and then, after I'm married—well, don't blame me for anything that happens."

"I'm sure you'll be happy with him—it's only your silly notions. He's in love with you."

"That makes me hesitate. He really is a man—I like him—see this letter—a long review from the Arcady *Lyre* of the 'poem' he wrote, a poem consisting of 'Avice Milbrey.' The reviewer has been quite enthusiastic over it, too,—written from some awful place in Montana."

"What more could you ask? He'll be kind."

"You don't understand, Mütterchen. He seems too decent to marry that way—and yet it's the only way I could marry him. And after he found me out—oh, think of what marriage *is*—he'd *have* to find it out—I couldn't *act* long—doubtless he wouldn't even be kind to me then."

"You are morbid, child."

"But I will do it; I shall; I will be a credit to my training—and I shall learn to hate him and he will have to learn—well, a great deal that he doesn't know about women."

She stared into the fire and added, after a moment's silence:

"Oh, if a man only *could* live up to the verses he cuts out of magazines!"

CHAPTER XVI.

With the Barbaric Hosts

History repeats itself so cleverly, with a variance of stage-settings and accessories so cunning, that the repetition seldom bores, and is, indeed, frequently undetected. Thus, the descent of the Barbarians upon a decadent people is a little *tour de force* that has been performed again and again since the oldest day. But because the assault nowadays is made not with force of arms we are prone to believe it is no longer made at all;—as if human ways had changed a bit since those ugly, hairy tribes from the Northern forests descended upon the Roman empire. And yet the mere difference that the assault is now made with force of money in no way alters the process nor does it permit the result to vary. On the surface all is cordiality and peaceful negotiation. Beneath is the same immemorial strife, the life-and-death struggle,—pitiless, inexorable.

What would have been a hostile bivouac within the city's gates, but for the matter of a few centuries, is now, to select an example which remotely concerns us, a noble structure on Riverside Drive, facing the lordly Hudson and the majestic Palisades that form its farther wall. And, for the horde of Goths and Visigoths, Huns and Vandals, drunkenly reeling in the fitful light of camp-fires, chanting weird battle-runes, fighting for captive vestals, and bickering in uncouth tongues over the golden spoils, what have we now to make the parallel convince? Why, the same Barbarians, actually; the same hairy rudeness, the same unrefined, all-conquering, animal force; a red-faced, big-handed lot, imbued with hearty good nature and an easy tolerance for the ways of those upon whom they have descended.

Here are chiefs of renown from the farthest fastnesses; they and their curious households: the ironmonger from Pittsburg, the gold-miner from Dawson, the copper chief from Butte, the silver chief from Denver, the cattle chief from Oklahoma, lord of three hundred thousand good acres and thirty thousand cattle, the lumber prince from Michigan, the founder of a later dynasty in oil, from Texas. And, for the unaesthetic but effective Attila, an able fashioner of pork products from Chicago.

Here they make festival, carelessly, unafraid, unmolested. For, in the lapse of time, the older peoples have learned not only the folly of resisting inevitables, but that the huge and hairy invaders may be treated and bartered with not unprofitably. Doubtless it often results from this amity that the patrician strain is corrupted by the alien admixture,—but business has been business since as many as two persons met on the face of the new earth.

For example, this particular shelter is builded upon land which one of the patrician families had held for a century solely because it could not be disposed of. Yet the tribesmen came, clamouring for palaces, and now this same land, with some adjoining areas of trifling extent, produces an income that will suffice to maintain that family almost in its ancient and befitting estate.

In this mammoth pile, for the petty rental of ten or fifteen thousand dollars a year, many tribes of the invaders have found shelter and entertainment in apartments of many rooms. Outwardly, in details of ornamentation, the building is said to duplicate the Chateaux Blois, those splendid palaces of Francis I. Inside are all the line and colour and device of elegant opulence, modern to the last note.

To this palace of an October evening comes the tribe of Bines, and many another such, for a triumphal feast in the abode of Barbarian Silas Higbee. The carriages pass through a pair of lordly iron gates, swung from massive stone pillars, under an arch of wrought iron with its antique lamp, and into the echoing courtyard flanked by trim hedges of box.

Alighting, the barbaric guests of Higbee are ushered through a marble-walled vestibule, from which a wrought-iron and bronze screen gives way to the main entrance-hall. The ceiling here reproduces that of a feudal castle in Rouen, with some trifling and effective touches of decoration in blue, scarlet, and gold. The walls are of white Caen stone, with ornate windows and balconies jutting out above. In one corner is a stately stone mantel with richly carved hood, bearing in its central panel the escutcheon of the gallant French monarch. Up a little flight of marble steps, guarded by its hand-rail of heavy metal, shod with crimson velvet, one reaches the elevator. This pretty enclosure of iron and glass, of classic detail in the period of Henry II., of Circassian walnut trim, with crotch panels, has more the aspect of boudoir than elevator. The deep seat is of walnut, upholstered with fat cushions of crimson velvet edged in dull gold galloon. Over the seat is a mirror cut into small squares by wooden muntins. At each side are electric candles softened by red silk shades. One's last view before the door closes noiselessly is of a bay-window opposite, set with cathedral glass casement-lights, which sheds soft colours upon the hall-bench of carven stone and upon the tessellated floor.

The door to the Higbee domain is of polished mahogany, set between lights of antique verte Italian glass, and bearing an ancient brass knocker. From the reception-room, with its walls of green empire silk, one passes through a foyer hall, of Cordova leather hangings, to the drawing-room with its three broad windows. Opposite the entrance to this superb room is a mantel of carved Caen stone, faced with golden Pavanazza marble, with old Roman andirons of gold ending in the fleur-de-lis. The walls are hung with blue Florentine silk, embossed in silver. Beyond a bronze grill is the music-room, a library done in Austrian oak with stained burlap panelled by dull-forged nails, a conservatory, a billiard-room, a smoking-room. This latter has walls of red damask and a mantel with "*Post Tenebras Lux*" cut into one of its marble panels,—a legend at which the worthy lessee of all this splendour is wont often to glance with respectful interest.

The admirable host—if one be broad-minded—is now in the drawing-room, seconding his worthy wife and pretty daughter who welcome the dinner-guests.

For a man who has a fad for ham and doesn't care who knows it, his bearing is all we have a right to expect that it should be. Among the group of arrivals, men of his own sort, he is speaking of the ever-shifting fashion in beards, to the evangel of a Texas oil-field who flaunts to the world one of those heavy moustaches spuriously extended below the corners of the mouth by means of the chin-growth of hair. Another, a worthy tribesman from Snohomish, Washington, wears a beard which, for a score of years, has been let to be its own true self; to express, fearlessly, its own unique capacity for variation from type. These two have rallied their host upon his modishly trimmed side-whiskers.

"You're right," says Mr. Higbee, amiably, "I ain't stuck any myself on this way of trimming up a man's face, but the madam will have it this way—says it looks more refined and New Yorky. And now, do you know, ever since I've wore 'em this way—ever since I had 'em scraped from around under my neck here—I have to go to Florida every winter. Come January or February, I get bronchitis every blamed year!"

Two of the guests only are alien to the barbaric throng.

There is the noble Baron Ronault de Palliac, decorated, reserved, observant,—almost wistful. For the moment he is picturing dutifully the luxuries a certain marriage would enable him to procure for his noble father and his aged mother, who eagerly await the news of his quest for the golden fleece. For the baron contemplates, after the fashion of many conscientious explorers, a marriage with a native woman; though he permits himself to cherish the hope that it may not be conditioned upon his adopting the manners and customs of the particular tribe that he means to honour. Monsieur the Baron has long since been obliged to confess that a suitable *mesalliance* is none too easy of achievement, and, in testimony of his vicissitudes, he has written for a Paris comic paper a series of grimly satiric essays upon New York society. Recently, moreover, he has been upon the verge of accepting employment in the candy factory of a bourgeois compatriot. But hope has a little revived in the noble breast since chance brought him and his title under the scrutiny of the bewitching Miss Millicent Higbee and her appreciative mother.

And to-night there is not only the pretty Miss Higbee, but the winning Miss Bines, whose *dot*, the baron has been led to understand, would permit his beloved father unlimited piquet at his club, to say nothing of regenerating the family chateau. Yet these are hardly matters to be gossiped of. It is enough to know that the Baron Ronault de Palliac when he discovers himself at table between Miss Bines and the adorable Miss Higbee, becomes less saturnine than has for some time been his wont. He does not forget previous disappointments, but desperately snaps his swarthy jaws in commendable superiority to any adverse fate.

"*Je ne donne pas un damn*," he says to himself, and translates, as was his practice, to better his English—"I do not present a damn. I shall take what it is that it may be."

The noble Baron de Palliac at this feast of the tribesmen was like the captive patrician of old led in chains that galled. The other alien, Launton Oldaker, was present under terms of honourable truce, willingly and without ulterior motive saving—as he confessed to himself—a consuming desire to see "how the other half lives." He was no longer the hunted and dismayed being Percival had met in that far-off and impossible Montana; but was now untroubled, remembering, it is true, that this "slumming expedition," as he termed it, had taken him beyond the recognised bounds of his beloved New York, but serene in the consciousness that half an hour's drive would land him safely back at his club.

Oldaker observed Miss Psyche Bines approvingly.

"We are so glad to be in New York!" she had confided to him, sitting at her right.

"My dear young woman," he warned her, "you haven't reached New York yet." The talk being general and loud, he ventured further.

"This is Pittsburg, Chicago, Kansas City, Denver—almost anything but New York."

"Of course I know these are not the swell old families."

Oldaker sipped his glass of old Oloroso sherry and discoursed.

"And our prominent families, the ones whose names you read, are not New York any more, either. They are rather London and Paris. Their furniture, clothing, plate, pictures, and servants come from one or the other. Yes, and their manners, too, their interests and sympathies and concerns, their fashions—and—sometimes, their—er—morals. They are assuredly not New York any more than Gobelin tapestries and Fortuny pictures and Louis Seize chairs are New York."

"How queerly you talk. Where is New York, then?"

Oldaker sighed thoughtfully between two spoonfuls of *tortue verte, claire.*

"Well, I suppose the truth is that there isn't much of New York left in New York. As a matter of fact I think it died with the old Volunteer Fire Department. Anyway the surviving remnant is coy. Real old New Yorkers like myself—neither poor nor rich—are swamped in these days like those prehistoric animals whose bones we find. There comes a time when we can't live, and deposits form over us and we're lost even to memory."

But this talk was even harder for Miss Bines to understand than the English speech of the Baron Ronault de Palliac, and she turned to that noble gentleman as the turbot with sauce Corail was served.

The dining-room, its wall wainscotted from floor to ceiling in Spanish oak, was flooded with soft light from the red silk dome that depended from its crown of gold above the table. The laughter and talk were as little subdued as the scheme of the rooms. It was an atmosphere of prodigal and confident opulence. From the music-room near by came the soft strains of a Haydn quartet, exquisitely performed by finished and expensive artists.

"Say, Higbee!" it was the oil chief from Texas, "see if them fiddlers of yours can't play 'Ma Honolulu Lulu!'"

Oldaker, wincing and turning to Miss Bines for sympathy, heard her say:

"Yes, do, Mr. Higbee! I do love those ragtime songs—and then have them play 'Tell Me, Pretty Maiden,' and the 'Intermezzo.'"

He groaned in anguish.

The talk ran mostly on practical affairs: the current values of the great staple commodities; why the corn crop had been light; what wheat promised to bring; how young Burman of the Chicago Board of Trade had been pinched in his own wheat corner for four millions—"put up" by his admiring father; what beef on the hoof commanded; how the Federal Oil Company would presently own the State of Texas.

Almost every Barbarian at the table had made his own fortune. Hardly one but could recall early days when he toiled on farm or in shop or forest, herded cattle, prospected, sought adventure in remote and hazardous wilds.

"'Tain't much like them old days, eh, Higbee?" queried the Crown Prince of Cripple Creek—"when you and me had to walk from Chicago to Green Bay, Wisconsin, because we didn't have enough shillings for stage-fare?" He gazed about him suggestively.

"Corn-beef and cabbage was pretty good then, eh?" and with sure, vigorous strokes he fell to demolishing his *filet de dinde a la Perigueux*, while a butler refilled his glass with Chateau Malescot, 1878.

"Well, it does beat the two rooms the madam and me started to keep house in when we was married," admitted the host. "That was on the banks of the Chicago River, and now we got the Hudson flowin' right through the front yard, you might say, right past our own yacht-landing."

From old days of work and hardship they came to discuss the present and their immediate surroundings, social and financial.

Their daughters, it appeared, were being sought in marriage by the sons of those among whom they sojourned.

"Oh, they're a nice band of hand-shakers, all right, all right," asserted the gentleman from Kansas City. "One of 'em tried to keep company with our Caroline, but I wouldn't stand for it. He was a crackin' good shinny player, and he could lead them cotillion-dances blowin' a whistle and callin', 'All right, Up!' or something, like a car-starter,—but, 'Tell me something good about him,' I says to an old friend of his family. Well, he hemmed and hawed—he was a New York gentleman, and says he, 'I don't know whether I could make you understand or not,' he says, 'but he's got Family,' jest like that, bearin' down hard on 'Family'—'and you've got money,' he says, 'and Money and Family need each other badly in this town,' he says. 'Yes,' says I, 'I met up with a number of people here,' I says, 'but I ain't met none yet that you'd have to blindfold and back into a lot of money,' I says, 'family or no family,' I says. 'And that young man,' he says, 'is a pleasant, charming fellow; why,' he says, 'he's the best-coated man in New York.' Well, I looked at him and I says, 'Well,' says I, 'he may be the best-coated man in New York, but he'll be the best-booted man in New York, too,' I says, 'if he comes around trying to spark Caroline any more,—or would be if I had my way. His chin's pushed too far back under his face,' I says, 'and besides,' I says, 'Caroline is being waited on by a young hardware drummer, a good steady young fellow travelling out of little old K.C.,' I says, 'and while he ain't much for fam'ly,' I says, he'll have one of his own before he gets through,' I says; 'we start fam'lies where I come from,' I says."

"Good boy! Good for you," cheered the self-made Barbarians, and drank success to the absent disseminator of hardware.

With much loud talk of this unedifying character the dinner progressed to an end; through *selle d'agneau*, floated in '84 champagne, terrapin convoyed by a special Madeira of 1850, and canvas-back duck with *Romanee Conti*, 1865, to a triumphant finale of Turkish coffee and 1811 brandy.

After dinner the ladies gossiped of New York society, while the barbaric males smoked their big oily cigars and bandied reminiscences. Higbee showed them through every one of the apartment's twenty-two rooms, from reception-hall to laundry, manipulating the electric lights with the skill of a stage-manager.

The evening ended with a cake-walk, for the musical artists had by rare wines been mellowed from their classic reserve into a mood of ragtime abandon. And if Monsieur the Baron with his ceremonious grace was less exuberant than the Crown Prince of Cripple Creek, who sang as he stepped the sensuous measure, his pleasure was not less. He joyed to observe that these men of incredible millions had no hauteur.

"I do not," wrote the baron to his noble father the marquis, that night, "yet understand their joke; why should it be droll to wish that the man whose coat is of the best should also wear boots of the best? but as for what they call *une promenade de gateau*, I find it very enjoyable. I have met a Mlle. Bines to whom I shall at once pay my addresses. Unlike Mlle. Higbee, she has not the father from Chicago nor elsewhere. *Quel diable d'homme!*"

CHAPTER XVII.

The Patricians Entertain

To reward the enduring who read politely through the garish revel of the preceding chapter, covers for fourteen are now laid with correct and tasteful quietness at the sophisticated board of that fine old New York family, the Milbreys. Shaded candles leave all but the glowing table in a gloom discreetly pleasant. One need not look so high as the old-fashioned stuccoed ceiling. The family portraits tone agreeably into the halflight of the walls; the huge old-fashioned walnut sideboard, soberly ornate with its mirrors, its white marble top and its wood-carved fruit, towers majestically aloft in proud scorn of the frivolous Chippendale fad.

Jarvis, the accomplished and incomparable butler, would be subdued and scholarly looking but for the flagrant scandal of his port-wine nose. He gives finishing little fillips to the white chrysanthemums massed in the central epergne on the long silver plateau, and bestows a last cautious survey upon the cut-glass and silver radiating over the dull white damask. Finding the table and its appointments faultless, he assures himself once more that the sherry will come on irreproachably at a temperature of 60 degrees; that the Burgundy will not fall below 65 nor mount above 70; for Jarvis wots of a palate so acutely sensitive that it never fails to record a variation of so much as one degree from the approved standard of temperature.

How restful this quiet and reserve after the colour and line tumult of the Higbee apartment. There the flush and bloom of newness were oppressive to the right-minded. All smelt of the shop. Here the dull tones and decorous lines caress and soothe instead of overwhelming the imagination with effects too grossly literal. Here is the veritable spirit of good form.

Throughout the house this contrast might be noted. It is the brown-stone, high-stoop house, guarded by a cast-iron fence, built in vast numbers when the world of fashion moved North to Murray Hill and Fifth Avenue a generation ago. One of these houses was like all the others inside and out, built of unimaginative "builder's architecture." The hall, the long parlour, the back parlour or library, the high stuccoed ceilings—not only were these alike in all the houses, but the furnishings, too, were apt to be of a sameness in them all, rather heavy and tasteless, but serving the ends that such things should be meant to serve, and never flamboyant. Of these relics of a simpler day not many survive to us, save in the shameful degeneracy of boarding-houses. But in such as are left, we may confidently expect to find the traditions of that more dignified time kept unsullied;—to find, indeed, as we find in the house of Milbrey, a settled air of gloom that suggests insolvent but stubbornly determined exclusiveness.

Something of this air, too, may be noticed in the surviving tenants of these austere relics. Yet it would hardly be observed in this house on this night, for not only do arriving guests bring the aroma of a later prosperity, but the hearts of our host and hostess beat high with a new hope. For the fair and sometimes uncertain daughter of the house of Milbrey, after many ominous mutterings, delays, and frank rebellions, has declared at last her readiness to be a credit to her training by conferring her family prestige, distinction of manner and charms of person upon one equipped for their suitable maintenance.

Already her imaginative father is ravishing in fancy the mouldiest wine-cellars of Continental Europe. Already the fond mother has idealised a house in "Millionaire's Row" east of the Park, where there shall be twenty servants instead of three, and there shall cease that gnawing worry lest the treacherous north-setting current sweep them west of the Park into one of those hideously new apartment houses, where the halls are done in marble that seems to have been sliced from a huge Roquefort cheese, and where one must vie, perhaps, with a shop-keeper for the favours of an irreverent and materialistic janitor.

The young woman herself entertains privately a state of mind which she has no intention of making public. It is enough, she reasons, that her action should outwardly accord with the best traditions of her class; and indeed, her family would never dream of demanding more.

Her gown to-night is of orchard green, trimmed with apple-blossoms, a single pink spray of them caught in her hair. The rounding, satin grace of her slender arms, sloping to the opal-tipped fingers, the exquisite line from ear to shoulder strap, the melting ripeness of her chin and throat, the tender pink and white of her fine skin, the capricious, inciting tilt of her small head, the dainty lift of her short nose,—these allurements she has inventoried with a calculating and satisfied eye. She is glad to believe that there is every reason why it will soon be over.

And, since the whole loaf is notoriously better than a half, here is the engaging son of the house, also firmly bent upon the high emprise of matrimony; handsome, with the chin, it may be, slightly receding; but an unexcelled leader of cotillions, a surpassing polo-player, clever, winning, and dressed with an effect that has long made him remarked in polite circles, which no mere money can achieve. Money, indeed, if certain ill-natured gossip of tradesmen be true, has been an inconsiderable factor in the encompassment of this sartorial distinction. He waits now, eager for a first glimpse of the young woman whose charms, even by report, have already won the best devotion he has to give. A grievous error it is to suppose that Cupid's artillery is limited to bow and arrows.

And now, instead of the rude commercial horde that laughed loudly and ate uncouthly at the board of the Barbarian, we shall sit at table with people born to the only manner said to be worth possessing;—if we except, indeed, the visiting tribe of Bines, who may be relied upon, however, to behave at least unobtrusively.

As a contrast to the oppressively Western matron from Kansas City, here is Mistress Fidelia Oldaker on the arm of her attentive son. She would be very old but for the circumstance that she began early in life to be a belle, and age cannot stale such women. Brought up with board at her back, books on her head, to guard her complexion as if it were her fair name, to be diligent at harp practice and conscientious with the dancing-master, she is almost the last of a school that nursed but the single aim of subjugating man. To-night, at seventy-something, she is a bit of pink bisque fragility, bubbling tirelessly with reminiscence, her vivacity unimpaired, her energy amazing, and her coquetry faultless. From which we should learn, and be grateful therefor, that when a girl is brought up in the way she ought to go she will never be able to depart from it.

Here also is Cornelia Van Geist, sister of our admirable hostess—relict of a gentleman who had been first or second cousin to half the people in society it were really desirable to know, and whose taste in wines, dinners, and sports had been widely praised at his death by those who had had the fortune to be numbered among his friends. Mrs. Van Geist has a kind, shrewd face, and her hair, which turned prematurely grey while she was yet a wife, gives her a look of age that her actual years belie.

Here, too, is Rulon Shepler, the money-god, his large, round head turning upon his immense shoulders without the aid of a neck—sharp-eyed, grizzled, fifty, short of stature, and with as few illusions concerning life as the New York financier is apt to retain at his age.

If we be forced to wait for another guest of note, it is hardly more than her due; for Mrs. Gwilt-Athelstan is truly a personage, and the best people on more than one continent do not become unduly provoked at being made to wait for her. Those less than the very best frankly esteem it a privilege. Yet the great lady is not careless of engagements, and the wait is never prolonged. Mrs. Milbrey has time to say to her sister, "Yes, we think it's going; and really, it will do very well, you know. The girl has had some nonsense in her mind for a year past—none of us can tell what—but now she seems actually sensible, and she's promised to accept when the chap proposes." But there is time for no more gossip.

The belated guest arrives, enveloped in a vast cloak, and accompanied by her two nephews, whom Percival Bines recognises for the solemn and taciturn young men he had met in Shepler's party at the mine.

Mrs. Gwilt-Athelstan, albeit a decorative personality, is constructed on the same broad and generously graceful lines as her own victoria. The great lady has not only two chins, but what any fair-minded observer would accept as sufficient promise of a good third. Yet hardly could a slighter person display to advantage the famous Gwilt-Athelstan jewels. The rope of pierced diamonds with pigeon-blood rubies strung between them, which she wears wound over her corsage, would assuredly overweight the frail Fidelia Oldaker; the tiara of emeralds and diamonds was never meant for a brow less majestic; nor would the stomacher of lustrous grey pearls and glinting diamonds ever have clasped becomingly a figure that was *svelte*—or "skinny," as the great lady herself is frank enough to term all persons even remotely inclined to be *svelte*.

But let us sit and enliven a proper dinner with talk upon topics of legitimate interest and genuine propriety.

Here will be no discussion of the vulgar matter of markets, staples, and prices, such as we perforce endured through the overwined and too-abundant repast of Higbee. Instead of learning what beef on the hoof brings per hundred-weight, f.o.b. at Cheyenne, we shall here glean at once the invaluable fact that while good society in London used to be limited to those who had been presented at court, the presentations have now become so numerous that the limitation has lost its significance. Mrs. Gwilt-Athelstan thus discloses, as if it were a trifle, something we should never learn at the table of Higbee though we ate his heavy dinners to the day of ultimate chaos. And while we learned at that distressingly new table that one should keep one's heifers and sell off one's steer calves, we never should have been informed there that Dinard had just enjoyed the gayest season of its history under the patronage of this enterprising American; nor that Lady de Muzzy had opened a tea-room in Grafton Street, and Cynthia, Marchioness of Angleberry, a beauty-improvement parlour on the Strand "because she needs the money."

"Lots of 'em takin' to trade nowadays; it's a smart sayin' there now that all the peers are marryin' actresses and all the peeresses goin' into business." Mrs. Gwilt-Athelstan nodded little shocks of brilliance from her tiara and hungrily speared another oyster.

"Only trouble is, it's such rotten hard work collectin' bills from their intimate friends; they simply *won't* pay."

Nor at the barbaric Higbee's should we have been vouchsafed, to treasure for our own, the knowledge that Mrs. Gwilt-Athelstan had merely run over for the cup-fortnight, meaning to return directly to her daughter, Katharine, Duchess of Blanchmere, in time for the Melton Mowbray hunting-season; nor that she had been rather taken by the new way of country life among us, and so tempted to protract her gracious sojourn.

"Really," she admits, "we're comin' to do the right thing over here; a few years were all we needed. Hardly a town-house to be opened before Thanksgivin', I understand; and down at the Hills some of the houses will stay open all winter. It's coachin', ridin', and golf and auto-racin' and polo and squash; really the young folks don't go in at all except to dance and eat; and it's quite right, you know. It's quite decently English, now. Why, at Morris Park the other day, the crowd on the lawn looked quite like Ascot, actually."

Nor could we have learned in the hostile camp the current gossip of Tuxedo, Meadowbrook, Lenox, Morristown, and Ardsley; of the mishap to Mrs. "Jimmie" Whettin, twice unseated at a recent meet; of the woman's championship tournament at Chatsworth; or the good points of the new runner-up at Baltusrol, daily to be seen on the links. Where we might incur knowledge of Beaumont "gusher" or Pittsburg mill we should never have discovered that teas and receptions are really falling into disrepute; that a series of dinner-dances will be organised by the mothers of debutantes to bring them forward; and that big subscription balls are in disfavour, since they benefit no one but the caterers who serve poor suppers and bad champagne.

Mrs. takes only Scotch whiskey and soda.

"But I'm glad," she confides to Horace Milbrey on her left, "that you haven't got to followin' this fad of havin' one wine at dinner; I know it's English, but it's downright shoddy."

Her host's eyes swam with gratitude for this appreciation.

"I stick to my peg," she continued; "but I like to see a Chablis with the oysters and good dry sherry with the soup, and a Moselle with the fish, and then you're ready to be livened with a bit of champagne for the roast, and steadied a bit by Burgundy with the game. Phim sticks to it, too; tells me my peg is downright encouragement to the bacteria. But I tell him I've no quarrel with *my* bacteria. 'Live and let live' is my motto, I tell him,—and if the microbes and I both like Scotch and soda, why, what harm. I'm forty-two and not so much of a fool that I ain't a little bit of a physician. I know my stomach, I tell him."

"What about these Western people?" she asked Oldaker at her other side, after a little.

"Decent, unpretentious folks, somewhat new, but with loads of money."

"I've heard how the breed's stormin' New York in droves; but they tell me some of us need the money."

"I dined with one last night, a sugar-cured ham magnate from Chicago."

"*Dear* me! how shockin'!"

"But they're good, whole-souled people."

"And well-*heeled*—and that's what we need, it seems. Some of us been so busy bein' well-familied that we've forgot to make money."

"It's a good thing, too. Nature has her own building laws about fortunes. When they get too sky-scrapy she topples them over. These people with their thrifty habits would have *all* the money in time if their sons and daughters didn't marry aristocrats with expensive tastes who know how to be spenders. Nature keeps things fairly even, one way or another."

"You're thinkin' about Kitty and the duke."

"No, not then I wasn't, though that's one of the class I mean. I was thinking especially about these Westerners."

"Well, my grandfather made the best barrels in New York, and I'm mother-in-law of a chap whose ancestors for three hundred and fifty years haven't done a stroke of work; but he's the Duke of Blanchmere, and I hope our friends here will come as near gettin' the worth of their money as we did. And if that chap"—she glanced at Percival—"marries a certain young woman, he'll never have a dull moment. I'd vouch for that. I'm quite sure she's the devil in her."

"And if the yellow-haired girl marries the fellow next her—"

"He might do worse."

"Yes, but might *she*? He's already doing worse, and he'll keep on doing it, even if he does marry her."

"Nonsense—about that, you know; all rot! What can you expect of these chaps? So does the duke do worse, but you'll never hear Kitty complain so long as he lets her alone and she can wear the strawberry leaves. I fancy I'll have those young ones down to the Hills for Hallowe'en and the week-end. Might as well help 'em along."

At the other end of the table, the fine old ivory of her cheeks gently suffused with pink until they looked like slightly crumpled leaves of a la France rose, Mrs. Oldaker was flirting brazenly with Shepler, and prattling impartially to him and to one of the twin nephews of old days in social New York; of a time when the world of fashion occupied a little space at the Battery and along Broadway; of its migration to the far north of Great Jones Street, St. Mark's Place, and Second Avenue. In Waverly Place had been the flowering of her belle-hood, and the day when her set moved on to Murray Hill was to her still recent and revolutionary.

Between the solemn Angstead twins, Mrs. Bines had sat in silence until by some happy chance it transpired that "horse" was the word to unlock their lips. As Mrs. Bines knew all about horses the twins at once became voluble, showing her marked attention. The twins were notably devoid of prejudice if your sympathies happened to run with theirs.

Miss Bines and young Milbrey were already on excellent terms. Percival and Miss Milbrey, on the other hand, were doing badly. Some disturbing element seemed to have put them aloof. Miss Milbrey wondered somewhat; but her mind was easy, for her resolution had been taken.

Mrs. Gwilt-Athelstan extended her invitation to the young people, who accepted joyfully.

"Come down and camp with us, and help Phim keep the batteries of his autos run out. You know they deteriorate when they're left half-charged, and it's one of the cares of his life to see to the whole six of 'em when they come in. He gets in one and the men get in the others, and he leads a solemn parade around the stables until they've been run out. Tell me the leisure class isn't a hard-workin' class, now."

Over coffee and chartreuse in the drawing-room there was more general talk of money and marriage, and of one for the other.

"And so he married money," concluded Mrs. Gwilt-Athelstan of one they had discussed.

"Happy marriage!" Shepler called out.

"No; money talks! and this time, on my word, now, it made you want to put on those thick sealskin ear-muffs. Poor chap, and he'd been talkin' to me about the monotony of married life. 'Monotony, my boy,' I said to him, 'you don't *know* lovely woman!' and now he wishes jolly well that he'd not done it, you know."

Here, too, was earned by Mrs. Bines a reputation for wit that she was never able quite to destroy. There had been talk of a banquet to a visiting celebrity the night before, for which the *menu* was one of unusual costliness.

Mr. Milbrey had dwelt with feeling upon certain of its eminent excellences, such as loin of young bear, a la Granville, and the boned quail, stuffed with goose-livers.

"Really," he concluded, "from an artistic standpoint, although large dinners are apt to be slurred and slighted, it was a creation of undoubted worth."

"And the orchestra," spoke up Mrs. Bines, who had read of the banquet, "played 'Hail to the *Chef!*'"

The laughter at this sally was all it should have been, even the host joining in it. Only two of those present knew that the good woman had been warned not to call "chef" "chief," as Silas Higbee did. The fact that neither should "chief" be called "chef" was impressed upon her later, in a way to make her resolve ever again to eschew both of the troublesome words.

When the guests had gone Miss Milbrey received the praise of both parents for her blameless attitude toward young Bines.

"It will be fixed when we come back from Wheatly," said that knowing young woman, "and now don't worry any more about it."

"And, Fred," said the mother, "do keep straight down there. She's a commonplace girl, with lots of mannerisms to unlearn, but she's pretty and sweet and teachable."

"And she'll learn a lot from Fred that she doesn't know now," finished that young man's sister from the foot of the stairway.

Back at their hotel Psyche Bines was saying:

"Isn't it queer about Mrs. Gwilt-Athelstan? We've read so much about her in the papers. I thought she must be some one awful to meet—I was that scared—and instead, she's like any one, and real chummy besides; and, actually, ma, don't you think her dress was dowdy—all except the diamonds? I suppose that comes from living in England so much. And hasn't Mrs. Milbrey twice as grand a manner, and the son—he's a precious—he knows everything and everybody; I shall like him."

Her brother, who had flung himself into a cushioned corner, spoke with the air of one who had reluctantly consented to be interviewed and who was anxious to be quoted correctly:

"Mrs. Gwilt-Athelstan is all right. She reminds me of what Uncle Peter writes about that new herd of short-horns: 'This breed has a mild disposition, is a good feeder, and produces a fine quality of flesh.' But I'll tell you one thing, sis," he concluded with sudden emphasis, "with all this talk about marrying for money I'm beginning to feel as if you and I were a couple of white rabbits out in the open with all the game laws off!"

CHAPTER XVIII.

The Course of True Love at a House Party

Among sundry maxims and observations of King Solomon, collated by the discerning men of Hezekiah, it will be recalled that the way of a man with a maid is held up to wonder. "There be," says the wise king, who composed a little in the crisp manner of Mr. Kipling, "three things which are too wonderful for me; yea, four which I know not: the way of an eagle in the air; the way of a serpent upon a rock; the way of a ship in the midst of the sea; and the way of a man with a maid." Why he neglected to include the way of a maid with a man is not at once apparent. His unusual facilities for observation must seemingly have inspired him to wonder at the maid's way even more than at the man's; and wise men later than he have not hesitated to confess their entire lack of understanding in the matter. But if Solomon included this item in his summary, the men of Hezekiah omitted to report the fact, and by their chronicles we learn only that the woman "eateth and wipeth her mouth and saith 'I have done no wickedness.'" Perhaps it was Solomon's mischance to observe phenomena of this character too much in the mass.

Miss Milbrey's way, at any rate, with the man she had decided to marry, would undoubtedly have made more work for the unnamed Boswells of the king, could it have been brought to his notice.

For, as she journeyed to the meeting-place on a bright October afternoon, she confessed to herself that it was of a depth beyond her own fathoming. Lolling easily back in the wicker chair of the car that bore her, and gazing idly out over the brown fields and yellow forests of Long Island as they swirled by her, she found herself wishing once that her eyes were made like those of a doll. She had lately discovered of one that when it appeared to fall asleep, it merely turned its eyes around to look into its own head. With any lesser opportunity for introspection she felt that certain doubts as to her own motives and processes would remain for ever unresolved. It was not that she could not say "I have done no wickedness;" let us place this heroine in no false light. She was little concerned with the morality of her course as others might appraise it. The fault, if fault it be, is neither ours nor hers, and Mr. Darwin wrote a big book chiefly to prove that it isn't. From the force of her environment and heredity Miss Milbrey had debated almost exclusively her own chances of happiness under given conditions; and if she had, for a time, questioned the wisdom of the obvious course, entirely from her own selfish standpoint, it is all that, and perhaps more than, we were justified in expecting from her. Let her, then, cheat the reader of no sympathy that might flow to a heroine struggling for a high moral ideal. Merely is she clear-headed enough to have discovered that selfishness is not the thing of easy bonds it is reputed to be; that its delights are not certain; that one does not unerringly achieve happiness by the bare circumstance of being uniformly selfish. Yet even this is a discovery not often made, nor one to be lightly esteemed; for have not the wise ones of Church and State ever implied that the way of selfishness is a way of sure delight, to be shunned only because its joys endure not? So it may be, after all, no small merit we claim for this girl in that, trained to selfishness and a certain course, she yet had the wit to suspect that its joys have been overvalued even by its professional enemies. It is no small merit, perhaps, even though, after due and selfish reflection, she determined upon the obvious course.

If sometimes her heart was sick with the hunger to love and be loved by the one she loved, so that there were times when she would have bartered the world for its plenary feeding, it is all that, we insist, and more, than could be expected of this sort of heroine.

And so she had resolved upon surrender—upon an outward surrender. Inwardly she knew it to be not more than a capitulation under duress, whose terms would remain for ever secret except to those clever at induction. And now, as the train took her swiftly to her fate, she made the best of it.

There would be a town-house fit for her; a country-house at Tuxedo or Lenox or Westbury, a thousand good acres with greeneries, a game preserve, trout pond, and race-course; a cottage at Newport; a place in Scotland; a house in London, perhaps. Then there would be jewels such as she had longed for, a portrait by Chartran, she thought. And there was the dazzling thought of going to Felix or Doucet with credit unlimited.

And he—would the thought of him as it had always come to her keep on hurting with a hurt she could neither explain nor appease? Would he annoy her, enrage her perhaps, or even worse, tire her? He would be very much in earnest, of course, and so few men could be in earnest gracefully. But would he be stupid enough to stay so? And if not, would he become brutal? She suspected he might have capacities for that. Would she be able to hide all but her pleasant emotions from him,—hide that want, the great want, to which she would once have done sacrifice?

Well, it was easier to try than not to try, and the sacrifice—one could always sacrifice if the need became imperative.

"And I'm making much of nothing," she concluded. "No other girl I know would do it. And papa shall 'give me away.' What a pretty euphemism that is, to be sure!"

But her troubled musings ended with her time alone. From a whirl over the crisp, firm macadam, tucked into one of Phimister Gwilt-Athelstan's automobiles with four other guests, with no less a person than her genial host for chauffeur, she was presently ushered into the great hall where a huge log-fire crackled welcome, and where blew a lively little gale of tea-chatter from a dozen people.

Tea Miss Milbrey justly reckoned among the little sanities of life. Her wrap doffed and her veil pushed up, she was in a moment restored to her normal ease, a part of the group, and making her part of the talk that touched the latest news from town, the flower show, automobile show, Irving and Terry, the morning's meet, the weekly musicale and dinner-dance at the club; and at length upon certain matters of marriage and divorce.

"Ladies, ladies—this is degenerating into a mere hammer-fest." Thus spoke a male wit who had listened. "Give over, and be nice to the absent."

"The end of the fairy story was," continued the previous speaker, unheeding, "and so they were divorced and lived happily ever after."

"I think she took the Chicago motto, 'Marry early and often,'" said another, "but here she comes."

And as blond and fluffy little Mrs. Akemit, a late divorcee, joined the group the talk ranged back to the flourishing new hunt at Goshen, the driving over of Tuxedo people for the meet, the nasty accident to Warner Ridgeway when his blue-ribbon winner Musette fell upon him in taking a double-jump.

Miss Milbrey had taken stock of her fellow guests. Especially was she interested to note the presence of Mrs. Drelmer and her protege, Mauburn. It meant, she was sure, that her brother's wooing of Miss Bines would not be uncontested.

Another load of guests from a later train bustled in, the Bineses among them, and there was more tea and fresher gossip, while the butler circulated again with his tray for the trunk-keys.

The breezy hostess now took pains to impress upon all that only by doing exactly as they pleased, as to going and coming, could they hope to please her. Had she not, by this policy, conquered the cold, Scottish exclusiveness of Inverness-shire, so that the right sort of people fought to be at her house-parties during the shooting, even though she would persist in travelling back and forth to London in gowns that would be conspicuously elaborate at an afternoon reception, and even though, in any condition of dress, she never left quite enough of her jewels in their strong-box?

During the hour of dressing-sacque and slippers, while maids fluttered through the long corridors on hair-tending and dress-hooking expeditions, Mrs. Drelmer favoured her hostess with a confidential chat in that lady's boudoir, and, over Scotch and soda and a cigarette, suggested that Mr. Mauburn, in a house where he could really do as he pleased, would assuredly take Miss Bines out to dinner.

Mrs. Gwilt-Athelstan was instantly sympathetic.

"Only I can't take sides, you know, my dear, and young Milbrey will think me shabby if he doesn't have first go; but I'll be impartial; Milbrey shall take her in, and Mauburn shall be at her other side, and may God have mercy on her soul! These people have so much money, I hear, it amounts to financial embarrassment, but with those two chaps for the girl, and Avice Milbrey for that decent young chap, I fancy they'll be disembarrassed, in a measure. But I mustn't 'play favourites,' as those slangy nephews of mine put it."

And so it befell at dinner in the tapestried dining-room that Psyche Bines received assiduous attention from two gentlemen whom she considered equally and superlatively fascinating. While she looked at one, she listened to the other, and her neck grew tired with turning. Of anything, save the talk, her mind was afterward a blank; but why is not that the ideal dinner for any but mere feeders?

Nor was the dazzled girl conscious of others at the table,—of Florence Akemit, the babyish blond, listening with feverish attention to the German savant, Doctor von Herzlich, who had translated Goethe's "Iphigenie in Tauris" into Greek merely as recreation, and who was now justifying his choice of certain words and phrases by citing passages from various Greek authors; a choice which the sympathetic listener, after discreet intervals for reflection, invariably commended.

"Oh, you wonderful, wonderful man, you!" she exclaimed, resolving to sit by some one less wonderful another time.

Or there was Mrs. Gwilt-Athelstan, like a motherly Venus rising from a sea of pink velvet and white silk lace, asserting that some one or other would never get within sniffing-distance of the Sandringham set.

Or her husband, whose face, when he settled it in his collar, made the lines of a perfect lyre, and of whom it would presently become inaccurate to say that he was getting bald. He was insisting that "too many houses spoil the home," and that, with six establishments, he was without a place to lay his head, that is, with any satisfaction.

Or there was pale, thin, ascetic Winnie Wilberforce, who, as a theosophist, is understood to believe that, in a former incarnation, he came near to having an affair with a danseuse; he was expounding the esoterics of his cult to a high-coloured brunette with many turquoises, who, in turn, was rather inclined to the horse-talk of one of the nephews.

Or there were Miss Milbrey and Percival Bines, of whom the former had noted with some surprise that the latter was studying her with the eyes of rather cold calculation, something she had never before detected in him.

After dinner there were bridge and music from the big pipe-organ in the music-room, and billiards and some dancing.

The rival cavaliers of Miss Bines, perceiving simultaneously that neither would have the delicacy to withdraw from the field, cunningly inveigled each other into the billiard-room, where they watchfully consumed whiskey and soda together with the design of making each other drunk. This resulted in the two nephews, who invariably hunted as a pair, capturing Miss Bines to see if she could talk horse as ably as her mother, and, when they found that she could, planning a coaching trip for the morrow.

It also resulted in Miss Bines seeing no more of either cavalier that night, since they abandoned their contest only after every one but a sleepy butler had retired, and at a time when it became necessary for the Englishman to assist the American up the stairs, though the latter was moved to protest, as a matter of cheerful generality, that he was "aw ri'—entirely cap'le." At parting he repeatedly urged Mauburn, with tears in his eyes, to point out one single instance in which he had ever proved false to a friend.

To herself, when the pink rose came out of her hair that night, Miss Milbrey admitted that it wasn't going to be so bad, after all.

She had feared he might rush his proposal through that night; he had been so much in earnest. But he had not done so, and she was glad he could be restrained and deliberate in that "breedy" sort of way. It promised well, that he could wait until the morrow.

CHAPTER XIX.

An Afternoon Stroll and an Evening Catastrophe

Miss Milbrey, the next morning, faced with becoming resignation what she felt would be her last day of entire freedom. She was down and out philosophically to play nine holes with her host before breakfast.

Her brother, awakening less happily, made a series of discoveries regarding his bodily sensations that caused him to view life with disaffection. Noting that the hour was early, however, he took cheer, and after a long, strong, cold drink, which he rang for, and a pricking icy shower, which he nerved himself to, he was ready to ignore his aching head and get the start of Mauburn.

The Englishman, he seemed to recall, had drunk even more than he, and, as it was barely eight o'clock, would probably not come to life for a couple of hours yet. He made his way to the breakfast-room. The thought of food was not pleasant, but another brandy and soda, beading vivaciously in its tall glass, would enable him to watch with fortitude the spectacle of others who might chance to be eating. And he would have at least two hours of Miss Bines before Mauburn's head should ache him back to consciousness.

He opened the door of the spacious breakfast-room. Through the broad windows from the south-east came the glorious shine of the morning sun to make him blink; and seated where it flooded him as a calcium was Mauburn, resplendent in his myriad freckles, trim, alive, and obviously hungry. Around his plate were cold mutton, a game pie, eggs, bacon, tarts, toast, and sodden-looking marmalade. Mauburn was eating of these with a voracity that published his singleness of mind to all who might observe.

Milbrey steadied himself with one hand upon the door-post, and with the other he sought to brush this monstrous illusion from his fickle eyes. But Mauburn and the details of his deadly British breakfast became only more distinct. The appalled observer groaned and rushed for the sideboard, whence a decanter, a bowl of cracked ice, and a siphon beckoned.

Between two gulps of coffee Mauburn grinned affably.

"Mornin', old chap! Feelin' a bit seedy? By Jove! I don't wonder. I'm not so fit myself. I fancy, you know, it must have been that beastly anchovy paste we had on the biscuits."

Milbrey's burning eyes beheld him reach out for another slice of the cold, terrible mutton.

"Life," said Milbrey, as he inflated his brandy from the siphon, "is an empty dream this morning."

"Wake up then, old chap!" Mauburn cordially urged, engaging the game pie in deadly conflict; "try a rasher; nothing like it; better'n peggin' it so early. Never drink till dinner-time, old chap, and you'll be able to eat in the morning like—like a blooming baby." And he proceeded to crown this notion of infancy's breakfast with a jam tart of majestic proportions.

"Where are the people?" inquired Milbrey, eking out his own moist breakfast with a cigarette.

"All down and out except some of the women. Miss Bines just drove off a four-in-hand with the two Angsteads—held the reins like an old whip, too, by Jove; but they'll be back for luncheon;—and directly after luncheon she's promised to ride with me. I fancy we'll have a little practice over the sticks."

"And I fancy I'm going straight back to bed,—that is, if it's all right to fancy a thing you're certain about."

Outside most of the others had scattered for life in the open, each to his taste. Some were on the links. Some had gone with the coach. A few had ridden early to the meet of the Essex hounds near Easthampton, where a stiff run was expected. Others had gone to follow the hunt in traps. A lively group came back now to read the morning papers by the log-fire in the big cheery hall. Among these were Percival and Miss Milbrey. When they had dawdled over the papers for an hour Miss Milbrey grew slightly restive.

"Why doesn't he have it over?" she asked herself, with some impatience. And she delicately gave Percival, not an opportunity, but opportunities to make an opportunity, which is a vastly different form of procedure.

But the luncheon hour came and people straggled back, and the afternoon began, and the request for Miss Milbrey's heart and hand was still unaccountably deferred. Nor could she feel any of those subtle premonitions that usually warn a woman when the event is preparing in a lover's secret heart.

Reminding herself of his letters, she began to suspect that, while he could write unreservedly, he might be shy and reluctant of speech; and that shyness now deterred him. So much being clear, she determined to force the issue and end the strain for both.

Percival had shown not a little interest in pretty Mrs. Akemit, and was now talking with that fascinating creature as she lolled on a low seat before the fire in her lacy blue house-gown. At the moment she was adroitly posing one foot and then the other before the warmth of the grate. It may be disclosed without damage to this tale that the feet of Mrs. Akemit were not cold; but that they were trifles most daintily shod, and, as her slender silken ankles curved them toward the blaze from her froth of a petticoat, they were worth looking at.

Miss Milbrey disunited the chatting couple with swiftness and aplomb.

"Come, Mr. Bines, if I'm to take that tramp you made me promise you, it's time we were off."

Outside she laughed deliciously. "You know you did make me promise it mentally, because I knew you'd want to come and want me to come, but I was afraid Mrs. Akemit mightn't understand about telepathy, so I pretended we'd arranged it all in words."

"Of course! Great joke, wasn't it?" assented the young man, rather awkwardly.

Down the broad sweep of roadway, running between its granite coping, they strode at a smart pace.

"You know you complimented my walking powers on that other walk we took, away off there where the sun goes down."

"Yes, of course," he replied absently.

"Now, he's beginning," she said to herself, noting his absent and somewhat embarrassed manner.

In reality he was thinking how few were the days ago he would have held this the dearest of all privileges, and how strange that he should now prize it so lightly, almost prefer, indeed, not to have it; that he should regard her, of all women, "the fairest of all flesh on earth" with nervous distrust.

She was dressed in tan corduroy; elation was in her face; her waist, as she stepped, showed supple as a willow; her suede-gloved little hands were compact and tempting to his grasp. His senses breathed the air of her perfect and compelling femininity. But sharper than all these impressions rang the words of the worldly-wise Higbee: *"She's hunting night and day for a rich husband; she tries for them as fast as they come; she'd rather marry a sub-treasury—she'd marry me in a minute—she'd marry* YOU; *but if you were broke she'd have about as much use for you...."*

Her glance was frank, friendly, and encouraging. Her deep eyes were clear as a trout-brook. He thought he saw in them once almost a tenderness for him.

She thought, "He *does* love me!"

Outside the grounds they turned down a bridle-path that led off through the woods—off through the golden sun-wine of an October day. The air bore a clean autumn spice, and a faint salty scent blended with it from the distant Sound. The autumn silence, which is the only perfect silence in all the world, was restful, yet full of significance, suggestion, provocation. From the spongy lowland back of them came the pleading sweetness of a meadow-lark's cry. Nearer they could even hear an occasional leaf flutter and waver down. The quick thud of a falling nut was almost loud enough to earn its echo. Now and then they saw a lightning flash of vivid turquoise and heard a jay's harsh scream.

In this stillness their voices instinctively lowered, while their eyes did homage to the wondrous play of colour about them. Over a yielding brown carpet they went among maple and chestnut and oak, with their bewildering changes through crimson, russet, and amber to pale yellow; under the deep-stained leaves of the sweet-gum they went, and past the dogwood with scarlet berries gemming the clusters of its dim red leaves.

But through all this waiting, inciting silence Miss Milbrey listened in vain for the words she had felt so certain would come.

Sometimes her companion was voluble; again he was taciturn—and through it all he was doggedly aloof.

Miss Milbrey had put herself bravely in the path of Destiny. Destiny had turned aside. She had turned to meet it, and now it frankly fled. Destiny, as she had construed it, was turned a fugitive. She was bruised, puzzled, and not a little piqued. During the walk back, when this much had been made clear, the silence was intolerably oppressive. Without knowing why, they understood perfectly now that neither had been ingenuous.

"She would love the money and play me for a fool," he thought, under the surface talk. Youth is prone to endow its opinions with all the dignity of certain knowledge.

"Yet I am certain he loves me," thought she. On the other hand, youth is often gifted with a credulity divine and unerring.

At the door as they came up the roadway a trap was depositing a man whom Miss Milbrey greeted with evident surprise and some restraint. He was slight, dark, and quick of movement, with finely cut nostrils that expanded and quivered nervously like those of a high-bred horse in tight check.

Miss Milbrey introduced him to Percival as Mr. Ristine.

"I didn't know you were hereabouts," she said.

"I've run over from the Bloynes to dine and do Hallowe'en with you," he answered, flashing his dark eyes quickly over Percival and again lighting the girl with them.

"Surprises never come singly," she returned, and Percival noted a curious little air of defiance in her glance and manner.

Now it is possible that Solomon's implied distinction as to the man's way with a maid was not, after all, so ill advised.

For young Bines, after dinner, fell in love with Miss Milbrey all over again. The normal human mind going to one extreme will inevitably gravitate to its opposite if given time. Having put her away in the conviction that she was heartless and mercenary—having fasted in the desert of doubt—he now found himself detecting in her an unmistakable appeal for sympathy, for human kindness, perhaps for love. He forgot the words of Higbee and became again the confident, unquestioning lover. He noted her rather subdued and reserved demeanour, and the suggestions of weariness about her eyes. They drew him. He resolved at once to seek her and give his love freedom to tell itself. He would no longer meanly restrain it. He would even tell her all his distrust. Now that they had gone she should know every ignoble suspicion; and, whether she cared for him or not, she would comfort him for the hurt they had been to him.

The Hallowe'en frolic was on. Through the long hall, lighted to pleasant dusk by real Jack-o'-lanterns, stray couples strolled, with subdued murmurs and soft laughter. In the big white and gold parlour, in the dining-room, billiard-room, and in the tropic jungle of the immense palm-garden the party had bestowed itself in congenial groups, ever intersecting and forming anew. Little flutters of high laughter now and then told of tests that were being made with roasting chestnuts, apple-parings, the white of an egg dropped into water, or the lighted candle before an open window.

Percival watched for the chance to find Miss Milbrey alone. His sister had just ventured alone with a candle into the library to study the face of her future husband in a mirror. The result had been, in a sense, unsatisfactory. She had beheld looking over her shoulder the faces of Mauburn, Fred Milbrey, and the Angstead twins, and had declared herself unnerved by the weird prophecy.

Before the fire in the hall Percival stood while Mrs. Akemit reclined picturesquely near by, and Doctor von Herzlich explained, with excessive care as to his enunciation, that protoplasm can be analysed but cannot be reconstructed; following this with his own view as to why the synthesis does not produce life.

"You wonderful man!" from Mrs. Akemit; "I fairly tremble when I think of all you know. Oh, what a delight science must be to her votaries!"

The Angstead twins joined the group, attracted by Mrs. Akemit's inquiry of the savant if he did not consider civilisation a failure. The twins did. They considered civilisation a failure because it was killing off all the big game. There was none to speak of left now except in Africa; and they were pessimistic about Africa.

Percival listened absently to the talk and watched Miss Milbrey, now one of the group in the dining-room. Presently he saw her take a lighted candle from one of the laughing girls and go toward the library.

His heart-beats quickened. Now she should know his love and it would be well. He walked down the hall leisurely, turned into the big parlour, momentarily deserted, walked quickly but softly over its polished floor to a door that gave into the library, pushed the heavy portiere aside and stepped noiselessly in.

The large room was lighted dimly by two immense yellow pumpkins, their sides cut into faces of grinning grotesqueness. At the far side of the room Miss Milbrey had that instant arrived before an antique oval mirror whose gilded carvings reflected the light of the candle. She held it above her head with one rounded arm. He stood in deep shadow and the girl had been too absorbed in the play to note his coming. He took one noiseless step toward her, but then through the curtained doorway by which she had come he saw a man enter swiftly and furtively.

Trembling on the verge of laughing speech, something held him back, some unexplainable instinct, making itself known in a thrill that went from his feet to his head; he could feel the roots of his hair tingle. The newcomer went quickly, with catlike tread, toward the girl. Fascinated he stood, wanting to speak, to laugh, yet powerless from the very swiftness of what followed.

In the mirror under the candle-light he saw the man's dark face come beside the other, heard a little cry from the girl as she half-turned; then he saw the man take her in his arms, saw her head fall on to his shoulder, and her face turn to his kiss.

He tried to stop breathing, fearful of discovery, grasping with one hand the heavy fold of the curtain back of him to steady himself.

There was the space of two long, trembling breaths; then he heard her say, in a low, tense voice, as she drew away:

"Oh, you are my bad angel—why?—why?"

She fled toward the door to the hall.

"Don't come this way," she called back, in quick, low tones of caution.

The man turned toward the door where Percival stood, and in the darkness stumbled over a hassock. Instantly Percival was on the other side of the portiere, and, before the other had groped his way to the dark corner where the door was, had recrossed the empty parlour and was safely in the hall.

He made his way to the dining-room, where supper was under way.

"Mr. Bines has seen a ghost," said the sharp-eyed Mrs. Drelmer.

"Poor chap's only starved to death," said Mrs. Gwilt-Athelstan. "Eat something, Mr. Bines; this supper is go-as-you-please. Nobody's to wait for anybody."

Strung loosely about the big table a dozen people were eating hot scones and bannocks with clotted cream and marmalade, and drinking mulled cider.

"And there's cold fowl and baked beans and doughnuts and all, for those who can't eat with a Scotch accent," said the host, cheerfully.

Percival dropped into one of the chairs.

"I'm Scotch enough to want a Scotch high-ball."

"And you're getting it so high it's top-heavy," cautioned Mrs. Drelmer.

Above the chatter of the table could be heard the voices of men and the musical laughter of women from the other rooms.

"I simply can't get 'em together," said the hostess.

"It's nice to have 'em all over the place," said her husband, "fair women and brave men, you know."

"The men *have* to be brave," she answered, shortly, with a glance at little Mrs. Akemit, who had permitted Percival to seat her at his side, and was now pleading with him to agree that simple ways of life are requisite to the needed measure of spirituality.

Then came strains of music from the rich-toned organ.

"Oh, that dear Ned Ristine is playing," cried one; and several of the group sauntered toward the music-room.

The music flooded the hall and the room, so that the talk died low.

"He's improvising," exclaimed Mrs. Akemit. "How splendid! He seems to be breathing a paean of triumph, some high, exalted spiritual triumph, as if his soul had risen above us—how precious!"

When the deep swell had subsided to silvery ripples and the last cadence had fainted, she looked at Percival with moistened parted lips and eyes half-shielded, as if her full gaze would betray too much of her quivering soul.

Then Percival heard the turquoised brunette say: "What a pity his wife is such an unsympathetic creature!"

"But Mr. Ristine is unmarried, is he not?" he asked, quickly.

There was a little laugh from Mrs. Drelmer.

"Not yet—not that I've heard of."

"I beg pardon!"

"There have been rumours lots of times that he was going to be *unmarried*, but they always seem to adjust their little difficulties. He and his wife are now staying over at the Bloynes."

"Oh! I see," answered Percival; "you're a jester, Mrs. Drelmer."

"Ristine," observed the theosophic Wilberforce, in the manner of a hired oracle, "is, in his present incarnation, imperfectly monogamous."

Some people came from the music-room.

"Miss Milbrey has stayed by the organist," said one; "and she's promised to make him play one more. Isn't he divine?"

The music came again.

"Oh!" from Mrs. Akemit, again in an ecstasy, "" he's playing that heavenly stuff from the second act of 'Tristan and Isolde'—the one triumphant, perfect love-poem of all music."

"That Scotch whiskey is good in some of the lesser emergencies," remarked Percival, turning to her; "but it has its limitations. Let's you and me trifle with a nice cold quart of champagne!"

CHAPTER XX.

Doctor Von Herzlich Expounds the Hightower Hotel and Certain Allied Phenomena

The Hightower Hotel is by many observers held to be an instructive microcosm of New York, more especially of upper Broadway, with correct proportions of the native and the visiting provincial. With correct proportions, again, of the money-making native and the money-spending native, male and female. A splendid place is this New York; splendid but terrible. London for the stranger has a steady-going, hearty hospitality. Paris on short notice will be cosily and coaxingly intimate. New York is never either. It overwhelms with its lavish display of wealth, it stuns with its tireless, battering energy. But it stays always aloof, indifferent if it be loved or hated; if it crush or sustain.

The ground floor of the Hightower Hotel reproduces this magnificent, brutal indifference. One might live years in its mile or so of stately corridors and its acre or so of resplendent cafes, parlours, reception-rooms, and restaurants, elbowed by thousands, suffocated by that dense air of human crowdedness, that miasma of brain emanations, and still remain in splendid isolation, as had he worn the magic ring of Gyges. Here is every species of visitor: the money-burdened who "stop" here and cultivate an air of being blase to the wealth of polished splendours; and the less opulent who "stop" cheaply elsewhere and venture in to tread the corridors timidly, to stare with honest, drooping-jawed wonder at its marvels of architecture and decoration, and to gaze with becoming reverence at those persons whom they shrewdly conceive to be social celebrities.

This mixture of many and strange elements is never at rest. Its units wait expectantly, chat, drink, eat, or stroll with varying airs through reception-room, corridor, and office. It is an endless function, attended by all of Broadway, with entertainment diversely contrived for every taste by a catholic-minded host with a sincere desire to please the paying public.

"Isn't it a huge bear-garden, though?" asks Launton Oldaker of the estimable Doctor von Herzlich, after the two had observed the scene in silence for a time.

The wise German dropped an olive into his Rhine wine, and gazed reflectively about the room. Men and women sat at tables drinking. Beyond the tables at the farther side of the room, other men were playing billiards. It was four o'clock and the tide was high.

"It is yet more," answered the doctor. "In my prolonged studies of natural phenomena this is the most valuable of all which I have been privileged to observe."

He called them "brifiletched" and "awbsairf" with great nicety. Perhaps his discernment was less at fault.

"Having," continued the doctor, "granted myself some respite from toil in the laboratory at Marburg, I chose to pleasure voyage, to study yet more the social conditions in this loveworthy land. I suspected that much tiredness of travel would be involved. Yet here I find all conditions whatsoever—here in that which you denominate 'bear-garden'. They have been reduced here for my edification, yes? But your term is a term of inadequate comprehensiveness. It is to me more what you call a 'beast-garden,' to include all species of fauna. Are there not here moths and human flames? are there not cunning serpents crawling with apples of knowledge to unreluctant, idling Eves, yes? Do we not hear the amazing converse of parrots and note the pea-fowl negotiating admiration from observers? Mark at that yet farther table also the swine and the song-bird; again, mark our draught-horses who have achieved a competence, yes? You note also the presence of wolves and lambs. And, endly, mark our tailed arborean ancestors, trained to the wearing of garments and a single eye-glass. May I ask, have you bestowed upon this diversity your completest high attention? *Hanh!*"

This explosion of the doctor's meant that he invited and awaited some contradiction. As none ensued, he went on:

"For wolf and lamb I direct your attention to the group at yonder table. I notice that you greeted the young man as he entered—a common friend to us then—Mr. Bines, with financial resources incredibly unlimited? Also he is possessed of an unexperienced freedom from suspectedness-of-ulterior-motive-in-others—one may not in English as in German make the word to fit his need of the moment—that unsuspectedness, I repeat, which has ever characterised the lamb about to be converted into nutrition. You note the large, loose gentleman with wide-brimmed hat and beard after my own, somewhat, yes? He would dispose of some valuable oil-wells which he shall discover at Texas the moment he shall have sufficiently disposed of them. A wolf he is, yes? The more correctly attired person at his right, with the beak of a hawk and lips so thin that his big white teeth gleam through them when they are yet shut, he is what he calls himself a promoter. He has made sundry efforts to promote myself. I conclude 'promoter' is one other fashion of wolf-saying. The yet littler and yet younger man at his left of our friend, the one of soft voice and insinuating manner, much resembling a stray scion of aristocracy, discloses to those with whom he affably acquaints himself the location of a luxurious gaming house not far off; he will even consent to accompany one to its tables; and still yet he has but yesterday evening invited me the all-town to see.

"As a scientist, I remind you, I permit myself no prejudices. I observe the workings of unemotional law and sometimes record them. You have a saying here that there are three generations between shirt-sleeves and shirt-sleeves. I observe the process of the progress. It is benign as are all processes. I have lately observed it in England. There, by their law of entail, the same process is unswifter,—yet does it unvary. The poor aristocrats, almost back to shirt-sleeves, with their taxes and entailed lands, seek for the money in shops of dress and bonnet and ale, and graciously rent their castles to the but-newly-opulent in American oil or the diamonds of South Africa. Here the posterity of your Mynherr Knickerbocker do likewise. The ancestor they boast was a toiler, a market-gardener, a fur-trader, a boatman, hardworking, simple-wayed, unspending. The woman ancestor kitchen-gardened, spun, wove, and nourished the poultry. Their descendants upon the savings of these labours have forgotten how to labour themselves. They could not yet produce should they even relinquish the illusion that to produce is of a baseness, that only to consume is noble. I gather reports that a few retain enough of the ancient strain to become sturdy tradesmen and gardeners once more. Others seek out and assimilate this new-richness, which, in its turn, will become impoverished and helpless. Ah, what beautiful showing of Evolution!

"See the pendulum swing from useful penury to useless opulence. Why does it not halt midway, you inquire? Because the race is so young. Ach! a mere two hundred and forty million years from our grandfather-grandmother amoeba in the ancestral morass! What can one be expecting? Certain faculties develop in response to the pressure of environment. Omit the pressure and the faculties no longer ensue. Yes? Withdraw the pressure, and the faculties decay. Sightless moles, their environment demands not the sight; nor of the fishes that inhabit the streams of your Mammoth Cave. Your aristocrats between the sleeve-of-the-shirt periods likewise degenerate. There is no need to work, they lose the power. No need to sustain themselves, they become helpless. They are as animals grown in an environment that demands no struggle of them. Yet their environment is artificial. They live on stored energy, stored by another. It is exhausted, they perish. All but the few that can modify to correspond with the changed environment, as when your social celebrities venture into trade, and the also few that in their life of idleness have acquired graces of person and manner to let them find pleasure in the eyes of marryers among the but-now-rich."

The learned doctor submitted to have his glass refilled from the cooler at his side, dropped another olive into the wine, and resumed before Oldaker could manage an escape.

"And how long, you ask, shall the cosmic pendulum swing between these extremes of penurious industry and opulent idleness?"

Oldaker had not asked it. But he tried politely to appear as if he had meant to. He had really meant to ask the doctor what time it was and then pretend to recall an engagement for which he would be already late.

"It will so continue," the doctor placidly resumed, "until the race achieves a different ideal. Now you will say, but there can be no ideal so long as there is no imagination; and as I have directly—a moment-soon—said, the race is too young to have achieved imagination. The highest felicity which we are yet able to imagine is a felicity based upon much money; our highest pleasures the material pleasures which money buys, yes? We strive for it, developing the money-getting faculty at the expense of all others; and when the money is obtained we cannot enjoy it. We can imagine to do with it only delicate-eating and drinking and dressing for show-to-others and building houses immense and splendidly uncalculated for homes of rational dwelling. Art, science, music, literature, sociology, the great study and play of our humanity, they are shut to us.

"Our young friend Bines is a specimen. It is as if he were a child, having received from another a laboratory full of the most beautiful instruments of science. They are valuable, but he can do but common things with them because he knows not their possibilities. Or, we may call it stored energy he has; for such is money, the finest, subtlest, most potent form of stored energy; it may command the highest fruits of genius, the lowest fruits of animality; it is also volatile, elusive. Our young friend has many powerful batteries of it. But he is no electrician. Some he will happily waste without harm to himself. Much of it, apparently, he will convert into that champagne he now drinks. For a week since I had the pleasure of becoming known to him he has drunk it here each day, copiously. He cannot imagine a more salutary mode of exhausting his force. I am told he comes of a father who died at fifty, and who did in many ways like that. This one, at the rate I have observed, will not last so long. He will not so long correspond with an environment even so unexacting as this. And his son, perhaps his grandson, will become what you call broke; will from lack of pressure to learn some useful art, and from spending only, become useless and helpless. For besides drink, there is gambling. He plays what you say, the game of poker, this Bines. You see the gentleman, rounded gracefully in front, who has much the air of seeming to stand behind himself,—he drinks whiskey at my far right, yes? He is of a rich trust, the magnate-director as you say, and plays at cards nightly with our young friend. He jested with him in my presence before you entered, saying, 'I will make you look like'—I forget it now, but his humourous threat was to reduce our young friend to the aspect of some inconsiderable sum in the money of your country. I cannot recall the precise amount, but it was not so much as what you call one dollar. Strange, is it not, that the rich who have too much money gamble as feverishly as the poor who have none, and therefore have an excuse? And the love of display-for-display. If one were not a scientist one might be tempted to say there is no progress. The Peruvian grandee shod his mules with pure gold, albeit that metal makes but inferior shodding for beasts of burden. The London factory girl hires the dyed feathers of the ostrich to make her bonnet gay; and your money people are as display-loving. Lucullus and your latest millionaire joy in the same emotion of pleasure at making a show. Ach! we are truly in the race's childhood yet. The way of evolution is so unfast, yes? Ah! you will go now, Mr. Oldaker. I shall hope to enjoy you more again. Your observations have interested me deeply; they shall have my most high attention. Another time you shall discuss with me how it must be that the cosmic process shall produce a happy mean between stoic and epicure, by learning the valuable arts of compromise, yes? How Zeno with his bread and dates shall learn not to despise a few luxuries, and Vitellius shall learn that the mind may sometimes feast to advantage while the body fasts."

Through the marbled corridors and regal parlours, down long perspectives of Persian rugs and onyx pillars, the function raged.

The group at Percival's table broke up. He had an appointment to meet Colonel Poindexter the next morning to consummate the purchase of some oil stock certain to appreciate fabulously in value. He had promised to listen further to Mr. Isidore Lewis regarding a plan for obtaining control of a certain line of one of the metal stocks. And he had signified his desire to make one of a party the affable younger man would guide later in the evening to a sumptuous temple of chance, to which, by good luck, he had gained the entree. The three gentlemen parted most cordially from him after he had paid the check.

To Mr. Lewis, when Colonel Poindexter had also left, the young man with a taste for gaming remarked, ingenuously:

"Say, Izzy, on the level, there's the readiest money that ever registered at this joint. You don't have to be Mr. William Wisenham to do business with him. You can have all you want of that at track odds."

"I'm making book that way myself," responded the cheerful Mr. Lewis; "fifty'll get you a thousand any time, my lad. It's a lead-pipe at twenty to one. But say, with all these Petroleum Pete oil-stock grafters and Dawson

City Daves with frozen feet and mining-stock in their mitts, a man's got to play them close in to his bosom to win out anything. Competition is killing this place, my boy."

In the Turkish room Percival found Mrs. Akemit, gowned to perfection, glowing, and wearing a bunch of violets bigger than her pretty head.

"I've just sent cards to your mother and sister," she explained, as she made room for him upon the divan.

To them came presently Mrs. Drelmer, well-groomed and aggressively cheerful.

"How de do! Just been down to Wall Street seeing how my other half lives, and now I'm famished for tea and things. Ah! here are your mother and our proud Western beauty!" And she went forward to greet them.

"It's more than *her* other half knows about her," was Mrs. Akemit's observation to the violets on her breast.

"Come sit with me here in this corner, dear," said Mrs. Drelmer to Psyche, while Mrs. Bines joined her son and Mrs. Akemit. "I've so much to tell you. And that poor little Florence Akemit, isn't it too bad about her. You know one of those bright French women said it's so inconvenient to be a widow because it's necessary to resume the modesty of a young girl without being able to feign her ignorance. No wonder Florence has a hard time of it; but isn't it wretched of me to gossip? And I wanted to tell you especially about Mr. Mauburn. You know of course he'll be Lord Casselthorpe when the present Lord Casselthorpe dies; a splendid title, really quite one of the best in all England; and, my dear, he's out-and-out smitten with you; there's no use in denying it; you should hear him rave to me about you; really these young men in love are so inconsiderate of us old women. Ah! here is that Mrs. Errol who does those fascinating miniatures of all the smart people. Excuse me one moment, my dear; I want her to meet your mother."

The fashionable miniature artist was presently arranging with the dazed Mrs. Bines for miniatures of herself and Psyche. Mrs. Drelmer, beholding the pair with the satisfied glance of one who has performed a kindly action, resumed her *tete-a-tete* with Psyche.

Percival, across the room, listened to Mrs. Akemit's artless disclosure that she found life too complex—far too hazardous, indeed, for a poor little creature in her unfortunate position, so liable to cruel misjudgment for thoughtless, harmless acts, the result of a young zest for life. She had often thought most seriously of a convent, indeed she had—"and, really, Mr. Bines, I'm amazed that I talk this way—so freely to you—you know, when I've known you so short a time; but something in you compels my confidences, poor little me! and my poor little confidences! One so seldom meets a man nowadays with whom one can venture to talk about any of the *real* things!"

A little later, as Mrs. Drelmer was leaving, the majestic figure of the Baron Ronault de Palliac framed itself in the handsome doorway. He sauntered in, as if to give the picture tone, and then with purposeful air took the seat Mrs. Drelmer had just vacated. Miss Bines had been entertained by involuntary visions of herself as Lady Casselthorpe. She now became in fancy the noble Baroness de Palliac, speaking faultless French and consorting with the rare old families of the Faubourg St. Germain. For, despite his artistic indirection, the baron's manner was conclusive, his intentions unmistakable.

And this day was much like many days in the life of the Bines and in the life of the Hightower Hotel. The scene from parlour to cafe was surveyed at intervals by a quiet-mannered person with watchful eyes, who appeared to enjoy it as one upon whom it conferred benefits. Now he washed his hands in the invisible sweet waters of satisfaction, and murmured softly to himself, "Setters and Buyers!" Perhaps the term fits the family of Bines as well as might many another coined especially for it.

When the three groups in the Turkish room dissolved, Percival with his mother and sister went to their suite on the fourth floor.

"Think of a real live French nobleman!" cried Psyche, with enthusiasm, "and French must be such a funny language—he talks such funny English. I wish now I'd learned more of it at the Sem, and talked more with that French Delpasse girl that was always toasting marshmallows on a hat-pin."

"That lady Mrs. Drelmer introduced me to," said Mrs. Bines, "is an artist, miniature artist, hand-painted you know, and she's going to paint our miniatures for a thousand dollars each because we're friends of Mrs. Drelmer."

"Oh, yes," exclaimed Psyche, with new enthusiasm, "and Mrs. Drelmer has promised to teach me bridge whist if I'll go to her house to-morrow. Isn't she kind? Really, every one must play bridge now, she tells me."

"Well, ladies," said the son and brother, "I'm glad to see you both getting some of the white meat. I guess we'll do well here. I'm going into oil stock and lead, myself."

"How girlish your little friend Mrs. Akemit is!" said his mother. "How did she come to lose her husband?"

"Lost him in South Dakota," replied her son, shortly.

"Divorced, ma," explained Psyche, "and Mrs. Drelmer says her family's good, but she's too gay."

"Ah!" exclaimed Percival, "Mrs. Drelmer's hammer must be one of those cute little gold ones, all set with precious stones. As a matter of fact, she's anything but gay. She's sad. She couldn't get along with her husband because he had no dignity of soul."

He became conscious of sympathising generously with all men not thus equipped.

CHAPTER XXI.

The Diversions of a Young Multi-millionaire

To be idle and lavish of money, twenty-five years old, with the appetites keen and the need for action always pressing; then to have loved a girl with quick, strong, youthful ardour, and to have had the ideal smirched by gossip, then shattered before his amazed eyes,—this is a situation in which the male animal is apt to behave inequably. In the language of the estimable Herr Doctor von Herzlich, he will seek those avenues of modification in which the least struggle is required. In the simpler phrasing of Uncle Peter Bines, he will "cut loose."

During the winter that now followed Percival Bines behaved according to either formula, as the reader may prefer. He early ascertained his limitations with respect to New York and its people.

"Say, old man," he asked Herbert Delancey Livingston one night, across the table at their college club, "are all the people in New York society impecunious?"

Livingston had been with him at Harvard, and Livingston's family was so notoriously not impecunious that the question was devoid of any personal element. Livingston, moreover, had dined just unwisely enough to be truthful.

"Well, to be candid with you, Bines," the young man had replied, in a burst of alcoholic confidence, "about all that you are likely to meet are broke— else you wouldn't meet 'em, you know," he explained cheerfully. "You know, old chap, a few of you Western people have got into the right set here; there's the Nesbits, for instance. On my word the good wife and mother hasn't the kinks out of her fingers yet, nor the callouses from her hands, by Jove! She worked so hard cooking and washing woollen shirts for miners before Nesbit made his strike. As for him—well caviare, I'm afraid, will always be caviare to Jimmy Nesbit. And now the son's married a girl that had everything but money—my boy, Nellie Wemple has fairly got that family of Nesbits awestricken since she married into it, just by the way she can spend money—but what was I saying, old chap? Oh, yes, about getting in—it takes time, you know; on my word, I think they were as much as eight years, and had to start in abroad at that. At first, you know, you can only expect to meet a crowd that can't afford to be exclusive any longer."

From which friendly counsel, and from certain confirming observations of his own, Percival had concluded that his lot in New York was to spend money. This he began to do with a large Western carelessness that speedily earned him fame of a sort. Along upper Broadway, his advent was a golden joy. Tradesmen learned to love him; florists, jewelers, and tailors hailed his coming with honest fervour; waiters told moving tales of his tips; cabmen fought for the privilege of transporting him; and the hangers-on of rich young men picked pieces of lint assiduously and solicitously from his coat.

One of his favourite resorts was the sumptuous gambling-house in Forty-fourth Street. The man who slides back the panel of the stout oaken door early learned to welcome him through the slit, barred by its grill of wrought iron. The attendant who took his coat and hat, the waiter who took his order for food, and the croupier who took his money, were all gladdened by his coming; for his gratuities were as large when he lost as when he won Even the reserved proprietor, accustomed as he was to a wealthy and careless clientele, treated Percival with marked consideration after a night when the young man persuaded him to withdraw the limit at roulette, and spent a large sum in testing a system for breaking the wheel, given to him by a friend lately returned from Monte Carlo.

"I think, really the fellow who gave me that system is an ass," he said, lighting a cigarette when the play was done. "Now I'm going down and demolish eight dollars' worth of food and drink—you won't be all to the good on that, you know."

His host decided that a young man who was hungry, after losing a hundred thousand dollars in five hours' play, was a person to be not lightly considered.

And, though he loved the rhythmic whir and the ensuing rattle of the little ivory ball at the roulette wheel, he did not disdain the quieter faro, playing that dignified game exclusively with the chocolate-coloured chips, which cost a thousand dollars a stack. Sometimes he won; but not often enough to disturb his host's belief that there is less of chance in his business than in any other known to the captains of industry.

There were, too, sociable games of poker, played with Garmer, of the Lead Trust, Burman, the intrepid young wheat operator from Chicago, and half a dozen other well-moneyed spirits; games in which the limit, to use the Chicagoan's phrase, was "the beautiful but lofty North Star." At these games he lost even more regularly than at those where, with the exception of a trifling percentage, he was solely at the mercy of chance. But he was a joyous loser, endearing himself to the other players; to Garmer, whom Burman habitually accused of being "closer than a warm night," as well as to the open-handed son of the chewing-gum magnate, who had been raised abroad and who protested nightly that there was an element of beastly American commercialism in the game. When Percival was by some chance absent from a sitting, the others calculated the precise sum he probably would have lost and humourously acquainted him with the amount by telegraph next morning,—it was apt to be nine hundred and some odd dollars,—requesting that he cover by check at his early convenience.

Yet the diversion was not all gambling. There were Jong sessions at all-night restaurants where the element of chance in his favour, inconspicuous elsewhere, was wholly eliminated; suppers for hungry Thespians and thirsty parasites, protracted with song and talk until the gas-flames grew pale yellow, and the cabmen, when the party went out into the wan light, would be low-voiced, confidential, and suggestive in their approaches.

Broadway would be weirdly quiet at such times, save for the occasional frenzied clatter of a hurrying milk-wagon. Even the cars seemed to move with less sound than by day, and the early-rising workers inside, holding dinner-pails and lunch-baskets, were subdued and silent, yet strangely observing, as if the hour were one in which the vision was made clear to appraise the values of life justly. To the north, whence the cars bulked silently, would be an awakening sky of such tender beauty that the revellers often paid it the tribute of a moment's notice.

"Pure turquoise," one would declare.

"With just a dash of orange bitters in it," another might add.

And then perhaps they burst into song under the spell, blending their voices into what the professional gentlemen termed "barber-shop harmonies," until a policeman would saunter across the street, pretending, however, that he was not aware of them.

Then perhaps a ride toward the beautiful northern sky would be proposed, whereupon three or four hansom or coupe loads would begin a journey that wound up through Central Park toward the northern light, but which never attained a point remoter than some suburban road-house, where sleepy cooks and bartenders would have to be routed out to collaborate toward breakfast.

Oftener the party fell away into straggling groups with notions for sleep, chanting at last, perhaps:

"While beer brings gladness, don't forget That water only makes you wet!"

Percival would walk to the hotel, sobered and perhaps made a little reflective by the unwonted quiet. But they were pleasant, careless folk, he concluded always. They permitted him to spend his money, but he was quite sure they would spend it as freely as he if they had it. More than one appreciative soubrette, met under such circumstances, was subsequently enabled to laud the sureness of his taste in jewels,—he cared little for anything but large diamonds, it transpired. It was a feeling tribute paid to his munificence by one of these in converse with a sister artist, who had yet to meet him:

"Say, Myrtle, on the dead, he spends money just like a young Jew trying to be white!"

Under this more or less happy surface of diversion, however, was an experience decidedly less felicitous. He knew he should not, must not, hold Avice Milbrey in his mind; yet when he tried to put her out it hurt him.

At first he had plumed himself upon his lucky escape that night, when he would have declared his love to her. To have married a girl who cared only for his money; that would have been dire enough. But to marry a girl like *that!* He had been lucky indeed!

Yet, as the weeks went by the shock of the scene wore off. The scene itself remained clear, with the grinning grotesquerie of the Jack-o'-lanterns lighting it and mocking his simplicity. But the first sharp physical hurt had healed. He was forced to admit that the girl still had power to trouble him. At times his strained nerves would relax to no other device than the picturing of her as his own. Exactly in the measure that he indulged this would his pride smart. With a budding gift for negation he could imagine her caring for nothing but his money; and there was that other picture, swift and awful, a pantomime in shadow, with the leering yellow faces above it.

In the far night, when he awoke to sudden and hungry aloneness, he would let his arms feel their hunger for her. The vision of her would be flowers and music and sunlight and time and all things perfect to mystify and delight, to satisfy and—greatest of all boons—to unsatisfy. The thought of her became a rest-house for all weariness; a haven where he was free to choose his nook and lie down away from all that was not her, which was all that was not beautiful. He would go back to seek the lost sweetness of their first meeting; to mount the poor dead belief that she would care for him— that he could make her care for him—and endow the thing with artificial life, trying to capture the faint breath of it; but the memory was always fleeting, attenuated, like the spirit of the memory of a perfume that had been elusive at best. And always, to banish what joy even this poor device might bring, came the more vivid vision of the brutal, sordid facts. He forced himself to face them regularly as a penance and a corrective.

They came before him with especial clearness when he met her from time to time during the winter. He watched her in talk with others, noting the contradiction in her that she would at one moment appear knowing and masterful, with depths of reserve that the other people neither fathomed nor knew of; and at another moment frankly girlish, with an appealing feminine helplessness which is woman's greatest strength, coercing every strong masculine instinct.

When the reserve showed in her, he became afraid. What was she not capable of? In the other mood, frankly appealing, she drew him mightily, so that he abandoned himself for the moment, responding to her fresh exulting youth, longing to take her, to give her things, to make her laugh, to enfold and protect her, to tell her secrets, to feather her cheek with the softest kiss, to be the child-mate of her.

Toward him, directly, when they met she would sometimes be glacial and forbidding, sometimes uninterestedly frank, as if they were but the best of commonplace friends. Yet sometimes she made him feel that she, too, threw herself heartily to rest in the thought of their loving, and cheated herself, as he did, with dreams of comradeship. She left him at these times with the feeling that they were deaf, dumb, and blind to each other; that if some means of communication could be devised, something surer than the invisible play of secret longings, all might yet be well. They talked as the people about them talked, words that meant nothing to either, and if there were mute questionings, naked appeals, unuttered declarations, they were only such as language serves to divert attention from. Speech, doubtless, has its uses as well as its abuses. Politics, for example, would be less entertaining without it. But in matters of the heart, certain it is that there would be fewer misunderstandings if it were forbidden between the couple under the penalty of immediate separation. In this affair real meanings are rarely conveyed except by silences. Words are not more than tasteless drapery to obscure their lines. The silence of lovers is the plainest of all speech, warning, disconcerting indeed, by its very bluntness, any but the truly mated. An hour's silence with these two people by themselves might have worked wonders.

Another diversion of Percival's during this somewhat feverish winter was Mrs. Akemit. Not only was she a woman of finished and expert daintiness in dress and manner and surroundings, but she soothed, flattered, and stimulated him. With the wisdom of her thirty-two years, devoted chiefly to a study of his species, she took care never to be exigent. She had the way of referring to herself as "poor little me," yet she never made demands or allowed him to feel that she expected anything from him in the way of allegiance.

Mrs. Akemit was not only like St. Paul, "all things to all men," but she had gone a step beyond that excellent theologue. She could be all things to one man. She was light-heartedly frivolous, soberly reflective, shallow, profound, cynical or naive, ingenuous, or inscrutable. She prized dearly the ecclesiastical background provided by her uncle, the bishop, and had him to dine with the same unerring sense of artistry that led her to select swiftly the becoming shade of sofa-cushion to put her blond head back upon.

The good bishop believed she had jeopardised her soul with divorce. He feared now she meant to lose it irrevocably through remarriage. As a foil to his austerity, therefore, she would be audaciously gay in his presence.

"Hell," she said to him one evening, "is given up *so* reluctantly by those who don't expect to go there." And while the bishop frowned into his salad she invited Percival to drink with her in the manner of a woman who is mad to invite perdition. If the good man could have beheld her before a background of frivolity he might have suffered less anxiety. For there her sense of contrast-values led her to be grave and deep, to express distaste for society with its hollowness, and to expose timidly the cruel scars on a soul meant for higher things.

Many afternoons Percival drank tea with her in the little red drawing-room of her dainty apartment up the avenue. Here in the half light which she had preferred since thirty, in a soft corner with which she harmonised faultlessly, and where the blaze from the open fire coloured her animated face just enough, she talked him usually into the glow of a high conceit with himself. When she dwelt upon the shortcomings of man, she did it with the air of frankly presuming him to be different from all others, one who could sympathise with her through knowing the frailties of his sex, yet one immeasurably superior to them. When he was led to talk of himself—of whom, it seemed, she could never learn enough—he at once came to take high views of himself: to gaze, through her tactful prompting, with a gentle, purring appreciation upon the manifest spectacle of his own worth.

Sometimes, away from her, he wondered how she did it. Sometimes, in her very presence, his sense of humour became alert and suspicious. Part of the time he decided her to be a charming woman, with a depth and quality of sweetness unguessed by the world. The rest of the time he remembered a saying about alfalfa made by Uncle Peter: "It's an innocent lookin', triflin' vegetable, but its roots go right down into the ground a hundred feet."

"My dear," Mrs. Akemit had once confided to an intimate in an hour of *negligee*, "to meet a man, any man, from a red-cheeked butcher boy to a bloodless monk, and not make him feel something new for you— something he never before felt for any other woman—really it's as criminal as a wrinkled stocking, or for blondes to wear shiny things. Every woman can do it, if she'll study a little how to reduce them to their least common denominator—how to make them primitive."

Of another member of Mrs. Akemit's household Percival acknowledged the sway with never a misgiving. He had been the devoted lover of Baby Akemit from the afternoon when he had first cajoled her into autobiography—a vivid, fire-tipped little thing with her mother's piquancy. He gleaned that day that she was "a quarter to four years old;" that she was mamma's girl, but papa was a friend of Santa Claus; that she went to "ball-dances" every day clad in "dest a stirt 'cause big ladies don't ever wear waist-es at night;" that she had once ridden in a merry-go-round and it made her "all homesick right here," patting her stomach; and that "elephants are horrid, but you mustn't be cruel to them and cut their eyes out. Oh, no!"

Her Percival courted with results that left nothing to be desired. She fell to the floor in helpless, shrieking laughter when he came. In his honour she composed and sang songs to an improvised and spirited accompaniment upon her toy piano. His favourites among these were "'Cause Why I Love You" and "Darling, Ask Myself to Come to You." She rendered them with much feeling. If he were present when her bed-time came she refused to sleep until he had consented to an interview.

Avice Milbrey had the fortune to witness one of these bed-time *causeries*. One late afternoon the young man's summons came while he was one of a group that lingered late about Mrs. Akemit's little tea-table, Miss Milbrey being of the number.

He followed the maid dutifully out through the hall to the door of the bedroom, and entered on all-fours with what they two had agreed was the growl of a famished bear.

The familiar performance was viewed by the mother and by Miss Milbrey, whom the mother had urged to follow. Baby Akemit in her crib, modestly arrayed in blue pajamas, after simulating the extreme terror required by the situation, fell to chatting, while her mother and Miss Milbrey looked on from the doorway.

Miss Akemit had once been out in the woods, it appeared, and a "biting-wolf" chased her, and she ran and ran until she came to a river all full of pigs and fishes and berries, so she jumped in and had supper, and it wasn't a "biting-wolf" at all—and then—

But the narrative was cut short by her mother.

"Come, Pet! Mr. Bines wishes to go now."

Miss Akemit, it appeared, was bent upon relating the adventures of Goldie Locks, subsequent to her leap from the window of the bears' house. She had, it seemed, been compelled to ride nine-twenty miles on a trolley, and, reaching home too late for luncheon, had been obliged to eat in the kitchen with the cook.

"Mr. Bines can't stay, darling!"

Baby Akemit calculated briefly, and consented to his departure if Mr. Bines would bring her something next time.

Mr. Bines promised, and moved away after the customary embrace, but she was not through:

"Oh! oh! go out like a bear! dere's a bear come in here!"

And so, having brought the bear in, he was forced to drop again and growl the beast out, whereupon, appeased by this strict observance of the unities, the child sat up and demanded:

"You sure you'll bring me somefin next time?"

"Yes, sure, Lady Grenville St. Clare." "Well, you sure you're *comin'* next time?"

Being reassured on this point, and satisfied that no more bears were at large, she lay down once more while Percival and the two observers returned to the drawing-room.

"You love children so!" Miss Milbrey said. And never had she been so girlishly appealing to all that was strong in him as a man. The frolic with the child seemed to have blown away a fog from between them. Yet never had the other scene been more vivid to him, and never had the pain of her heartlessness been more poignant.

When he "played" with Baby Akemit thereafter, the pretence was not all with the child. For while she might "play" at giving a vexatiously large dinner, for which she was obliged to do the cooking because she had discharged all the servants, or when they "played" that the big couch was a splendid ferry-boat in which they were sailing to Chicago where Uncle David lived—with many stern threats to tell the janitor of the boat if the captain didn't behave himself and sail faster—Percival "played" that his companion's name was Baby Bines, and that her mother, who watched them with loving eyes, was a sweet and gracious young woman named Avice. And when he told Baby Akemit that she was "the only original sweetheart" he meant it of some one else than her.

When the play was over he always conducted himself back to sane reality by viewing this some one else in the cold light of truth.

CHAPTER XXII.

The Distressing Adventure of Mrs. Bines

The fame of the Bines family for despising money was not fed wholly by Percival's unremitting activities. Miss Psyche Bines, during the winter, achieved wide and enviable renown as a player of bridge whist. Not for the excellence of her play; rather for the inveteracy and size of her losses and the unconcerned cheerfulness with which she defrayed them. She paid the considerable sums with an air of gratitude for having been permitted to lose them. Especially did she seem grateful for the zealous tutelage and chaperonage of Mrs. Drelmer.

"Everybody in New York plays bridge, my dear, and of course you must learn," that capable lady had said in the beginning.

"But I never was bright at cards," the girl confessed, "and I'm afraid I couldn't learn bridge well enough to interest you good players."

"Nonsense!" was Mrs. Drelmer's assurance. "Bridge is easy to learn and easy to play. I'll teach you, and I promise you the people you play with shall never complain."

Mrs. Drelmer, it soon appeared, knew what she was talking about.

Indeed, that well-informed woman was always likely to. Her husband was an intellectual delinquent whom she spoke of largely as being "in Wall Street," and in that feat of jugglery known as "keeping up appearances," his wife had long been the more dexterous performer.

She was apt not only to know what she talked about, but she was a woman of resource, unafraid of action. She drilled Miss Bines in the rudiments of bridge. If the teacher became subsequently much the largest winner of the pupil's losings, it was, perhaps, not more than her fit recompense. For Miss Bines enjoyed not only the sport of the game, but her manner of playing it, combined with the social prestige of her amiable sponsor, procured her a circle of acquaintances that would otherwise have remained considerably narrower. An enthusiastic player of bridge, of passable exterior, mediocre skill, and unlimited resources, need never want in New York for very excellent society. Not only was the Western girl received by Mrs. Drelmer's immediate circle, but more than one member of what the lady called "that snubby set" would now and then make a place for her at the card-table. A few of Mrs. Drelmer's intimates were so wanting in good taste as to intimate that she exploited Miss Bines even to the degree of an understanding expressed in bald percentage, with certain of those to whom she secured the girl's society at cards. Whether this ill-natured gossip was true or false, it is certain that the exigencies of life on next to nothing a year, with a husband who could boast of next to nothing but Family, had developed an unerring business sense in Mrs. Drelmer; and certain it also is that this winter was one when the appearances with which she had to strive were unwontedly buoyant.

Miss Bines tirelessly memorised rules. She would disclose to her placid mother that the lead of a trump to the third hand's go-over of hearts is of doubtful expediency; or that one must "follow suit with the smallest, except when you have only two, neither of them better than the Jack. Then play the higher first, so that when the lower falls your partner may know you are out of the suit, and ruff it."

Mrs. Bines declared that it did seem to her very much like out-and-out gambling. But Percival, looking over the stubs of his sister's check-book, warmly protested her innocence of this charge.

"Heaven knows sis has her shortcomings," he observed, patronisingly, in that young woman's presence, "but she's no gambler; don't say it, ma, I beg of you! She only knows five rules of the game, and I judge it's cost her about three thousand dollars each to learn those. And the only one she never forgets is, 'When in doubt, lead your highest check.' But don't ever accuse her of gambling. Poor girl, if she keeps on playing bridge she'll have writer's cramp; that's all I'm afraid of. I see there's a new rapid-fire check-book on the market, and an improved fountain pen that doesn't slobber. I'll have to get her one of each."

Yet Psyche Bines's experience, like her brother's, was not without a proper leaven of sentiment. There was Fred Milbrey, handsome, clever, amusing, knowing every one, and giving her a pleasant sense of intimacy with all that was worth while in New York. Him she felt very friendly to.

Then there was Mauburn, presently to be Lord Casselthorpe, with his lazy, high-pitched drawl; good-natured, frank, carrying an atmosphere of high-class British worldliness, and delicately awakening within her while she was with him a sense of her own latent superiority to the institutions of her native land. She liked Mauburn, too.

More impressive than either of these, however, was the Baron Ronault de Palliac. Tall, swarthy, saturnine, a polished man of all the world, of manners finished, elaborate, and ceremonious, she found herself feeling foreign and distinguished in his presence, quite as if she were the heroine of a romantic novel, and might at any instant be called upon to assist in royalist intrigues. The baron, to her intuition, nursed secret sorrows. For these she secretly worshipped him. It is true that when he dined with her and her mother, which he was frequently gracious enough to do, he ate with a heartiness that belied this secret sorrow she had imagined. But he was fascinating at all times, with a grace at table not less finished than that with which he bowed at their meetings and partings. It was not unpleasant to think of basking daily in the shine of that grand manner, even if she did feel friendlier with Milbrey, and more at ease with Mauburn.

If the truth must be told, Miss Bines was less impressionable than either of the three would have wished. Her heart seemed not easy to reach; her impulses were not inflammable. Young Milbrey early confided to his family a suspicion that she was singularly hard-headed, and the definite information that she had "a hob-nailed Western way" of treating her admirers.

Mauburn, too, was shrewd enough to see that, while she frankly liked him, he was for some reason less a favourite than the Baron de Palliac.

"It'll be no easy matter marrying that girl," he told Mrs. Drelmer. "She's really a dear, and awfully good fun, but she's not a bit silly, and I dare say she'll marry some chap because she likes him, and not because he's anybody, you know."

"Make her like you," insisted his adviser.

"On my word, I wish she did. And I'm not so sure, you know, she doesn't fancy that Frenchman, or even young Milbrey."

"I'll keep you before her," promised Mrs. Drelmer, "and I wish you'd not think you can't win her. 'Tisn't like you."

Miss Bines accordingly heard that it was such a pity young Milbrey drank so, because his only salvation lay in making a rich marriage, and a young man, nowadays, had to keep fairly sober to accomplish that. Really, Mrs. Drelmer felt sorry for the poor weak fellow. "Good-hearted chap, but he has no character, my dear, so I'm afraid there's no hope for him. He has the soul of a merchant tailor, actually, but not the tailor's manhood. Otherwise he'd be above marrying some unsuspecting girl for her money and breaking her heart after marriage. Now, Mauburn is a type so different; honest, unaffected, healthy, really he's a man for any girl to be proud of, even if he were not heir to a title—one of the best in all England, and an ornament of the most exclusively correct set; of a line, my dear, that is truly great—not like that shoddy French nobility, discredited in France, that sends so many of its comic-opera barons here looking for large dowries to pay their gambling debts and put furniture in their rattle-trap old chateaux, and keep them in absinthe and their other peculiar diversions. And Mauburn, you lucky minx, simply adores you—he's quite mad about you, really!"

In spite of Mrs. Drelmer's two-edged sword, Miss Bines continued rather more favourable to the line of De Palliac. The baron was so splendid, so gloomy, so deferential. He had the air of laying at her feet, as a rug, the whole glorious history of France. And he appeared so well in the victoria when they drove in the park.

It is true that the heart of Miss Bines was as yet quite untouched; and it was not more than a cool, dim, aesthetic light in which she surveyed the three suitors impartially, to behold the impressive figure of the baron towering above the others. Had the baron proposed for her hand, it is not impossible that, facing the question directly, she would have parried or evaded.

But certain events befell unpropitiously at a time when the baron was most certain of his conquest; at the very time, indeed, when he had determined to open his suit definitely by extending a proposal to the young lady through the orthodox medium of her nearest male relative.

"I admit," wrote the baron to his expectant father, "that it is what one calls '*very chances*' in the English, but one must venture in this country, and your son is not without much hope. And if not, there is still Mlle. Higbee."

The baron shuddered as he wrote it. He preferred not to recognise even the existence of this alternative, for the reason that the father of Mlle. Higbee distressed him by an incompleteness of suavity.

"He conducts himself like a pork," the baron would declare to himself, by way of perfecting his English.

The secret cause of his subsequent determination not to propose for the hand of Miss Bines lay in the hopelessly middle-class leanings of the lady who might have incurred the supreme honour of becoming his mother-in-law. Had Mrs. Bines been above talking to low people, a catastrophe might have been averted. But Mrs. Bines was not above it. She was quite unable to repress a vulgar interest in the menials that served her.

She knew the butler's life history two days after she had ceased to be afraid of him. She knew the distressing family affairs of the maids; how many were the ignoble progeny of the elevator-man, and what his plebeian wife did for their croup; how much rent the hall-boy's low-born father paid for his mean two-story dwelling in Jersey City; and how many hours a day or night the debased scrub-women devoted to their unrefining toil.

Brazenly, too, she held converse with Philippe, the active and voluble Alsatian who served her when she chose to dine in the public restaurant instead of at her own private table. Philippe acquainted her with the joys and griefs of his difficult profession. There were fourteen thousand waiters in New York, if, by waiters, you meant any one. Of course there were not so many like Philippe, men of the world who had served their time as assistants and their three years as sub-waiters; men who spoke English, French, and German, who knew something of cooking, how to dress a salad, and how to carve. Only such, it appeared, could be members of the exclusive Geneva Club that procured a place for you when you were idle, and paid you eight dollars a week when you were sick.

Having the qualifications, one could earn twenty-five dollars a month in salary and three or four times as much in gratuities. Philippe's income was never less than one hundred and twenty dollars a month; for was he not one who had come from Europe as a master, after two seasons at Paris where a man acquires his polish—his perfection of manner, his finish, his grace? Philippe could never enough prize that post-graduate course at the *Maison d'Or*, where he had personally known—madame might not believe it—the incomparable Casmir, a *chef* who served two generations of epicures, princes, kings, statesmen, travelling Americans,—all the truly great.

With his own lips Casmir had told him, Philippe, of the occasion when Dumas, *pere*, had invited him to dinner that they might discuss the esoterics of salad dressing and sauces; also of the time when the Marquis de St. Georges embraced Casmir for inventing the precious soup that afterwards became famous as *Potage Germine*. And now the skilled and puissant Casmir had retired. It was a calamity. The *Maison d'Or*—Paris—would no longer be what they had been.

For that matter, since one must live, Philippe preferred it to be in America, for in no other country could an adept acquire so much money. And Philippe knew the whole dining world. With Celine and the baby, Paul, Philippe dwelt in an apartment that would really amaze madame by its appointments of luxury, in East 38th Street, and only the four flights to climb. And Paul was three, the largest for his age, quite the largest, that either Philippe or Celine had ever beheld. Even the brother of Celine and his wife, who had a restaurant of their own—serving the *table d'hote* at two and one-half francs the plate, with wine—even these swore they had never seen an infant so big, for his years, as Paul.

And so Mrs. Bines grew actually to feel an interest in the creature and his wretched affairs, and even fell into the deplorable habit of saying, "I must come to see you and your wife and Paul some pleasant day, Philippe," and Philippe, being a man of the world, thought none the less of her for believing that she did not mean it.

Yet it befell on an afternoon that Mrs. Bines found herself in a populous side-street, driving home from a visit to the rheumatic scrub-woman who had now to be supported by the papers her miserable offspring sold. Mrs. Bines had never seen so many children as flooded this street. She wondered if an orphan asylum were in the neighbourhood. And though the day was pleasantly warm, she decided that there were about her at least a thousand cases of incipient pneumonia, for not one child in five had on a hat. They raged and dashed and rippled from curb to curb so that they might have made her think of a swift mountain torrent at the bottom of a gloomy canyon, but that the worthy woman was too literal-minded for such fancies. She only warned the man to drive slowly.

And then by a street sign she saw that she was near the home of Philippe. It was three o'clock, and he would be resting from his work. The man found the number. The waves parted and piled themselves on either side in hushed wonder as she entered the hallway and searched for the name on the little cards under the bells. She had never known the surname, and on two of the cards "Ph." appeared. She rang one of the bells, the door mysteriously opened with a repeated double click, and she began the toilsome climb. The waves of children fell together behind her in turbulent play again.

At the top she breathed a moment and then knocked at a door before her. A voice within called:

"*Entrez!*" and Mrs. Bines opened the door.

It was the tiny kitchen of Philippe. Philippe, himself, in shirt-sleeves, sat in a chair tilted back close to the gas-range, the *Courier des Etats Unis* in his hands and Paul on his lap. Celine ironed the bosom of a gentleman's white shirt on an ironing board supported by the backs of two chairs.

Hemmed in the corner by this board and by the gas-range, seated at a table covered by the oilcloth that simulates the marble of Italy's most famous quarry, sat, undoubtedly, the Baron Ronault de Palliac. A steaming plate of spaghetti *a la Italien* was before him, to his left a large bowl of salad, to his right a bottle of red wine.

For a space of three seconds the entire party behaved as if it were being photographed under time-exposure. Philippe and the baby stared, motionless. Celine stared, resting no slight weight on the hot flat-iron. The Baron Ronault de Palliac stared, his fork poised in mid-air and festooned with gay little streamers of spaghetti.

Then came smoke, the smell of scorching linen, and a cry of horror from Celine.

"*Ah, la seule chemise blanche de Monsieur le Baron!*"

The spell was broken. Philippe was on his feet, bowing effusively.

"Ah! it is Madame Bines. *Je suis tres honore*—I am very honoured to welcome you, madame. It is madame, *ma femme*, Celine,—and—Monsieur le Baron de Palliac—"

Philippe had turned with evident distress toward the latter. But Philippe was only a waiter, and had not behind him the centuries of schooling that enable a gentleman to remain a gentleman under adverse conditions.

The Baron Ronault de Palliac arose with unruffled aplomb and favoured the caller with his stateliest bow. He was at the moment a graceful and silencing rebuke to those who aver that manner and attire be interdependent. The baron's manner was ideal, undiminished in volume, faultless as to decorative qualities. One fitted to savour its exquisite finish would scarce have noted that above his waist the noble gentleman was clad in a single woollen undergarment of revolutionary red.

Or, if such a one had observed this trifling circumstance, he would, assuredly, have treated it as of no value to the moment; something to note, perhaps, and then gracefully to forget.

The baron's own behaviour would have served as a model. One swift glance had shown him there was no way of instant retreat. That being impossible, none other was graceful; hence none other was to be considered. He permitted himself not even a glance at the shirt upon whose fair, defenceless bosom the iron of the overcome Celine had burned its cruel brown imprimature. Mrs. Bines had greeted him as he would have wished, unconscious, apparently, that there could be cause for embarrassment.

"Ah! madame," he said, handsomely, "you see me, I unfast with the fork. You see me here, I have envy of the simple life. I am content of to do it— *comme ca*—as that, see you," waving in the direction of his unfinished repast. "All that magnificence of your grand hotel, there is not the why of it, the most big of the world, and suchly stupefying, with its 'infernil rackit' as you say. And of more—what droll of idea, enough curious, by example! to dwell with the good Philippe and his *femme aimable*. Their hotel is of the most littles, but I rest here very volunteerly since longtime. Is it that one can to comprehend liking the vast hotel American?"

"Monsieur le Baron lodges with us; we have so much of the chambers," ventured Celine.

"Monsieur le Baron wishes to retire to his apartment," said Philippe, raising the ironing-board. "Will madame be so good to enter our *petit salon* at the front, *n'est-ce-pas?*"

The baron stepped forth from his corner and bowed himself graciously out.

"Madame, my compliments—and to the adorable Mademoiselle Bines! *Au revoir*, madame—to the soontime—*avant peu*—before little!"

On the farther side of his closed door the Baron Ronault de Palliac swore—once. But the oath was one of the most awful that a Frenchman may utter in his native tongue: "Sacred Name of a Name!"

"But the baron wasn't done eating," protested Mrs. Bines.

"Ah, yes, madame!" replied Philippe. "Monsieur le Baron has consumed enough for now. *Paul, mon enfant, ne touche pas la robe de madame!* He is large, is he not, madame, as I have told you? A monster, yes?"

Mrs. Bines, stooping, took the limp and wide-eyed Paul up in her arms. Whereupon he began to talk so fast to her in French that she set him quickly down again, with the slightly helpless air of one who has picked up an innocent-looking clock only to have the clanging alarm go suddenly off.

"Madame will honour our little salon," urged Philippe, opening the door and bowing low.

"*Quel dommage!*" sighed Celine, moving after them; "*la seule chemise blanche de Monsieur le Baron. Eh bien! il faut lui en acheter une autre!*"

At dinner that evening Mrs. Bines related her adventure, to the unfeigned delight of her graceless son, and to the somewhat troubled amazement of her daughter.

"And, do you know," she ventured, "maybe he isn't a regular baron, after all!"

"Oh, I guess he's a regular one all right," said Percival; "only perhaps he hasn't worked at it much lately."

"But his sitting there eating in that—that shirt—" said his sister.

"My dear young woman, even the nobility are prey to climatic rigours; they are obliged, like the wretched low-born such as ourselves, to wear—pardon me—undergarments. Again, I understand from Mrs. Cadwallader here that the article in question was satisfactory and fit—red, I believe you say, Mrs. Terwilliger?"

"Awful red!" replied his mother—"and they call their parlour a saloon."

"And of necessity, even the noble have their moments of *deshabille*."

"They needn't eat their lunch that way," declared his sister.

"Is *deshabille* French for underclothes?" asked Mrs. Bines, struck by the word.

"Partly," answered her son.

"And the way that child of Philippe's jabbered French! It's wonderful how they can learn so young."

"They begin early, you know," Percival explained. "And as to our friend the baron, I'm ready to make book that sis doesn't see him again, except at a distance."

Sometime afterwards he computed the round sum he might have won if any such bets had been made; for his sister's list of suitors, to adopt his own lucent phrase, was thereafter "shy a baron."

CHAPTER XXIII.

The Summer Campaign Is Planned

Winter waned and spring charmed the land into blossom. The city-pent, as we have intimated, must take this season largely on faith. If one can find a patch of ground naked of stone or asphalt one may feel the heart of the earth beat. But even now the shop-windows are more inspiring. At least they copy the outer show. Tender-hued shirt-waists first push up their sprouts of arms through the winter furs and woollens, quite as the first violets out in the woodland thrust themselves up through the brown carpet of leaves. Then every window becomes a summery glade of lawn, tulle, and chiffon, more lavish of tints, shades, and combinations, indeed, than ever nature dared to be.

Outside, where the unspoiled earth begins, the blossoms are clouding the trees with a mist of pink and white, and the city-dweller knows it from the bloom and foliage of these same windows.

Then it is that the spring "get away" urge is felt by each prisoner, by those able to obey it, and by those, alike, who must wear it down in the groomed and sophisticated wildness of the city parks.

On a morning late in May Mrs. Bines and her daughter were at breakfast.

"Isn't Percival coming?" asked his mother. "Everything will be cold."

"Can't say," Psyche answered. "I don't even know if he came in last night. But don't worry about cold things. You can't get them too cold for Perce at breakfast, nowadays. He takes a lot of ice-water and a little something out of the decanter, and maybe some black coffee."

"Yes, and I'm sure it's bad for him. He doesn't look a bit healthy and hasn't since he quit eating breakfast. He used to be such a hearty eater at breakfast, steaks and bacon and chops and eggs and waffles. It was a sight to see him eat; and since he's quit taking anything but that cold stuff he's lost his colour and his eyes don't look right. I know what he's got hold of—it's that 'no-breakfast' fad. I heard about it from Mrs. Balldridge when we came here last fall. I never did believe in it, either."

The object of her solicitude entered in dressing-gown and slippers.

"I'm just telling Psyche that this no-breakfast fad is hurting your health, my son. Now do come and eat like you used to. You began to look bad as soon as you left off your breakfast. It's a silly fad, that's what it is. You can't tell *me!*"

The young man stared at his mother until he had mastered her meaning. Then he put both hands to his head and turned to the sideboard as if to conceal his emotion.

"That's it," he said, as he busied himself with a tall glass and the cracked ice. "It's that 'no-breakfast' fad. I didn't think you knew about it. The fact is," he continued, pouring out a measure of brandy, and directing the butler to open a bottle of soda, "we all eat too much. After a night of sound sleep we awaken refreshed and buoyant, all our forces replenished; thirsty, of course, but not hungry"—he sat down to the table and placed both hands again to his head—"and we have no need of food. Yet such is the force of custom that we deaden ourselves for the day by tanking up on coarse, loathsome stuff like bacon. Ugh! Any one would think, the way you two eat so early in the day, that you were a couple of cave-dwellers,—the kind that always loaded up when they had a chance because it might be a week before they got another."

He drained his glass and brightened visibly.

"Now, why not be reasonable?" he continued, pleadingly. "You know there is plenty of food. I have observed it being brought into town in huge wagon-loads in the early morning on many occasions. Why do you want to eat it all at one sitting? No one's going to starve you. Why stupefy yourselves when, by a little nervy self-denial, you can remain as fresh and bright and clear-headed as I am at this moment? Why doesn't a fire make its own escape, Mrs. Carstep-Jamwuddle?"

"I don't believe you feel right, either. I just know you've got an awful headache right now. Do let the man give you a nice piece of this steak."

"Don't, I beg of you, Lady Ashmorton! The suggestion is extremely repugnant to me. Besides, I'm behaving this way because I arose with the purely humourous fancy that my head was a fine large accordeon, and that some meddler had drawn it out too far. I'm sportively pretending that I can press it back into shape. Now you and sis never get up with any such light poetic notion as that. You know you don't—don't attempt to deceive me." He glanced over the table with swift disapproval.

"Strawberries, oatmeal, rolls, steak three inches thick, bacon, omelette—oh, that I should live to see this day! It's disgraceful! And at your age—before your own innocent woman-child, and leading her into the same excesses. Do you know what that breakfast is? No; I'll tell you. That breakfast is No. 78 in that book of Mrs. Rorer's, and she expressly warns everybody that it can be eaten safely only by steeple-climbers, piano-movers, and sea-captains. Really, Mrs. Wrangleberry, I blush for you."

"I don't care how you go on. You ain't looked well for months."

"But think of my great big heart—a heart like an ox,"—he seemed on the verge of tears—"and to think that you, a woman I have never treated with anything but respect since we met in Honduras in the fall of '93—to think *you* should throw it up to my own face that I'm not beautiful. Others there are, thank God, who can look into a man's heart and prize him for what he is—not condemn him for his mere superficial blemishes."

"And I just know you've got in with a fast set. I met Mr. Milbrey yesterday in the corridor—"

"Did he tell you how to make a lovely asparagus short-cake or something?"

"He told me those men you go with so much are dreadful gamblers, and that when you all went to Palm Beach last February you played poker for money night and day, and you told me you went for your health!"

"Oh, he did, did he? Well, I didn't get anything else. He's a dear old soul, if you've got the copper handy. If that man was a woman he'd be a warm neighbourhood gossip. He'd be the nice kind old lady that *starts* things, that's what Hoddy Milbrey would be."

"And you said yourself you played poker most of the time when you went to Aiken on the car last month."

"To be honest with you, ma, we did play poker. Say, they took it off of me so fast I could feel myself catching cold."

"There, you see—and you really ought to wear one of those chamois-skin chest protectors in this damp climate."

"Well, we'll see. If I can find one that an ace-full won't go through I'll snatch it so quick the man'll think he's being robbed. Now I'll join you ladies to the extent of some coffee, and then I want to know what you two would rather do this summer *than*."

"Of course," said Psyche, "no one stays in town in summer."

"Exactly. And I've chartered a steam yacht as big as this hotel—all but— But what I want to know is whether you two care to bunk on it or whether you'd rather stay quietly at some place, Newport perhaps, and maybe take a cruise with me now and then."

"Oh, that would be good fun. But here's ma getting so I can't do a thing with her, on account of all those beggars and horrid people down in the slums."

Mrs. Bines looked guilty and feebly deprecating. It was quite true that in her own way she had achieved a reputation for prodigality not inferior to that acquired by her children in ways of their own.

"You know it's so, ma," the daughter went on, accusingly. "One night last winter when you were away we dined at the Balldridge's, in Eighty-sixth Street, and the pavements were so sleety the horses couldn't stand, so Colonel Balldridge brought us home in the Elevated, about eleven o'clock. Well, at one of the stations a big policeman got on with a little baby all wrapped up in red flannel. He'd found it in an area-way, nearly covered with snow—where some one had left it, and he was taking it down to police-headquarters, he said. Well, ma went crazy right away. She made him undo it, and then she insisted on holding it all the way down to Thirty-third Street. One man said it might be President of the United States, some day; and Colonel Balldridge said, 'Yes, it has unknown possibilities—it may even be a President's wife'—just like that. But I thought ma would be demented. It was all fat and so warm and sleepy it could hardly hold its eyes open, and I believe she'd have kept it then and there if the policeman would have let her. She made him promise to get it a bottle of warm milk the first thing, and borrowed twenty dollars of the colonel to give to the policeman to get it things with, and then all the way down she talked against the authorities for allowing such things—as if they could help it—and when we got home she cried—you _know_ you did, ma—and you pretended it was toothache—and ever since then she's been perfectly daft about babies. Why, whenever she sees a woman going along with one she thinks the poor thing is going to leave it some place; and now she's in with those charity workers and says she won't leave New York at all this summer."

"I don't care," protested the guilty mother, "it would have frozen to death in just a little while, and it's done so often. Why, up at the Catholic Protectory they put out a basket at the side door, so a body can leave their baby in it and ring the bell and run away; and they get one twice a week sometimes; and this was such a sweet, fat little baby with big blue eyes, and its forehead wrinkled, and it was all puckered up around its little nose—"

"And that isn't the worst of it," the relentless daughter broke in. "She gets begging letters by the score and gives money to all sorts of people, and a man from the Charities Organisation, who had heard about it, came and warned her that they were impostors—only she doesn't care. Do you know, there was a poor old blind woman with a dismal, wheezy organ down at Broadway and Twenty-third Street—the organ would hardly play at all, and just one wretched tune—only the woman wasn't blind at all we found out—and ma bought her a nice new organ that cost seventy-five dollars and had it taken up to her. Well, she found out through this man from the Organisation that the woman had pawned the new organ for twenty dollars and was still playing on the old one. She didn't want a new one because it was too cheerful; it didn't make people sad when they heard it, like her old one did. And yesterday ma bought an Indian—"

"A what?" asked her brother, in amazement.

"An Indian—a tobacco sign."

"You don't mean it? One of those lads that stand out in front and peer under their hands to see what palefaces are moving into the house across the street? Say, ma, what you going to do with him? There isn't much room here, you know."

"I didn't buy him for myself," replied Mrs. Bines, with dignity; "I wouldn't want such an object."

"She bought it," explained his sister, "for an Italian woman who keeps a little tobacco-shop down in Rivington Street. A man goes around to repaint them, you know, but hers was so battered that this man told her it wasn't worth painting again, and she'd better get another, and the woman said she didn't know what to do because they cost twenty-five dollars and one doesn't last very long. The bad boys whittle him and throw him down, and the people going along the street put their shoes up to tie them and step on his feet, and they scratch matches on his face, and when she goes out and says that isn't right they tell her she's too fresh. And so ma gave her twenty-five dollars for a new one."

"But she has to support five children, and her husband hasn't been able to work for three years, since he fell through a fire-escape where he was sleeping one hot night," pleaded Mrs. Bines, "and I think I'd rather stay here this summer. Just think of all those poor babies when the weather gets hot. I never thought there were so many babies in the world."

"Well, have your own way," said her son. "If you've started out to look after all the babies in New York you won't have any time left to play the races, I'll promise you that."

"Why, my son, I never—"

"But sis here would probably rather do other things."

"I think," said Psyche, "I'd like Newport—Mrs. Drelmer says I shouldn't think of going any place else. Only, of course, I can't go there alone. She says she would be glad to chaperone me, but her husband hasn't had a very good year in Wall Street, and she's afraid she won't be able to go herself."

"Maybe," began Mrs. Bines, "if you'd offer—"

"Oh! she'd be offended," exclaimed Psyche.

"I'm not so sure of that," said her brother, "not if you suggest it in the right way—put it on the ground that you'll be quite helpless without her, and that she'd oblige you world without end and all that. The more I see of people here the more I think they're quite reasonable in little matters like that. They look at them in the right light. Just lead up to it delicately with Mrs. Drelmer and see. Then if she's willing to go with you, your summer will be provided for; except that we shall both have to look in upon Mrs. Juzzlebraggin here now and then to see that she doesn't overplay the game and get sick herself, and make sure that they don't get her vaccination mark away from her. And, ma, you'll have to come off on the yacht once or twice, just to give it tone."

It appeared that Percival had been right in supposing that Mrs. Drelmer might be led to regard Psyche's proposal in a light entirely rational. She was reluctant, at first, it is true.

"It's awfully dear of you to ask me, child, but really, I'm afraid it will be quite impossible. Oh!—for reasons which you, of course, with your endless bank-account, cannot at all comprehend. You see we old New York families have a secure position *here* by right of birth; and even when we are forced to practice little economies in dress and household management it doesn't count against us—so long as we *stay* here. Now, Newport is different. One cannot economise gracefully there—not even one of *us*. There are quiet and very decent places for those of us that must. But at Newport one must not fall behind in display. A sense of loyalty to the others, a *noblesse oblige*, compels one to be as lavish as those flamboyant outsiders who go there. One doesn't want them to report, you know, that such and such families of our smart set are falling behind for lack of means. So, while we of the real stock are chummy enough here, where there is only *us* in a position to observe ourselves, there is a sort of tacit agreement that only those shall go to Newport who are able to keep up the pace. One need not, for one season or so, be a cottager; but, for example, in the matter of dress, one must be sinfully lavish. Really, child, I could spend three months in the Engadine for the price of one decent month at Newport; the parasols, gloves, fans, shoes, 'frillies'—enough to stock the Rue de la Paix, to say nothing of gowns—but why do I run on? Here am I with a few little simple summer things, fit enough indeed for the quiet place we shall reach for July and August, but ab-so-lute-ly impossible for Newport—so say no more about it, dear. You're a sweet—but it's madness to think of it."

"And I had," reported Psyche to her mother that night, "such a time getting her to agree. At first she wouldn't listen at all. Then, after I'd just fairly begged her, she admitted she might because she's taken such a fancy to me and hates to leave me—but she was sensitive about what people might say. I told her they'd never have a chance to say a word; and she was anxious

Perce shouldn't know, because she says he's so cynical about New York people since that Milbrey girl made such a set for him; and at last she called me a dear and consented, though she'd been looking forward to a quiet summer. To-morrow early we start out for the shops."

So it came that the three members of the Bines family pursued during the summer their respective careers of diversion under conditions most satisfactory to each.

The steam yacht *Viluca*, chartered by Percival, was put into commission early in June. Her first cruise of ten days was a signal triumph. His eight guests were the men with whom he had played poker so tirelessly during the winter. Perhaps the most illuminating log of that cruise may be found in the reply of one of them whom Percival invited for another early in July.

"Much obliged, old man, but I haven't touched a drop now in over three weeks. My doctor says I must let it be for at least two months, and I mean to stick by him. Awfully kind of you, though!"

CHAPTER XXIV.

The Sight of a New Beauty, and Some Advice from Higbee

From the landing on a still morning in late July, Mrs. Drelmer surveyed the fleet of sailing and steam yachts at anchor in Newport harbour. She was beautifully and expensively gowned in nun's grey chiffon; her toque was of chiffon and lace, and she held a pale grey parasol, its ivory handle studded with sapphires. She fixed a glass upon one of the white, sharp-nosed steam yachts that rode in the distance near Goat Island. "Can you tell me if that's the *Viluca?*" she asked a sailor landing from a dinghy, "that boat just astern of the big schooner?"

"No ma'am; that's the *Alta*, Commodore Weckford."

"Looking for some one?" inquired a voice, and she turned to greet Fred Milbrey descending the steps.

"Oh! Good-morning! yes; but they've not come in, evidently. It's the *Viluca*—Mr. Bines, you know; he's bringing his sister back to me. And you?"

"I'm expecting the folks on Shepler's craft. Been out two weeks now, and were to have come down from New London last night. They're not in sight either. Perhaps the gale last night kept them back."

Mrs. Drelmer glanced above to where some one seemed to be waiting for him.

"Who's your perfectly gorgeous companion? You've been so devoted to her for three days that you've hardly bowed to old friends. Don't you want her to know any one?"

The young man laughed with an air of great shrewdness.

"Come, now, Mrs. Drelmer, you're too good a friend of Mauburn's—about his marrying, I mean. You fixed him to tackle me low the very first half of one game we know about, right when I was making a fine run down the field, too. I'm going to have better interference this time."

"Silly! Your chances are quite as good as his there this moment."

"You may think so; I know better."

"And of course, in any other affair, I'd never think of—"

"P'r'aps so; but I'd rather not chance it just yet."

"But who is she? What a magnificent mop of hair. It's like that rich piece of ore Mr. Bines showed us, with copper and gold in it."

"Well, I don't mind telling you she's the widow of a Southern gentleman, Colonel Brench Wybert."

"Ah, indeed! I did notice that two-inch band of black at the bottom of her accordeon-plaited petticoat. I'll wager that's a *Rue de la Paix* idea of mourning for one's dead husband. And she confides her grief to the world with such charming discretion. Half the New York women can't hold their skirts up as daintily as she does it. I dare say, now, her tears could be dried?—by the right comforter?"

Milbrey looked important.

"And I don't mind telling you the late Colonel Brench Wybert left her a fortune made in Montana copper. Can't say how much, but two weeks ago she asked the governor's advice about where to put a spare million and a half in cash. Not so bad, eh?"

"Oh, this new plutocracy! Where *do* they get it?"

"How old, now, should you say she was?"

Mrs. Drelmer glanced up again at the colour-scheme of heliotrope seated in a victoria upholstered in tan brocade.

"Thirty-five, I should say—about."

"Just twenty-eight."

"Just about what I should say—she'd say."

"Come now, you women can't help it, can you? But you can't deny she's stunning?"

"Indeed I can't! She's a beauty—and, good luck to you. Is that the *Viluca* coming in? No; it has two stacks; and it's not your people because the *Lotus* is black. I shall go back to the hotel. Bertie Trafford brought me over on the trolley. I must find him first and do an errand in Thames Street."

At the head of the stairs they parted, Milbrey joining the lady who had waited for him.

Hers was a person to gladden the eye. Her figure, tall and full, was of a graceful and abundant perfection of contours; her face, precisely carved and showing the faintly generous rounding of maturity, was warm in colouring, with dark eyes, well shaded and languorous; her full lips betrayed their beauty in a ready and fascinating laugh; her voice was a rich, warm contralto; and her speech bore just a hint of the soft r-less drawl of the South.

She had blazed into young Milbrey's darkness one night in the palm-room of the Hightower Hotel, escorted by a pleased and beefy youth of his acquaintance, who later told him of their meeting at the American Embassy in Paris, and who unsuspectingly presented him. Since their meeting the young man had been her abject cavalier. The elder Milbrey, too, had met her at his son's suggestion. He had been as deeply impressed by her helplessness in the matter of a million and a half dollars of idle funds as she had been by his aristocratic bearing and enviable position in New York society.

"Sorry to have kept you waiting. The *Lotus* hasn't come in sight yet. Let's loaf over to the beach and have some tall, cold ones."

"Who was your elderly friend?" she asked, as they were driven slowly up the old-fashioned street.

"Oh! that's Joe Drelmer. She's not so old, you know; not a day over forty, Joe can't be; fine old stock; she was a Leydenbroek and her husband's family is one of the very oldest in New York. Awfully exclusive. Down to meet friends, but they'd not shown up, either. That reminds me; they're friends of ours, too, and I must have you meet them. They're from your part of the country—the Bines."

"The—ah—"

"Bines; family from Montana; decent enough sort; didn't know but you might have heard of them, being from your part of the country."

"Ah, I never think of that vulgar West as 'my part of the country' at all. *My* part is dear old Virginia, where my father, General Tulver, and his father and his father's father all lived the lives of country gentlemen, after the family came here from Devonshire. It was there Colonel Wybert wooed me, though we later removed to New Orleans." Mrs. Wybert called it "New *Aw*-leens."

"But it was not until my husband became interested in Montana mines that we ventured into that horrid West. So *do* remember not to confound me with your Western—ah—Bones,—was it not?"

"No, Bines; they'll be here presently, and you can meet them, anyway."

"Is there an old fellow—a queer old character, with them?"

"No, only a son and daughter and the mother."

"Of course I sha'n't mind meeting any friends of yours," she said, with charming graciousness, "but, really, I always understood that you Knickerbockers were so vastly more exclusive. I do recall this name now. I remember hearing tales of the family in Spokane. They're a type, you know. One sees many of the sort there. They make a strike in the mines and set up ridiculous establishments regardless of expense. You see them riding in their carriages with two men in the box—red-handed, grizzled old vulgarians who've roughed it in the mountains for twenty years with a pack-mule and a ham and a pick-axe—with their jug of whiskey—and their frowsy red-faced wives decked out in impossible finery. Yes, I do recall this family. There is a daughter, you say?"

"Yes; Miss Psyche Bines."

"Psyche; ah, yes; it's the same family. I recollect perfectly now. You know they tell the funniest tales of them out there. Her mother found the name 'Psyche' in a book, and liked it, but she pronounced it 'Pishy,' and so the girl was called until she became old enough to go to school and learned better."

"Dear me; fancy now!"

"And there are countless tales of the mother's queer sayings. Once a gentleman whom they were visiting in San Francisco was showing her a cabinet of curios. 'Now, don't you find the Pompeiian figurines exquisite?' he asked her. The poor creature, after looking around her helplessly, declared that she *did* like them; but that she liked the California nectarines better—they were so much juicier."

"You don't tell me; gad! that was a good one. Oh, well, she's a meek, harmless old soul, and really, my family's not the snobbish sort, you know."

In from the shining sea late that afternoon steamed the *Viluca*. As her chain was rattling through the hawse-hole, Percival, with his sister and Mauburn, came on deck.

"Why, there's the *Chicago*—Higbee's yacht."

"That's the boat," said Mauburn, "that's been piling the white water up in front of her all afternoon trying to overhaul us."

"There's Millie Higbee and old Silas, now."

"And, as I live," exclaimed Psyche, "there's the Baron de Palliac between them!"

"Sure enough," said her brother. "We must call ma up to see him dressed in those sweet, pretty yachting flannels. Oh, there you are!" as Mrs. Bines joined them. "Just take this glass and treat yourself to a look at your old friend, the baron. You'll notice he has one on—see—they're waving to us."

"Doesn't the baron look just too distinguished beside Mr. Higbee?" said Psyche, watching them.

"And doesn't Higbee look just too Chicago beside the baron?" replied her brother.

The Higbee craft cut her way gracefully up to an anchorage near the *Viluca*, and launches from both yachts now prepared to land their people. At the landing Percival telephoned for a carriage. While they were waiting the Higbee party came ashore.

"Hello!" said Higbee; "if I'd known that was you we was chasing I'd have put on steam and left you out of sight."

"It's much better you didn't recognise us; these boiler explosions are so messy."

"Know the baron here?"

"Of course we know the baron. Ah, baron!"

"Ah, ha! very charmed, Mr. Bines and Miss Bines; it is of a long time that we are not encountered."

He was radiant; they had never before seen him thus. Mrs. Higbee hovered near him with an air of proud ownership. Pretty Millie Higbee posed gracefully at her side.

"This your carriage?" asked Higbee; "I must telephone for one myself. Going to the Mayson? So are we. See you again to-night. We're off for Bar Harbour early to-morrow."

"Looks as if there were something doing there," said Percival, as they drove off the wharf.

"Of course, stupid!" said his sister; "that's plain; only it isn't doing, it's already done. Isn't it funny, ma?"

"For a French person," observed Mrs. Bines, guardedly, "I always liked the baron."

"Of course," said her son, to Mauburn's mystification, "and the noblest men on this earth have to wear 'em."

The surmise regarding the Baron de Palliac and Millie Higbee proved to be correct. Percival came upon Higbee in the meditative enjoyment of his after-dinner cigar, out on the broad piazza.

"I s'pose you're on," he began; "the girl's engaged to that Frenchy."

"I congratulate him," said Percival, heartily.

"A real baron," continued Higbee. "I looked him up and made sure of that; title's good as wheat. God knows that never would 'a' got me, but the madam was set on it, and the girl too, and I had to give in. It seemed to be a question of him or some actor. The madam said I'd had my way about Hank, puttin' his poor stubby nose to the grindstone out there in Chicago, and makin' a plain insignificant business man out of him, and I'd ought to let her have her way with the girl, being that I couldn't expect her to go to work too. So Mil will work the society end. I says to the madam, I says, 'All right, have your own way; and we'll see whether you make more out of the girl than I make out of the boy,' I says. But it ain't going to be *all* digging up. I've made the baron promise to go into business with me, and though I ain't told him yet, I'm going to put out a line of Higbee's thin-sliced ham and bacon in glass jars with his crest on 'em for the French trade. This baron'll cost me more'n that sign I showed you coming out of the old town, and he won't give any such returns, but the crest on them jars, printed in three colours and gold, will be a bully ad; and it kept the women quiet," he concluded, apologetically.

"The baron's a good fellow," said Percival.

"Sure," replied Higbee. "They're all good fellows. Hank had the makin's of a good fellow in him. And say, young man, that reminds me; I hear all kinds of reports about your getting to be one yourself. Now I knew your father, Daniel J. Bines, and I liked him, and I like you; and I hope you won't get huffy, but from what they tell me you ain't doing yourself a bit of good."

"Don't believe all you hear," laughed Percival.

"Well, I'll tell you one thing plain, if you was my son, you'd fade right back to the packing-house along with Henry-boy. It's a pity you ain't got some one to shut down on you that way. They tell me you got your father's capacity for carrying liquor, and I hear you're known from one end of Broadway to the other as the easiest mark that ever came to town. They say you couldn't walk in your sleep without spending money. Now, excuse my plain speaking, but them are two reputations that are mighty hard to live up to beyond a certain limit. They've put lots of good weight-carriers off the track before they was due to go. I hear you got pinched in that wheat deal of Burman's?"

"Oh, only for a few hundred thousand. The reports of our losses were exaggerated. And we stood to win over—"

"Yes—you stood to win, and then you went 'way back and set down,' as the saying is. But it ain't the money. You've got too much of that, anyway, Lord knows. It's this everlasting hullabaloo and the drink that goes with it, and the general trifling sort of a dub it makes out of a young fellow. It's a pity you ain't my son; that's all I got to say. I want to see you again along in September after I get back from San Francisco; I'm going to try to get you interested in some business. That'd be good for you."

"You're kind, Mr. Higbee, and really I appreciate all you say; but you'll see me settle down pretty soon, quick as I get my bearings, and be a credit to the State of Montana."

"I say," said Mauburn, coming up, "do you see that angel of the flaming hair with that young Milbrey chap?"

The two men gazed where he was indicating.

"By Jove! she *is* a stunner, isn't she?" exclaimed Percival.

"Might be one of Shepler's party," suggested Higbee. "He has the Milbrey family out with him, and I see they landed awhile ago. You can bet that party's got more than her good looks, if the Milbreys are taking any interest in her. Well, I've got to take the madam and the young folks over to the Casino. So long!"

Fred Milbrey came up.

"Hello, you fellows!"

"Who is she?" asked the two in faultless chorus.

"We're going over to hear the music awhile. Come along and I'll present you."

"Rot the luck!" said Mauburn; "I'm slated to take Mrs. Drelmer and Miss Bines to a musicale at the Van Lorrecks, where I'm certain to fall asleep trying to look as if I quite liked it, you know."

"You come," Milbrey urged Percival. "My sister's there and the governor and mother."

But for the moment Percival was reflecting, going over in his mind the recent homily of Higbee. Higbee's opinion of the Milbreys also came back to him.

"Sorry, old man, but I've a headache, so you must excuse me for to-night. But I'll tell you, we'll all come over in the morning and go for a dip with you."

"Good! Stop for us at the Laurels, about eleven, or p'r'aps I'll stroll over and get you. I'm expecting some mail to be forwarded to this hotel."

He rejoined his companion, who had been chatting with a group of women near the door, and they walked away.

"*Isn't* she a stunner!" exclaimed Mauburn.

"She is a *peach!*" replied Percival, in tones of deliberate and intense conviction. "Whoever she is, I'll meet her to-morrow and ask her what she means by pretending to see anything in Milbrey. This thing has gone too far!"

Mauburn looked wistful but said nothing. After he had gone away with Mrs. Drelmer and Psyche, who soon came for him, Percival still sat revolving the paternal warnings of Higbee. He considered them seriously. He decided he ought to think more about what he was doing and what he should do. He decided, too, that he could think better with something mechanical to occupy his hands. He took a cab and was driven to the local branch of his favourite temple of chance. His host welcomed him at the door.

"Ah, Mr. Bines, a little recreation, eh? Your favourite dealer, Dutson, is here to-night, if you prefer bank."

Passing through the crowded, brightly-lighted rooms to one of the faro tables, where his host promptly secured a seat for him, he played meditatively until one o'clock; adding materially to his host's reasons for believing he had done wisely to follow his New York clients to their summer annex.

CHAPTER XXV.

Horace Milbrey Upholds the Dignity of His House

In the shade of the piazza at the Hotel Mayson next morning there was a sorting out of the mail that had been forwarded from the hotel in New York. The mail of Mrs. Bines was a joy to her son. There were three conventional begging letters, heart-breaking in their pathos, and composed with no mean literary skill. There was a letter from one of the maids at the Hightower for whose mother Mrs. Bines had secured employment in the family of a friend; a position, complained the daughter, "in which she finds constant hard labour caused by the quantity expected of her to attend to." There was also a letter from the lady's employer, saying she would not so much mind her laziness if she did not aggravate it by drink. Mrs. Bines sighed despairingly for the recalcitrant.

"And who's this wants more help until her husband's profession picks up again?" asked Percival.

"Oh, that's a poor little woman I helped. They call her husband 'the Terrible Iceman.'"

"But this is just the season for icemen!"

"Well," confessed his mother, with manifest reluctance, "he's a prize-fighter or something."

Percival gasped.

"—and he had a chance to make some money, only the man he fought against had some of his friends drug this poor fellow before their their meeting—and so of course he lost. If he hadn't been drugged he would have won the money, and now there's a law passed against it, and of course it isn't a very nice trade, but I think the law ought to be changed. He's got to live."

"I don't see why; not if he's the man I saw box one night last winter. He didn't have a single excuse for living. And what are these tickets,—'Grand Annual Outing and Games of the Egg-Candlers & Butter Drivers' Association at Sulzer's Harlem River Park. Ticket Admitting Lady and Gent, One dollar.' Heavens! What is it?"

"I promised to take ten tickets," said Mrs. Bines. "I must send them a check."

"But what are they?" her son insisted; "egg-candlers may be all right, but what are butter-drivers? Are you quite sure it's respectable? Why, I ask you, should an honest man wish to drive butter? That shows you what life in a great city does for the morally weak. Look out you don't get mixed up in it yourself, that's all I ask. They'll have you driving butter first thing you know. Thank heaven! thus far no Bines has ever candled an egg—and as for driving butter—" he stopped, with a shudder of extreme repugnance.

"And here's a notice about the excursions of the St. John's Guild. I've been on four already, and I want you to get me back to New York right away for the others. If you could only see all those babies we take out on the floating hospital, with two men in little boats behind to pick up those that fall overboard—and really it's a wonder any of them live through the summer in that cruel city. Down in Hester Street the other day four of them had a slice of watermelon from Mr. Slivinsky's stand on the corner, and when I saw them they were actually eating the hard, green rind. It was enough to kill a horse."

"Well, have your own fun," said her son, cheerfully. "Here's a letter from Uncle Peter I must read."

He drew his chair aside and began the letter:

"MONTANA CITY, July 21st, 1900.

"DEAR PETE:—Your letter and Martha's rec'd, and glad to hear from you. I leave latter part of this week for the mtns. Late setting out this season acct. rhumatiz caught last winter that laid me up all spring. It was so mortal dull here with you folks gone that I went out with a locating party to get the M. P. branch located ahead of the Short Line folks. So while you were having your fun there I was having mine here, and I had it good and plenty.

"The worst weather I ever did see, and I have seen some bad. Snow six to eight feet on a level and the mercury down as low as 62 with an ornery fierce wind. We lost four horses froze to death, and all but two of the men got froze up bad. We reached the head of Madison Valley Feb. 19, north of Red Bank Canyon, but it wasn't as easy as it sounds.

"Jan. 8, after getting out of supplies, we abandoned our camp at Riverside and moved 10 m. down the river carrying what we could on our backs. Met pack train with a few supplies that night, and next day I took part of the force in boat to meet over-due load of supplies. We got froze in the ice. Left party to break through and took Billy Brue and went ahead to hunt team. Billy and me lived four days on one lb. bacon. The second day Billy took some sickness so he could not eat hardly any food; the next day he was worse, and the last day he was so bad he said the bare sight of food made him gag. I think he was a liar, because he wasn't troubled none after we got to supplies again, but I couldn't do anything with him, and so I lived high and come out slick and fat. Finally we found the team coming in. They had got stuck in the river and we had to carry out the load on our backs, waist-deep in running water. I see some man in the East has a fad for breaking the ice in the river and going swimming. I would not do it for any fad. Slept in snow-drift that night in wet clothes, mercury 40 below. Was 18 days going 33 miles. Broke wagon twice, then broke sled and crippled one horse. Packed the other five and went on till snow was too deep. Left the horses where four out of five died and carried supplies the rest of the way on our backs. Moved camp again on our backs and got caught in a blizzard and nearly all of us got our last freezeup that time. Finally a Chinook opened the river and I took a boat up to get the abandoned camp. Got froze in harder than ever and had to walk out. Most of the men quit on account of frozen feet, etc., etc. They are a getting to be a sissy lot these days, rather lie around a hot stove all winter.

"I had to pull chain, cut brush, and shovel snow after the 1st Feb. Our last stage was from Fire Hole Basin to Madison Valley, 45 m. It was hell. Didn't see the sun but once after Feb. 1, and it stormed insessant, making short sights necessary, and with each one we would have to dig a hole to the ground and often a ditch or a tunnel through the snow to look through. The snow was soft to the bottom and an instrument would sink through."

"Here's a fine letter to read on a hot day," called Percival. "I'm catching cold." He continued.

"We have a very good line, better than from Beaver Canon, our maps filed and construction under way; all grading done and some track laid. That's what you call hustling. The main drawback is that Red Bank Canon. It's a regular avalanche for eight miles. The snow slides just fill the river. One just above our camp filled it for 1/4 mile and 40 feet deep and cut down 3 ft. trees like a razor shaves your face. I had to run to get out of the way. Reached Madison Valley with one tent and it looked more like mosquito bar than canvas. The old cloth wouldn't hardly hold the patches together. I slept out doors for six weeks. I got frost-bit considerable and the rhumatiz. I tell you, at 75 I ain't the man I used to be. I find I need a stout tent and a good warm sleeping bag for them kind of doings nowdays.

"Well, this Western country would be pretty dull for you I suppose going to balls and parties every night with the Astors and Vanderbilts. I hope you ain't cut loose none.

"By the way, that party that ground-sluiced us, Coplen he met a party in Spokane the other day that seen her in Paris last spring. She was laying in a stock of duds and the party gethered that she was going back to New York—"

The Milbreys, father and son, came up and greeted the group on the piazza.

"I've just frozen both ears reading a letter from my grandfather," said Percival. "Excuse me one moment and I'll be done."

"All right, old chap. I'll see if there's some mail for me. Dad can chat with the ladies. Ah, here's Mrs. Drelmer. Mornin'!"

Percival resumed his letter:

"—going back to New York and make the society bluff. They say she's got the face to do it all right. Coplen learned she come out here with a gambler from New Orleans and she was dealing bank herself up to Wallace for a spell while he was broke. This gambler he was the slickest short-card player ever struck hereabouts. He was too good. He was so good they shot him all up one night last fall over to Wardner. She hadn't lived with him for some time then, though Coplen says they was lawful man and wife, so I guess maybe she was glad when he got it good in the chest-place—"

Fred Milbrey came out of the hotel office.

"No mail," he said. "Come, let's be getting along. Finish your letter on the way, Bines."

"I've just finished," said Percival, glancing down the last sheet.

"—Coplen says she is now calling herself Mrs. Brench Wybert or some such name. I just thought I'd tell you in case you might run acrost her and—"

"Come along, old chap," urged Milbrey; "Mrs. Wybert will be waiting." His father had started off with Psyche. Mrs. Bines and Mrs. Drelmer were preparing to follow.

"I beg your pardon," said Percival, "I didn't quite catch the name."

"I say Mrs. Wybert and mother will be waiting—come along!"

"What name?"

"Wybert—Mrs. Brench Wybert—my friend—what's the matter?"

"We can't go;—that is—we can't meet her. Sis, come back a moment," he called to Psyche, and then:

"I want a word with you and your father, Milbrey."

The two joined the elder Milbrey and the three strolled out to the flower-bordered walk, while Psyche Bines went, wondering, back to her mother.

"What's all the row?" inquired Fred Milbrey.

"You've been imposed upon. This woman—this Mrs. Brench Wybert—there can be no mistake; you are sure that's the name?"

"Of course I'm sure; she's the widow of a Southern gentleman, Colonel Brench Wybert, from New Orleans."

"Yes, the same woman. There is no doubt that you have been imposed upon. The thing to do is to drop her quick—she isn't right."

"In what way has my family been imposed upon, Mr. Bines?" asked the elder Milbrey, somewhat perturbed; "Mrs. Wybert is a lady of family and large means—"

"Yes, I know, she has, or did have a while ago, two million dollars in cold cash."

"Well, Mr. Bines—?"

"Can't you take my word for it, that she's not right—not the woman for your wife and daughter to meet?"

"Look here, Bines," the younger Milbrey spluttered, "this won't do, you know. If you've anything to say against Mrs. Wybert, you'll have to say it out and you'll have to be responsible to me, sir."

"Take my word that you've been imposed upon; she's not—not the kind of person you would care to know, to be thrown—"

"I and my family have found her quite acceptable, Mr. Bines," interposed the father, stiffly. "Her deportment is scrupulously correct, and I am in her confidence regarding certain very extensive investments—she cannot be an impostor, sir!"

"But I tell you she isn't right," insisted Percival, warmly.

"Oh, I see," said the younger Milbrey—his face clearing all at once. "It's all right, dad, come on!"

"If you insist," said Percival, "but none of us can meet her."

"It's all right, dad—I understand—"

"Nor can we know any one who receives her."

"Really, sir," began the elder Milbrey, "your effrontery in assuming to dictate the visiting list of my family is overwhelming."

"If you won't take my word I shall have to dictate so far as I have any personal control over it."

"Don't mind him, dad—I know all about it, I tell you—I'll explain later to you."

"Why," exclaimed Percival, stung to the revelation, "that woman, this woman now waiting with your wife and daughter, was my—"

"Stop, Mr. Bines—not another word, if you please!" The father raised his hand in graceful dismissal. "Let this terminate the acquaintance between our families! No more, sir!" and he turned away, followed by his son. As they walked out through the grounds and turned up the street the young man spoke excitedly, while his father slightly bent his head to listen, with an air of distant dignity.

"What's the trouble, Perce?" asked his sister, as he joined the group on the piazza.

"The trouble is that we've just had to cut that fine old New York family off our list."

"What, not the Milbreys!" exclaimed Mrs. Drelmer.

"The same. Now mind, sis, and you, ma—you're not to know them again—and mind this—if any one else wants to present you to a Mrs. Wybert—a Mrs. Brench Wybert—don't you let them. Understand?"

"I thought as much," said Mrs. Drelmer; "she acted just the least little bit *too* right."

"Well, I haven't my hammer with me—but remember, now, sis, it's for something else than because her father's cravats were the ready-to-wear kind, or because her worthy old grandfather inhaled his soup. Don't forget that."

"As there isn't anything else to do," he suggested, a few moments later, "why not get under way and take a run up the coast?"

"But I must get back to my babies," said Mrs. Bines, plaintively. "Here I've been away four days."

"All right, ma, I suppose we shall have to take you there, only let's get out of here right away. We can bring sis and you back, Mrs. Drelmer, when those people we don't know get off again. There's Mauburn; I'll tell him."

"I'll have my dunnage down directly," said Mauburn.

Up the street driving a pony-cart came Avice Milbrey. Obeying a quick impulse, Percival stepped to the curb as she came opposite to him. She pulled over. She was radiant in the fluffs of summer white, her hat and gown touched with bits of the same vivid blue that shone in her eyes. The impulse that had prompted him to hail her now prompted wild words. His long habit of thought concerning her enabled him to master this foolishness. But at least he could give her a friendly word of warning. She greeted him with the pretty reserve in her manner that had long marked her bearing toward him.

"Good-morning! I've borrowed this cart of Elsie Vainer to drive down to the yacht station for lost mail. Isn't the day perfect—and isn't this the dearest fat, sleepy pony, with his hair in his eyes?"

"Miss Milbrey, there's a woman who seems to be a friend of your family—a Mrs.—"

"Mrs. Wybert; yes, you know her?"

"No, I'd never seen her until last night, nor heard that name until this morning; but I know of her."

"Yes?"

"It became necessary just now—really, it is not fair of me to speak to you at all—"

"Why, pray?—not fair?"

"I had to tell your father and brother that we could not meet Mrs. Wybert, and couldn't know any one who received her."

"There! I knew the woman wasn't right directly I heard her speak. Surely a word to my father was enough."

"But it wasn't, I'm sorry to say. Neither he nor your brother would take my word, and when I started to give my reasons—something it would have been very painful for me to do—your father refused to listen, and declared the acquaintance between our families at an end."

"Oh!"

"It hurt me in a way I can't tell you, and now, even this talk with you is off-side play. Miss Milbrey!"

"Mr. Bines!"

"I wouldn't have said what I did to your father and brother without good reason."

"I am sure of that, Mr. Bines."

"Without reasons I was sure of, you know, so there could be no chance of any mistake."

"Your word is enough for me, Mr. Bines."

"Miss Milbrey—you and I—there's always been something between us—something different from what is between most people. We've never talked straight out since I came to New York—I'll be sorry, perhaps, for saying as much as I am saying, after awhile—but we may not talk again at all—I'm afraid you may misunderstand me—but I must say it—I should like to go away knowing you would have no friendship,—no intimacy whatever with that woman."

"I promise you I shall not, Mr. Bines; they can row if they like."

"And yet it doesn't seem fair to have you promise as if it were a consideration for *me*, because I've no right to ask it. But if I felt sure that you took my word quite as if I were a stranger, and relied upon it enough to have no communication or intercourse of any sort whatsoever with her, it would be a great satisfaction to me."

"I shall not meet her again. And—thank you!" There was a slight unsteadiness once in her voice, and he could almost have sworn her eyes showed that old brave wistfulness.

"—and quite as if you were a stranger."

"Thank you! and, Miss Milbrey?"

"Yes?"

"Your brother may become entangled in some way with this woman."

"It's entirely possible."

Her voice was cool and even again.

"He might even marry her."

"She has money, I believe; he might indeed."

"Always money!" he thought; then aloud:

"If you find he means to, Miss Milbrey, do anything you can to prevent it. It wouldn't do at all, you know."

"Thank you, Mr. Bines; I shall remember."

"I—I think that's all—and I'm sorry we're not—our families are not to be friends any more."

She smiled rather painfully, with an obvious effort to be conventional.

"*So* sorry! Good-bye!"

He looked after her as she drove off. She sat erect, her head straight to the front, her trim shoulders erect, and the whip grasped firmly. He stood motionless until the fat pony had jolted sleepily around the corner.

"Bines, old boy!" he said to himself, "you nearly *made* one of yourself there. I didn't know you had such ready capabilities for being an ass."

CHAPTER XXVI.

A Hot Day in New York, with News of an Interesting Marriage

At five o'clock that day the prow of the *Viluca* cut the waters of Newport harbour around Goat Island, and pointed for New York.

"Now is your time," said Mrs. Drelmer to Mauburn. "I'm sure the girl likes you, and this row with the Milbreys has cut off any chance that cub had. Why not propose to her to-night?"

"I *have* seemed to be getting on," answered Mauburn. "But wait a bit. There's that confounded girl over there. No telling what she'll do. She might knock things on the head any moment."

"All the more reason for prompt action, and there couldn't very well be anything to hurt you."

"By Jove! that's so; there couldn't, very well, could there? I'll take your advice."

And so it befell that Mauburn and Miss Bines sat late on deck that night, and under the witchery of a moon that must long since have become hardened to the spectacle, the old, old story was told, to the accompaniment of the engine's muffled throb, and the soft purring of the silver waters as they slipped by the boat and blended with the creamy track astern. So little variation was there in the time-worn tale, and in the maid's reception of it, that neither need here be told of in detail.

Nor were the proceedings next morning less tamely orthodox. Mrs. Bines managed to forget her relationship of elder sister to the poor long enough to behave as a mother ought when the heart of her daughter has been given into a true-love's keeping. Percival deported himself cordially.

"I'm really glad to hear it," he said to Mauburn. "I'm sure you'll make sis as good a husband as she'll make you a wife; and that's very good, indeed. Let's fracture a cold quart to the future Lady Casselthorpe."

"And to the future Lord Casselthorpe!" added Mrs. Drelmer, who was warmly enthusiastic.

"Such a brilliant match," she murmured to Percival, when they had touched glasses in the after-cabin. "I know more than one New York girl who'd have jumped at the chance."

"We'll try to bear our honours modestly," he answered her.

The yacht lay at her anchorage in the East River. Percival made preparations to go ashore with his mother.

"Stay here with the turtle-doves," he said to Mrs. Drelmer, "far enough off, of course, to let them coo, and I'll be back with any people I can pick up for a cruise."

"Trust me to contract the visual and aural infirmities of the ideal chaperone," was Mrs. Drelmer's cheerful response. "And if you should run across that poor dear of a husband of mine, tell him not to slave himself to death for his thoughtless butterfly of a wife, who toils not, neither does she spin. Tell him," she added, "that I'm playing dragon to this engaged couple. It will cheer up the poor dear."

The city was a fiery furnace. But its prisoners were not exempt from its heat, like certain holy ones of old. On the dock where Percival and his mother landed was a listless throng of them, gasping for the faint little breezes that now and then blew in from the water. A worn woman with unkempt hair, her waist flung open at the neck, sat in a spot of shade, and soothed a baby already grown too weak to be fretful. Mrs. Bines spoke to her, while Percival bought a morning paper from a tiny newsboy, who held his complete attire under one arm, his papers under the other, and his pennies in his mouth, keeping meantime a shifty side-glance on the policeman a block away, who might be expected to interfere with his contemplated plunge.

"That poor soul's been there all night," said Mrs. Bines. "She's afraid her baby's going to die; and yet she was so cheerful and polite about it, and when I gave her some money the poor thing blushed. I told her to bring the baby down to the floating hospital to-morrow, but I mistrust it won't be alive, and—oh, there's an ambulance backed up to the sidewalk; see what the matter is."

As Percival pushed through the outer edge of the crowd, a battered wreck of a man past middle age was being lifted into the ambulance. His eyes were closed, his face a dead, chalky white, and his body hung limp.

"Sunstroke?" asked Percival.

The overworked ambulance surgeon, who seemed himself to be in need of help, looked up.

"Nope; this is a case of plain starvation. I'm nearer sunstroke myself than he is—not a wink of sleep for two nights now. Fifty-two runs since yesterday at this time, and the bell still ringing. Gee! but it's hot. This lad won't ever care about the weather again, though," he concluded, jumping on to the rear step and grasping the rails on either side while the driver clanged his gong and started off.

"Was it sunstroke?" asked Mrs. Bines.

"Man with stomach trouble," answered her son, shortly.

"They're so careless about what they eat this hot weather," Mrs. Bines began, as they walked toward a carriage; "all sorts of heavy foods and green fruit—"

"Well, if you must know, this one had been careless enough not to eat anything at all. He was starved."

"Oh, dear! What a place! here people are starving, and look at us! Why, we wasted enough from breakfast to feed a small family. It isn't right. They never would allow such a thing in Montana City."

They entered the carriage and were driven slowly up a side street where slovenly women idled in windows and doorways and half-naked children chased excitedly after the ice-wagons.

"I used to think it wasn't right myself until I learned not to question the ways of Providence."

"Providence, your grandmother! Look at those poor little mites fighting for that ice!"

"We have to accept it. It seems to be proof of the Creator's versatility. It isn't every one who would be nervy enough and original enough to make a world where people starve to death right beside those who have too much."

"That's rubbish!"

"You're blasphemous! and you're overwrought about the few cases of need here. Think of those two million people that have just starved to death in India."

"That wasn't my fault."

"Exactly; if you'd been there the list might have been cut down four or five thousand; not more. It was the fault of whoever makes the weather. It didn't rain and their curry crop failed—or whatever they raise—and there you are; and we couldn't help matters any by starving ourselves to death."

"Well, I know of a few matters here I can help. And just look at all those empty houses boarded up!" she cried later, as they crossed Madison Avenue. "Those poor things bake themselves to death down in their little ovens, and these great cool places are all shut up. Why, that poor little baby's hands were just like bird's claws."

"Well, don't take your sociology too seriously," Percival warned her, as they reached the hotel. "Being philanthropic is obeying an instinct just as selfish as any of the others. A little of it is all right—but don't be a slave to your passions. And be careful of your health."

In his mail at the Hightower was a note from Mrs. Akemit:

"NEW LONDON, July 29th.

"You DEAR THOUGHTFUL MAN: I'll be delighted, and the aunt, a worthy sister of the dear bishop, has consented. She is an acidulous maiden person with ultra-ritualistic tendencies. At present she is strong on the reunion of Christendom, and holds that the Anglican must be the unifying medium of the two religious extremes. So don't say I didn't warn you fairly. She will, however, impart an air of Episcopalian propriety to that naughty yacht of yours—something sadly needed if I am to believe the tales I hear about its little voyages to nowhere in particular.

"Babe sends her love, and says to tell 'Uncle Percibal' that the ocean tastes 'all nassy.' She stood upon the beach yesterday after making this discovery involuntarily, and proscribed it with one magnificent wave of her hand and a brief exclamation of disgust—turned her back disrespectfully upon a body of water that is said to cover two-thirds—or is it three-fourths?—of the earth's surface. Think of it! She seemed to suspect she had been imposed upon in the matter of its taste, and is going to tell the janitor directly we get home, in order that the guilty ones may be seen to. Her little gesture of dismissal was superbly contemptuous. I wish you had been with me to watch her. Yes, the bathing-suit does have little touches of red, and red—but this will never do. Give us a day's notice, and believe me,

"Sincerely,

"FLORENCE VERDON AKEMIT.

"P.S. Babe is on the back of my chair, cuddling down in my neck, and says, 'Send him your love, too, Mommie. Now don't you forget.'"

He telegraphed Mrs. Akemit: "Will reach New London to-morrow. Assure your aunt of my delight at her acceptance. I have long held that the reunion must come as she thinks it will."

Then he ventured into the heat and glare of Broadway where humanity stewed and wilted. At Thirty-second Street he ran into Burman, with whom he had all but cornered wheat.

"You're the man I wanted to see," said Percival.

"Hurry and look! I'm melting fast."

"Come off on the yacht."

"My preserver! I was just going down to the Oriental, but your dug-out wins me hands down. Come into this poor-man's club. I must have a cold drink taller than a church steeple."

"Anybody else in town we can take?"

"There's Billy Yelverton—our chewing-gum friend; just off the *Lucania* last night; and Eddie Arledge and his wife. They're in town because Eddie was up in supplementary or something—some low, coarse brute of a tradesman wanted his old bill paid, and wouldn't believe Eddie when he said he couldn't spare the money. Eddie is about as lively as a dish of cold breakfast food, but his wife is all right, all right. Retiring from the footlights' glare didn't spoil Mrs. E. Wadsworth Arledge,—not so you could notice it."

"Well, see Eddie if you can, and I'll find Yelverton; he's probably at the hotel yet; and meet me there by five, so we can get out of this little amateur hell."

"And quit trying to save that collar," urged Burman, as they parted; "you look foolisher than a horse in a straw hat with it on anyway. Let it go and tuck in your handkerchief like the rest of us. See you at five!"

At the hour named the party had gathered. Percival, Arledge and his lively wife, Yelverton, who enjoyed the rare distinction of having lost money to Percival, and Burman. East they drove through the street where less fortunate mortals panted in the dead afternoon shade, and out on to the dock, whence the *Viluca's* naphtha launch presently put them aboard that sumptuous craft. A little breeze there made the heat less oppressive.

"We'll be under way as soon as they fetch that luggage out," Percival assured his guests.

"It's been frightfully oppressive all day, even out here," said Mrs. Drelmer, "but the engaged ones haven't lost their tempers once, even if the day was trying. And really they're the most unemotional and matter-of-fact couple I ever saw. Oh! do give me that stack of papers until I catch up with the news again."

Percival relinquished to her the evening papers he had bought before leaving the hotel, and Mrs. Drelmer in the awninged shade at the stern of the boat was soon running through them.

The others had gone below, where Percival was allotting staterooms, and urging every one to "order whatever cold stuff you like and get into as few things as the law allows. For my part, I'd like to wear nothing but a cold bath."

Mrs. Drelmer suddenly betrayed signs of excitement. She sat up straight in the wicker deck-chair, glanced down a column of her newspaper, and then looked up.

Mauburn's head appeared out of the cabin's gloom. He was still speaking to some one below. Mrs. Drelmer rattled the paper and waved it at him. He came up the stairs.

"What's the row?"

"Read it!"

He took the paper and glanced at the headlines. "I knew she'd do it. A chap always comes up with something of that sort, and I was beginning to feel so chippy!" He read:

"London, July 30th.—Lord Casselthorpe to-day wed Miss 'Connie' Burke, the music-hall singer who has been appearing at the Alhambra. The marriage was performed, by special license, at St. Michael's Church, Chester Square, London, the Rev. Canon Mecklin, sub-dean of the Chapel Royal, officiating. The honeymoon will be spent at the town-house of the groom, in York Terrace. Lord Casselthorpe has long been known as the blackest sheep of the British Peerage, being called the 'Coster Peer' on account of his unconventional language, his coarse manner, and slovenly attire. Two years ago he was warned off Newmarket Heath and the British turf by the Jockey Club. He is eighty-eight years old. The bride, like some other lights of the music-hall who have become the consorts of Britain's hereditary legislators, has enjoyed considerable ante-nuptial celebrity among the gilded youth of the metropolis, and is said to have been especially admired at one time by the next in line of this illustrious family, the Hon. Cecil G.H. Mauburn.

"The Hon. Cecil G. H. Mauburn, mentioned in the above cable despatch, has been rather well-known in New York society for two years past. His engagement to the daughter of a Montana mining magnate, not long deceased, has been persistently rumoured."

Mauburn was pale under his freckles.

"Have they seen it yet?"

"I don't think so," she answered. "We might drop these papers over the rail here."

"That's rot, Mrs. Drelmer; it's sure to be talked of, and anyway I don't want to be sneaky, you know."

Percival came up from the cabin with a paper in his hand.

"I see you have it, too," he said, smiling. "Burman just handed me this."

"Isn't it perfectly disreputable!" exclaimed Mrs. Drelmer.

"Why? I only hope I'll have as much interest in life by the time I'm that age."

"But how will your sister take it?" asked Mauburn; "she may be afraid this will knock my title on the head, you know."

"Oh, I see," said Percival; "I hadn't thought of that."

"Only it can't," continued Mauburn. "Hang it all, that blasted old beggar will be eighty-nine, you know, in a fortnight. There simply can't be any issue of the marriage, and that—that blasted—"

"Better not try to describe her—while I'm by, you know," said Mrs. Drelmer, sympathetically.

"Well—his wife—you know, will simply worry him into the grave a bit sooner, I fancy—that's all can possibly come of it."

"Well, old man," said Percival, "I don't pretend to know the workings of my sister's mind, but you ought to be able to win a girl on your own merits, title or no title."

"Awfully good of you, old chap. I'm sure she does care for me."

"But of course it will be only fair to sis to lay the matter before her just as it is."

"To be sure!" Mauburn assented.

"And now, thank the Lord, we're under way. Doesn't that breeze save your life, though? We'll eat here on deck."

The *Viluca* swung into mid-stream, and was soon racing to the north with a crowded Fall River boat.

"But anyway," concluded Percival, after he had explained Mauburn's position to his sister, "he's a good fellow, and if you suit each other even the unexpected wouldn't make any difference."

"Of course not," she assented, "'the rank is but the guinea's stamp,' I know—but I wasn't meaning to be married for quite a time yet, anyway,—it's such fun just being engaged."

"A mint julep?" Mauburn was inquiring of one who had proposed it. "Does it have whiskey in it?"

"It does," replied Percival, overhearing the question; "whiskey may be said to pervade, even to infest it. Try five or six, old man; that many make a great one-night trouble cure. And I can't have any one with troubles on this Cunarder—not for the next thirty days. I need cheerfulness and rest for a long time after this day in town. Ah! General Hemingway says that dinner is served; let's be at it before the things get all hot!"

CHAPTER XXVII.

A Sensational Turn in the Milbrey Fortunes

It was a morning early in November. In the sedate Milbrey dining-room a brisk wood-fire dulled the edge of the first autumn chill. At the breakfast-table, comfortably near the hearth, sat Horace Milbrey. With pointed spoon he had daintily scooped the golden pulp from a Florida orange, touched the tips of his slender white fingers to the surface of the water in the bowl, and was now glancing leisurely at the headlines of his paper, while his breakfast appetite gained agreeable zest from the acid fruit.

On the second page of the paper the names in a brief item arrested his errant glance. It disclosed that Mr. Percival Bines had left New York the day before with a party of guests on his special car, to shoot quail in North Carolina. Mr. Milbrey glanced at the two shells of the orange which the butler was then removing.

"What a hopeless brute that fellow was!" he reflected.. He was recalling a dictum once pronounced by Mr. Bines. "Oranges should never be eaten in public," he had said with that lordly air of dogmatism characteristic of him. "The only right way to eat a juicy orange is to disrobe, grasp the fruit firmly in both hands and climb into a bath-tub half full of water."

The finished epicure shuddered at the recollection, poignantly, quite as if a saw were being filed in the next room.

The disagreeable emotion was allayed, however, by the sight of his next course—*oeufs aux saucissons*. Tender, poetic memories stirred within him. The little truffled French sausages aroused his better nature. Two of them reposed luxuriously upon an egg-divan in the dainty French baking-dish of dull green. Over them—a fitting baptism, was the rich wine sauce of golden brown—a sauce that might have been the tears of envious angels, wept over a mortal creation so faultlessly precious.

Mrs. Milbrey entered, news of importance visibly animating her. Her husband arose mechanically, placed the chair for her, and resumed his fork in an ecstasy of concentration. Yet, though Mrs. Milbrey was full of talk, like a charged siphon, needing but a slight pressure to pour forth matters of grave moment, she observed the engrossment of her husband, and began on the half of an orange. She knew from experience that he would be deaf, for the moment, to anything less than an alarm of fire.

When he had lovingly consumed the last morsel he awoke to her presence and smiled benignantly.

"My dear, don't fail to try them, they're exquisitely perfect!"

"You really *must* talk to Avice," his wife replied.

Mr. Milbrey sighed, deprecatingly. He could remember no time within five years when that necessity had not weighed upon his father's sense of duty like a vast boulder of granite. He turned to welcome the diversion provided by the *rognons sautees* which Jarvis at that moment uncovered before him with a discreet flourish.

"Now you really must," continued his wife, "and you'll agree with me when I tell you why."

"But, my dear, I've already talked to the girl exhaustively. I've pointed out that her treatment of Mrs. Wybert—her perverse refusal to meet the lady at all, is quite as absurd as it is rude, and that if Fred chooses to marry Mrs. Wybert it is her duty to act the part of a sister even if she cannot bring herself to feel it. I've assured her that Mrs. Wybert's antecedents are all they should be; not illustrious, perhaps, but eminently respectable. Indeed, I quite approve of the Southern aristocracy. But she constantly recalls what that snobbish Bines was unfair enough to tell her. I've done my utmost to convince her that Bines spoke in the way he did about Mrs. Wybert because he knew she was aware of those ridiculous tales of his mother's illiteracy. But Avice is—er—my dear, she is like her mother in more ways than one. Assuredly she doesn't take it from me."

He became interested in the kidneys. "If Marie had been a man," he remarked, feelingly, "I often suspect that her fame as a *chef* would have been second to none. Really, the suavity of her sauces is a never-ending delight to me."

"I haven't told you yet the reason—a new reason—why you must talk to Avice."

"The money—yes, yes, my dear, I know, we all know. Indeed, I've put it to her plainly. She knows how sorely Fred needs it. She knows how that beast of a tailor is threatening to be nasty—and I've explained how invaluable Mrs. Wybert would be, reminding her of that lady's generous hint about the rise in Federal Steel, which enabled me to net the neat little profit of ten thousand dollars a month ago, and how, but for that, we might have been acutely distressed. Yet she stubbornly clings to the notion that this marriage would be a *mesalliance* for the Milbreys."

"I agree with her," replied his wife, tersely.

Mr. Milbrey looked perplexed but polite.

"I quite agree with Avice," continued the lady. "That woman hasn't been right, Horace, and she isn't right. Young Bines knew what he was talking about. I haven't lived my years without being able to tell that after five minutes with her, clever as she is. I can read her. Like so many of those women, she has an intense passion to be thought respectable, and she's come into money enough—God only knows how—to gratify it. I could tell it, if nothing else showed it, by the way in which she overdoes respectability. She has the thousand and one artificial little rules for propriety that one never does have when one has been bred to it. That kind of woman is certain to lapse sooner or later. She would marry Fred because of his standing, because he's a favourite with the smart people she thinks she'd like to be pally with. Then, after a little she'd run off with a German-dialect comedian or something, like that appalling person Normie Whitmund married."

"But the desire to be respectable, my dear—and you say this woman has it—is a mighty lever. I'm no cynic about your sex, but I shudder to think of their—ah—eccentricities if it should cease to be a factor in the feminine equation."

"It's nothing more than a passing fad with this person—besides, that's not what I've to tell you."

"But you, yourself, were not averse to Fred's marrying her, in spite of these opinions you must secretly have held."

"Not while it seemed absolutely necessary—not while the case was so brutally desperate, when we were actually pressed—"

"Remember, my dear, there's nothing magic in those ten thousand dollars. They're winged dollars like all their mates, and most of them, I'm sorry to say, have already flown to places where they'd long been expected."

Mrs. Milbrey's sensation was no longer to be repressed. She had toyed with the situation sufficiently. Her husband was now skilfully dissecting the devilled thighs of an immature chicken.

"Horace," said his wife, impressively, "Avice has had an offer of marriage—from—"

He looked up with new interest.

"From Rulon Shepler."

He dropped knife and fork. Shepler, the man of mighty millions! The undisputed monarch of finance! The cold-blooded, calculating sybarite in his lighter moments, but a man whose values as a son-in-law were so ideally superb that the Milbrey ambition had never vaulted high enough even to overlook them for one daring moment! Shepler, whom he had known so long and so intimately, with never the audacious thought of a union so stupendously glorious!

"Margaret, you're jesting!"

Mrs. Milbrey scorned to be dazzled by her triumph.

"Nonsense! Shepler asked her last night to marry him."

"It's bewildering! I never dreamed—"

"I've expected it for months. I could tell you the very moment when the idea first seized the man—on the yacht last summer. I was sure she interested him, even before his wife died two years ago."

"Margaret, it's too good to be true!"

"If you think it is I'll tell you something that isn't: Avice practically refused him."

Her husband pushed away his plate; the omission of even one regretful glance at its treasures betrayed the strong emotion under which he laboured.

"This is serious," he said, quietly. "Let us get at it. Tell me if you please!"

"She came to me and cried half the night. She refused him definitely at first, but he begged her to consider, to take a month to think it over—"

Milbrey gasped. Shepler, who commanded markets to rise and they rose, or to fall and they fell—Shepler begging, entreating a child of his! Despite the soul-sickening tragedy of it, the situation was not without its element of sublimity.

"She will consider; she *will* reflect?"

"You're guessing now, and you're as keen at that as I. Avice is not only amazingly self-willed, as you intimated a moment since, but she is intensely secretive. When she left me I could get nothing from her whatever. She was wretchedly sullen and taciturn."

"But why *should* she hesitate? Shepler—Rulon Shepler! My God! is the girl crazy? The very idea of hesitation is preposterous!"

"I can't divine her. You know she has acted perversely in the past. I used to think she might have some affair of which we knew nothing—something silly and romantic. But if she had any such thing I'm sure it was ended, and she'd have jumped at this chance a year ago. You know yourself she was ready to marry young Bines, and was really disappointed when he didn't propose."

"But this is too serious." He tinkled the little silver bell.

"Find out if Miss Avice will be down to breakfast."

"Yes, sir."

"If she's not coming down I shall go up," declared Mr. Milbrey when the man had gone.

"She's stubborn," cautioned his wife.

"Gad! don't I know it?"

Jarvis returned.

"Miss Avice won't be down, sir, and I'm to fetch her up a pot of coffee, sir."

"Take it at once, and tell her I shall be up to see her presently." Jarvis vanished.

"I think I see a way to put pressure on her, that is if the morning hasn't already brought her back to her senses."

At four o'clock that afternoon, Avice Milbrey's ring brought Mrs. Van Geist's butler to the door.

"Sandon, is Aunt Cornelia at home?"

"Yes, Miss Milbrey, she's confined to her room h'account h'of a cold, miss."

"Thank heaven!"

"Yes, miss—certainly! will you go h'up to her?"

"And Mutterchen, dear, it was a regular bombshell," she concluded after she had fluttered some of the November freshness into Mrs. Van Geist's room, and breathlessly related the facts.

"You demented creature! I should say it must have been."

"Now, don't lecture!"

"But Shepler is one of the richest men in New York."

"Dad already suspects as much."

"And he's kind, he's a big-hearted chap, a man of the world, generous—a—"

"'A woman fancier,' Fidelia Oldaker calls him."

"My dear, if he fancies you—"

"There, you old conservative, I've heard all his good points, and my duty has been written before me in letters of fire. Dad devoted three hours to writing it this morning, so don't, please, say over any of the moral maxims I'm likely to have heard."

"But why are you unwilling?"

"Because—because I'm wild, I fancy—just because I don't like the idea of marrying that man. He's such a big, funny, round head, and positively no neck—his head just rolls around on his big, pillowy shoulders—and then he gets little right at once, tapers right off to a point with those tiny feet."

"It isn't easy to have everything."

"It wouldn't be easy to have him, either."

Mrs. Van Geist fixed her niece with a sudden look of suspicion.

"Has—has that man anything to do with your refusal?"

"No—not a thing—I give you my word, auntie. If he had been what I once dreamed he was no one would be asking me to marry him now, but—do you know what I've decided? Why, that he is a joke—that's all—just a joke. You needn't think of him, Mutterchen—I don't, except to think it was funny that he should have impressed me so—he's simply a joke."

"I could have told you as much long ago."

"Tell me something now. Suppose Fred marries that Wybert woman."

"It will be a sorry day for Fred."

"Of course! Now see how I'm pinned. Dad and the mater both say the same now—they're more severe than I was. Only we were never in such straits for money. It must be had. So this is the gist of it: I ought to marry Rulon Shepler in order to save Fred from a marriage that might get us into all sorts of scandal."

"Well?"

"Well, I would do a lot for Fred. He has faults, but he's always been good to me."

"And so?"

"And so it's a question whether he marries a very certain kind of woman or whether I marry a very different kind of man."

"How do you feel?"

"For one thing Fred sha'n't get into that kind of muss if I can save him from it."

"Then you'll marry Shepler?"

"I'm still uncertain about Mr. Shepler."

"But you say—"

"Yes, I know, but I've reasons for being uncertain. If I told you you'd say they're like the most of a woman's reasons, mere fond, foolish hopes, so I won't tell you."

"Well, dear, work it out by your lonely if you must. I believe you'll do what's best for everybody in the end. And I am glad that your father and Margaret take your view of that woman."

"I was sure she wasn't right—and I knew Mr. Bines was too much of a man to speak of her as he did without positive knowledge. Now please give me some tea and funny little cakes; I'm famished."

"Speaking of Mr. Bines," said Mrs. Van Geist, when the tea had been brought by Sandon, "I read in the paper this morning that he'd taken a party to North Carolina for the quail shooting, Eddie Arledge and his wife and that Mr. and Mrs. Garmer, and of course Florence Akemit. Should you have thought she'd marry so soon after her divorce? They say Bishop Doolittle is frightfully vexed with her."

"Really I hadn't heard. Whom is Florence to marry?"

"Mr. Bines, to be sure! Where have you been? You know she was on his yacht a whole month last summer—the bishop's sister was with her— highly scandalised all the time by the drinking and gaiety, and now every one's looking for the engagement to be announced. Here, what did I do with that *Town Topics* Cousin Clint left? There it is on the tabouret. Read the paragraph at the top of the page." Avice read:

"An engagement that is rumoured with uncommon persistence will put society on the *qui vive* when it is definitely announced. The man in the case is the young son of a mining Croesus from Montana, who has inherited the major portion of his father's millions and who began to dazzle upper Broadway about a year since by the reckless prodigality of his ways. His blond *innamorata* is a recent *divorcee* of high social standing, noted for her sparkling wit and an unflagging exuberance of spirits. The interest of the gossips, however, centres chiefly in the uncle of the lady, a Right Reverend presiding over a bishopric not a thousand miles from New York, and in the attitude he will assume toward her contemplated remarriage. At the last

Episcopal convention this godly and well-learned gentleman was a vehement supporter of the proposed canon to prohibit absolutely the marriage of divorced persons; and though he stoutly championed his bewitching niece through the infelicities that eventuated in South Dakota, *on dit* that he is highly wrought up over her present intentions, and has signified unmistakably his severest disapproval. However, *nous verrons ce que nous verrons.*"

"But, Mutterchen, that's only one of those absurd, vulgar things that wretched paper is always printing. I could write dozens of them myself. Tom Banning says they keep one man writing them all the time, out of his own imagination, and then they put them in like raisins in a cake."

"But, my dear, I'm quite sure this is authentic. I know from Fidelia Oldaker that the bishop began to cut up about it to Florence, and Florence defied him. That ancient theory that most gossip is without truth was exploded long ago. As a matter of fact most gossip, at least about the people we know, doesn't do half justice to the facts. But, really, I can't see why he fancied Florence Akemit. I should have thought he'd want some one a bit less fluttery."

"I dare say you're right, about the gossip, I mean—" Miss Milbrey remarked when she had finished her tea, and refused the cakes. "I remember, now, one day when we met at her place, and he seemed so much at home there. Of course, it must be so. How stupid of me to doubt it! Now I must run. Good-bye, you old dear, and be good to the cold."

"Let me know what you do."

"Indeed I shall; you shall be the first one to know. My mind is really, you know, *almost* made up."

A week later Mr. and Mrs. Horace Milbrey announced in the public prints the engagement of their daughter Avice to Mr. Rulon Shepler.

CHAPTER XXVIII.

Uncle Peter Bines Comes to Town With His Man

One day in December Peter Bines of Montana City dropped in on the family,—came with his gaunt length of limb, his kind, brown old face with eyes sparkling shrewdly far back under his grizzled brows, with his rough, resonant, musical voice, the spring of youth in his step, and the fresh, confident strength of the big hills in his bearing.

He brought Billy Brue with him, a person whose exact social status some of Percival's friends were never able to fix with any desirable certainty. Thus, Percival had presented the old man, the morning after his arrival, to no less a person than Herbert Delancey Livingston, with whom he had smoked a cigar of unusual excellence in the *cafe* of the Hightower Hotel.

"If you fancy that weed, Mr. Bines," said Livingston, graciously, to the old man, "I've a spare couple of hundred I'd like to let you have. The things were sent me, but I find them rather stiffish. If your man's about the hotel I'll give him a card to my man, and let him fetch them."

"My man?" queried Uncle Peter, and, sighting Billy Brue at that moment, "why, yes, here's my man, now. Mr. Brue, shake hands with Mr. Livingston. Billy, go up to the address he gives you, and get some of these se-gars. You'll relish 'em as much as I do. Now don't talk to any strangers, don't get run over, and don't lose yourself."

Livingston had surrendered a wavering and uncertain hand to the warm, reassuring clasp of Mr. Brue.

"He ain't much fur style, Billy ain't," Uncle Peter explained when that person had gone upon his errand, "he ain't a mite gaudy, but he's got friendly feelings."

The dazed scion of the Livingstons had thereupon made a conscientious tour of his clubs in a public hansom, solely for the purpose of relating this curious adventure to those best qualified to marvel at it.

The old man's arrival had been quite unexpected. Not only had he sent no word of his coming, but he seemed, indeed, not to know what his reasons had been for doing a thing so unusual.

"Thought I'd just drop in on your all and say 'howdy,'" had been his first avowal, which was lucid as far as it went. Later he involved himself in explanations that were both obscure and conflicting. Once it was that he had felt a sudden great longing for the life of a gay city. Then it was that he would have been content in Montana City, but that he had undertaken the winter in New York out of consideration for Billy Brue.

"Just think of it," he said to Percival, "that poor fellow ain't ever been east of Denver before now. It wa'n't good for him to be holed up out there in them hills all his life. He hadn't got any chance to improve his mind."

"He'd better improve his whiskers first thing he does," suggested Percival. "He'll be gold-bricked if he wears 'em scrambled that way around this place."

But in neither of these explanations did the curious old man impress Percival as being wholly ingenuous.

Then he remarked casually one day that he had lately met Higbee, who was on his way to San Francisco.

"I only had a few minutes with him while they changed engines at Green River, but he told me all about you folks—what a fine time you was havin', yachts and card-parties, and all like that. Higbee said a man had ought to come to New York every now and then, jest to keep from gettin' rusty."

Back of this Percival imagined for a time that he had discovered Uncle Peter's true reason for descending upon them. Higbee would have regaled him with wild tales of the New York dissipations, and Uncle Peter had come promptly on to pull him up. Percival could hear the story as Higbee would word it, with the improving moral incident of his own son snatched as a brand from the "Tenderloin," to live a life of impecunious usefulness in far Chicago. But, when he tried to hold this belief, and to prove it from his observations, he was bound to admit its falsity. For Uncle Peter had shown no inclination to act the part of an evangel from the virtuous West. He had delivered no homilies, no warnings as to the fate of people who incontinently "cut loose." He had evinced not the least sign of any disposition even to criticise.

On the contrary, indeed, he appeared to joy immensely in Percival's way of life. He manifested a willingness and a capacity for unbending in boon companionship that were, both of them, quite amazing to his accomplished grandson. By degrees, and by virtue of being never at all censorious, he familiarised himself with the young man's habits and diversions. He listened delightedly to the tales of his large gambling losses, of the bouts at poker, the fruitless venture in Texas Oil land, the disastrous corner in wheat, engineered by Burman, and the uniformly unsuccessful efforts to "break the bank" in Forty-fourth Street. He never tired of hearing whatever adventures Percival chose to relate; and, finding that he really enjoyed them, the young man came to confide freely in him, and to associate with him without restraint.

Uncle Peter begged to be introduced at the temple of chance, and spent a number of late evenings there with his popular grandson. He also frequently made himself one of the poker coterie, and relished keenly the stock jokes as to his grandson's proneness to lose.

"Your pa," he would say, "never *could* learn to stay out of a Jack-pot unless he had Jacks or better; he'd come in and draw four cards to an ace any time, and then call it 'hard luck' when he didn't draw out. And he just loved straights open in the middle; said anybody could fill them that's open at both ends; but, after all, I guess that's the only way to have fun at the game. If a man ain't got the sperrit to overplay aces-up when he gets 'em, he might as well be clerkin' in a bank for all the fun he'll have out of the game."

The old man's endurance of late suppers and later hours, and his unsuspected disposition to "cut loose," became twin marvels to Percival. He could not avoid contrasting this behaviour with his past preaching. After a few weeks he was forced to the charitable conclusion that Uncle Peter's faculties were failing. The exposure and hardships of the winter before had undoubtedly impaired his mental powers.

"I can't make him out," he confided to his mother. "He never wants to go home nights; he can drink more than I can without batting an eye, and show up fresher in the morning, and he behaves like a young fellow just out of college. I don't know where he would bring up if he didn't have me to watch over him."

"I think it's just awful—at his time of life, too," said Mrs. Bines.

"I think that's it. He's getting old, and he's come along into his second childhood. A couple of more months at this rate, and I'm afraid I'll have to ring up one of those nice shiny black wagons to take him off to the foolish-house."

"Can't you talk to him, and tell him better?"

"I could. I know it all by heart—all the things to say to a man on the downward path. Heaven knows I've heard them often enough, but I'd feel ashamed to talk that way to Uncle Peter. If he were my son, now, I'd cut off his allowance and send him back to make something of himself, like Sile Higbee with little Hennery; but I'm afraid all I can do is to watch him and see that he doesn't marry one of those little pink-silk chorus girls, or lick a policeman, or anything."

"You're carryin' on the same way yourself," ventured his mother.

"That's different," replied her perspicacious son.

Uncle Peter had refused to live at the Hightower after three days in that splendid and populous caravansary.

"It suits me well enough," he explained to Percival, "but I have to look after Billy Brue, and this ain't any place for Billy. You see Billy ain't city broke yet. Look at him now over there, the way he goes around butting into strangers. He does that way because he's all the time looking down at his new patent-leather shoes—first pair he ever had. He'll be plumb stoop-shouldered if he don't hurry up and get the new kicked off of 'em. I'll have to get him a nice warm box-stall in some place that ain't so much on the band-wagon as this one. The ceilings here are too high fur Billy. And I found him shootin' craps with the bell-boy this mornin'. The boy thinks Billy, bein' from the West, is a stage robber, or somethin' like he reads about in the Cap' Collier libr'ies, and follows him around every chance he gets. And Billy laps up too many of them little striped drinks; and them French-cooked dishes ain't so good fur him, either. He caught on to the bill-of-fare right away. Now he won't order anything but them allas—them dishes that has 'a la' something or other after 'em," he explained, when Percival looked puzzled. "He knows they'll always be something all fussed up with red, white, and blue gravy, and a little paper bouquet stuck into 'em. I never knew Billy was such a fancy eater before."

So Uncle Peter and his charge had established themselves in an old-fashioned but very comfortable hotel down on one of the squares, a dingy monument to the time when life had been less hurried. Uncle Peter had stayed there thirty years before, and he found the place unchanged. The carpets and hangings were a bit faded, but the rooms were generously broad, the chairs, as the old man remarked, were "made to sit in," and the *cuisine* was held, by a few knowing old epicures who still frequented the place, to be superior even to that of the more pretentious Hightower. The service, it is true, was apt to be slow. Strangers who chanced in to order a meal not infrequently became enraged, and left before their food came, trailing plain short words of extreme dissatisfaction behind them as they went. But the elect knew that these delays betokened the presence of an artistic conscience in the kitchen, and that the food was worth tarrying for. "They know how to make you come back hungry for some more the next day," said Uncle Peter Bines.

From this headquarters the old man went forth to join in the diversions of his grandson. And here he kept a watchful eye upon the uncertain Billy Brue; at least approximately. Between them, his days and nights were occupied to crowding. But Uncle Peter had already put in some hard winters, and was not wanting in fortitude.

Billy Brue was a sore trouble to the old man. "I jest can't keep him off the streets nights," was his chief complaint. By day Billy Brue walked the streets in a decent, orderly trance of bewilderment. He was properly puzzled and amazed by many strange matters. He never could find out what was "going on" to bring so many folks into town. They all hurried somewhere constantly, but he was never able to reach the centre of excitement. Nor did he ever learn how any one could reach those high clothes-lines, strung forty feet above ground between the backs of houses; nor how there could be "so many shows in town, all on one night;" nor why you should get so many good things to eat by merely buying a "slug of whiskey;" nor why a thousand people weren't run over in Broadway each twenty-four hours.

At night, Billy Brue ceased to be the astounded alien, and, as Percival said Dr. Von Herzlich would say, "began to mingle and cooperate with his environment." In the course of this process he fell into adventures, some of them, perhaps, unedifying. But it may be told that his silver watch with the braided leather fob was stolen from him the second night out; also that the following week, in a Twenty-ninth Street saloon, he accepted the hospitality of an affable stranger, who had often been in Montana City. His explanation of subsequent events was entirely satisfactory, at least, from the time that he returned to consciousness of them.

"I only had about thirty dollars in my clothes," he told Percival, "but what made me so darned hot, he took my breastpin, too, made out of the first nugget ever found in the Early Bird mine over Silver Bow way. Gee! when I woke up I couldn't tell where I was. This cop that found me in a hallway, he says I must have been give a dose of Peter. I says, 'All right—I'm here to go against all the games,' I says, 'but pass me when the Peter comes around again,' I says. And he says Peter was knockout drops. Say, honestly, I didn't know my own name till I had a chanst to look me over. The clothes and my hands looked like I'd seen 'em before, somehow—and then I come to myself."

After this adventure, Uncle Peter would caution him of an evening:

"Now, Billy, don't stay out late. If you ain't been gone through by eleven, just hand what you got on you over to the first man you meet—none of 'em'll ask any questions—and then pike fur home. The later at night it gets in New York the harder it is fur strangers to stay alive. You're all right in Wardner or Hellandgone, Billy, but in this here camp you're jest a tender little bed of pansies by the wayside, and these New Yorkers are terrible careless where they step after dark."

Notwithstanding which, Mr. Brue continued to behave uniformly in a manner to make all judicious persons grieve. His place of supreme delight was the Hightower. Its marble splendours, its myriad lights, the throngs of men and women in evening dress, made for him a scene of unfailing fascination. The evenings when he was invited to sit in the *café* with Uncle Peter and Percival made memories long to be cherished.

He spent such an evening there at the end of their first month in New York. Half a dozen of Percival's friends sat at the table with them from time to time. There had been young Beverly Van Arsdel, who, Percival disclosed, was heir to all the Van Arsdel millions, and no end of a swell. And there was big, handsome, Eddie Arledge, whose father had treated him shabbily. These two young gentlemen spoke freely about the inferiority of many things "on this side"—as they denominated this glorious Land of Freedom—of many things from horses to wine. The country was rapidly becoming, they agreed, no place for a gentleman to live. Eddie Arledge confessed that, from motives of economy, he had been beguiled into purchasing an American claret.

"I fancied, you know," he explained to Uncle Peter, "that it might do for an ordinary luncheon claret, but on my sacred honour, the stuff is villainous. Now you'll agree with me, Mr. Bines, I dare say, that a Bordeaux of even recent vintage is vastly superior to the very best so-called American claret."

Whereupon Beverly Van Arsdel having said, "To be sure—fancy an American Burgundy, now! or a Chablis!" Uncle Peter betrayed the first sign of irritation Percival had detected since his coming.

"Well, you see, young men, we're not much on vintages in Montana. Whiskey is mostly our drink—whiskey and spring water—and if our whiskey is strong, it's good enough. When we want to test a new barrel, we inject three drops of it into a jack-rabbit, and if he doesn't lick a bull clog in six seconds, we turn down the goods. That's as far's our education has ever gone in vintages."

It sounded like the old Uncle Peter, but he was afterward so good natured that Percival concluded the irritation could have been but momentary.

CHAPTER XXIX.

Uncle Peter Bines Threatens to Raise Something

Uncle Peter and Billy Brue left the Hightower at midnight. Billy Brue wanted to walk down to their hotel, on the plea that they might see a fight or a fire "or something." He never ceased to feel cheated when he was obliged to ride in New York. But Uncle Peter insisted on the cab.

"Say, Uncle Peter," he said, as they rode down, "I got a good notion to get me one of them first-part suits—like the minstrels wear in the grand first part, you know—only I'd never be able to git on to the track right without a hostler to harness me and see to all the buckles and cinch the straps right. They're mighty fine, though."

Finding Uncle Peter uncommunicative, he mused during the remainder of the ride, envying the careless ease with which Percival and his friends, and even Uncle Peter, wore the prescribed evening regalia of gentlemen, and yearning for the distinguished effect of its black and white elegance upon himself.

They went to their connecting rooms, and Billy Brue regretfully sought his bed, marvelling how free people in a town like New York could ever bring themselves to waste time in sleep. As he dozed off, he could hear the slow, measured tread of Uncle Peter pacing the floor in the next room.

He was awakened by hearing his name called. Uncle Peter stood in a flood of light at the door of his room. He was fully dressed.

"Awake, Billy?"

"Is it gittin'-up time?"

The old man came into the room and lighted a gas-jet. He looked at his watch.

"No; only a quarter to four. I ain't been to bed yet."

Billy Brue sat up and rubbed his eyes.

"Rheumatiz again, Uncle Peter?"

"No; I been thinkin', Billy. How do you like the game?"

He began to pace the floor again from one room to the other.

"What game?"! Billy Brue had encountered a number in New York.

"This whole game—livin' in New York."

Mr. Brue became judicial.

"It's a good game as long as you got money to buy chips. I'd hate like darnation to go broke here. All the pay-claims have been located, I guess."

"I doubt it's bein' a good game any time, Billy. I been actin' as kind of a lookout now fur about forty days and forty nights, and the chances is all in favour of the house. You don't even get half your money on the high card when the splits come."

Billy Brue pondered this sentiment. It was not his own.

"The United States of America is all right, Billy."

This was safe ground.

"Sure!" His mind reverted to the evening just past. "Of course there was a couple of Clarences in high collars there to-night that made out like they was throwin' it down; but they ain't the whole thing, not by a long shot."

"Yes, and that young shrimp that was talkin' about 'vintages' and 'trouserings.'" The old man paused in his walk.

"What *are* 'trouserings,' Billy?"

Mr. Brue had not looked into shop windows day after day without enlarging his knowledge.

"Trouserings," he proclaimed, rather importantly, "is the cloth they make pants out of."

"Oh! is that all? I didn't know but it might be some new kind of duds. And that fellow don't ever get up till eleven o'clock A.M. I don't reckon I would myself if I didn't have anything but trouserings and vintages to worry about. And that Van Arsdel boy!"

"Say!" said Billy, with enthusiasm, "I never thought I'd be even in the same room with one of that family, 'less I prized open the door with a jimmy."

"Well, who's *he*? My father knew his grandfather when he kep' tavern over on the Raritan River, and his grandmother!—this shrimp's grandmother!—she tended bar."

"Gee!"

"Yes, they kep' tavern, and the old lady passed the rum bottle over the bar, and took in the greasy money. This here fellow, now, couldn't make an honest livin' like that, I bet you. He's like a dogbreeder would say—got the pedigree, but not the points."

Mr. Brue emitted a high, throaty giggle.

"But they ain't all like that here, Uncle Peter. Say, you come out with me some night jest in your workin' clothes. I can show you people all right that won't ask to see your union card. Say, on the dead, Uncle Peter, I wish you'd come. There's a lady perfessor in a dime museum right down here on Fourteenth Street that eats fire and juggles the big snakes;—say, she's got a complexion—"

"There's enough like that kind, though," interrupted Uncle Peter. "I could take a double-barrel shotgun up to that hotel and get nine with each barrel around in them hallways; the shot wouldn't have to be rammed, either; 'twouldn't have to scatter so blamed much."

"Oh, well, them society sports—there's got to be some of *them*—"

"Yes, and the way they make 'em reminds me of what Dal Mutzig tells about the time they started Pasco. 'What you fellows makin' a town here fur?' Dal says he asked 'em, and he says they says, 'Well, why not? The land ain't good fur anything else, is it?' they says. That's the way with these shrimps; they ain't good fur anything else. There's that Arledge, the lad that keeps his mouth hangin' open all the time he's lookin' at you—he'll catch cold in his works, first thing *he* knows—with his gold monogram on his cigarettes."

"He said he was poor," urged Billy, who had been rather taken with the ease of Arledge's manner.

"Fine, big, handsome fellow, ain't he? Strong as an ox, active, and perfectly healthy, ain't he? Well, he's a *pill*! But *his* old man must 'a' been on to him. Here, here's a piece in the paper about that fine big strappin' giant—it's partly what got me to thinkin' to-night, so I couldn't sleep. Just listen to this," and Uncle Peter read:

"E. Wadsworth Arledge, son of the late James Townsend Arledge, of the dry-goods firm of Arledge & Jackson, presented a long affidavit to Justice Dutcher, of the Supreme Court, yesterday, to show why his income of six thousand dollars a year from his father's estate should not be abridged to pay a debt of $489.32. Henry T. Gotleib, a grocer, who obtained a judgment for that amount against him in 1895, and has been unable to collect, asked the Court to enjoin Judge Henley P. Manderson, and the Union Fidelity Trust Company, as executors of the Arledge estate, from paying Mr. Arledge his full income until the debt has been discharged. Gotleib contended that Arledge could sustain the reduction required.

"James T. Arledge died about two years ago, leaving an estate of about $3,000,000. He had disapproved of the marriage of his son and evinced his displeasure in his will. The son had married Flora Florenza, an actress. To the son was given an income of $6,000 a year for life. The rest of the estate went to the testator's widow for life, and then to charity.

"Here is the affidavit of E. Wadsworth Arledge:

"'I have been brought up in idleness, under the idea that I was to inherit a large estate. I have never acquired any business habits so as to fit me to acquire property, or to make me take care of it.

"'I have never been in business, except many years ago, when I was a boy, when I was for a short time employed in one of the stores owned by my father. For many years prior to my father's death I was not employed, but lived on a liberal allowance made to me by him. I am a married man, and in addition to my wife have a family of two children to support from my income.

"'All our friends are persons of wealth and of high social standing, and we are compelled to spend money in entertaining the many friends who entertain us. I am a member of many expensive clubs. I have absolutely no income except the allowance I receive from my father's estate, and the same is barely sufficient to support my family.

"'I have received no technical or scientific education, fitting me for any business or profession, and should I be deprived of any portion of my income, I will be plunged in debt anew.'

"The Court reserved decision."

"You hear that, Billy? The Court reserved decision. Mr. Arledge has to buy so many gold cigarettes and vintages and trouserings, and belong to so many clubs, that he wants the Court to help him chouse a poor grocer out of his money. Say, Billy, that judge could fine me for contempt of court, right now, fur reservin' his decision. You bet Mr. Arledge would 'a' got my decision right hot off the griddle. I'd 'a' told him, 'You're the meanest kind of a crook I ever heard of fur wantin' to lie down on your fat back and whine out of payin' fur the grub you put in your big gander paunch,' I'd tell him, 'and now you march to the lock-up till you can look honest folks in the face,' I'd tell him. Say, Billy, some crooks are worse than others. Take Nate Leverson out there. Nate set up night and day for six years inventin' a process fur sweatin' gold into ore; finally he gets it; how he does it, nobody knows, but he sweat gold eighteen inches into the solid rock. The first few holes he salted he gets rid of all right, then of course they catch him, and Nate's doin' time now. But say, I got respect fur Nate since readin' that piece. There's a good deal of a man about him, or about any common burglar or sneak thief, compared to this duck. They take chances, say nothin' of the hard work they do. This fellow won't take a chance and won't work a day. Billy, that's the meanest specimen of crook I ever run against, bar none, and that crook is produced and tolerated in a place that's said to be the centre of 'culture and refinement and practical achievement.' Billy, he's a pill!"

"That's right," said Billy Brue, promptly throwing the recalcitrant Arledge overboard.

"But it ain't none of my business. What I do spleen again, is havin' a grandson of mine livin' in a community where a man that'll act like that is actually let in their houses by honest folks. Think of a son of Daniel J. Bines treatin' folks like that as if they was his equals. Say, Dan'l had a line of faults, all right—but, by God! he'd a trammed ore fur two twenty-five a day any time in his life rather'n not pay a dollar he owed. And think of this lad making his bed in this kind of a place where men are brought up to them ways; and that name; think of a husky, two-fisted boy like him lettin' himself be called by a measly little gum-drop name like Percival, when he's got a right to be called Pete. And he's right in with 'em. He'd be jest as bad—give him a little time; and Pishy engaged to a damned fortune-hunting Englishman into the bargain. It's all Higbee said it was, only it goes double. Say, Billy, I been thinkin' this over all night."

"'Tis mighty worryin', ain't it, Uncle Peter?"

"And I got it thought out."

"Sure, you must 'a' got it down to cases."

"Billy,' listen now. There's a fellow down in Wall Street. His name is Shepler, Rulon Shepler. He's most the biggest man down there."

"Sure! I heard of him."

"Listen! I'm goin' to bed now. I can sleep since I got my mind made up. But I want to see Shepler in private to-morrow. Don't wake me up in the morning. But get up yourself, and go find his office—look in a directory, then ask a policeman. Shepler's a busy man. You tell the clerk or whoever holds you up that Mr. Peter Bines wants an appointment with Mr. Shepler as soon as he can make it—Mr. Peter Bines, of Montana City. Be there by 9.30 so's to get him soon as he comes. He knows me; tell him I want to see him on business soon as possible, and find out when he can give me time. And don't you say to any one else that I ever seen him or sent you there. Understand? Don't ever say a word to any one. Remember, now, be there at 9.30, and don't let any clerk put you off, and ask him what hour'll be convenient for him. Now get what sleep's comin' to you. It's five o'clock."

At noon Billy Brue returned to the hotel to find Uncle Peter finishing a hearty breakfast.

"I found him all right, Uncle Peter. The lookout acted suspicious, but I saw the main guy himself come out of a door—like I'd seen his picture in the papers, so I just called to him, and said, 'Mr. Peter Bines wants to see you,' like that. He took me right into his office, and I told him what you said, and he'll be ready for you at two o'clock. He knows mines, all right, out our way, don't he?—and he crowded a handful of these tin-foil cigars on to me, and acted real sociable. Told me to drop in any time. Say, he'd run purty high in the yellow stuff all right."

"At two o'clock, you say?"

"Yes."

"And what's his number?"

"Gee, I forgot; I can tell you, though. You go down Broadway to that old church—say, Uncle Peter, there's folks in that buryin'-ground been dead over two hundred years, if you can go by their gravestones. Gee! I didn't s'pose *anybody'd* been dead that long—then you turn down the gulch right opposite, until you come to the Vandevere Building, a few rods down on the left. Shepler's there. Git into the bucket and go up to the second level, and you'll find him in the left-hand back stope—his name's on the door in gold letters."

"All right. And look here, Billy, keep your head shut about all I said last night about anything. Don't you ever let on to a soul that I ain't stuck on this place and its people—no matter what I do."

"Sure not! What *are* you going to do, Uncle Peter?"

The old man's jaws were set for some seconds in a way to make Billy Brue suspect he might be suffering from cramp. It seemed, however, that he had merely been thinking intently. Presently he said:

"I'm goin' to raise hell, Billy."

"Sure!" said Mr. Brue—approvingly on general principles. "Sure! Why not?"

CHAPTER XXX.

Uncle Peter Inspires His Grandson to Worthy Ambitions

On three successive days the old man held lengthy interviews with Shepler in the latter's private office. At the close of the third day's interview, Shepler sent for Relpin, of the brokerage firm of Relpin and Hendricks. A few days after this Uncle Peter said to Percival one morning:

"I want to have a talk with you, son."

"All right, Uncle Peter," was the cheerful answer. He suspected the old man might at last be going to preach a bit, since for a week past he had been rather less expansive. He resolved to listen with good grace to any homilies that might issue. He took his suspicion to be confirmed when Uncle Peter began:

"You folks been cuttin' a pretty wide swath here in New York."

"That's so, Uncle Peter,—wider than we could have cut in Montana City."

"Been spendin' money purty free for a year."

"Yes; you need money here."

"I reckon you can't say about how much, now?"

"Oh, I shouldn't wonder," Percival answered, going over to the escritoire, and taking out some folded sheets and several check-books. "Of course, I haven't it all here, but I have the bulk of it. Let me figure a little."

He began to work with a pencil on a sheet of paper. He was busy almost half an hour, while Uncle Peter smoked in silence.

"It struck me the other night we might have been getting a little near to the limit, so I figured a bit then, too, and I guess this will give you some idea of it. Of course this isn't all mine; it includes ma's and Psyche's. Sis has been a mark for every bridge-player between the Battery and the Bronx, and the way ma has been plunging on her indigent poor is a caution,—she certainly does hold the large golden medal for amateur cross-country philanthropy. Now here's a rough expense account—of course only approximate, except some of the items I happened to have." Uncle Peter took the statement, and studied it carefully.

Paid Hightower Hotel................ $ 42,983.75

Keep of horses, and extra horse and carriage hire....................... 5,628.50

Chartering steam-yacht *Viluca* three months............................. 24,000.00

Expenses running yacht.............. 46,850.28

W. U. Telegraph Company............. 32.65

Incidentals......................... 882,763.90

Total $1,002,259.08

His sharp old eyes ran up and down the column of figures. Something among the items seemed to annoy him.

"Looking at those 'incidentals'? I took those from the check-books. They are pretty heavy."

"It's an outrage!" exclaimed the old man, indignantly, "that there $32.50 to the telegraph company. How's it come you didn't have a Western Union frank this year? I s'posed you had one. They sent me mine."

"Oh, well, they didn't send me one, and I didn't bother to ask for it," the young man answered in a tone of relief. "Of course the expenses have been pretty heavy, coming here strangers as we did. Now, another year—"

"Oh, that ain't anything. Of course you got to spend money. I see one of them high-toned gents that died the other day said a gentleman couldn't possibly get along on less'n two thousand dollars a day and expenses. I'm glad to see you ain't cut under the limit none—you got right into his class jest like you'd always lived here, didn't you? But, now, I been kind of lookin' over the ground since I come here, and it's struck me you ain't been gettin' enough for your money. You've spent free, but the goods ain't been delivered. I'm talkin' about yourself. Both your ma and Pishy has got more out of it than you have. Why, your ma gets her name in the papers as a philanthropist along with that—how do the papers call her?—'the well-known club woman' that Mrs. Helen Wyot Lamson that always has her name spelled out in full? Your ma is getting public recognition fur her money, and look at Pishy. What's she gone and done while you been laxin' about? Why, she's got engaged to a lord, or just as good. Look at the prospects she's got! She'll enter the aristocracy of England and have a title. But look at you! Really, son, I'm ashamed of you. People over there'll be sayin' 'Lady What's-her-name? Oh, yes! She *has* got a brother, but he don't amount to shucks—he ain't much more'n a three-spot. He can't do anything but play bank and drink like a fish. He's throwed away his opportunities'—that's what them dukes and counts will be sayin' about you behind your back."

"I understood you didn't think much of sis's choice."

"Well, of course, he wouldn't be much in Montana City, but he's all right in his place, and he seems to be healthy. What knocks *me* is how he ever got all them freckles. He never come by 'em honestly, I bet. He must 'a' got caught in an explosion of freckles sometime. But that ain't neither here nor there. He has the goods and Pish'll get 'em delivered. She's got something to show fur her dust. But what *you* got to show? Not a blamed thing but a lot of stubs in a check-book, and a little fat. Now I ain't makin' any kick. I got no right to; but I do hate to see you leadin' this life of idleness and dissipation when you might be makin' something of yourself. Your pa was quite a man. He left his mark out there in that Western country. Now you're here settled in the East among big people, with a barrel of money and fine chances to do something, and you're jest layin' down on the family name. You wouldn't think near so much of your pa if he'd laid down before his time; and your own children will always have to say 'Poor pa—he had a good heart, but he never could amount to anything more'n a threespot; he didn't have any stuff in him,' they'll be sayin'. Now, on the level, you don't want to go through life bein' just known as a good thing and easy money, do you?"

"Why, of course not, Uncle Peter; only I had to look around some at first,—for a year or so."

"Well, if you need to look any more, then your eyes ain't right. That's my say. I ain't askin' you to go West. I don't expect that!"

Percival brightened.

"But I am tryin' to nag you into doin' something here. People can say what they want to about you," he continued, stubbornly, as one who confesses the most arrant bigotry, "but I know you *have* got some brains, some ability—I really believe you got a whole lot—and you got the means to take your place right at the top. You can head 'em all in this country or any other. Now what you ought to do, you ought to take your place in the world of finance—put your mind on it night and day—swing out—get action—and set the ball to rolling. Your pa was a big man in the West, and there ain't any reason as I can see of why you can't be just as big a man in proportion here. People can talk all they want to about your bein' just a dub—I won't believe 'em. And there's London. You ain't been ambitious enough. Get a down-hill pull on New York, and then branch out. Be a man of affairs like your pa, and like that fellow Shepler. Let's *be* somebody. If Montana City was too small fur us, that's no reason why New York should be too big."

Percival had walked the floor in deep attention to the old man's words.

"You've got me right, Uncle Peter," he said at last. "And you're right about what I ought to do. I've often thought I'd go into some of these big operations here. But for one thing I was afraid of what you'd say. And then, I didn't know the game very well. But I see I ought to do something. You're dead right."

"And we need more money, too," urged the old man. "I was reading a piece the other day about the big fortunes in New York. Why, we ain't one, two, three, with the dinky little twelve or thirteen millions we could swing. You don't want to be a piker, do you? If you go in the game at all, play her open and high. Make 'em take the ceiling off. You can just as well get into the hundred million class as not, and I know it. They needn't talk to *me*—I know you *have* got some brains. If you was to go in now it would keep you straight and busy, and take you out of this pin-head class that only spends their pa's money."

"You're all right, Uncle Peter! I certainly did need you to come along right now and set me straight. You founded the fortune, pa trebled it, and now I'll get to work and roll it up like a big snowball."

"That's the talk. Get into the hundred million class, and show these wise folks you got something in you besides hot air, like the sayin' is. *Then* they won't always be askin' who your pa was—they'll be wantin' to know who you are, by Gripes! Then you can have the biggest steam yacht afloat, two or three of 'em, and the best house in New York, and palaces over in England; and Pish'll be able to hold up her head in company over there. You can finance *that* proposition right up to the nines."

"By Jove! but you're right. You're a wonder, Uncle Peter. And that reminds me—"

He stopped in his walk.

"I gave it hardly any thought at the time, but now it looks bigger than a mountain. I know just the things to start in on systematically. Now don't breathe a word of this, but there's a big deal on in Consolidated Copper. I happened on to the fact in a queer way the other night. There's a broker I've known down-town—fellow by the name of Relpin. Met him last summer. He does most of Shepler's business; he's supposed to be closer to Shepler and know more about the inside of his deals than any man in the Street. Well, I ran across Relpin down in the cafe the other night and he was wearing one of those gents' nobby three-button souses. Nothing would do but I should dine with him, so I did. It was the night you and the folks went to the opera with the Oldakers. Relpin was full of lovely talk and dark hints about a rise in copper stock, and another rise in Western Trolley, and a bigger rise than either of them in Union Cordage. How that fellow can do

Shepler's business and drink the stuff that makes you talk I don't see. Anyway he said—and you can bet what he says goes—that the Consolidated is going to control the world's supply of copper inside of three months, and the stock is bound to kite, and so are these other two stocks; Shepler's back of all three. The insiders are buying up now, slowly and cautiously, so as not to start any boom prematurely. Consolidated is no now, and it'll be up to 150 by April at the latest. The others may go beyond that. I wasn't looking for the game at the time, so I didn't give it any thought, but now, you see, there's our chance. We'll plunge in those three lines before they start to rise, and be in on the ground floor." "Now don't you be rash! That Shepler's old enough to suck eggs and hide the shells. I heard a man say the other day copper was none too good at no."

"Exactly. You can hear anything you're looking to hear, down there. But I tell you this was straight. Don't you suppose Shepler knows what he's about?—there's a boy that won't be peddling shoe-laces and gum-drops off one of these neat little bosom-trays—not for eighty-five or ninety-thousand years yet—and Relpin, even if he was drunk, knows Shepler's deals like you know Skiplap. They'll bear the stocks all they can while they're buying up. I wouldn't be surprised if the next Consolidated dividend was reduced. That would send her down a few points, and throw more stock on the market. Meantime, they're quietly workin' to get control of the European mines—and as to Western Trolley and Union Cordage—say, Relpin actually got to crying—they're so good—he had one of those loving ones, the kind where you want to be good to every one in the world. I'm surprised he didn't get into a sandwich sign and patrol Broadway, giving those tips to everybody.".

"Course, we're on a proposition now that you know more about it than I do; you certainly do take right hold at once—that was your pa's way, too. Daniel J. could look farther ahead in a minute than most men could in a year. I got to trust you wholly in these matters, and I know I can do it, too. I got confidence in you, no matter *what* other people say. They don't know you like I do. And if there's any other things you know about fur sure—"

"Well, there's Burman. He's plunging in corn now. His father has staked him, and he swears he can't lose. He was after me to put aside a million. Of course if he does win out it would be big money."

"Well, son, I can't advise you none—except I know you have got a head on you, no matter how people talk. You know about this end of the game, and I'll have to be led entirely by you. If you think Burman's got a good proposition, why, there ain't anything like gettin' action all along the layout, from ace down to seven-spot and back to the king card."

"That's the talk. I'll see Relpin to-day or to-morrow. I'll bet he tries to hedge on what he said. But I got him too straight—let a drunken man alone for telling the truth when he's got it in him. We'll start in buying at once."

"It does sound good. I must say you take hold of it considerable like Dan'l J. would 'a' done—and use my money jest like your own. I do want to see you takin' your place where you belong. This life of idleness you been leadin'—one continual potlatch the whole time—it wa'n't doin' you a bit of good."

"We'll get action, don't you worry. Now let's have lunch down-stairs, and then go for a drive. It's too fine a day to stay in. I'll order the cart around and show you that blue-ribbon cob I bought at the horse show. I just want you to see his action. He's a beaut, all right. He's been worked a half in 1.17, and he can go to his speed in ten lengths, any time."

In the afternoon they fell into the procession of carriages streaming toward the park. The day was pleasantly sharp, the clear sunshine enlivening, and the cob was one with the spirit of the occasion, alertly active, from his rubber-shod, varnished hoofs to the tips of his sensitive ears.

"Central Park," said Uncle Peter, "always seems to me just like a tidy little parlour, livin' around in them hills the way I have."

He watched the glinting of varnished spokes, and listened absently to the rhythmic "click-clump" of trotting horses, with its accompanying jingle of silver harness trappings.

"These people must have lots of money," he observed. "But you'll go in and outdo 'em all."

"That's what! Uncle Peter."

Toward the upper end of the East Drive they passed a victoria in which were Miss Milbrey and her mother with Rulon Shepler. The men raised their hats. Miss Milbrey flashed the blue of her eyes to them and pointed down her chin in the least bit of a bow. Mrs. Milbrey stared.

"Wa'n't that Shepler?"

"Yes, Shepler and the Milbreys. That woman certainly has the haughtiest lorgnon ever built."

"She didn't speak to us. Is her eyes bad?"

"Yes, ever since that time at Newport. None of them has spoken to me but the girl—she's engaged to Shepler."

"She's a right nice lookin' little lady. I thought you was kind of taken there."

"She would have married me for my roll. I got far enough along to tell that. But that was before Shepler proposed. I'd give long odds she wouldn't consider me now. I haven't enough for her with him in the game."

"Well, you go in and make her wish she'd waited for you."

"I'll do that; I'll make Shepler look like a well-to-do business man from Pontiac, Michigan."

"Is that brother of hers you told me about still makin' up to that party?"

"Can't say. I suppose he'll be a little more fastidious, as the brother-in-law of Shepler. In fact I heard that the family had shut down on any talk of his marrying her."

"Still, she ought to be able to do well here. Any man that would marry a woman fur money wouldn't object to her. One of these fortune-hunting Englishmen, now, would snap her up."

"She hasn't quite enough for that. Two millions isn't so much here, you know, and she must have spent a lot of hers. I hear she has a very expensive suite back there at the Arlingham, and lives high. I did hear, too, that she takes a flyer in the Street now and then. She'll be broke soon if she keeps that up."

"Too bad she ain't got a few more millions," said Uncle Peter, ruminantly. "Take one of these titled Englishmen looking for an heiress to keep 'em— she'd make just the kind of a wife he'd ought to get. She certainly ought to have a few more millions. If she had, now, she might cure some decent girl of her infatuation. Where'd you say she was stoppin'?"

"Arlingham—that big private hotel I showed you back there."

Percival confessed to his mother that night that he had wronged Uncle Peter.

"That old boy is all right yet," he said, with deep conviction. "Don't make any mistake there. He has bigger ideas than I gave him credit for. I suggested branching out here in a business way, to-day, and the old fellow got right in line. If anybody tells you that old Petie Bines hasn't got the leaves of his little calendar torn off right up to date you just feel wise inside, and see what odds are posted on it!"

CHAPTER XXXI.

Concerning Consolidated Copper and Peter Bines as Matchmakers

Consolidated copper at 110. The day after his talk with Uncle Peter, Percival through three different brokers gave orders to buy ten thousand shares.

"I tried to give Relpin an order for five thousand shares over the telephone," he said to Uncle Peter; "but they're used to those fifty and a hundred thousand dollar pikers down in that neighbourhood. He seemed to think I was joshing him. When I told him I meant it and was ready to take practically all he could buy for the next few weeks or so, I think he fell over in the booth and had to be helped out."

Orders for twenty thousand more shares in thousand share lots during the next three weeks sent the stock to 115. Yet wise men in the Street seemed to fear the stock. They were waiting cautiously for more definite leadings. The plunging of Bines made rather a sensation, and when it became known that his holdings were large and growing almost daily larger, the waning confidence of a speculator here and there would be revived.

At 115 the stock rested again, with few sales recorded. A certain few of the elect regarded this calm as ominous. It was half believed by others that the manipulations of the inner ring would presently advance the stock to a sensational figure, and that the reckless young man from Montana might be acting upon information of a definite character. But among the veteran speculators the feeling was conservative. Before buying they preferred to await some sign that the advance had actually begun. The conservatives were mostly the bald old fellows. Among the illusions that rarely survive a man's hair in Wall Street is the one that "sure things" are necessarily sure.

Percival watched Consolidated Copper go back to 110, and bought again— ten thousand shares. The price went up two points the day after his orders were placed, and two days later dropped back to 110. The conservatives began to agree with the younger set of speculators, in so far as both now believed that the stock was behaving in an unnatural manner, indicating that "something was doing"—that manipulation behind the scenes was under way to a definite end. The conservatives and the radicals differed as to what this end was. But then, Wall Street is nourished almost exclusively upon differences of opinion.

Percival now had accounts with five firms of brokers.

"Relpin," he explained to Uncle Peter, "is a foxy boy. He's foxier than a fox. He not only tried to hedge on what he told me,—said he'd been drinking absinthe *frappé* that day, and it always gets him dreamy,—but he actually had the nerve to give me the opposite steer. Of course he knows the deal clear to the centre, and Shepler knows that he knows, and he must have been afraid Shepler would suspect he'd been talking. So I only traded a few thousand shares with him. I didn't want to embarrass him. Funny about him, too. I never heard before of his drinking anything to speak of. And there isn't a man in the Street comes so near to knowing what the big boys are up to. But we're on the winning cards all right. I get exactly the same information from a dozen confidential sources; some of it I can trace to Relpin, and some of it right to Shepler himself." "Course I'm leavin' it all to you," answered Uncle Peter; "and I must say I do admire the way you take hold and get things on the move. You don't let any grass grow under *your* heels. You got a good head fur them things. I can tell by the way you start out—just like your pa fur all the world. I'll feel safe enough about my money as long as you keep your health. If only you got the nerve. I've known men would play a big proposition half-through and then get scared and pull out. Your pa wa'n't that way. He could get a proposition right by its handle every time, and they never come any too big fur him; the bigger they was, better he liked 'em. That's the kind of genius I think you got. You ain't afraid to take a chance."

Percival beamed modestly under praise of this sort which now came to him daily.

"It's good discipline for me, too, Uncle Peter. It's what I needed, something to put my mind on. I needed a new interest in life. You had me down right. I wasn't doing myself a bit of good with nothing to occupy my mind."

"Well, I'm mighty glad you thought up this stock deal. It'll give you good business habits and experience, say nothing of doubling your capital."

"And I've gone in with Burman on his corn deal. He's begun to buy, and he has it cinched this time. He'll be the corn king all right by June 1st; don't make any mistake on that. I thought as long as we were plunging so heavy in Western Trolley and Union Cordage, along with the copper, we might as well take the side line of corn. Then we won't have our eggs all in one basket."

"All right, son, all right! I'm trustin' you. A corner in corn is better'n a corner in wild-oats any day; anything to keep you straight, and doin' something. I don't care *how* many millions you pile up! I hear the Federal Oil people's back of the copper deal."

"That's right; the oil crowd and Shepler. I had it straight from Relpin that night. They're negotiating now with the Rothschilds to limit the output of the Rio Tinto mines. They'll end by controlling them, and then—well, we'll have a roll of the yellow boys—say, we'll have to lay quiet for a year just to count it."

"Do it good while you're doin' it," urged Uncle Peter, cheerfully. "I rely so much on your judgment, I want you to get action on my stuff, too. I got a couple millions that ought to be workin' harder than they are."

"Good; I didn't think you had so much gambler in you."

"It's fur a worthy purpose, son. And it seems too bad that Pishy can't pull out something with her bit, when it's to be had so easy. From what that spangle-faced beau of hers tells me there's got to be some expensive plumbing done in that castle he gets sawed off on to him."

"We'll let sis in, too," exclaimed her brother, generously, "and ma could use a little more in her business. She's sitting up nights to corner all the Amalgamated Hard-luck on the island. We'll pool issue, and say, we'll make those Federal Oil pikers think we've gnawed a corner off the subtreasury. I'll put an order in for twenty thousand more shares to-morrow—among the three stocks. And then we'll have to see about getting all our capital here. We'll need every cent of it that's loose; and maybe we better sell off some of those dead-wood stocks."

The twenty thousand shares were bought by the following week, five thousand of them being Consolidated Copper, ten thousand Western Trolley, and five thousand Union Cordage. Consolidated Copper fell off two points, upon rumours, traceable to no source, that the company had on hand a large secret supply of copper, and was producing largely in excess of the demand every month.

Percival told Uncle Peter of these rumours, and chuckled with the easy confidence of a man who knows secrets.

"You see, it's coming the way Relpin said. The insiders are hammering down the stock with those reports, hammering with one hand, and buying up small lots quietly with the other. But you'll notice the price of copper doesn't go down any. They keep it at seventeen cents all right. Now, the moment they get control of the European supply they'll hold the stuff, force up the selling price to awful figures, and squeeze out dividends that will make you wear blue glasses to look at them."

"You certainly do know your business, son," said Uncle Peter, fervently. "You certainly got your pa's head on you. You remind me more and more of Dan'l J. Bines every day. I'd rather trust your judgment now than lots of older men down there. You know their tricks all right. Get in good and hard so long as you got a sure thing. I'd hate to have you come meachin' around after that stock has kited, and be kickin' because you hadn't bet what your hand was worth."

"Trust me for that, Uncle Peter. Garmer tried to steer me off this line of stocks the other night. He'd heard these rumours about a slump, and he's fifty years old at that. I thanked him for his tip and coppered it with another thousand shares all around next day. The way Garmer can tell when you're playing a busted flush makes you nervous, but I haven't looked over his license to know everything down in the Street yet."

The moral gain to Percival from his new devotion to the stock market was commented upon approvingly both by Uncle Peter and by his mother. It was quite as tangible as his money profits promised to be. He ceased to frequent the temple of chance in Forty-fourth Street, to the proprietor's genuine regret. The poker-games at the hotel he abandoned as being trivial. And the cabmen along upper Broadway had seldom now the opportunity to compete for his early morning patronage. He began to keep early hours and to do less casual drinking during the day. After three weeks of this comparatively regular living his mother rejoiced to note signs that his breakfast-appetite was returning.

"You see," he explained earnestly to Uncle Peter, "a man to make anything at this game must keep his head clear, and he must have good health to do that. I meet a lot of those fellows down there that queer themselves by drink. It doesn't do so much hurt when a man isn't needing his brains,— but no more of it for me just now!"

"That's right, son. I knew I could make something more than a polite sosh out of you. I knew you'd pull up if you got into business like you been doin'."

"Come down-town with me this afternoon, and see me make a play, Uncle Peter. I think I'll begin now to buy on a margin. The rise can't hold off much longer."

"I'd like to, son, but I'd laid out to take a walk up to the park this afternoon, and look in at the monkeys awhile. I need the out-doors, and anyway you don't need me down there. You know *your* part all right. My! but I'd begin to feel nervous with all that money up, if it was anybody but you, now."

In pursuance of his pronounced plan, Uncle Peter walked up Fifth Avenue that afternoon. But he stopped short of the park. At the imposing entrance of the Arlingham he turned in. At the desk he asked for Mrs. Wybert.

"I'll see if Mrs. Wybert is in," said the clerk, handing him a blank card; "your name, please!"

The old man wrote, "Mr. Peter Bines of Montana City would like a few minutes' talk with Mrs. Wybert."

The boy was gone so long that Uncle Peter, waiting, began to suspect he would not be received. He returned at length with the message, "The lady says will you please step up-stairs."

Going up in the elevator, the old man was ushered by a maid into a violet-scented little nest whose pale green walls were touched discreetly with hangings of heliotrope. An artist, in Uncle Peter's place, might have fancied that the colour scheme of the apartment cried out for a bit of warmth. A glowing, warm-haired woman was needed to set the walls afire; and the need was met when Mrs. Wybert entered.

She wore a long coat of seal trimmed with chinchilla, and had been, apparently, about to go out.

Uncle Peter rose and bowed. Mrs. Wybert nodded rather uncertainly.

"You wished to see me, Mr. Bines?"

"I did want to have a little talk with you, Mrs. Wybert, but you're goin' out, and I won't keep you. I know how pressed you New York society ladies are with your engagements."

Mrs. Wybert had seemed to be puzzled. She was still puzzled but unmistakably pleased. The old man was looking at her with frank and friendly apology for his intrusion. Plainly she had nothing to fear from him. She became gracious.

"It was only a little shopping tour, Mr. Bines, that and a call at the hospital, where they have one of my maids who slipped on the avenue yesterday and fractured one of her—er—limbs. Do sit down."

Mrs. Wybert said "limb" for leg with the rather conscious air of escaping from an awkward situation only by the subtlest finesse.

She seated herself before a green and heliotrope background that instantly took warmth from her colour. Uncle Peter still hesitated.

"You see, I wanted kind of a long chat with you, Mrs. Wybert—a friendly chat if you didn't mind, and I'd feel a mite nervous if you're bundled up that way."

"I shall be delighted, Mr. Bines, to have a long, friendly chat. I'll send my cloak back, and you take your own time. There now, do be right comfortable!"

The old man settled himself and bestowed upon his hostess a long look of approval.

"The reports never done you justice, Mrs. Wybert, and they was very glowin' reports, too."

"You're very kind, Mr. Bines, awfully good of you!"

"I'm goin' to be more, Mrs. Wybert. I'm goin' to be a little bit confidential—right out in the straight open with you."

"I am sure of that."

"And if you want to, you can be the same with me. I ain't ever held anything against you, and maybe now I can do you a favour."

"It's right good of you to say so."

"Now, look here, ma'am, lets you and me get right down to cases about this society game here in New York."

Mrs. Wybert laughed charmingly and relaxed in manner.

"I'm with you, Mr. Bines. What about it, now?"

"Now don't get suspicious, and tell me to mind my own business when I ask you questions."

"I couldn't be suspicious of you—really I feel as if I'd have to tell you everything you asked me, some way."

"Well, there's been some talk of your marrying that young Milbrey. Now tell me the inside of it."

She looked at the old man closely. Her intuition confirmed his own protestations of friendliness.

"I don't mind telling you in strict confidence, there *was* talk of marriage, and his people, all but the sister, encouraged it. Then after she was engaged to Shepler they talked him out of it. Now that's the whole God's truth, if it does you any good."

"If you had married him you'd 'a' had a position, like they say here, right away."

"Oh, dear, yes! awfully swagger people—dead swell, every one of them. There's no doubt about that."

"Exactly; and there ain't really any reason why you can't be somebody here."

"Well, between you and I, Mr. Bines, I can play the part as well as a whole lot of these women here. I don't want to talk, of course, but—well!"

"Exactly, you can give half of 'em cards and spades and both casinos, Mrs. Wybert."

"And I'll do it yet. I'm not through by any means. They're not the only perfectly elegant people in this town!"

"Of course you'll do it, and you could do it better if you had three or four times the stake you got."

"Dollars are worth more apiece in New York than any town I've ever been in."

"Mrs. Wybert, I can put you right square into a good thing, and I'm going to do it. Heard anything about Consolidated Copper?"

"I've heard something big was doing in it; but nobody seems to know for certain. My broker is afraid of it."

"Very well. Now you do as I tell you, and you can clean up a big lot inside of the next two months. If you do as I tell you, mind, no matter *what* you hear, and if you don't talk."

Mrs. Wybert meditated.

"Mr. Bines, I'm—it's natural that I'm a little uneasy. Why should you want to see me do well, after our little affair? Now, out with it! What are you trying to do with me? What do you expect me to do for you? Get down to cases yourself, Mr. Bines!"

"I will, ma'am, in a few words. My granddaughter, you may have heard, is engaged to an Englishman. He's next thing to broke, but he's got a title coming. Naturally he's looking fur money. Naturally he don't care fur the girl. But I'm afraid she's infatuated with him. Now then, if he had a chance at some one with more money than she's got, why, naturally he'd jump at it."

"Aren't you a little bit wild?"

"Not a little bit. He saw you at Newport last summer, and he's seen you here. He was tearing the adjectives up telling me about you the other night, not knowing, you understand, that I'd ever heard tell of you before. You could marry him in a jiffy if you follow my directions."

"But your granddaughter has a fortune."

"You'll have as much if you play this the way I tell you. And—you never can tell in these times—she might lose a good bit of hers."

"It's very peculiar, Mr. Bines—your proposition."

"Look at what a brilliant match it would be fur you. Why, you'd be Lady Casselthorpe, with dukes and counts takin' off their crowns to you. And that other one—that Milbrey—from all I hear he's lighter'n cork—cut his galluses and he'd float right up into the sky. He ain't got anything but his good family and a thirst."

"I see. This Mauburn isn't good enough for your family, but you reckon he's good enough for me? Is that it, now?"

"Come, Mrs. Wybert, let's be broad. That's the game you like, and I don't criticise you fur it. It's a good game if that's the kind of a game you're huntin' fur. And you can play it better'n my granddaughter. She wa'n't meant fur it—and I'd rather have her marry an American, anyhow. Now you like it, and you got beauty—only you need more money. I'll put you in the way of it, and you can cut out my granddaughter."

"I must think about it. Suppose I plunge in copper, and your tip isn't straight. I've seen hard times, Mr. Bines, in my life. I haven't always wore sealskin and diamonds."

"Mrs. Wybert, you was in Montana long enough to know how I stand there?"

"I know you're A1, and your word's as good as another man's money. I don't question your good intentions."

"It's my judgment, hey? Now, look here, I won't tell you what I know and how I know it, but you can take my word that I know I do know. You plunge in copper right off, without saying a word to anybody or makin' any splurge, and here—"

From the little table at his elbow he picked up the card that had announced him and drew out his pencil.

"You said my word was as good as another man's money. Now I'm going to write on this card just what you have to do, and you're to follow directions, no matter what you hear about other people doing. There'll be all sorts of reports about that stock, but you follow my directions."

He wrote on the back of the card with his pencil.

"Consolidated Copper, remember—and now I'm a-goin' to write something else under them directions.

"'Do this up to the limit of your capital and I will make good anything you lose.' There, Mrs. Wybert, I've signed that 'Peter Bines.' That card wouldn't be worth a red apple in a court of law, but you know me, and you know it's good fur every penny you lose."

"Really, Mr. Bines, you half-way persuade me. I'll certainly try the copper play—and about the other—well,—we'll see; I don't promise, mind you!"

"You think over it. I'm sure you'll like the idea—think of bein' in that great nobility, and bein' around them palaces with their dukes and counts. Think how these same New York women will meach to you then!"

The old man rose.

"And mind, follow them directions and no other—makes no difference what you hear, or I won't be responsible. And I'll rely on you, ma'am, never to let anyone know about my visit, and to send me back that little document after you've cashed in."

He left her studying the card with a curious little flash of surprise.

CHAPTER XXXII.

Devotion to Business and a Chance Meeting

In the weeks that now followed, Percival became a model of sobriety and patient, unremitting industry, according to his own ideas of industry. He visited the offices of his various brokers daily, reading the tape with the single-hearted devotion of a veteran speculator. He acquired a general knowledge of the ebb and flow of popular stocks. He frequently saw opportunities for quick profit in other stocks than the three he was dealing in, but he would not let himself be diverted.

"I'm centering on those three," he told Uncle Peter. "When they win out we'll take up some other lines. I could have cleared a quarter of a million in that Northern Pacific deal last week, as easy as not. I saw just what was being done by that Ledrick combine. But we've got something better, and I don't want to take chances on tying up some ready money we might need in a hurry. If a man gets started on those little side issues he's too apt to lose his head. He jumps in one day, and out the next, and gets to be what they call a 'kangaroo,' down in the Street. It's all right for amusement, but the big money is in cinching one deal and pushing hard. It's a bull market now, too; buy A.O.T. is the good word—Any Old Thing—but I'm going to stay right by my little line."

"You certainly have a genius fur finance," declared Uncle Peter, with fervent admiration. "This going into business will be the makin' of you. You'll be good fur something else besides holdin' one of them dinky little teacups, and talking about 'trouserings'—no matter *what* people say. Let 'em *talk* about you—sayin' you'll never be anything like the man your pa was— *you'll* show 'em."

And Percival, important with his secret knowledge of the great *coup*, went back to the ticker, and laughed inwardly at the seasoned experts who frankly admitted their bewilderment as to what was "doing" in copper and Western Trolley.

"When it's all over," he confided gaily to the old man, "we ought to pinch off about ten per cent of the winnings, and put up a monument to absinthe *frappé*—the stuff Relpin had been drinking that day. They'll give us a fine public square for it in Paris if they won't here in New York. And it wouldn't do any good to give it to Relpin, who's really earned it—he'd only lush himself into one of those drunkard's graves—I understand there's a few left yet."

Early in March, Coplen, the lawyer, was sent for, and with him Percival spent two laborious weeks, going over inventories of the properties, securities, and moneys of the estate. The major portion of the latter was now invested in the three stocks, and the remainder was at hand where it could be conveniently reached.

Percival informed himself minutely as to the values of the different mining properties, railroad and other securities. A group of the lesser-paying mines was disposed of to an English syndicate, the proceeds being retained for the stock deal. All but the best paying of the railroad, smelting, and land-improvement securities were also thrown on the market.

The experience was a valuable one to the young man, enlarging greatly his knowledge of affairs, and giving him a needed insight into the methods by which the fortune had been accumulated.

"That was a slow, clumsy, old-fashioned way to make money," he declared to Coplen. "Nowadays it's done quicker."

His grasp of details delighted Uncle Peter and surprised Coplen.

"I didn't know but he might be getting plucked," said Coplen to the old man, "with all that money being drawn out so fast. If I hadn't known you were with him, I'd have taken it on myself to find out something about his operations. But he's all right, apparently. He had a scent like a hound for those dead-wood properties—got rid of them while we would have been making up our minds to. That boy will make his way unless I'm mistaken. He has a head for detail."

"I'll make him a bigger man than his pa was yet," declared Uncle Peter. "But I wouldn't want to let on that I'd had anything to do with it. He'll think he's done it all himself, and it's right he should. It stimulates 'em. Boys of his age need just about so much conceit, and it don't do to take it out of 'em."

Reports of the most encouraging character came from Burman. The deal in corn was being engineered with a riper caution than had been displayed in the ill-fated wheat deal of the spring before.

"Burman's drawn close up to a million already," said Percival to Uncle Peter, "and now he wants me to stand ready for another million."

"Is Burman," asked Uncle Peter, "that young fellow that had a habit of standin' pat on a pair of Jacks, and then bettin' everybody off the board?"

"Yes, that was Burman."

"Well, I liked his ways. I should say he could do you a whole lot of good in a corn deal."

"It certainly does look good—and Burman has learned the ropes and spars. They're already calling him the 'corn-king' out on the Chicago Board of Trade."

"Use your own judgment," Uncle Peter urged him. "You're the one that knows all about these things. My Lord! how you ever *do* manage to keep things runnin' in your head gets me. If you got confidence in Burman, all I can say is—well, your pa was a fine judge of men, and I don't see why you shouldn't have the gift."

"Between you and me, Uncle Peter, I *am* a good judge of human nature, and I know this much about Burman: when he does win out he'll win big. And I think he's going to whipsaw the market to a standstill this time, for sure. Here's a little item from this morning's paper that sounds right, all along the line."

"COPPER, CORN, AND CORDAGE.

"There are just now three great movements in the market, Copper Trust stock, corn, and cordage stock. The upward movement in corn seems to be in the main not speculative but natural—the result of a short supply and a long demand. The movements in Copper and Cordage Trust stocks are purely speculative. The copper movement is based on this proposition: Can the Copper Trust maintain the price for standard copper at seventeen cents a pound, in face of enormously increased supply and the rapidly decreasing demand, notably in Germany? The bears think not. The bulls, contrarily, persist in behaving as if they had inside information of a superior value. Just possibly a simultaneous rise in corn, copper, and cordage will be the next sensation in the trading world."

"You see?" said Percival. "They're beginning to wake up, down there—beginning to turn over in their sleep and mutter. Pretty soon they'll begin to stretch lazily; when they finally hear something drop and jump out of bed it will be too late. The bulls will be counting their chips to cash in, and the man waiting around to put out the lights. And I don't see why Burman isn't as safe as I am." "I don't, either," said Uncle Peter.

"'A short supply and a long demand,'—it would be a sin to let any one else in. I'll just wire him we're on, and that we need all of that good thing ourselves."

In the flush of his great plans and great expectations came a chance meeting with Miss Milbrey. He had seen her only at a distance since their talk at Newport. Yet the thought of her had persisted as a plaintive undertone through all the days after. Only the sharp hurt to his sensitive pride—from the conviction that she had found him tolerable solely because of the money—had saved him from the willing admission to himself that he had carried off too much of her ever to forget. In his quiet moments, the tones of her clear, low voice came movingly to his ears, and his eyes conjured involuntarily her girlish animation, her rounded young form, her colour and fire—the choked, smouldering fire of opals. He saw the curve of her wrist, the confident swing of her walk, the easy poise of her head, her bearing, at once girlish and womanly, the little air, half of wistful appeal, and half of self-reliant assertion. Yet he failed not to regard these indulgences as utter folly. It had been folly enough while he believed that she stood ready to accept him and his wealth. It was more flagrant, now that her quest for a husband with millions had been so handsomely rewarded.

But again, the fact that she was now clearly impossible for him, so that even a degrading submission on his part could no longer secure her, served only to bring her attractiveness into greater relief. With the fear gone that a sudden impulse to possess her might lead him to stultify himself, he could see more clearly than ever why she was and promised always to be to him the very dearest woman in the world—dearest in spite of all he could reason about so lucidly. He felt, then, a little shock of unreasoning joy to find one night that they were dining together at the Oldakers'.

At four o'clock he had received a hasty note signed "Fidelia Oldaker," penned in the fine, precise script of some young ladies' finishing school— perhaps extinct now for fifty years—imploring him, if aught of chivalry survived within his breast, to fetch his young grandfather and dine with her that evening. Two men had inconsiderately succumbed, at this eleventh hour, to the prevailing grip-epidemic, and the lady threw herself confidently on the well-known generosity of the Bines male—"like one of the big, stout nets those acrobatic people fall into from their high bars," she concluded.

Uncle Peter was more than willing. He liked the Oldakers.

"They're the only sane folks I've met among your friends," he had told his grandson. He had dined there frequently during the winter, and professed to be enamoured of the hostess. That fragile but sprightly bit of antiquity professed in turn to find Uncle Peter a very dangerous man among the ladies. They flirted outrageously at every opportunity, and Uncle Peter sent her more violets than many a popular *débutante* received that winter.

Percival, with his new air of Wall Street operator, was inclined to hesitate.

"You know I'm up early now, Uncle Peter, to get the day's run of the markets before I go downtown, and a man can't do much in the way of dinners when his mind is working all day. Perhaps Mauburn will go."

But Mauburn was taking Psyche and Mrs. Drelmer to the first night of a play, and Percival was finally persuaded by the old man to relax, for one evening, the austerity of his *régime.*

"But how your pa would love to see you so conscientious," he said, "and you with Wall Street, or a good part of it, right under your heel, just like *that,*" and the old man ground his heel viciously into the carpet.

When Percival found Shepler with Mrs. Van Geist and Miss Milbrey among the Oldakers' guests, he rejoiced. Now he would talk to her without any of that old awkward self-consciousness. He was even audacious enough to insist that Mrs. Oldaker direct him to take Miss Milbrey out to dinner.

"I claim it as the price of coming, you know, when I was only an afterthought."

"You shall be paid, sir," his hostess declared, "if you consider it pay to sit beside an engaged girl whose mind is full of her *trousseau.* And here's this captivating young scapegrace relative of yours. What price does he demand for coming?" and she glanced up at Uncle Peter with arch liberality in her bright eyes.

That gentleman bowed low—a bow that had been the admiration of the smartest society in Marietta County, Ohio, fifty years and more ago.

"I'm paid fur coming by coming," he replied, urbanely.

"There, now!" cried his hostess, "that's pretty, and means something. You shall take me in for that."

"I'll have to give you a credit-slip, ma'am. You've overpaid me." And Mrs. Oldaker, with a coy fillip of her fan, called him a naughty boy.

"Here, Rulon," she called to Shepler, "are two young daredevils who've been good enough to save me as many empty chairs. Now you shall take out Cornelia, and this juvenile sprig shall relieve you of Avice Milbrey. It's a providence. You engaged couples are always so dull when you're banished from your own *ciel à deux.*"

Shepler bowed and greeted the two men. Percival sought Miss Milbrey, who was with her aunt at the other side of the old-fashioned room, a room whose brocade hangings had been imported from England in the days of the Georges, and whose furniture was fabricated in the time when France was suffering its last kings.

He no longer felt the presence of anything overt between them. The girl herself seemed to have regained the charming frankness of her first manner with him. Their relationship was defined irrevocably. No uncertainty of doubt or false seeming lurked now under the surface to perplex and embarrass. The relief was felt at once by each.

"I'm to have the pleasure of taking you in, Miss Milbrey—hostess issues special commands to that effect."

"Isn't that jolly! We've not met for an age."

"And I've such an appetite for talk with you, I fear I won't eat a thing. If I'd known you were to be here I'd have taken the forethought to eat a gored ox, or something—what is the proverb, 'better a dinner of stalled ox where—'"

"'Where talk is,'" suggested Miss Milbrey, quickly.

"Oh, yes—.' than to have your own ox gored without a word of talk.' I remember it perfectly now. And—there—we're moving on to this feast of reason—"

"And the flow of something superior to reason," finished Shepler, who had come over for Mrs. Van Geist. "Oldaker has some port that lay in the wood in his cellar for forty years—and went around the world between keel and canvas."

"That sounds good," said Percival, and then to Miss Milbrey, "But come, let us reason together." His next sentiment, unuttered, was that the soft touch of her hand under his arm was headier than any drink, how ancient soever.

Throughout the dinner their entire absorption in each other was all but unbroken. Percival never could remember who had sat at his left; and Miss Milbrey's right-hand neighbour saw more than the winning line of her profile but twice. Percival began—

"Do you know, I've never been able to classify you at all. I never could tell how to take you."

"I'll tell you a secret, Mr. Bines; I think I'm not to be taken at all. I've begun to suspect that I'm like one of those words that haven't any rhyme—like 'orange' and 'month,' you know."

"But you find poetry in life? I do."

"Plenty of verse—not much poetry."

"How would you order life now, if the little old wishing-lady came to your door and knocked?"

And they plunged forthwith, buoyed by youth's divine effrontery, into mysteries that have vexed diners, not less than hermit sages, since "the fog of old time" first obscured truth. Of life and death—the ugliness of life, and the beauty of death—

"... even as death might smile, Petting the plumes of some surprised soul,"

quoted the girl. Of loving and hating, they talked; of trying and failing—of the implacable urge under which men must strive in the face of certain defeat—of the probability that men are purposely born fools, since, if they were born wise they would refuse to strive; whereupon life and death would merge, and naught would prevail but a vast indifference. In fact, they were very deep, and affected to consider these grave matters seriously. They affected that they never habitually thought of lesser concerns. And they had the air of listening to each other as if they were weighing the words judicially, and were quite above any mere sensuous considerations of personality.

Once they emerged long enough to hear the hostess speaking, as it were of yesterday, of a day when the new "German cotillion" was introduced, to make a sensation in New York; of a time when the best ballrooms were heated with wood stoves and lighted with lamps; and of a later but apparently still remote time when the Assemblies were "really, quite the smartest function of the season."

In another pause, they caught the kernel of a story being told by Uncle Peter:

"The girl was a half-breed, but had a fair skin and the biggest shock of hair you ever saw—bright yellow hair. She was awful proud of her hair. So when her husband, Clem Dewler, went to this priest, Father McNally, and complained that she *would* run away from the shack and hang around the dance-halls down at this mining-camp, Father McNally made up his mind to learn her a lesson. Well, he goes down and finds her jest comin' out of Tim Healy's place with two other women. He rushes up to her, catches hold of this big shock of hair that was trailin' behind her, and before she knew what was comin' he whipped out a big pair of sharp, shiny shears, and made as if he was going to give her a hair-cut. At that she begins to scream, but the priest he wouldn't let go. 'I'll cut it off,' he says, 'close,' he says, 'if you don't swear on this crucifix to be a good squaw to Clem Dewler, and never set so much as one of your little feet in these places again.' She could feel the shears against her hair, and she was so scared she swore like he told her. And so she was that afraid of losin' her fine yellow hair afterward, knowin' Father McNally was a man that didn't make no idle threats, that she kept prim and proper—fur a half-breed."

"That poor creature had countless sisters," was Miss Milbrey's comment to Percival. And they fell together once more in deciding whether, after all, the brightest women ever cease to believe that men are influenced most by surface beauties. They fired each other's enthusiasm for expressing opinions, and they took the opinions very seriously. Yet of their meeting, to an observer, their talk would have seemed the part least worth recording.

Twice Percival caught Shepler's regard bent upon them. It amused him to think he detected signs of uneasiness back of the survey, cool, friendly, and guarded as it was on the surface.

At parting, later, Percival spoke for the first time to Miss Milbrey of her engagement.

"You must know that I wish you all the happiness you hope for yourself; and if I were as lucky in love as Mr. Shepler has been, I surely would never dare to gamble in anything else—you know the saying."

"And you, Mr. Bines. I've been hearing so much of your marriage. I hope the rumour I heard to-day is true, that your engagement has been announced."

He laughed.

"Come, now! That's all gossip, you know; not a word of truth in it, and it's been very annoying to us both. Please demolish that rumour on my authority next time you hear it, thoroughly, so they can make nothing out of the pieces."

Miss Milbrey showed genuine disappointment.

"I had thought, naturally—"

"The only member of that household I could marry is not suited to my age."

Miss Milbrey was puzzled.

"But, really, she's not so old."

"No, not so very old. Still, she's going on five, and you know how time flies—and so much disparity in our ages—twenty-one years or so; no, she was no wife for me, although I don't mind confessing that there has been an affair between us, but—really you can't imagine what a frivolous and trifling creature she is."

Miss Milbrey laughed now, rather painfully he fancied.

"You mean the baby? Isn't she a little dear?"

"I'll tell you something, just between us—the baby's mother is—well, I like her—but she's a joke. That's all, a joke."

"I beg your pardon for talking of it. It had seemed so definite. They're waiting for me—good night—*so* glad to have seen you—and, nevertheless, she's a very *practical* joke!"

He watched her with frank, utter longing, as she moved over to Mrs. Oldaker, tender, girlish, appealing, with the old air of timid wistfulness, kept guard over by her woman's knowledge. His fingers still curved, as if they were loth to forget the clasp of her warm, firm little hand. She was gowned in white fleece, and she wore one pink rose where she could bend her blue eyes down upon it.

And she was going to marry Shepler for his millions. She might even yet regret that she had not waited for him, when his own name had been written up as the wizard of markets, and the master of millions. Since money was all she loved, he would show her that even in that he was pre-eminent; though he would still have none of her. And as for Shepler—he wondered if Shepler knew just what risks he might be taking on.

"Oh, Mütterchen! Wasn't it the jolliest evening?"

They were in the carriage.

"Did you and Mr. Bines enjoy yourselves as much as you seemed to?"

"And isn't his grandfather an old dear? What an interesting little story about that woman. I know just how she felt. You see, sir," she turned to Shepler, "there is always a way to manage a woman—you must find her weakness."

"He's a very unusual old chap," said Shepler. "I had occasion not long since to tell him that a certain business plan he proposed was entirely without precedent. His answer was characteristic. He said, 'We *make* precedents in the West when we can't find one to suit us.' It seemed so typical of the people to me. You never can tell what they may do. You see they were started out of old ruts by some form of necessity, almost every one of them, when they went West, and as necessity stimulates only the brightest people to action, those Westerners are apt to be of a pretty keen, active, and sturdy mental type. As this old chap says, they never hang back for lack of precedents; they go ahead and make them. They're not afraid to take sudden queer steps. But, really, I like them both."

"So do I," said his betrothed.

CHAPTER XXXIII.

The Amateur Napoleon of Wall Street

At the beginning of April, the situation in the three stocks Percival had bought so heavily grew undeniably tense. Consolidated Copper went from 109 to 103 in a week. But Percival's enthusiasm suffered little abatement from the drop. "You see," he reminded Uncle Peter, "it isn't exactly what I expected, but it's right in line with it, so it doesn't alarm me. I knew those fellows inside were bound to hammer it down if they could. It wouldn't phase me a bit if it sagged to 95."

"My! My!" Uncle Peter exclaimed, with warm approval, "the way you master this business certainly does win *me*. I tell you, it's a mighty good thing we got your brains to depend on. I'm all right the other side of Council Bluffs, but I'm a tenderfoot here, sure, where everybody's tryin' to get the best of you. You see, out there, everybody tries to make the best of it. But here they try to get the best of it. I told that to one of them smarties last night. But you'll put them in their place all right. You know both ends of the game and the middle. We certainly got a right to be proud of you, son. Dan'l J. liked big propositions himself—but, well, I'd just like to have him see the nerve you've showed, that's all."

Uncle Peter's professions of confidence were unfailing, and Percival took new hope and faith in his judgment from them daily.

Nevertheless, as the weeks passed, and the mysterious insiders succeeded in their design of keeping the stock from rising, he came to feel a touch of anxiety. More, indeed, than he was able to communicate to Uncle Peter, without confessing outright that he had lost faith in himself. That he was unable to do, even if it were true, which he doubted. The Bines fortune was now hanging, as to all but some of the Western properties, on the turning of the three stocks. Yet the old man's confidence in the young man's acumen was invulnerable. No shaft that Percival was able to fashion had point enough to pierce it. And he was both to batter it down, for he still had the gambler's faith in his luck.

"You got your father's head in business matters," was Uncle Peter's invariable response to any suggestion of failure. "I know that much—spite of what all these gossips say—and that's all I *want* to know. And of course you can't ever be no Shepler 'less you take your share of chances. Only don't ask *my* advice. You're master of the game, and we're all layin' right smack down on your genius fur it."

Whereupon the young man, with confidence in himself newly inflated, would hurry off to the stock tickers. He had ceased to buy the stocks outright, and for several weeks had bought only on margins.

"There was one rule in poker your pa had," said Uncle Peter. "If a hand is worth calling on, it's worth raising on. He jest never *would* call. If he didn't think a hand was worth raising, he'd bunch it in with the discards, and wait fur another deal. I don't know much about the game, but *he* said it was a sound rule, and if it was sound in poker, why it's got to be sound in this game. That's all I can tell you. You know what you hold, and if 'tain't a hand to lay down, it must be a hand to raise on. Of course, if you'd been brash and ignorant in your first calculations—if you'd made a fool of yourself at the start—but shucks! you're the son of Daniel J. Bines, ain't you?"

The rule and the clever provocation had their effect.

"I'll raise as long as I have a chip left, Uncle Peter. Why, only to-day I had a tip that came straight from Shepler, though he never dreamed it would reach me. That Pacific Cable bill is going to be rushed through at this session of Congress, sure, and that means enough increased demand to send Consolidated back where it was. And then, when it comes out that they've got those Rio Tinto mines by the throat, well, this anvil chorus will have to stop, and those Federal Oil sharks and Shepler will be wondering how I had the face to stay in."

The published rumours regarding Consolidated began to conflict very sharply. Percival read them all hungrily, disregarding those that did not confirm his own opinions. He called them irresponsible newspaper gossip, or believed them to be inspired by the clique for its own ends.

He studied the history of copper until he knew all its ups and downs since the great electrical development began in 1887. When Fouts, the broker he traded most heavily with, suggested that the Consolidated Company was skating on thin ice, that it might, indeed, be going through the same experience that shattered the famous Secretan corner a dozen years before, Percival pointed out unerringly the vital difference in the circumstances. The Consolidated had reduced the production of its controlled mines, and the price was bound to be maintained. When his adviser suggested that the companies not in the combine might cut the price, he brought up the very lively rumours of a "gentlemen's agreement" with the "non-combine" producers.

"Of course, there's Calumet and Hecla. I know that couldn't be gunned into the combination. They could pay dividends with copper at ten cents a pound. But the other independents know which side of their stock is spread with dividends, all right."

When it was further suggested that the Rio Tinto mines had sold ahead for a year, with the result that European imports from the United States had fallen off, and that the Consolidated could not go on for ever holding up the price, Percival said nothing.

The answer to that was the secret negotiations for control of the European output, which would make the Consolidated master of the copper world. Instead of disclosing this, he pretended craftily to be encouraged by the mere generally hopeful outlook in all lines. Western Trolley, too, might be overcapitalised, and Union Cordage might also be in the hands of a piratical clique; but the demand for trolley lines was growing every day, and cordage products were not going out of fashion by any means.

"You see," he said to his adviser, "here's what the most conservative man in the Street says in this afternoon's paper. 'That copper must necessarily break badly, and the whole boom collapse I do not believe. There is enough prosperity to maintain a strong demand for the metal through another year at least. As to Western Trolley and Union Cordage, the two other stocks about which doubt is now being so widely expressed in the Street, I am persuaded that they are both due to rise, not sensationally, but at a healthy upward rate that makes them sound investments!'

"There," said Percival, "there's the judgment of a man that knows the game, but doesn't happen to have a dollar in either stock, and he doesn't know one or two things that I know, either. Just hypothecate ten thousand of those Union Cordage shares and five thousand Western Trolley, and buy Consolidated on a twenty per cent margin. I want to get bigger action. There's a good rule in poker: if your hand is worth calling, it's worth raising."

"I like your nerve," said the broker.

"Well, I know some one who has a sleeve with something up it, that's all."

By the third week in April, it was believed that his holdings of Consolidated were the largest in the Street, excepting those of the Federal Oil people. Uncle Peter was delighted by the magnitude of his operations, and by his newly formed habits of industry.

"It'll be the makings of the boy," he said to Mrs. Bines in her son's presence. "Not that I care so much myself about all the millions he'll pile up, but it gives him a business training, and takes him out of the pin-head class. I bet Shepler himself will be takin' off his silk hat to your son, jest as soon as he's made this turn in copper—if he has enough of Dan'l J.'s grit to hang on—and I think he has."

"They needn't wait another day for me," Percival told him later. "The family treasure is about all in now, except ma's amethyst earrings, and the hair watch-chain Grandpa Cummings had. Of course I'm holding what I promised for Burman. But that rise can't hold off much longer, and the only thing I'll do, from now on, is to hock a few blocks of the stock I bought outright, and buy on margins, so's to get bigger action."

"My! My! you jest do fairly dazzle me," exclaimed the old man, delightedly. "Oh, I guess your pa wouldn't be at all proud of you if he could see it. I tell you, this family's all right while you keep hearty."

"Well, I'm not pushing my chest out any," said the young man, with becoming modesty, "but I don't mind telling you it will be the biggest thing ever pulled off down there by any one man."

"That's the true Western spirit," declared Uncle Peter, beside himself with enthusiasm. "We do things big when we bother with 'em at all. We ain't afraid of any pikers like Shepler, with his little two and five thousand lots. Oh! I can jest hear 'em callin' you hard names down in that Wall Street—Napoleon of Finance and Copper King and all like that—in about thirty days!"

He accepted Percival's invitation that afternoon to go down into the Street with him. They stopped for a moment in the visitors' gallery of the Stock Exchange and looked down into the mob of writhing, dishevelled, shouting brokers. In and out, the throng swirled upon itself, while above its muddy depths surged a froth of hands in frenzied gesticulation. The frantic movement and din of shrieks disturbed Uncle Peter.

"Faro is such a lot quieter game," was his comment; "so much more ca'm and restful. What a pity, now, 'tain't as Christian!"

Then they made the rounds of the brokers' offices in New, Broad, and Wall Streets.

They reached the office of Fouts, in the, latter street, just as the Exchange had closed. In the outer trading-room groups of men were still about the tickers, rather excitedly discussing the last quotations. Percival made his way toward one of them with a dim notion that he might be concerned. He was relieved when he saw Gordon Blythe, suave and smiling, in the midst of the group, still regarding the tape he held in his hands. Blythe, too, had plunged in copper. He had been one of the few as sanguine as Percival—and Blythe's manner now reassured him. Copper had obviously not gone wrong.

"Ah, Blythe, how did we close? Mr. Blythe, my grandfather, Mr. Bines."

Blythe was the model of easy, indolent, happy middle-age. His tall hat, frock coat with a carnation in the lapel, the precise crease of his trousers, the spickness of his patent-leathers and his graceful confidence of manner, proclaimed his mind to be free from all but the pleasant things of life. He greeted Uncle Peter airily.

"Come down to see how we do it, eh, Mr. Bines? It's vastly engrossing, on my word. Here's copper just closed at 93, after opening strong this morning at 105. I hardly fancied, you know, it could fall off so many of those wretched little points. Rumours that the Consolidated has made large sales of the stuff in London at sixteen, I believe. One never can be quite aware of what really governs these absurd fluctuations."

Percival was staring at Blythe in unconcealed amazement. He turned, leaving Uncle Peter still chatting with him, and sought Fouts in the inner office. When he came out ten minutes later Uncle Peter was waiting for him alone.

"Your friend Mr. Blythe is a clever sort of man, jolly and light-hearted as a boy."

"Let's go out and have a drink, before we go up-town."

In the *café* of the Savarin, to which he led Uncle Peter, they saw Blythe again. He was seated at one of the tables with a younger man. Uncle Peter and Percival sat down at a table near by.

Blythe was having trouble about his wine.

"Now, George," he was saying, "give us a real *lively* pint of wine. You see, yourself, that cork isn't fresh; show it to Frank there, and look at the wine itself—come now, George! Hardly a bubble in it! Tell Frank I'll leave it to him, by Gad! if this bottle is right."

The waiter left with the rejected wine, and they heard Blythe resume to his companion, with the relish of a connoisseur:

"It's simply a matter of genius, old chap—you understand?—to tell good wine—that is really to discriminate finely. If a chap's not born with the gift he's an ass to think he can acquire it. Sometime you've a setter pup that looks fit—head good, nose all right—all the markings—but you try him out and you know in half an hour he'll never do in the world. Then it's better to take him out back of the barn and shoot him, by Gad! Rather than have his strain corrupt the rest of the kennel. He can't acquire the gift, and no more can a chap acquire this gift. Ah! I was right, was I, George? Look how different that cork is."

He sipped the bubbling amber wine with cautious and exacting appreciation. As the waiter would have refilled the glasses, Blythe stopped him.

"Now, George, let me tell you something. You're serving at this moment the only gentleman's drink. Do it right, George. Listen! Never refill a gentleman's glass until it's quite empty. Do you know why? Think, George! You pour fresh wine into stale wine and what have you?—neither. I've taught you something, George. Never fill a glass till it's empty."

"It beats me," said Uncle Peter, when Blythe and his companion had gone, "how easy them rich codgers get along. That fellow must 'a' made a study of wines, and nothing worse ever bothers him than a waiter fillin' his glass wrong."

"You'll be beat more," answered Percival, "when I tell you this slump in copper has just ruined him—wiped out every cent he had. He'd just taken it off the ticker when we found him in Fouts's place there. He's lost a million and a half, every cent he had in the world, and he has a wife and two grown daughters."

"Shoo! you don't say! And I'd have sworn he didn't care a row of pins whether copper went up or down. He was a lot more worried about that champagne. Well, well! he certainly is a game loser. I got more respect fur him now. This town does produce thoroughbreds, you can't deny that."

"Uncle Peter, she's down to 93, and I've had to margin up a good bit. I didn't think it could get below 95 at the worst."

"Oh, I can't bother about them things. Just think of when she booms."

"I do—but say—do you think we better pinch our bets?"

Uncle Peter finished his glass of beer.

"Lord! don't ask *me*," he replied, with the unconcern of perfect trust. "Of course if you've lost your nerve, or if you think all these things you been tellin' me was jest some one foolin' you—"

"No, I know better than that, and I haven't lost my nerve. After all, it only means that the crowd is looking for a bigger rake-off."

"Your pa always kept *his* nerve," said Uncle Peter. "I've known him to make big money by keepin' it when other men lost theirs. Of course he had genius fur it, and you're purty young yet—"

"I only thought of it for a minute. I didn't really mean it."

They read the next afternoon that Gordon Blythe had been found dead of asphyxiation in a little down-town hotel under circumstances that left no doubt of his suicide.

"That man wa'n't so game as we thought," said Uncle Peter. "He's left his family to starve. Now your pa was a game loser fur fair. Dan'l J. would'a' called fur another deck."

"And copper's up two points to-day," said Percival, cheerfully. He had begun to be depressed with forebodings of disaster, and this slight recovery was cheering.

"By the way," he continued, "there may be another gas-jet blown out in a few days. That party, you know, our friend from Montana, has been selling Consolidated right and left. Where do you suppose she got any such tip as that? Well, I'm buying and she's selling, and we'll have that money back. She'll be wiped off the board when Consolidated soars."

CHAPTER XXXIV.

How the Chinook Came to Wall Street

The loss of much money is commonly a subject to be managed with brevity and aversion by one who sits down with the right reverence for sheets of clean paper. To bewail is painful. To affect lightness, on the other hand, would, in this age, savour of insincerity, if not of downright blasphemy. More than a bare recital of the wretched facts, therefore, is not seemly.

The Bines fortune disappeared much as a heavy fall of snow melts under the Chinook wind.

That phenomenon is not uninteresting. We may picture a far-reaching waste of snow, wind-furrowed until it resembles a billowy white sea frozen motionless. The wind blows half a gale and the air is full of fine ice-crystals that sting the face viciously. The sun, lying low on the southern horizon, seems a mere frozen globe, with lustrous pink crescents encircling it.

One day the wind backs and shifts. A change portends. Even the herds of half-frozen range cattle sense it by some subtle beast-knowledge. They are no longer afraid to lie down as they may have been for a week. The danger of freezing has passed. The temperature has been at fifty degrees below zero. Now, suddenly it begins to rise. The air is scarcely in motion, but occasionally it descends as out of a blast-furnace from overhead. To the southeast is a mass of dull black clouds. Their face is unbroken. But the upper edges are ragged, torn by a wind not yet felt below. Two hours later its warmth comes. In ten minutes the mercury goes up thirty-five degrees. The wind comes at a thirty-mile velocity. It increases in strength and warmth, blowing with a mighty roar.

Twelve hours afterward the snow, three feet deep on a level, has melted. There are bald, brown hills everywhere to the horizon, and the plains are flooded with water. The Chinook has come and gone. In this manner suddenly went the Bines fortune.

April 30th, Consolidated Copper closed at 91. Two days later, May 2d, the same ill-fated stock closed at 51—a drop of forty points. Roughly the decline meant the loss of a hundred million dollars to the fifteen thousand share-holders. From every city of importance in the country came tales more or less tragic of holdings wiped out, of ruined families, of defalcations and suicides. The losses in New York City alone were said to be fifty millions. A few large holders, reputed to enjoy inside information, were said to have put their stock aside and "sold short" in the knowledge of what was coming. Such tales are always popular in the Street.

Others not less popular had to do with the reasons for the slump. Many were plausible. A deal with the Rothschilds for control of the Spanish mines had fallen through. Or, again, the slaughter was due to the Shepler group of Federal Oil operators, who were bent on forcing some one to unload a great quantity of the stock so that they might absorb it. The immediate causes were less recondite. The Consolidated Company, so far from controlling the output, was suddenly shown to control actually less than fifty per cent of it. Its efforts to amend or repeal the hardy old law of Supply and Demand had simply met with the indifferent success that has marked all such efforts since the first attempted corner in stone hatchets, or mastodon tusks, or whatever it may have been. In the language of one of its newspaper critics, the "Trust" had been "founded on misconception and prompted along lines of self-destruction. Its fundamental principles were the restriction of product, the increase of price, and the throttling of competition, a trinity that would wreck any combination, business, political, or social."

With this generalisation we have no concern. As to the copper situation, the comment was pat. It had been suddenly disclosed, not only that no combination could be made to include the European mines, but that the Consolidated Company had an unsold surplus of 150,000,000 pounds of copper; that it was producing 20,000,000 pounds a month more than could be sold, and that it had made large secret sales abroad at from two to three cents below the market price.

As if fearing that these adverse conditions did not sufficiently ensure the stock's downfall, the Shepler group of Federal Oil operators beat it down further with what was veritably a golden sledge. That is, they exported gold at a loss. At a time when obligations could have been met more cheaply with bought bills they sent out many golden cargoes at an actual loss of three hundred dollars on the half million. As money was already dear, and thus became dearer, the temptation and the means to hold copper stock, in spite of all discouragements, were removed from the paths of hundreds of the harried holders.

Incidentally, Western Trolley had gone into the hands of a receiver, a failure involving another hundred million dollars, and Union Cordage had fallen thirty-five points through sensational disclosures as to its overcapitalisation.

Into this maelstrom of a panic market the Bines fortune had been sucked with a swiftness so terrible that the family's chief advising member was left dazed and incredulous.

For two days he clung to the ticker tape as to a life line. He had committed the millions of the family as lightly as ever he had staked a hundred dollars on the turn of a card or left ten on the change-tray for his waiter.

Then he had seen his cunningly built foundations, rested upon with hopes so high for three months, melt away like snow when the blistering Chinook comes.

It has been thought wise to adopt two somewhat differing similes in the foregoing, in order that the direness of the tragedy may be sufficiently apprehended.

The morning of the first of the two last awful days, he was called to the office of Fouts and Hendricks by telephone.

"Something going to happen in Consolidated to-day."

He had hurried down-town, flushed with confidence. He knew there was but one thing *could* happen. He had reached the office at ten and heard the first vicious little click of the ticker—that beating heart of the Stock Exchange—as it began the unemotional story of what men bought and sold over on the floor. Its inventor died in the poorhouse, but Capital would fare badly without his machine. Consolidated was down three points. The crowd about the ticker grew absorbed at once. Reports came in over the telephone. The bears had made a set for the stock. It began to slump rapidly. As the stock was goaded down, point by point, the crowd of traders waxed more excited.

As the stock fell, the banks requested the brokers to margin up their loans, and the brokers, in turn, requested Percival to margin up his trades. The shares he had bought outright went to cover the shortage in those he had bought on a twenty per cent margin. Loans were called later, and marginal accounts wiped out with appalling informality.

Yet when Consolidated suddenly rallied three points just at the close of the day's trading, he took much comfort in it as an omen of the morrow. That night, however, he took but little satisfaction in Uncle Peter's renewed assurances of trust in his acumen. Uncle Peter, he decided all at once, was a fatuous, doddering old man, unable to realise that the whole fortune was gravely endangered. And with the gambler's inveterate hope that luck must change he forbore to undeceive the old man.

Uncle Peter went with him to the office next morning, serenely interested in the prospects.

"You got your pa's way of taking hold of big propositions. That's all I need to know," he reassured the young man, cheerfully.

Consolidated Copper opened that day at 78, and went by two o'clock to 51.

Percival watched the decline with a conviction that he was dreaming. He laughed to think of his relief when he should awaken. The crowd surged about the ticker, and their voices came as from afar. Their acts all had the weird inconsequence of the people we see in dreams. Yet presently it had gone too far to be amusing. He must arouse himself and turn over on his side. In five minutes, according to the dream, he had lost five million dollars as nearly as he could calculate. Losing a million a minute, even in sleep, he thought, was disquieting.

Then upon the tape he read another chapter of disaster. Western Trolley had gone into the hands of a receiver,—a fine, fat, promising stock ruined without a word of warning; and while he tried to master this news the horrible clicking thing declared that Union Cordage was selling down to 58,—a drop of exactly 35 points since morning.

Fouts, with a slip of paper in his hand, beckoned him from the door of his private office. He went dazedly in to him,—and was awakened from the dream that he had been losing a fortune in his sleep.

Coming out after a few moments, he went up to Uncle Peter, who had been sitting, watchful but unconcerned, in one of the armchairs along the wall. The old man looked up inquiringly.

"Come inside, Uncle Peter!"

They went into the private office of Fouts. Percival shut the door, and they were alone.

"Uncle Peter, Burman's been suspended on the Board of Trade; Fouts just had this over his private wire. Corn broke to-day."

"That so? Oh, well, maybe it was worth a couple of million to find out Burman plays corn like he plays poker; 'twas if you couldn't get it fur any less."

"Uncle Peter, we're wiped out."

"How, wiped out? What do you mean, son?"

"We're done, I tell you. We needn't care a damn now where copper goes to. We're out of it—and—Uncle Peter, we're broke."

"Out of copper? Broke? But you said—" He seemed to be making an effort to comprehend. His lack of grasp was pitiful.

"Out of copper, but there's Western Trolley and that Cordage stock—"

"Everything wiped out, I tell you—Union Cordage gone down thirty-five points, somebody let out the inside secrets—and God only knows how far Western Trolley's gone down."

"Are you all in?"

"Every dollar—you knew that. But say," he brightened out of his despair, "there's the One Girl—a good producer—Shepler knows the property—Shepler's in this block—" and he was gone.

The old man strolled out into the trading-room again. A curious grim smile softened his square jaw for a moment. He resumed his comfortable chair and took up a newspaper, glancing incidentally at the crowd of excited men about the tickers. He had about him that air of repose which comes to big men who have stayed much in big out-of-door solitudes.

"Ain't he a nervy old guy?" said a crisp little money-broker to Fouts. "They're wiped out, but you wouldn't think he cared any more about it than Mike the porter with his brass polish out there."

The old man held his paper up, but did not read.

Percival rushed in by him, beckoning him to the inner room.

"Shepler's all right about the One Girl. He'll take a mortgage on it for two hundred thousand if you'll recommend it—only he can't get the money before to-morrow. There's bound to be a rally in this stock, and we'll go right back for some of the hair of the—why,—what's the matter—Uncle Peter!"

The old man had reeled, and then weakly caught at the top of the desk with both hands for support.

"Ruined!" he cried, hoarsely, as if the extent of the calamity had just borne in upon him. "My God! Ruined, and at my time of life!" He seemed about to collapse. Percival quickly helped him into a chair, where he became limp.

"There, I'm all right. Oh, it's terrible! and we all trusted you so. I thought you had your pa's brains. I'd 'a' trusted you soon's I would Shepler, and now look what you led us into—fortune gone—broke—and all your fault!"

"Don't, Uncle Peter—don't, for God's sake—not when I'm down! I can't stand it!"

"Gamble away your own money—no, that wa'n't enough—take your poor ma's share and your sister's, and take what little I had to keep me in my old age—robbed us all—that's what comes of thinkin' a damned tea-drinkin' fop could have a thimble-full of brains!"

"Don't, please,—not just now—give it to me good later—to-morrow—all you want to!"

"And here I'm come to want in my last days when I'm too feeble to work. I'll die in bitter privation because I was an old fool, and trusted a young one."

"Please don't, Uncle Peter!"

"You led us in—robbed your poor ma and your sister. I told you I didn't know anything about it and you talked me into trusting you—I might 'a' known better."

"Can't you stop awhile—just a moment?"

"Of course I don't matter. Maybe I can hold a drill, or tram ore, or something, but I can't support your ma and Pishy like they ought to be, with my rheumatiz comin' on again, too. And your ma'll have to take in boarders, and do washin' like as not, and think of poor Pishy—prob'ly she'll have to teach school or clerk in a store—poor Pish—she'll be lucky now if she can marry some common scrub American out in them hills— like as not one of them shoe-clerks in the Boston Cash Store at Montana City! And jest when I was lookin' forward to luxury and palaces in England, and everything so grand! How much you lost?" "That's right, no use whining! Nearly as I can get the round figures of it, about twelve million."

"Awful—awful! By Cripes! that man Blythe that done himself up the other night had the right of it. What's the use of living if you got to go to the poorhouse?"

"Come, come!" said Percival, alarm over Uncle Peter crowding out his other emotions. "Be a game loser, just as you said pa would be. Sit up straight and make 'em bring on another deck."

He slapped the old man on the back with simulated cheerfulness; but the despairing one only cowered weakly under the blow.

"We can't—we ain't got the stake for a new deck. Oh, dear! think of your ma and me not knowin' where to turn fur a meal of victuals at our time of life."

Percival was being forced to cheerfulness in spite of himself.

"Come, it isn't as bad as that, Uncle Peter. We've got properties left, and good ones, too."

Uncle Peter weakly waved the hand of finished discouragement. "Hush, don't speak of that. Them properties need a manager to make 'em pay—a plain business man—a man to stay on the ground and watch 'em and develop 'em with his brains—a young man with his health! What good am I—a poor, broken-down old cuss, bent double with rheumatiz—almost— I'm ashamed of you fur suggesting such a thing!"

"I'll do it myself—I never thought of asking you."

Uncle Peter emitted a nasal gasp of disgust.

"You—you—you'd make a purty manager of anything, wouldn't you! As if you could be trusted with anything again that needs a schoolboy's intelligence. Even if you had the brains, you ain't got the taste nor the sperrit in you. You're too lazy—too triflin'. *You*, a-goin' back there, developin' mines, and gettin' out ties, and lumber, and breeding shorthorns, and improvin' some of the finest land God ever made—*you* bein' sober and industrious, and smart, like a business man has got to be out there nowadays. That ain't any bonanza country any more; 1901 ain't like 1870; don't figure on that. You got to work the low-grade ore now for a few dollars a ton, and you got to work it with brains. No, sir, that country ain't what it used to be. There might 'a' been a time when you'd made your board and clothes out there when things come easier. Now it's full of men that hustle and keep their mind on their work, and ain't runnin' off to pink teas in New York. It takes a man with some of the brains your pa had to make the game pay now. But *you*—don't let me hear any more of *that* nonsense!"

Percival had entered the room pale. He was now red. The old man's bitter contempt had flushed him into momentary forgetfulness of the disaster.

"Look here, Uncle Peter, you've been telling me right along I *did* have my father's head and my father's ways and his nerve, and God knows what I *didn't* have that he had!"

"I was fooled,—I can't deny it. What's the use of tryin' to crawl out of it? You did fool me, and I own up to it; I thought you had some sense, some capacity; but you was only like him on the surface; you jest got one or two little ways like his, that's all—Dan'l J. now was good stuff all the way through. He might 'a' guessed wrong on copper, but he'd 'a' saved a get-away stake or borrowed one, and he'd 'a' piked back fur Montana to make his pile right over—and he'd 'a' *made* it, too—that was the kind of man your pa was—he'd 'a' made it!"

"I *have* saved a get-away stake."

"Your pa had the head, I tell you—and the spirit—"

"And, by God, I'll show you I've got the head. You think because I wanted to live here, and because I made this wrong play that I'm like all these pinheads you've seen around here. I'll show you different!—I'll fool you."

"Now don't explode!" said the old man, wearily. "You meant well, poor fellow—I'll say that fur you; you got a good heart. But there's lots of good men that ain't good fur anything in particular. You've got a good heart—yes—you're all right from the neck down."

"See here," said Percival, more calmly, "listen: I've got you all into this thing, and played you broke against copper; and I'm going to get you out—understand that?"

The old man looked at him pityingly.

"I tell you I'm going to get you out. I'm going back there, and get things in action, and I'm going to stay by them. I've got a good idea of these properties—and you hear me, now—I'll finish with a bank-roll that'll choke Red Bank Cañon."

Fouts knocked and came in.

"Now you go along up-town, Uncle Peter. I want a few minutes with Mr. Fouts, and I'll come to your place at seven."

The old man arose dejectedly.

"Don't let me interfere a minute with your financial operations. I'm too old a man to be around in folks' way."

He slouched out with his head bent.

A moment later Percival remembered his last words, also his reference to Blythe. He was seized with fear for what he might do in his despair. Uncle Peter would act quickly if his mind had been made up.

He ran out into Wall Street, and hurried up to Broadway. A block off on that crowded thoroughfare he saw the tall figure of Uncle Peter turning into the door of a saloon. He might have bought poison. He ran the length of the block and turned in.

Uncle Peter stood at one end of the bar with a glass of creamy beer in front of him. At the moment Percival entered he was enclosing a large slab of Swiss cheese between two slices of rye bread.

He turned and faced Percival, looking from him to his sandwich with vacant eyes.

"I'm that wrought up and distressed, son, I hardly know what I'm doin'! Look at me now with this stuff in my hands."

"I just wanted to be sure you were all right," said Percival, greatly relieved.

"All right," the old man repeated. "All right? My God,—ruined! There's nothin' left to do now."

He looked absently at the sandwich, and bit a generous semicircle into it.

"I don't see how you can eat, Uncle Peter. It's so horrible!"

"I don't myself; it ain't a healthy appetite—can't be—must be some kind of a fever inside of me—I s'pose—from all this trouble. And now I've come to poverty and want in my old age. Say, son, I believe there's jest one thing you can do to keep me from goin' crazy."

"Name it, Uncle Peter. You bet I'll do it!"

"Well, it ain't much—of course I wouldn't expect you to do all them things you was jest braggin' about back there—about goin' to work the properties and all that—you would do it if you could, I know—but it ain't that. All I ask is, don't play this Wall Street game any more. If we can save out enough by good luck to keep us decently, so your ma won't have to take boarders, why, don't you go and lose that, too. Don't mortgage the One Girl. I may be sort of superstitious, but somehow, I don't believe Wall Street is your game. Course, I don't say you ain't got a game—of some kind—but I got one of them presentiments that it ain't Wall Street." "I don't believe it is, Uncle Peter—I won't touch another share, and I won't go near Shepler again. We'll keep the One Girl."

He called a cab for the old man, and saw him started safely off up-town.

At the hotel Uncle Peter met Billy Brue flourishing an evening paper that flared with exclamatory headlines.

"It's all in the papers, Uncle Peter!"

"Dead broke! Ain't it awful, Billy!"

"Say, Uncle Peter, you said you'd raise hell, and you done it. You done it good, didn't you?"

CHAPTER XXXV.

The News Broken, Whereupon an Engagement is Broken

At seven Percival found Uncle Peter at his hotel, still in abysmal depths of woe. Together they went to break the awful news to the unsuspecting Mrs. Bines and Psyche.

"If you'd only learned something useful while you had the chance," began Uncle Peter, dismally, as they were driven to the Hightower, "how to do tricks with cards, or how to sing funny songs, like that little friend of yours from Baltimore you was tellin' me about. Look at him, now. He didn't have anything but his own ability. He could tell you every time what card you was thinkin' about, and do a skirt dance and give comic recitations and imitate a dog fight out in the back yard, and now he's married to one of the richest ladies in New York. Why couldn't you 'a' been learnin' some of them clever things, so you could 'a' married some good-hearted woman with lots of money—but no—" Uncle Peter's tones were bitter to excess— "you was a rich man's son and raised in idleness—and now, when the rainy day's come, you can't even take a white rabbit out of a stove-pipe hat!"

To these senile maunderings Percival paid no attention. When they came into the crowd and lights of the Hightower, he sent the old man up alone.

"You go, please, and break it to them, Uncle Peter. I'd rather not be there just at first. I'll come along in a little bit."

So Uncle Peter went, protesting that he was a broken old man and a cumberer of God's green earth.

Mrs. Bines and Psyche had that moment sat down to dinner. Uncle Peter's manner at once alarmed them.

"It's all over," he said, sinking into a chair.

"Why, what's the matter, Uncle Peter?"

"Percival has—"

Mrs. Bines arose quickly, trembling.

"There—I just knew it—it's all over?—he's been struck by one of those terrible automobiles—Oh, take me to where he is!"

"He ain't been run over—he's gone broke-lost all our money; every last cent."

"He hasn't been run over and killed?"

"He's ruined us, I tell you, Marthy,—lost every cent of our money in Wall Street."

"Hasn't he been hurt at all?—not even his leg broke or a big gash in his head and knocked senseless?"

"That boy never had any sense. I tell you he's lost all our money."

"And he ain't a bit hurt—nothing the matter with him?"

"Ain't any more hurt than you or me this minute."

"You're not fooling his mother, Uncle Peter?"

"I tell you he's alive and well, only he's lost your money and Pish's and mine and his own."

Mrs. Bines breathed a long, trembling sigh of relief, and sat down to the table again.

"Well, no need to scare a body out of their wits—scaring his mother to death won't bring his money back, will it? If it's gone it's gone."

"But ma, it *is* awful!" cried Psyche. "Listen to what Uncle Peter says. We're poor! Don't you understand? Perce has lost all our money."

Mrs. Bines was eating her soup defiantly.

"Long's he's got his health," she began.

"And me windin' up in the poorhouse," whined Uncle Peter.

"Think of it, ma! Oh, what shall we do?"

Percival entered. Uncle Peter did not raise his head. Psyche stared at him. His mother ran to him, satisfied herself that he was sound in wind and limb, that he had not treacherously donned his summer underwear, and that his feet were not wet. Then she led him to the table.

"Now you sit right down here and take some food. If you're all right, everything is all right."

With a weak attempt at his old gaiety he began: "Really, Mrs. Crackenthorpe—" but he caught Psyche's look and had to stop.

"I'm sorry, sis, clear into my bones. I made an ass of myself—a regular fool right from the factory."

"Never mind, my son; eat your soup," said his mother. And then, with honest intent to comfort him, "Remember that saying of your pa's, 'it takes all kinds of fools to make a world.'"

"But there ain't any fool like a damn fool!" said Uncle Peter, shortly. "I been a-tellin' him."

"Well, you just let him alone; you'll spoil his appetite, first thing you know. My son, eat your soup, now before it gets cold."

"If I only hadn't gone in so heavy," groaned Percival. "Or, if I'd only got tied up in some way for a few weeks—something I could tide over."

"Yes," said Uncle Peter, with a cheerful effort at sarcasm, "it's always easy to think up a lot of holes you *could* get out of—some different kind of a hole besides the one you're in. That's all some folks can do when they get in one hole, they say, 'Oh, if I was only in that other one, now, how slick I could climb out!' I ain't ever met a person yet was satisfied with the hole they was in. Always some complaint to make about 'em."

"And I had a chance to get out a week ago."

"Yes, and you wouldn't take it, of course—you knew too much—swellin' around here about bein' a Napoleon of finance—and a Shepler and a Wizard of Wall Street, and all that kind of guff—and you wouldn't take your chance, and old Mr. Chance went right off and left you, that's what. I tell you, what some folks need is a breed of chances that'll stand without hitchin'."

Percival braced himself and began on his soup.

"Never you mind, Uncle Peter. You remember what I told you."

"That takes a different man from what you are. If your pa was alive now—"

"But what are we going to do?" cried Psyche.

"First thing you'll do," said Uncle Peter, promptly, "you go write a letter to that beau of your'n, tellin' him it's all off. You don't want to let him be the one to break it because you lost your money, do you? You go sign his release right this minute."

"Yes—you're right, Uncle Peter—I suppose it must be done—but the poor fellow really cares for me."

"Oh, of course," answered the old man, "it'll fairly break his heart. You do it just the same!"

She withdrew, and presently came back with a note which she despatched to Mauburn.

Percival and his mother had continued their dinner, the former shaking his head between the intervals of the old man's lashings, and appearing to hold silent converse with himself.

This was an encouraging sign. It is a curious fact that people never talk to themselves except triumphantly. In moments of real despair we are inwardly dumb. But observe the holders of imaginary conversations. They are conquerors to the last one. They administer stinging rebukes that leave the adversary writhing. They rise to Alpine heights of pure wisdom and power, leaving him to flounder ignobly in the mire of his own fatuity.

They achieve repartee the brilliance of which dazzles him to contemptible silence. If statistics were at hand we should doubtless learn that no man has ever talked to himself save by way of demonstrating his own godlike superiority, and the tawdry impotence of all obstacles and opponents. Percival talked to himself and mentally lived the next five years in a style that reduced Uncle Peter to grudging but imperative awe for his superb gifts of administration. He bathed in this imaginary future as in the waters of omnipotence. As time went on he foresaw the shafts of Uncle Peter being turned back upon him with such deadliness that, by the time the roast came, his breast was swelling with pity for that senile scoffer.

Uncle Peter had first declared that the thought of food sickened him. Prevailed upon at last by Mrs. Bines to taste the soup, he was soon eating as those present had of late rarely seen him eat.

"'Tain't a natural appetite, though," he warned them. "It's a kind of a mania before I go all to pieces, I s'pose."

"Nonsense! We'll have you all right in a week," said Percival. "Just remember that I'm going to take care of you."

"My son can do anything he makes up his mind to," declared Mrs. Bines— "just anything he lays out to do."

They talked until late into the night of what he should "lay out" to do.

Meantime the stronghold of Mauburn's optimism was being desperately stormed.

In an evening paper he had read of Percival's losses. The afternoon press of New York is not apt to understate the facts of a given case. The account

Mauburn read stated that the young Western millionaire had beggared his family.

Mauburn had gone to his room to be alone with this bitter news. He had begun to face it when Psyche's note of release came. While he was adjusting this development, another knock came on his door. It was the same maid who had brought Psyche's note. This time she brought what he saw to be a cablegram.

"Excuse me, Mr. Mauburn,—now this came early to-day and you wasn't in your room, and when you came in Mrs. Ferguson forgot it till just now."

He tore open the envelope and read:

"Male twins born to Lady Casselthorpe. Mother and sons doing finely.

"HINKIE."

Mauburn felt the rock foundations of Manhattan Island to be crumbling to dust. For an hour he sat staring at the message. He did not talk to himself once.

Then he hurriedly dressed, took the note and the cablegram, and sought Mrs. Drelmer.

He found that capable lady gowned for the opera. She received his bits of news with the aplomb of a resourceful commander.

"Now, don't go seedy all at once—you've a chance."

"Hang it all, Mrs. Drelmer, I've not. Life isn't worth living—"

"Tut, tut! Death isn't, either!"

"But we'd have been so nicely set up, even without the title, and now Bines, the clumsy ass, has come this infernal cropper, and knocked everything on the head. I say, you know, it's beastly!"

"Hush, and let me think!"

He paced the floor while his matrimonial adviser tapped a white kidded foot on the floor, and appeared to read plans of new battle in a mother-of-pearl paper-knife which she held between the tips of her fingers.

"I have it—and we'll do it quickly!—Mrs. Wybert!"

Mauburn's eyes opened widely.

"That absurd old Peter Bines has spoken to me of her three times lately. She's made a lot more money than she had in this same copper deal, and she'd a lot to begin with. I wondered why he spoke so enthusiastically of her, and I don't see now, but—"

"Well?"

"She'll take you, and you'll be as well set up as you were before. Listen. I met her last week at the Critchleys. She spoke of having seen you. I could see she was dead set to make a good marriage. You know she wanted to marry Fred Milbrey, but Horace and his mother wouldn't hear of it after Avice became engaged to Rulon Shepler. I'm in the Critchleys' box to-night and I understand she's to be there. Leave it to me. Now it's after nine, so run along."

"But, Mrs. Drelmer, there's that poor girl—she cares for me, and I like her immensely, you know—truly I do—and she's a trump—see where she says here she couldn't possibly leave her people now they've come down—even if matters were not otherwise impossible."

"Well, you see they're not only otherwise impossible, but every wise impossible. What could you do? Go to Montana with them and learn to be an Indian? Don't for heaven's sake sentimentalise! Go home and sleep like a rational creature. Come in by eleven to-morrow. Even without the title you'll be a splendid match for Mrs. Wybert, and she must have a tidy lot of millions after this deal."

Sorely distressed, he walked back to his lodgings in Thirty-second Street. Wild, Quixotic notions of sacrifice flooded his mood of dejection. If the worst came, he could go West with the family and learn how to do something. And yet—Mrs. Wybert. Of course it must be that. The other idea was absurd—too wild for serious consideration. He was thirty years old, and there was only one way for an English gentleman to live—even if it must break the heart of a poor girl who had loved him devotedly, and for whom he had felt a steady and genuine affection. He passed a troubled night.

Down at the hotel of Peter Bines was an intimation from Mrs. Wybert herself, bearing upon this same fortuity. When Uncle Peter reached there at 2 A.M., he found in his box a small scented envelope which he opened with wonder.

Two enclosures fell out. One was a clipping from an evening paper, announcing the birth of twin sons to Lord Casselthorpe. The other was the card he had left with Mrs. Wybert on the day of his call; his name on one side, announcing him; on the other the words he had written:

"Sell Consolidated Copper all you can until it goes down to 65. Do this up to the limit of your capital and I will make good anything you lose.

"PETER BINES."

He read the note:

"ARLINGHAM HOTEL—7.30.

"MR. PETER BINES:

"*Dear Sir.*—You funny old man, you. I don't pretend to understand your game, but you may rely on my secrecy. I am more grateful to you than words can utter—and I will always be glad to do anything for you.

"*Yours very truly,*

"BLANCHE CATHERTON WYBERT.

"P. S. About that other matter—him you know—you will see from this notice I cut from the paper that the party won't get any title at all now, so a dead swell New York man is in every way more eligible. In fact the other party is not to be thought of for one moment, as I am positive you would agree with me."

He tore the note and the card to fine bits.

"It does beat all," he complained later to Billy Brue. "Put a beggar on horseback and they begin right away to fuss around because the bridle ain't set with diamonds—give 'em a little, and they want the whole ball of wax!"

"That's right," said Billy Brue, with the quick sympathy of the experienced. "That guy that doped me, he wa'n't satisfied with my good thirty-dollar wad. Not by no means! He had to go take my breast-pin nugget from the Early Bird."

At eleven o'clock the next morning Mauburn waited in Mrs. Drelmer's drawing-room for the news she might have.

When that competent person sailed in, he saw temporary defeat written on her brow. His heart sank to its low level of the night before.

"Well, I saw the creature," she began, "and it required no time at all to reach a very definite understanding with her. I had feared it might be rather a delicate matter, talking to her at once, you know—and we needed to hurry—but she's a woman one can talk to. She's made heaps of money, and the poor thing is society-mad—*so* afraid the modish world won't take her at her true value—but she talked very frankly about marriage—really she's cool-headed for all the fire she seems to have—and the short of it is that she's determined to marry some one of the smart men here in New York. The creature's fascinated by the very idea."

"Did you mention me?"

"You may be sure I did, but she'd read the papers, and, like so many of these people, she has no use at all for an Englishman without a title. Of course I couldn't be too definite with her, but she understood perfectly, and she let me see she wouldn't hear of it at all. So she's off the list. But don't give up. Now, there's—"

But Mauburn was determinedly downcast.

"It's uncommon handsome of you, Mrs. Drelmer, really, but we'll have to leave off that, you know. If a chap isn't heir to a peerage or a city fortune there's no getting on that way."

"Why, the man is actually discouraged. Now you need some American pluck, old chap. An American of your age wouldn't give up."

"But, hang it all! an American knows how to do things, you know, and like as not he'd nothing to begin with, by Jove! Now I'd a lot to begin with, and here it's all taken away."

"Look at young Bines. He's had a lot taken away, but I'll wager he makes it all back again and more too before he's forty."

"He might in this country; he'd never do it at home, you know."

"This country is for you as much as for him. Now, there's Augusta Hartong—those mixed-pickle millionaires, you know. I was chatting with Augusta's mother only the other day, and if I'd only suspected this—"

"Awfully kind of you, Mrs. Drelmer, but it's no use. I'm fairly played out. I shall go to see Miss Bines, and have a chat with her people, you know."

"Now, for heaven's sake, don't make a silly of yourself, whatever you do! Mind, the girl released you of her own accord!"

"Awfully obliged. I'll think about it jolly well, first. See you soon. Good-bye!" And Mauburn was off.

He was reproaching himself. "That poor girl has been eating her heart out for a word of love from me. I'm a brute!"

CHAPTER XXXVI.

The God in the Machine

Uncle Peter next morning was up to a late breakfast with the stricken family. Percival found him a trifle less bitter, but not less convinced in his despair. The young man himself had recovered his spirits wonderfully. The utter collapse of the old man, always so reliant before, had served to fire all his latent energy. He was now voluble with plans for the future; not only determined to reassure Uncle Peter that the family would be provided for, but not a little anxious to justify the old man's earlier praise, and refute his calumnies of the night before.

Mrs. Bines, so complacent overnight, was the most disconsolate one of the group. With her low tastes she was now regarding the loss of the fortune as a calamity to the worthy infants of her own chosen field.

"And there, I'd promised to give five thousand dollars to the new home for crippled children, and five thousand to St. John's Guild for the floating hospitals this summer—just yesterday—and I do declare, I just couldn't stay in New York without money, and see those poor babies suffer."

"You couldn't stay in New York without money. Mrs. Good-thing," said her son,—"not even if you couldn't see a thing; but don't you welsh on any of your plays—we'll make that ten thousand good if I have to get a sand-bag, and lay out a few of these lads around here some dark night."

"But anyway you can't do much to relieve them. I don't know but what it's honester to be poor while the authorities allow such goings on."

"You have the makings of a very dangerous anarchist in you, ma. I've seen that for some time. But we're an honest family all right now, with the exception of a few properties that I'll have to sit up with nights—sit right by their sick-beds and wake them up to take their meddy every half hour—"

"Now, my son, don't you get to going without your sleep," began his mother.

"And wasn't it lucky about my sending that note to George!" said Psyche. "Here in this morning's paper we find he isn't going to be Lord Casselthorpe, after all. What *could* I have done if we hadn't lost the money?" From which it might be inferred that certain people who had declared Miss

Bines to be very hard-headed were not so far wrong as the notorious "casual observer" is very apt to be.

"Never you mind, sis," said her brother, cheerfully, "we'll be all right yet. You wait a little, and hear Uncle Peter take back what he's said about me. Uncle Peter, I'll have you taking off that hat of yours every time you get sight of me, in about a year."

He went again over the plans. The income from the One Girl was to be used in developing the other properties: the stock ranch up on the Bitter Root, the other mines that had been worked but little and with crude appliances; the irrigation and land-improvement enterprises, and the big timber tracts.

"I got something of an idea of it when Uncle Peter took me around summer before last, and I learned a lot more getting the stuff together with Coplen. Now, I'm ready to buckle down to it." He looked at Uncle Peter, hungry for a word of encouragement to soothe the hurts the old man had put upon him.

But all Uncle Peter would say was, "That *sounds* very well," compelling the inference that he regarded sound and substance as phenomena not necessarily related.

"But give me a chance, Uncle Peter. Just don't jump on me too hard for a year!"

"Well, I know that country. There's big chances for a young man with brains—understand?—that has got all the high-living nonsense blasted out of his upper levels—but it takes work. You *may* do something—there *are* white blackbirds—but you're on a nasty piece of road-bed—curves all down on the outside—wheels flatted under every truck, and you've had her down in the corner so long I doubt if you can even slow up, say nothin' of reversin'. And think of me gettin' fooled that way at *my* time of life," he continued, as if in confidence to himself. "But then, I always was a terrible poor judge of human nature."

"Well, have your own way; but I'll fool you again, while you're coppering me. You watch, that's all I ask. Just sit around and talk wise about me all you want to, but watch. Now, I must go down and get to work with Fouts. Thank the Lord, we didn't have to welsh either, any more than Mrs. Give-up there did."

"You won't touch any more stock; you won't get that money from Shepler?"

"I won't; I won't go near Shepler, I promise you. Now you'll believe me in one thing, I know you will, Uncle Peter." He went over to the old man.

"I want to thank you for pulling me up on that play as you did last night. You saved me, and I'm more grateful to you than I can say. But for you I'd have gone in and dug the hole deeper." He made the old man shake hands with him—though Uncle Peter's hand remained limp and cheerless. "You can shake on that, at least. You saved me, and I thank you for it."

"Well, I'm glad you got *some* sense," answered the old man, grudgingly. "It's always the way in that stock game. There's always goin' to be a big killing made in Wall Street to-morrow, only to-morrow never comes. Reminds me of Hollings's old turtle out at Spokane—Hollings that keeps the Little Gem restaurant. He's got an enormous big turtle in his cellar that he's kept to my knowledge fur fifteen years. Every time he gets a little turtle from the coast he takes a can of red paint down cellar, and touches up the sign on old Ben's back—they call the turtle Ben, after Hollings's father-in-law that won't do a thing but lay around the house all the time, and kick about the meals. Well, the sign on Ben's back is, 'Green Turtle Soup To-morrow,' and Ben is drug up to the sidewalk in front of the Little Gem. And Hollings does have turtle-soup next day, but it's always the little turtles that's killed, and old Ben is hiked back to his boudoir until another killing comes off. It's a good deal like that in Wall Street; there's killings made, but the big fellers with the signs on their back don't worry none."

"You're right, Uncle Peter. It certainly wasn't my game. Will you come down with me?"

"Me? Shucks, no! I'm jest a poor, broken old man, now. I'm goin' down to the square if I can walk that fur, and set on a bench in the sun."

Uncle Peter did succeed in walking as far as Madison Square. He walked, indeed, with a step of amazing springiness for a man of his years. But there, instead of reposing in the sun, he entered a cab and was driven to the Vandevere Building, where he sent in his name to Rulon Shepler.

He was ushered into Shepler's office after a little delay. The two men shook hands warmly. Uncle Peter was grinning now with rare enjoyment—he who had in the presence of the family shown naught but broken age and utter despondency.

"You rough-housed the boy considerable yesterday."

"I never believed the fellow would hold on," said Shepler. "I'm sure you're right in a way about the West. There isn't another man in this

He handed the old man a dozen or so certified checks on as many different banks. Each check had many figures on it. Uncle Peter placed them in his old leather wallet.

"I knew he'd plunge," he said, taking the chair proffered him, near Shepler's desk. "I knew he was a natural born plunger, and I knew that once he gets an idea in his head you can't blast it out; makes no difference what he starts on he'll play the string out. His pa was jest that way. Then of course he wa'n't used to money, and he was ignorant of this game, and he didn't realise what he was doin'. He sort of distrusted himself along toward the last—but I kept him swelled up good and plenty."

"Well, I'm glad it's over, Mr. Bines. Of course I concede the relative insignificance of money to a young man of his qualities—"

"Not its relative insignificance, Mr. Shepler—it's plain damned insignificance, if you'll excuse the word. If that boy'd gone on he'd 'a' been one of what Billy Brue calls them high-collared Clarences—no good fur anything but to spend money, and get apoplexy or worse by forty. As it is now, he'll be a man. He's got his health turned on like a steam radiator, he's full of responsibility, and he's really long-headed."

"How did he take the loss?"

"He acted jest like a healthy baby does when you take one toy away from him. He cries a minute, then forgets all about it, and grabs up something else to play with. His other toy was bad. What he's playin' with now will do him a lot of good."

"He's not discouraged, then—he's really hopeful?"

"That ain't any name fur it. Why, he's actin' this mornin' jest like the world's his oyster—and every month had an 'r' in it at that."

"I'm delighted to hear it. I've always been taken with the chap; and I'm very glad you read him correctly. It seemed to me you were taking a risk. It would have broken the spirit of most men."

"Well, you see I knew the stock. It's pushin', fightin' stock. My grandfather fought his way west to Pennsylvania when that country was wilder'n Africa, and my father fought his way to Ohio when that was the frontier. I seen some hard times myself, and this boy's father was a fighter, too. So I knew the boy had it in him, all right. He's got his faults, but they don't hurt him none."

"Will he return West?"

"He will that—and the West is the only place fur him. He was gettin' bad notions about his own country here from them folks that's always crackin' up the 'other side' 'sif there wa'n't any 'this side,' worth speakin' of in company. This was no place fur him. Mr. Shepler, this whole country is God's country. I don't talk much about them things, but I believe in God—

a man has to if he lives so much alone in them wild places as I have—and I believe this country is His favourite. I believe He set it apart fur great works. The history of the United States bears me out so fur. And I didn't want any of my stock growin' up without feelin' that he had the best native land on earth, and without bein' ready to fight fur it at the drop of the hat. And jest between you and me, I believe we can raise that kind in the West better'n you can here in New York. You got a fine handsome town here, it's a corkin' good place to see—and get out of—but it ain't any breedin' place—there ain't the room to grow. Now we produce everything in the West, includin' men. Here you don't do anything but consume—includin' men. If the West stopped producin' men fur you, you'd be as bad off as if it stopped producin' food. You can't grow a big man on this island any more than you can grow wheat out there on Broadway. You're all right. You folks have your uses. I ain't like one of these crazy Populists that thinks you're rascals and all like that; but my point is that you don't get the fun out of life. You don't get the big feelin's. Out in the West they're the flesh and blood and bone; and you people here, meanin' no disrespect—you're the dimples and wrinkles and—the warts. You spend and gamble back and forth with that money we raise and dig out of the ground, and you think you're gettin' the best end of it, but you ain't. I found that out thirty-two years ago this spring. I had a crazy fool notion then to go back there even when I hadn't gone broke—and I done well to go. And that's why I wanted that boy back there. And that's why I'm mighty proud of him, to see he's so hot to go and take hold, like I knew he would be."

"That's excellent. Now, Mr. Bines, I like him and I dare say you've done the best thing for him, unusual as it was. But don't grind him. Might it not be well to ease up a little after he's out there? You might let it be understood that I am willing to finance any of those propositions there liberally—"

"No, no—that ain't the way to handle him. Say, I don't expect to quit cussin' him fur another thirty days yet. I want him to think he ain't got a friend on earth but himself. Why, I'd have made this play just as I have done, Mr. Shepler, if there hadn't been a chance to get back a cent of it—if we'd had to go plumb broke—back to the West in an emigrant car, with bologna and crackers to eat, that's what I'd have done. No, sir, no help fur him!"

"Aren't you a little hard on him?"

"Not a bit; don't I know the stock, and know just what he needs? Most men you couldn't treat as I'm treatin' him; but with him, the harder you bear down on him the more you'll get out of him. That was the way with his pa—he was a different man after things got to comin' too easy fur him. This fellow, the way I'm treatin' him, will keep his head even after he gets things comin' easy again, or I miss my guess. He thinks I despise him now. If you told him I was proud of him, I almost believe you could get a bet out of him, sick as he is of gamblin'."

"Has he suspected anything?"

"Sure, not! Why, he just thanked me about an hour ago fur savin' him— made me shake hands with him—and I could see the tears back in his eyes."

The old man chuckled.

"It was like Len Carey's Nigger Jim. Len had Jim set apart on the plantation fur his own nigger. They fished and went huntin' and swimmin' together. One day they'd been swimmin', and was lyin' up on the bank. Len got thinkin' he'd never seen any one drown. He knew Jim couldn't swim a lick, so he thought he'd have Jim go drown. He says to him, 'Jim, go jump off that rock there!' That was where the deep hole was. Jim was scar't, but he had to go. After he'd gone down once, Len says to him, 'Drown, now, you damn nigger!' and Jim come up and went down twice more. Then Len begun to think Jim was worth a good bit of money, and mebbe he'd be almighty walloped if the truth come out, so he dives in after Jim and gets him shore, and after while he brought him to. Anyway, he said, Jim had already sure-enough drowned as fur as there was any fun in it. Well, Len Carey is an old man now, and Jim is an old white-headed nigger still hangin' around the old place, and when Len goes back there to visit his relatives, old Nigger Jim hunts him up with tears in his eyes, and thanks Mister Leonard fur savin' his life that time. Say, I felt this mornin' like Len Carey must feel them times when Jim's thankin' him."

Shepler laughed.

"You're a rare man, Mr. Bines. I'll hope to have your cheerful, easy views of life if I ever lose my hold here in the Street. I hope I'll have the old Bines philosophy and the young Bines spirit. That reminds me," he continued as Uncle Peter rose to go, "we've been pretty confidential, Mr. Bines, and I don't mind telling you I was a bit afraid of that young man until yesterday. Oh, not on the stock proposition. On another matter. You may have noticed that night at the Oldakers'—well, women, Mr. Bines, are uncertain. I know something about markets and the ways of a dollar, but all I know about women is that they're good to have. You can't know any more about them, because they don't know any more themselves. Just between us, now, I never felt any too sure of a certain young woman's state of mind until copper reached 51 and Union Cordage had been blown up from inside."

They parted with warm expressions of good-will, and Uncle Peter, in high spirits at the success of his machinations, had himself driven up-town.

The only point where his plans had failed was in Mrs. Wybert's refusal to consider Mauburn after the birth of the Casselthorpe twins. Yet he felt that matters, in spite of this happening, must go as he wished them to. The Englishman-Uncle Peter cherished the strong anti-British sentiment peculiar to his generation—would surely never marry a girl who was all but penniless, and the consideration of an alliance with Mrs. Wybert, when the fortune should be lost, had, after all, been an incident—a means of showing the girl, if she should prove to be too deeply infatuated with Mauburn for her own peace of mind—how unworthy and mercenary he was; for he had meant, in that event, to disillusion her by disclosing something of Mrs. Wybert's history—the woman Mauburn should prefer to her. He still counted confidently on the loss of the fortune sufficing to break the match.

When he reached the Hightower that night for dinner, he found Percival down-stairs in great glee over what he conceived to be a funny situation.

"Don't ask me, Uncle Peter. I couldn't get it straight; but as near as I could make out, Mauburn came up here afraid the blow of losing him was going to kill sis with a broken heart, and sis was afraid the blow was going to kill Mauburn, because she wouldn't have married him anyway, rich or poor, after he'd lost the title. They found each other out some way, and then Mauburn accused her of being heartless, of caring only for his title, and she accused him of caring only for her money, and he insisted she ought to marry him anyway, but she wouldn't have it because of the twins—"

Uncle Peter rubbed his big brown hands with the first signs of cheerfulness he had permitted Percival to detect in him.

"Good fur Pish—that's the way to take down them conceited Britishers—"

"But then they went at matters again from a new standpoint, and the result is they've made it up."

"What? Has them precious twin Casselthorpes perished?"

"Not at all, both doing finely—haven't even had colic—growing fast—probably learned to say 'fancy, now,' by this time. But Mauburn's going West with us if we'll take him."

"Get out!"

"Fact! Say, it must have been an awful blow to him when he found sis wouldn't think of him at all without his title, even if she was broke. They had a stormy time of it from all I can hear. He said he was strong enough to work and all that, and since he'd cared for her, and not for her money, it was low down of her to throw him over; then she said she wouldn't leave her mother and us, now that we might need her, not for him or any other man—and he said that only made him love her all the more, and then he got chesty, and said he was just as good as any American, even if he never would have a title; so pretty soon they got kind of interested in each other again, and by the time I came home it was all over. They ratified the preliminary agreement for a merger."

"Well, I snum!"

"That's right, go ahead and snum. I'd snum myself if I knew how—it knocked me. Better come up-stairs and congratulate the happy couple."

"Shoo, now! I certainly am mighty disappointed in that fellow. Still he *is* well spotted, and them freckles mean iron in the blood. Maybe we can develop him along with the other properties."

They found Psyche already radiant, though showing about her eyes traces of the storm's devastations. Mauburn was looking happy; also defiant and stubborn.

"Mr. Bines," he said to Uncle Peter, "I hope you'll side with me. I know something about horses, and I've nearly a thousand pounds that I'll be glad to put in with you out there if you can make a place for me."

The old man looked him over quizzically. Psyche put her arm through Mauburn's.

"I'd *have* to marry some one, you know, Uncle Peter!"

"Don't apologise, Pish. There's room for men that can work out there, Mr. Mauburn, but there ain't any vintages or trouserings to speak of, and the hours is long."

"Try me, Mr. Bines!"

"Well, come on! If you can't skin yourself you can hold a leg while somebody else skins. But you ain't met my expectations, I'll say that." And he shook hands cordially with the Englishman.

"I say, you know," said Mauburn later to Psyche, "why *should* I skin myself? Why should I be skinned at all, you know?"

"You shouldn't," she reassured him. "That's only Uncle Peter's way of saying you can help the others, even if you can't do much yourself at first. And won't Mrs. Drelmer be delighted to know it's all settled?"

"Well," said Uncle Peter to Percival, later in the evening, "Pish has done better than you have here. It's a pity you didn't pick out some good sensible girl, and marry her in the midst of your other doings."

"I couldn't find one that liked cats. I saw a lot that suited every other way but I always said to myself, 'Remember Uncle Peter's warning!' so I'd go to an animal store and get a basket of kittens and take them around, and not one of the dozen stood your test. Of course I'd never disregard your advice."

"Hum," remarked Uncle Peter, in a tone to be noticed for its extreme dryness. "Too bad, though—you certainly need a wife to take the conceit out of you."

"I lost that in the Street, along with the rest."

"Well, son, I ain't no ways alarmed but what you'll soon be on your feet again in that respect—say by next Tuesday or Wednesday. I wish the money was comin' back as easy."

"Well, there are girls in Montana City."

"You could do worse. That reminds me—I happened to meet Shepler to-day and he got kind of confidential,—talkin' over matters. He said he'd never really felt sure about the affections of a certain young woman, especially after that night at the Oldakers'—he'd never felt dead sure of her until you went broke. He said you never could know anything about a woman—not really."

"He knows something about that one, all right, if he knows she wouldn't have any use for me now. Shepler's coming on with the ladies. I feel quite hopeful about him."

CHAPTER XXXVII.

The Departure of Uncle Peter—And Some German Philosophy

The Bineses, with the exception of Psyche, were at breakfast a week later. Miss Bines had been missing since the day that Mr. and Mrs. Cecil G. H. Mauburn had left for Montana City to put the Bines home in order.

Uncle Peter and Mrs. Bines had now determined to go, leaving Percival to follow when he had closed his business affairs.

"It's like starting West again to make our fortune," said Uncle Peter. He had suffered himself to regain something of his old cheerfulness of manner.

"I wish you two would wait until they can get the car here, and go back with me," said Percival. "We can go back in style even if we didn't save much more than a get-away stake."

But his persuasions were unavailing.

"I can't stand it another day," said Mrs. Bines, "and those letters keep coming in from poor suffering people that haven't heard the news."

"I'm too restless to stay," declared Uncle Peter. "I declare, with spring all greenin' up this way I'd be found campin' up in Central Park some night and took off to the calaboose. I just got to get out again where you can feel the wind blow and see a hundred miles and don't have to dodge horseless horse-cars every minute. It's a wonder one of 'em ain't got me in this town. You come on in the car, and do the style fur the family. One of them common Pullmans is good enough fur Marthy and me. And besides, I got to get Billy Brue back. He's goin' plumb daft lookin' night and day fur that man that got his thirty dollars and his breastpin. He says there'll be an ambulance backed up at the spot where he meets him—makes no difference if it's right on Fifth Avenue. Billy's kind of nearsighted at that, so I'm mortal afraid he'll make a mistake one of these nights and take some honest man's money and trinkets away from him."

"Well, here's a *Sun* editorial to take back with us," said Percival; "you remember we came East on one." He read aloud:

"The great fall in the price of copper, Western Trolley, and cordage stocks has ruined thousands of people all over this country. These losses are doubtless irreparable so far as the stocks in question are concerned. The losers will have to look elsewhere for recovery. That they will do so with good courage is not to be doubted. It might be argued with reasonable plausibility that Americans are the greatest fatalists in the world; the readiest to take chances and the least given to whining when the cards go against them.

"A case in point is that of a certain Western family whose fortune has been swept away by the recent financial hurricane. If ever a man liked to match with Destiny, not 'for the beers,' but for big stakes, the young head of the family in question appears to have been that man. He persisted in believing that the power and desire of the rich men controlling these three stocks were great enough to hold their securities at a point far above their actual value. In this persistence he displayed courage worthy of a better reward. A courage, moreover —the gambler's courage—that is typically American. Now he has had a plenty of that pleasure of losing which, in Mr. Fox's estimation, comes next to the pleasure of winning.

"From the point of view of the political economist or the moralist, thrift, saving, and contentment with a modest competence are to be encouraged, and the propensity to gamble is to be condemned. We stand by the copy-book precepts. Yet it is only honest to confess that there is something of this young American's love for chances in most of us. American life is still so fluid, the range of opportunity so great, the national temperament so buoyant, daring, and hopeful, that it is easier for an American to try his luck again than to sit down snugly and enjoy what he has. The fun and the excitement of the game are more than the game. There are Americans and plenty of them who will lose all they have in some magnificent scheme, and make much less fuss about it than a Paris shopkeeper would over a bad twenty-franc piece.

"Our disabled young Croesus from the West is a luminous specimen of the type. The country would be less interesting without his kind, and, on the whole, less healthy—for they provide one of the needed ferments. May the young man make another fortune in his own far West—and come once more to rattle the dry bones of our Bourse!"

"He'll be too much stuck on Montana by the time he gets that fortune," observed Uncle Peter.

"I will *that,* Uncle Peter. Still it's pleasant to know we've won their good opinion."

"Excuse me fur swearin', Marthy," said Uncle Peter, turning to Mrs. Bines, "but he can win a better opinion than that in Montana fur a damn sight less money."

"That editor is right," said Mrs. Bines, "what he says about American life being 'fluid.' There's altogether too much drinking goes on here, and I'm glad my son quit it."

Percival saw them to the train.

"Take care of yourself," said Uncle Peter at parting. "You know I ain't any good any more, and you got a whole family, includin' an Englishman, dependin' on you—we'll throw him on the town, though, if he don't take out his first papers the minute I get there."

His last shot from the rear platform was:

"Change your name back to 'Pete,' son, when you get west of Chicago. 'Tain't anything fancy, but it's a crackin' good business name fur a hustler!"

"All right, Uncle Peter,—and I hope I'll have a grandson that thinks as much of it as I do of yours."

When they had gone, he went back to the work of final adjustment. He had the help of Coplen, whom they had sent for. With him he was busy for a week. By lucky sales of some of the securities that had been hypothecated they managed to save a little; but, on the whole, it was what Percival described it, "a lovely autopsy."

At last the vexatious work was finished, and he was free again. At the end of the final day's work he left the office of Fouts in Wall Street, and walked up Broadway. He went slowly, enjoying the freedom from care. It was the afternoon of a day when the first summer heat had been felt, and as he loitered before shop windows or walked slowly through that street where all move quickly and most very hurriedly, a welcome little breeze came up from the bay to fan him and encourage his spirit of leisure.

At Union Square, when he would have taken a car to go the remainder of the distance, he saw Shepler, accompanied by Mrs. Van Geist and Miss Milbrey, alight from a victoria and enter a jeweller's.

He would have passed on, but Miss Milbrey had seen him, and stood waiting in the doorway while Shepler and Mrs. Van Geist went on into the store.

"Mr. Bines—I'm *so* glad!"

She stood, flushed with pleasure, radiant in stuff of filmy pink, with little flecks at her throat and waist of the first tender green of new leaves. She was unaffectedly delighted to see him.

"You are Miss Spring?" he said when she had given him her hand—"and you've come into all your mother had that was worth inheriting, haven't you?"

"Mr. Bines, shall we not see you now? I wanted so much to talk with you when I heard everything. Would it be impertinent to say I sympathised with you?"

He looked over her shoulder, in where Shepler and Mrs. Van Geist were inspecting a tray of jewels.

"Of course not impertinent—very kind—only I'm really not in need of any sympathy at all. You won't understand it; but we don't care so much for money in the West—for the loss of it—not so much as you New Yorkers would. Besides we can always make a plenty more."

The situation was, emphatically, not as he had so often dreamed it when she should marvel, perhaps regretfully, over his superiority to her husband as a money-maker. His only relief was to belittle the importance of his loss.

"Of course we've lost everything, almost—but I've not been a bit downcast about it. There's more where it came from, and no end of fun going after it. I'm looking forward to the adventures, I can tell you. And every one will be glad to see me there; they won't think the less of me, I assure you, because I've made a fluke here!"

"Surely, Mr. Bines, no one here could think less of you. Indeed, I think more of you. I think it's fine and big to go back with such courage. Do you know, I wish I were a man—I'd show them!"

"Really, Miss Milbrey—"

He looked over her shoulder again, and saw that Shepler was waiting for her.

"I think your friends are impatient."

"They can wait. Mr. Bines, I wonder if you have quite a correct idea of all New York people."

"Probably not; I've met so few, you know."

"Well, of course,—but of those you've met?"

"You can't know what my ideas are."

"I wish we might have talked more—I'm sure—when are you leaving?"

"I shall leave to-morrow."

"And we're leaving for the country ourselves. Papa and mamma go to-morrow—and, Mr. Bines, I *should* have liked another talk with you—I wish we were dining at the Oldakers' again."

He observed Shepler strolling toward them.

"I shall be staying with Aunt Cornelia a few days after to-morrow."

Shepler came up.

"And I shall be leaving to-morrow, Miss Milbrey."

"Ah, Bines, glad to see you!"

The accepted lover looked Miss Milbrey over with rather a complacent air—with the unruffled confidence of assured possession. Percival fancied there was a look almost of regret in the girl's eyes.

"I'm afraid," said Shepler, "your aunt doesn't want to be kept waiting. And she's already in a fever for fear you won't prefer the necklace she insists you ought to prefer."

"Tell Aunt Cornelia, please, that I shall be along in just a moment." "She's quite impatient, you know," urged Shepler.

Percival extended his hand.

"Good-bye, Miss Milbrey. Don't let me detain you. Sorry I shall not see you again."

She gave him her hand uncertainly, as if she had still something to say, but could find no words for it.

"Good-bye, Mr. Bines."

"Good-bye, young man," Shepler shook hands with him cordially, "and the best of luck to you out there. I shall hope to hear good reports from you. And mind, you're to look us up when you're in town again. We shall always be glad to see you. Good-bye!"

He led the girl back to the case where the largest diamonds reposed chastely on their couches of royal velvet.

Percival smiled as he resumed his walk—smiled with all that bitter cynicism which only youth may feel to its full poignance. Yet, heartless as she was, he recalled that while she talked to him he had imprinted an imaginary kiss deliberately upon her full scarlet lips. And now, too, he was forced to confess that, in spite of his very certain knowledge about her, he would actually prefer to have communicated it through the recognised physical media. He laughed again, more cheerfully.

"The spring has gotten a strangle-hold on my judgment," he said to himself.

At dinner that night he had the company of that estimable German savant, the Herr Doctor von Herzlich. He did not seek to incur the experience, but the amiable doctor was so effusive and interested that he saw no way of avoiding it gracefully. Returned from his archaeological expedition to Central America, the doctor was now on his way back to Marburg.

"I pleasure much in your news," said the cheerful man over his first glass of Rhine wine with the olive in it. "You shall now, if I have misapprehended you not, develop a new strongness of the character."

Percival resigned himself to listen. He was not unfamiliar with the lot of one who dines with the learned Von Herzlich.

"Now he's off," he said to himself.

"Ach! It is but now that you shall begin to live. Is it not that while you planned the money-amassing you were deferring to live—ah, yes—until some day when you had so much more? Yes? A common thought-failure it is—a common failure of the to-take-thoughtedness of life—its capacities and the intentions of the scheme under which we survive. Ach! So few humans learn that this invitation to live specifies not the hours, like a five-o'clock. It says—so well as Father-Mother Nature has learned to write the words to our unseeing eyes—'at once,' but we ever put off the living we are invited to at once—until to-morrow-next day, next year—until this or that be done or won. So now you will find this out. Before, you would have waited for a time that never came—no matter the all-money you gathered.

"Nor yet, my young friend, shall you take this matter to be of a seriousness, to be sorrow-worthy. If you take of the courage, you shall find the world to smile to your face, and father-mother you. You recall what the English Huxley says—Ah! what fine, dear man, the good Huxley—he says, yes, in the 'Genealogy of the Beasts,' 'It is a probable hypothesis that what the world is to organisms in general, each organism is to the molecules of which it is composed.' So you laugh at the world, the world it laugh back 'ha! ha! ha!'—then—soly—all your little molecules obediently respond—you thrill with the happiness—with the power—the desire—the capacity—you out-go and achieve. Yes? So fret not. Ach! we fret so much of what it shall be unwise to fret of. It is funny to fret. Why? Why fret? Yet but the month last, they have excavated at Nippur, from the pre-Sargonic strata, a lady and a gentleman of the House of Ptah. What you say in New York—'a damned fine old family,' yes, is it not? I am read their description, and seen of the photographs.

"They have now the expressions of indifference—of disinterest—without the prejudice—as if they say, 'Ach! those troubles of ours, three thousand eight hundred years in the B.C.—nearly come to six thousand years before now—Ach! those troubles,' say this philosophic-now lady and gentleman, of the House of Ptah of Babylonia—'such a silliness—those troubles and frets; it was not the while-worth that we should ever have sorrowed, because the scheme of time and creation is suchly big; had we grasped but its bigness, and the littleness of our span, should we have felt griefs? Nay, nay—*nit*,' like the street-youths say—would say the lady and gentleman now so passionless as to have philosophers become. And you, it should mean to you much. Humans are funniest when they weep and tremble before, like you say, 'the facts in the case.' Ha! I laugh to myself at them often when I observe. Their funniness of the beards and eyebrows, the bald head, of the dress, the solemnities of manner, as it were they were persons of weight. Ah, they are of their insignificance so loftily unconscious. Was it not great skill—to compel the admiration of the love-worthiest scientist— to create a unit of a numberless mass of units and then to enable it to feel each one the importance of the whole, as if each part were big as the whole? So you shall not fret I say.

"If the fret invade you, you shall do well to lie out in the friendly space, and look at this small topspinning of a world through the glass that reduces.

Yes? You had thought it of such bigness—its concerns of a sublime tragicness? Yet see now, these funny little animals on the surface of the spinning-ball. How frantic, as if all things were about to eventuate, remembering not that nothing ends. So? Observe the marks of their silliness, their unworthiness. You have reduced the ball to so big as a melon, yes? Watch the insects run about in the craziness, laughing, crying, loving their loves, hating their hates, fearing, fretting—killing one the other in such funny little clothes, made for such funny little purpose precisely— falling sick over the money-losings—and the ball so small, but one of such many—as many stars under the earth, remember, as above it.

"So! you are back to earth; you are a human like the rest, so foolish, so funny as any—so you say, 'Well, I shall not be more troubled again yet. I play the same game, but it is only a game, a little game to last an afternoon—I play my part—yes—the laughing part, crying part—loving, hating, killing part—what matter if I say it is good?' If the Maker there be to look down, what joys him most—the coward who fears and frets, and the whine makes for his soul or body? Ach! no, it is the one who say, it is *good*—I could not better have done myself—a great game, yes—'let her rip,' like you West-people remark—'let her rip—you cannot lose *me*,' like you say also. Ach, so! And then he say, the great Planner of it,' Ach! I am understood at last—good!—bright man that,' like you say, also—'bright man that—it is of a pleasure to see him do well!'

"So, my young friend, you shall pleasure yourself still much yet. It is of an excellence to pleasure one's self judiciously. The lotus is a leguminous plant—so excellent for the salad—not for the roast. You have of the salad overeaten—you shall learn of your successful capacity for it—you shall do well, then. You have been of the reckless deportment—you may still be of it. That is not the matter. You shall be reckless as you like—but without your stored energy surplus to harm you. Your environment from the now demands of you the faculties you will most pleasure yourself in developing. You shall produce what you consume. The gods love such. Ach, yes!"

CHAPTER XXXVIII.

Some Phenomena Peculiar to Spring

He awoke early, refreshed and intensely alive. With the work done he became conscious of a feeling of disassociation from the surroundings in which he had so long been at home. Many words of the talkative German were running in his mind from the night before. He was glad the business was off his mind. He would now go the pleasant journey, and think on the way.

His trunks were ready for the car; and before he went down-stairs his hand-bag was packed, and the preparations for the start completed. When, after his breakfast, he read the telegram announcing that the car had been delayed twenty-four hours in Chicago, he was bored by the thought that he must pass another day in New York. He was eager now to be off, and the time would hang heavily.

He tried to recall some forgotten detail of the business that might serve to occupy him. But the finishing had been thorough.

He ran over in his mind the friends with whom he could spend the time agreeably. He could recall no one he cared to see. He had no longer an interest in the town or its people.

He went aimlessly out on to Broadway in the full flood of a spring morning, breathing the fresh air hungrily. It turned his thought to places out of the grime and clamour of the city; to woods and fields where he might rest and feel the stimulus of his new plans. He felt aloof and sufficient unto himself.

He swung on to an open car bound north, and watched without interest the early quick-moving workers thronging south on the street, and crowding the cars that passed him. At Forty-second Street, he changed to a Boulevard car that took him to the Fort Lee Ferry at One Hundred and Twenty-fifth Street.

Out on the shining blue river he expanded his lungs to the clean, sweet air. Excursion boats, fluttering gay streamers, worked sturdily up the stream. Little yachts, in fresh-laundered suits of canvas, darted across their bows or slanted in their wakes, looking like white butterflies. The vivid blue of the sky was flecked with bits of broken fleece, scurrying like the yachts below. Across the river was a high-towering bank of green inviting him over its summit to the languorous freshness beyond.

He walked off the boat on the farther side and climbed a series of steep wooden stairways, past a tiny cataract that foamed its way down to the river. When he reached the top he walked through a stretch of woods and turned off to the right, down a cool shaded road that wound away to the north through the fresh greens of oak and chestnut.

He was entranced at once by the royal abandon of spring, this wondrous time of secret beginnings made visible. The old earth was become as a young wife from the arms of an ardent spouse, blushing into new life and beauty for the very joy of love. He breathed the dewy freshness, and presently he whistled the "Spring Song" of Mendelssohn, that bubbling, half-joyous, half-plaintive little prayer in melody.

He was well into the spirit of the time and place. His soul sang. The rested muscles of his body and mind craved the resistance of obstacles. He rejoiced. He had been wise to leave the city for the fresh, unspoiled country—the city with all its mean little fears, its petty immoralities, and its very trifling great concerns. He did not analyse, more than to remember, once, that the not reticent German would approve his mood. He had sought the soothing quiet with the unfailing instinct of the wounded animal.

The mysterious green life in the woods at either side allured him with its furtive pulsing. But he kept to the road and passed on. He was not yet far enough from the town.

Some words from a little song ran in his mind as he walked:

"The naked boughs into green leaves slipped,

The longing buds into flowers tripped,

The little hills smiled as if they were glad,

The little rills ran as if they were mad.

"There was green on the earth and blue in the sky,

The chrysalis changed to a butterfly,

And our lovers, the honey-bees, all a-hum,

To hunt for our hearts began to come."

When he came to a village with an electric car clanging through it, he skirted its borders, and struck off through a woodland toward the river. Even the village was too human, too modern, for his early-pagan mood.

In the woods he felt that curious thrill of stealth, that impulse to cautious concealment, which survives in man from the remote days when enemies beset his forest ways. On a southern hillside he found a dogwood-tree with its blossomed firmament of white stars. In low, moist places the violets had sprung through the thatch of leaves and were singing their purple beauties all unheard. Birds were nesting, and squirrels chattered and scolded.

Under these more obvious signs and sounds went the steady undertone of life in root and branch and unfurling leaf—provoking, inciting, making lawless whomsoever it thrilled.

He came out of the wood on to another road that ran not far from the river, and set off again to the north along the beaten track.

In an old-fashioned garden in front of a small house a girl bent over a flower bed, working with a trowel.

He stopped and looked at her over the palings. She was freshly pretty, with yellow hair blown about her face under the pushed back sunbonnet of blue. The look in her blue eyes was the look of one who had heard echoes; who had awakened with the spring to new life and longings, mysterious and unwelcome, but compelling.

She stood up when he spoke; her sleeves were turned prettily back upon her fair round arms.

"Yes, the road turns to the left, a bit ahead."

She was blushing.

"You are planting flower seeds."

"Yes; so many flowers were killed by the cold last winter."

"I see; there must a lot of them have died here, but their souls didn't go far, did they now?"

She went to digging again in the black moist earth. He lingered. The girl worked on, and her blush deepened. He felt a lawless impulse to vault the palings, and carry her off to be a flower for ever in some wooded glade near by. He dismissed it as impracticable. His intentions would probably be misconstrued.

"I hope your garden will thrive. It has a pretty pattern to follow."

"Thank you!"

He raised his hat and passed on, thinking; thinking of all the old dead flowers, and their pretty souls that had gone to bloom in the heaven of the maid's face.

Before the road turned to the left he found a path leading over to the top of the palisade. There on a little rocky shelf, hundreds of feet above the river, he lay a long time in the spring sun, looking over to the farther shore, where the city crept to the south, and lost its sharp lines in the smoky distance. There he smoked and gave himself up to the moment. He was glad to be out of that rush. He could see matters more clearly now— appraise values more justly. He was glad of everything that had come. Above all, glad to go back and carry on that big work of his father's—his father who had done so much to redeem the wilderness—and incidentally he would redeem his own manhood.

It will be recalled that the young man frequently expressed himself with regrettable inelegance; that he habitually availed himself, indeed, of a most infelicitous species of metaphor. It must not be supposed that this spring day in the spring places had reformed his manner of delivery. When he chose to word his emotions it was still done in a manner to make the right-spoken grieve. Thus, going back toward the road, after reviewing his great plans for the future, he spoke aloud: "I believe it's going to be a good game."

When he became hungry he thought with relief that he would not be compelled to seek one of those "hurry-up" lunch places with its clamour and crowd. What was the use of all that noise and crowding and piggish hurry? A remark of the German's recurred to him:

"It is a happy man who has divined the leisure of eternity, so he feels it, like what you say, 'in his bones.'"

When he came out on the road again he thought regretfully of the pretty girl and her flower bed. He would have liked to go back and suggest that she sing to the seeds as she put them to sleep in their earth cradle, to make their awakening more beautiful.

But he turned down the road that led away from the girl, and when he came to a "wheelman's rest," he ate many sandwiches and drank much milk.

The face of the maid that served him had been no heaven for the souls of dead flowers. Still she was a girl; and no girl could be wholly without importance on such a day. So he thought the things he would have said to her if matters had been different.

When he had eaten, he loafed off again down the road. Through the long afternoon he walked and lazed, turning into strange lanes and by-roads, resting on grassy banks, and looking far up. He followed Doctor von Herzlich's directions, and, going off into space, reduced the earth, watching its little continents and oceans roll toward him, and viewing the antics of its queer inhabitants in fancy as he had often in fact viewed a populous little ant-hill, with its busy, serious citizens. Then he would venture still farther—away out into timeless space, beyond even the starry refuse of creation, and insolently regard the universe as a tiny cloud of dust.

When the shadows stretched in the dusky languor of the spring evening, he began to take his bearings for the return. He heard the hum and clang of an electric car off through a chestnut grove.

The sound disturbed him, bringing premonitions of the city's unrest. He determined to stay out for the night. It was restful—his car would not arrive until late the next afternoon—there was no reason why he should not. He found a little wayside hotel whose weather-beaten sign was ancient enough to promise "entertainment for man and beast."

"Just what I want," he declared. "I'm both of them—man and beast."

Together they ate tirelessly of young chickens broiled, and a green salad, and a wonderful pie, with a bottle of claret that had stood back of the dingy little bar so long that it had attained, at least as to its label, a very fair antiquity.

This time the girl was pretty again, and, he at once discovered, not indisposed to light conversation. Yet she was a shallow creature, with little mind for the subtler things of life and the springtime. He decided she was much better to look at than to talk to. With a just appreciation of her own charms she appeared to pose perpetually before an imaginary mirror, regaling him and herself with new postures, tossing her brown head, curving her supple waist, exploiting her thousand coquetries. He was pained to note, moreover, that she was more than conscious of the red-cheeked youth who came in from the carriage shed, whistling.

When the man and the beast had been appeased they sat out under a blossomed apple-tree and smoked together in a fine spirit of amity.

He was not amazed when, in the gloom, he saw the red-cheeked youth with both arms about the girl—nor was he shocked at detecting instantly that her struggles were meant to be futile against her assailant's might. The birds were mating, life was forward, and Nature loves to be democratically lavish with her choicest secrets. Why not, then, the blooming, full curved kitchen-maid and the red-cheeked boy-of-all-work?

He smoked and saw the night fall. The dulled bronze jangle of cow-bells came soothingly to him. An owl called a little way off. Swallows flashed by in long graceful flights. A bat circled near, indecisively, as if with a message it hesitated to give. Once he heard the flute-like warble of a skylark.

He was under the clean, sharp stars of a moonless night. His keen senses tasted the pungent smoke and the softer feminine fragrance of the apple-blossoms. His nerves were stilled to pleasant ease, except when the laugh of the girl floated to him from the grape-arbour back of the house. That disturbed him to fierce longings—the clear, high measure of a woman's laugh floating to him in the night. And once she sang—some song common to her class. It moved him as her laugh did, making him vibrate to her, as when a practised hand flutters the strings of a harp. He was glad without knowing why when she stopped.

At ten o'clock he went in from under the peering little stars and fell asleep in an ancient four-poster. He dreamed that he had the world, a foot-ball, clasped to his breast, and was running down the field for a gain of a hundred yards. Then, suddenly, in place of the world, it was Avice Milbrey in his grasp, struggling frantically to be free; and instead of behaving like a gentleman he flung both arms around her and kissed her despite her struggles; kissed her time after time, until she ceased to strive against him, and lay panting and helpless in his arms.

CHAPTER XXXIX.

An Unusual Plan of Action Is Matured

He was awakened by the unaccustomed silence. As he lay with his eyes open, his first thought was that all things had stopped—the world had come to its end. Then remembrance came, and he stretched in lazy enjoyment of the stillness and the soft feather bed upon which he had slept. Finding himself too wide awake for more sleep, he went over to the little gable window and looked out. The unfermented wine of another spring day came to his eager nostrils. The little ball had made another turn. Its cheek was coming once more into the light. Already the east was flushing with a wondrous vague pink. The little animals in the city over there, he thought, would soon be tumbling out of their beds to begin another of their funny, serious days of trial and failure; to make ready for another night of forgetfulness, when their absurd little ant-hill should turn again away from the big blazing star. He sat a long time at the window, looking out to the east, where the light was showing; meditating on many idle, little matters, but conscious all the time of great power within himself.

He felt ready now for any conflict. The need for some great immediate action pressed upon him. He did not identify it. Something he must do—he must have action—and that at once. He was glad to think how Uncle Peter would begin to rejoice in him—secretly at first, and then to praise him. He was equal to any work. He could not begin it quickly enough. That queer need to do something at once was still pressing, still unidentified.

By five he was down-stairs. The girl, fresh as a dew-sprayed rose in the garden outside, brought him breakfast of fruit, bacon and eggs, coffee and waffles. He ate with relish, delighting meantime in the girl's florid freshness, and even in the assertive, triumphant whistle of the youth busy at his tasks outside.

When he set out he meant to reach the car and go back to town at once. Yet when he came to the road over which he had loitered the day before, he turned off upon it with slower steps. There was a confusing whirl of ideas in his brain, a chaos that required all his energy to feed it, so that the spring went from his step.

Then all at once, a new-born world cohered out of the nebula, and the sight of its measured, orderly whirling dazed him. He had been seized with a wish—almost an intention, so stunning in its audacity that he all but reeled under the shock. It seemed to him that the thing must have been germinated in his mind without his knowledge; it had lain there, gathering force while he rested, now to burst forth and dazzle him with its shine. All that undimmed freshness of longing he had felt the day before-all the unnamed, unidentified, nameless desires—had flooded back upon him, but now no longer aimless. They were acutely definite. He wanted Avice Milbrey,—wanted her with an intensity as unreasoning as it was resistless. This was the new world he had watched swimming out of the chaos in his mind, taking its allotted orbit in a planetary system of possible, rational, matter-of-course proceedings.

And Avice Milbrey was to marry Shepler, the triumphant money-king.

He sat down by the roadside, well-nigh helpless, surrendering all his forces to the want.

Then there came upon him to reinforce this want a burning sense of defeat. He remembered Uncle Peter's first warnings in the mine about "cupboard love;" the gossip of Higbee: "If you were broke, she'd have about as much use for you—" all the talk he had listened to so long about marriage for money; and, at the last, Shepler's words to Uncle Peter: "I was uncertain until copper went to 51." Those were three wise old men who had talked, men who knew something of women and much of the world. And they were so irritating in their certainty. What a fine play to fool them all!

The sense of defeat burned into him more deeply. He had been vanquished, cheated, scorned, shamefully flouted. The money was gone— all of Uncle Peter's complaints and biting sarcasms came back to him with renewed bitterness; but his revenge on Uncle Peter would be in showing him a big man at work, with no nonsense about him. But Shepler, who was now certain, and Higbee, who had always been certain,—especially Shepler, with his easy sense of superiority with a woman over any poor man. That was a different matter There was a thing to think about. And he wanted Avice Milbrey. He could not, he decided, go back without her.

Something of the old lawless spirit of adventure that had spurred on his reckless forbears urged him to carry the girl back with him. She didn't love him. He would take her in spite of that; overpower her; force her to go. It was a revenge of superb audacity. Shepler had not been sure of her until now. Well, Shepler might be hurled from that certainty by one hour of determined action.

The great wild wish narrowed itself into a definite plan. He recalled the story Uncle Peter had told at the Oldakers' about the woman and her hair. A woman could be coerced if a man knew her weakness. He could coerce her. He knew it instinctively; and the instinctive belief rallied to its support a thousand little looks from her, little intonations of her voice, little turnings of her head when they had been together. In spite of her calculations, in spite of her love of money, he could make her feel her weakness. He was a man with the power.

It was heady wine for the morning. He described himself briefly as a lunatic, and walked on again. But the crazy notion would not be gone. The day before he had been passive. Now he was active, acutely aware of himself and all his wants. He walked a mile trying to dismiss the idea. He sat down again, and it flooded back upon him with new force.

Her people were gone. She had even intimated a wish to talk with him again. It could be done quickly. He knew. He felt the primitive superiority of man's mere brute force over woman. He gloried in his knotted muscles and the crushing power of his desires.

Afterward, she would reproach him bitterly. They would both be unhappy. It was no matter. It was the present, the time when he should be living. He would have her, and Shepler—Shepler might have had the One Girl mine—but this girl, never!

Again he tried faithfully to walk off the obsession. Again were his essays at sober reason unavailing.

His mind was set as it had been when he bought the stocks day after day against the advice of the best judges in the Street. He could not turn himself back. There must be success. There could not be a giving up—and there must not be failure.

Hour after hour he alternately walked and rested, combating and favouring the mad project. It was a foolish little world, and people were always waiting for another time to begin the living of life. The German had quoted Martial: "To-morrow I will live, the fool says; to-day itself's too late. The wise lived yesterday."

If he did go away alone he knew he would always regret it. If he carried her triumphantly off, doubtless his regret for that would eventually be as great. The first regret was certain. The latter was equally plausible; but, if it came, would it not be preferable to the other? To have held her once—to have taken her away, to have triumphed over her own calculations, and, best of all, to have triumphed over the money-king resting fatuously confident behind his wealth, dignifying no man as rival who was not rich. The present, so, was more than any possible future, how dire soever it might be.

He was mad to prove to her—and to Shepler—that she was more a woman than either had supposed,—a woman in spite of herself, weak, unreasoning; to prove to them both that a determined man has a vital power to coerce which no money may ever equal.

Not until five o'clock had he by turns urged and fought himself to the ferry. By that time he had given up arguing. He was dwelling entirely upon his plan of action. Strive and grope as he would, the thing had driven him on relentlessly. His reason could not take him beyond the reach of its goad. Far as he went he loved her even farther. She belonged to him. He would have her. He seemed to have been storing, the day before, a vast quantity of energy that he was now drawing lavishly upon. For the time, he was pure, raw force, needing, to be resistless, only the guidance of a definite purpose.

He crossed the ferry and went to the hotel, where he shaved and freshened himself. He found Grant, the porter, waiting for him when he went downstairs, and gave him written directions to the railroad people to have the car attached to the Chicago Express leaving at eight the next morning; also instructions about his baggage.

"I expect there will be two of us, Grant; see that the car is well stocked; and here, take this; go to a florist's and get about four dozen pink roses—*la France*—can you remember?—pink—don't take any other colour, and be sure they're fresh. Have breakfast ready by the time the train starts."

"Yes, Mistah Puhs'val!" said Grant, and added to himself, "Yo' suttiny do ca'y yo'se'f mighty han'some, Mistah Man!"

Going out of the hotel, he met Launton Oldaker, with whom he chatted a few moments, and then bade good-bye.

Oldaker, with a sensitive regard for the decencies, refrained from expressing the hearty sympathy he felt for a man who would henceforth be compelled to live out of the world.

Percival walked out to Broadway, revolving his plan. He saw it was but six o'clock. He could do nothing for at least an hour. When he noted this he became conscious of his hunger. He had eaten nothing since morning. He turned into a restaurant on Madison Square and ordered dinner. When he had eaten, he sat with his coffee for a final smoke of deliberation. He went over once more the day's arguments for and against the novel emprise. He had become insensible, however, to all the dissenting ones. As a last rally, he tried to picture the difficulties he might encounter. He faced all he could imagine.

"By God, I'll do it!"

"*Oui, monsieur!*" said the waiter, who had been standing dreamily near, startled into attention by the spoken words.

"That's all—give me the check."

As he went out the door, a young woman passed him, looking him straight in the eyes. From her light swishing skirts came the faint perfume of the violet. It chilled the steel of his resolution.

He entered a carriage. It was a hot, humid night. Already the mist was making grey softness of the air, dulling the street lights to ruddy orange. Northward, over the breast of Murray Hill a few late carriages trickled down toward him. Their wheels, when they passed, made swift reflections in the damp glare of the asphalt.

He was pent force waiting to be translated into action.

He drove first to the Milbrey house, on the chance that she might be at home. Jarvis answered his ring.

"Miss Milbrey is with Mrs. Van Geist, sir."

Jarvis spoke regretfully. Pie had reasons of his own for believing that the severance of the Milbrey relationship with Mr. Bines had been nothing short of calamitous.

He rang Mrs. Van Geist's bell, five minutes later.

"The ladies haven't come back, sir. I don't know where they might be. Perhaps at the Valners', in Fifty-second Street, sir."

He rang the Valners' bell.

"Mrs. Van Geist and Miss Milbrey? They left at least half an hour ago, sir."

"Go down the avenue slowly, driver!"

At Fortieth Street he looked down to the middle of the block.

Mrs. Van Geist, alone, was just alighting from her coupé.

He signalled the driver.

"Go to the other address again, in Thirty-seventh Street."

Jarvis opened the door.

"Yes, sir—thank you, sir—Miss Milbrey is in, sir. I'll see, sir."

He crossed the Rubicon of a door-mat and stood in the unlighted hall. At the far end he saw light coming from a door that he knew opened into the library.

Jarvis came into the light. Behind him appeared Miss Milbrey in the doorway.

"Miss Milbrey says will you enter the library, Mr. Bines?"

CHAPTER XL.

Some Rude Behaviour, of Which Only a Western Man Could Be Guilty

He walked quickly back. At the doorway she gave him her hand, which he took in silence. "Why—Mr. Bines!—you wouldn't have surprised me last night. To-night I pictured you on your way West."

Her gown was of dull blue dimity. She still wore her hat, an arch of straw over her face, with ripe red cherries nodding upon it as she moved. He closed the door behind him.

"Do come in. I've been having a solitary rummage among old things. It is my last night here. We're leaving for the country to-morrow, you know."

She stood by the table, the light from a shaded lamp making her colour glow.

Now she noted that he had not spoken. She turned quickly to him as if to question.

He took a swift little step toward her, still without speaking. She stepped back with a sudden instinct of fright.

He took two quick steps forward and grasped one of her wrists. He spoke in cool, even tones, but the words came fast:

"I've come to marry you to-night; to take you away with me to that Western country. You may not like the life. You may grieve to death for all I know—but you're going. I won't plead, I won't beg, but I am going to take you."

She had begun to pull away in alarm when he seized her wrist. His grasp did not bruise, it did not seem to be tight; but the hand that held it was immovable.

"Mr. Bines, you forget yourself. Really, this is—"

"Don't waste time. You can say all that needs to be said—I'll give you time for that before we start—but don't waste the time saying all those useless things. Don't waste time telling me I'm crazy. Perhaps I am. We can settle that later."

"Mr. Bines—how absurd! Oh! let me go! You're hurting my wrist! Oh!— don't—don't—don't! Oh!"

When he felt the slender wrist trying to writhe from his grasp he had closed upon it more tightly, and thrusting his other arm quickly behind her, had drawn her closely to him. Her cries and pleadings were being smothered down on his breast. Her struggles met only the unbending, pitiless resistance of steel.

"Don't waste time, I tell you—can't you understand? Be sensible,—talk if you must—only talk sense."

"Let me go at once—I demand it—quick—oh!"

"Take this hat off!"

He forced the wrist he had been holding down between them, so that she could not free the hand, and, with his own hand thus freed, he drew out the two long hat-pins and flung the hat with its storm-tossed cherries across the room. Still holding her tightly, he put the free hand on her brow and thrust her head back, so that she was forced to look up at him.

"Let me see you—I want to see your eyes—they're my eyes now."

Her head strained against his hand to be down again, and all her strength was exerted to be away. She found she could not move in any direction.

"Oh, you're hurting my neck. What *shall* I do? I can't scream—think what it would mean!—you're hurting my neck!"

"You are hurting your *own* neck—stop it!"

He kissed her face, softly, her cheeks, her eyes, her chin.

"I've loved you so—don't—what's the use? Be sensible. My arms have starved for you so—do you think they're going to loosen now? Avice Milbrey—Avice Milbrey—Avice Milbrey!"

His arms tightened about her as he said the name over and over.

"That's poetry—it's all the poetry there is in the world. It's a verse I say over in the night. You can't understand it yet—it's too deep for you. It means I must have you—and the next verse means that you must have me—a poor man—be a poor man's wife—and all the other verses— millions of them—mean that I'll never give you up—and there's a lot more verses for you to write, when you understand—meaning that you'll never give *me* up—and there's one in the beginning means I'm going to carry you out and marry you to-night—*now*, do you understand?—right off—this very night!"

"Oh! Oh! this is so terrible! Oh, it's *so* awful!"

Her voice broke, and he felt her body quiver with sobs. Her face was pitifully convulsed, and tears welled in her eyes.

"Let me *go*—let—me—*go*!"

He released her head, but still held her closely to him. Her sobs had become uncontrollable.

"Here—" he reached for the little lace-edged handkerchief that lay beside her long gloves and her purse, on the table.

She took it mechanically.

"Please—oh, *please* let me go—I beg you." She managed it with difficulty between the convulsions that were rending her.

He put his lips down upon the soft hair.

"I *won't*—do you understand that? Stop talking nonsense."

He thought there would be no end to the sobs.

"Have it out, dear—there's plenty of time."

Once she seemed to have stopped the tears. He turned her face up to his own again, and softly kissed her wet eyes. Her full lips were parted before him, but he did not kiss them. The sobs came again.

"There—there!—it will soon be over."

At last she ceased to cry from sheer exhaustion, and when, with his hand under her chin, he forced up her head again, she looked at him a full minute and then closed her eyes.

He kissed their lids.

There came from time to time the involuntary quick little indrawings of breath,—the aftermath of her weeping.

He held her so for a time, while neither spoke. She had become too weak to struggle.

"My arms have starved for you so," he murmured. She gave no sign.

"Come over here." He led her, unresisting, around to the couch at the other side of the table.

"Sit here, and we'll talk it over sensibly, before you get ready."

When he released her, she started quickly up toward the door that led into the hall.

"*Don't* do that—please don't be foolish."

He locked the door, and put the key in his pocket. Then he went over to the big folding-doors, and satisfied himself they were locked from the other side. He went back and stood in front of her. She had watched him with dumb terror in her face.

"Now we can talk—but there isn't much to be said. How soon can you be ready?"

"You *are* crazy!"

"Possibly—believe what you like."

"How did you ever *dare?* Oh, how *awful!*"

"If you haven't passed that stage, I'll hold you again."

"No, no—*please* don't—please stand up again. Sit over there,—I can think better."

"Think quickly. This is Saturday, and to-morrow is their busy day. They may not sit up late to-night."

She arose with a little shrug of desperation that proclaimed her to be in the power of a mad man. She looked at her face in the oval mirror, wiping her eyes and making little passes and pats at her disordered hair. He went over to her.

"No, no—please go over there again. Sit down a moment—let me think. I'll talk to you presently."

There was silence for five minutes. He watched her, while she narrowed her eyes in deep thought.

Then he looked at his watch.

"I can give you an hour, if you've anything to say before it's done—not longer."

She drew a long breath.

"Mr. Bines, are you mad? Can't you be rational?"

"I haven't been irrational, I give you my word, not once since I came here."

He looked at her steadily. All at once he saw her face go crimson. She turned her eyes from his with an effort.

"I'm going back to Montana in the morning. I want you to marry me to-night—I won't even wait one more day—one more hour. I know it's a thing you never dreamt of—marrying a poor man. You'll look at it as the most disgraceful act of folly you could possibly commit, and so will every

- 274 -

one else here—but you'll *do* it. To-morrow at this time you'll be half-way to Chicago with me."

"Mr. Bines,—I'm perfectly reasonable and serious—I mean it—are you quite sure you didn't lose your wits when you lost your money?"

"It *may* be considered a witless thing to marry a girl who would marry for money—but never mind *that*—I'm used to taking chances."

She glanced up at him, curiously.

"You know I'm to marry Mr. Shepler the tenth of next month."

"Your grammar is faulty—tense is wrong—You should say 'I *was* to have married Mr. Shepler.' I'm fastidious about those little things, I confess."

"How can you jest?"

"I can't. Don't think this is any joke. *He'll* find out."

"Who will find out,—what, pray?"

"He will. He's already said he was afraid there might have been some nonsense between you and me, because we talked that evening at the Oldakers'. He told my grandfather he wasn't at all sure of you until that day I lost my money."

"Oh, I see—and of course you'd like your revenge—carrying me off from him just to hurt him."

"If you say that I'll hold you in my arms again." He started toward her. "I've loved you *so*, I tell you—all the time—all the time."

"Or perhaps it's a brutal revenge on me,—after thinking I'd only marry for money."

"I've loved you always, I tell you."

He came up to her, more gently now, and took up her hand to kiss it. He saw the ring.

"Take his ring off!"

She looked up at him with an amused little smile, but did not move. He reached for the hand, and she put it behind her.

"Take it off," he said, harshly.

He forced her hand out, took off the ring with its gleaming stone, none too gently, and laid it on the table behind him. Then he covered the hand with kisses.

"Now it's my hand. Perhaps there was a little of both those feelings you accuse me of—perhaps I *did* want to triumph over both you and Shepler—and the other people who said you'd never marry for anything but money—but do you think I'd have had either one of those desires if I hadn't loved you? Do you think I'd have cared how many Sheplers you married if I hadn't loved you so, night and day?—always turning to you in spite of everything,—loving you always, under everything—always, I tell you."

"Under what—what 'everything'?"

"When I was sure you had no heart—that you couldn't care for any man except a rich man—that you would marry only for money."

"You thought that?"

"Of course I thought it."

"What has changed you?"

"Nothing. I'm going to change it now by proving differently. I shall take you against your will—but I shall make you love me—in the end. I know you—you're a woman, in spite of yourself!"

"You were entirely right about me. I would even have married you because of the money—"

"Tell me what it is you're holding back—don't wait."

"Let me think—don't talk, please!"

She sat a long time silent, motionless, her eyes fixed ahead. At length she stirred herself to speak.

"You were right about me, partly—and partly wrong. I don't think I can make you understand. I've always wanted so much from life—so much more than it seemed possible to have. The only thing for a girl in my position and circumstances was to make what is called a good marriage. I wanted what that would bring, too. I was torn between the desires—or rather the natural instincts and the trained desires. I had ideals about loving and being loved, and I had the material ideals of my experience in this world out here.

"I was untrue to each by turns. Here—I want to show you something."

She took up a book with closely written pages.

"I came here to-night—I won't conceal from you that I thought of you when I came. It was my last time here, and you had gone, I supposed. Among other things I had out this old diary to burn, and I had found this, written on my eighteenth birthday, when I came out—the fond, romantic, secret ideal of a foolish girl—listen:

"The Soul of Love wed the Soul of Truth and their daughter, Joy, was born: who was immortal and in whom they lived for ever!'

"You see—that was the sort of moonshine I started in to live. Two or three times I was a grievous disappointment to my people, and once or twice, perhaps, I was disappointed myself. I was never quite sure what I wanted. But if you think I was consistently mercenary you are mistaken. "I shall tell you something more—something no one knows. There was a man I met while that ideal was still strong and beautiful to me—but after I'd come to see that here, in this life, it was not easily to be kept. He was older than I, experienced with women—a lover of women, I came to understand in time. I was a novelty to him, a fresh recreation—he enjoyed all those romantic ideals of mine. I thought then he loved me, and I worshipped him. He was married, but constantly said he was about to leave his wife, so she would divorce him. I promised to come to him when it was done. He had married for money and he would have been poor again. I didn't mind in the least. I tell you this to show you that I could have loved a poor man, not only well enough to marry him, but to break with the traditions, and brave the scandal of going to him in that common way. With all I felt for him I should have been more than satisfied. But I came in time to see that he was not as earnest as I had been. He wasn't capable of feeling what I felt. He was more cowardly than I—or rather, I was more reckless than he. I suspected it a long time; I became convinced of it a year ago and a little over. He became hateful to me. I had wasted my love. Then he became funny. But—you see—I am not altogether what you believed me. Wait a bit longer, please.

"Then I gave up, almost—and later, I gave up entirely. And when my brother was about to marry that woman, and Mr. Shepler asked me to marry him, I consented. It seemed an easy way to end it all. I'd quit fondling ideals. And you had told me I must do anything I could to keep Fred from marrying that woman—my people came to say the same thing—and so—"

"If he had married her—if they were married now—then you would feel free to marry me?"

"You would still be the absurdest man in New York—but we can't discuss that. He isn't going to marry her."

"But he *has* married her—"

"What do you mean?"

"I supposed you knew—Oldaker told me as I left the hotel. He and your father were witnesses. The marriage took place this afternoon at the Arlingham."

"You're not deceiving me?"

"Come, come!—*girl!*"

"Oh, *pardon* me! please! Of course I didn't mean it—but you stunned me. And papa said nothing to me about it before he left. The money must have been too great a temptation to him and to Fred. She has just made some enormous amount in copper stock or something."

"I know, she had better advice than I had. I'd like to reward the man who gave it to her."

"And I was sure you were going to marry that other woman."

"How could you think so?"

"Of course I'm not the least bit jealous—it isn't my disposition; but I *did* think Florence Akemit wasn't the woman to make you happy—of course I liked her immensely—and there were reports going about—everybody seemed so sure—and you were with her so much. Oh, how I did *hate* her!"

"I tell you she is a joke and always was."

"It's funny—that's exactly what I told Aunt Cornelia about that—that man."

"Let's stop joking, then."

"How absurd you are—with my plans all made and the day set—"

There was a knock at the door. He went over and unlocked it. Jarvis was there.

"Mr. Shepler, Miss Avice."

They looked at each other.

"Jarvis, shut that door and wait outside."

"Yes, Mr. Bines."

"You can't see him."

"But I must,—we're engaged, don't you understand?—of course I must!"

"I tell you I won't let you. Can't you understand that I'm not talking idly?"

She tried to evade him and reach the door, but she was caught again in his arms—held close to him.

"If you like he shall come in now. But he's not going to take you away from me, as he did in that jeweller's the other night—and you can't see him at all except as you are now."

She struggled to be free.

"Oh, you're so *brutal*!"

"I haven't begun yet—"

He drew her toward the door.

"Oh, not that—don't open it—I'll tell him—yes, I will!"

"I'm taking no more chances, and the time is short."

Still holding her closely with one arm, he opened the door. The man stared impassively above their heads—a graven image of unconsciousness.

"Jarvis."

"Yes, sir."

"Miss Milbrey wishes you to say to Mr. Shepler that she is engaged—"

"That I'm ill," she interrupted, still making little struggles to twist from his grasp, her head still bent down.

"That she is engaged with Mr. Bines, Jarvis, and can't see him. Say it that way—'Miss Milbrey is engaged with Mr. Bines, and can't see you.'".

"SAY IT THAT WAY—'MISS MILBREY IS ENGAGED WITH MR. BINES, AND CAN'T SEE YOU.'"

"Yes, sir!"

He remained standing motionless, as he had been, his eyes still fixed above them. But the eyes of Jarvis, from long training, did hot require to be bent upon those things they needed to observe. They saw something now that was at least two feet below their range.

The girl made a little move with her right arm, which was imprisoned fast between them, and which some intuition led her captor not to restrain. The firm little hand worked its way slowly up, went creepingly over his shoulder and bent tightly about his neck.

"Yes, sir," repeated Jarvis, without the quiver of an eyelid, and went.

He closed the door with his free hand, and they stood as they were until they heard the noise of the front door closing and the soft retreating footsteps of the butler.

"Oh, you were mean—*mean*—to shame me so," and floods of tears came again.

"I hated to do it, but I *had* to; it was a critical moment. And you couldn't have made up your mind without it."

She sobbed weakly in his arms, but her own arm was still tight about his neck. He felt it for the first time.

"But I *had* made up my mind—I did make it up while we talked."

They were back on the couch. He held her close and she no longer resisted, but nestled in his arms with quick little sighs, as if relieved from a great strain. He kissed her forehead and hair as she dried her eyes.

"Now, rest a little. Then we shall go."

"I've so much to tell you. That day at the jeweller's—well, what could I do but take one poor last little look of you—to keep?"

"Tell me if you care for me."

"Oh, I do, I do, I do care for you. I *have*—ever since that day we walked in the woods. I do, I *do*!"

She threw her head back and gave him her lips.

She was crying again and trying to talk.

"I did care for you, and that day I thought you were going to say something, but you didn't—you were so distant and troubled, and seemed not even to like me—though I felt sure you loved me. I had thought you were going to tell me, and I'd have accepted—yes, for the money—though I liked you so much. Why, when I first met you in that mine and thought you were a workman, I'm not sure I wouldn't have married you if you had asked me. But it was different again when I found out about you. And that day in the woods I thought something had come between us. Only after dinner you seemed kinder, and I knew at once you thought better of me, and might even seek me—I knew it in the way a woman knows things she doesn't know at all. I went into the library with a candle to look into the mirror, almost sure you were going to come. Then I heard your steps and I was so glad—but it wasn't you-I'd been mistaken again-you still disliked me. I was so disappointed and hurt and heartsick, and he kissed me and soothed me. And after that directly I saw through him, and I knew I truly did love you just as I'd wanted to love the man who would be my husband—only all that nonsense about money that had been dinned into me so long kept me from seeing it at first. But I was sure you didn't care for me when they talked so about you, and that—you never *did* care for her, did you—you *couldn't* have cared for her, could you?—and yet, after that night, I'd such a queer little feeling as if you *had* come for me, and had seen—"

"Surely a gentleman never sees anything he wasn't meant to see."

"I'm so glad—I should have been *so* ashamed—"

They were still a moment, while he stroked her hair.

"They'll be turning in early to-night, having to get up to-morrow and preach sermons—what a dreary place heaven must be compared with this!"

She sat up quickly.

"Oh, I'd forgotten. How awful it is. *Isn't* it awful?"

"It will soon be over."

"But think of my people, and what's expected of me—think of Mr. Shepler."

"Shepler's doing some hard thinking for himself by this time."

"Really, you're a dreadful person—"

There was a knock.

"The cabman outside, sir, says how long is he to wait, sir?"

"Tell him to wait all night if I don't come; tell him if he moves off that spot I'll have his license taken away. Tell him I'm the mayor's brother."

"Yes, sir."

"And, Jarvis, who's in the house besides you?"

"Miss Briggs, the maid, sir—but she's just ready to go out, sir."

"Stop her—say Miss Milbrey wishes to ask a favour of her; and Jarvis."

"Yes, sir!"

"Go put on that neat black street coat of yours that fits you so beautifully in the back, and a purple cravat, and your shiny hat, and wait for us with Briggs. We shall want you in a moment."

"Yes, Mr. Bines."

She looked at him wonderingly.

"We need two witnesses, you know. I learned that from Oldaker just now."

"But do give me a *moment*, everything is all so whirling and hazy."

"Yes, I know—like the solar system in its nebulous state. Well, hurry and make those worlds take shape. I can give you sixty seconds to find that I'm the North Star. Ach! I have the Doctor von Herzlich been ge-speaking with—come, come! What's the use of any more delay? I've wasted nearly three hours here now, dilly-dallying along. But then, a woman never does know her own mind.

"Put a thing before her—all as plain as the multiplication table—and she must use up just so much good time telling a man that he's crazy—and shedding tears because he won't admit that two times two are thirty-seven." She was silent and motionless for another five minutes, thinking intently. "Come, time's up."

She arose.

"I'm ready. I shall marry you, if you think I'm the woman to help you in that big, new life of yours. They meant me not to know about Fred's marriage until afterward."

He kissed her.

"I feel so rested and quiet now, as if I'd taken down a big old gate and let the peace rush in on me. I'm sure it's right. I'm sure I can help you."

She picked up her hat and gloves.

"Now I'll go bathe my eyes and fix my hair."

"I can't let you out of my sight, yet. I'm incredulous. Perhaps in seventy-five or eighty years—"

"I thought you were so sure."

"While I can reach you, yes."

She gave a low, delicious little laugh. She reached both arms up around him, pulled down his head and kissed him.

"There—*boy!*"

She took up the hat again.

"I'll be down in a moment."

"I'll be up in three, if you're not."

When she had gone he picked up an envelope and put a bill inside.

"Jarvis," he called.

The butler came up from below, dressed for the street.

"Jarvis, put this envelope in the inside of that excellent black coat of yours and hand it—afterward—to the gentleman we're going to do business with."

"Yes, Mr. Bines."

"And put your cravat down in the back, Jarvis—it makes you look excited the way it is now."

"Yes, sir; thank you, sir!"

"Is Briggs ready?" "She's waiting, sir."

"Go out and get in the carriage, both of you."

"Yes, sir!"

He stood in the hallway waiting for her. It was a quarter-past ten. In another moment she rustled softly down to him.

"I'm trusting so much to you, and you're trusting so much to me. It's *such* a rash step!"

"Must I—"

"No, I'm going. Couldn't we stop and take Aunt Cornelia?"

"Aunt Cornelia won't have a chance to worry about this until it's all over. We'll stop there then, if you like."

"We'll try Doctor Prendle, then. He's almost sure to be in."

"It won't make any difference if he isn't. We'll find one. Those horses are rested. They can go all night if they must."

"I have Grandmother Loekermann's wedding-ring—of course you didn't fetch one. Trust a man to forget anything of importance."

His grasp of her hand during the ride did not relax.

CHAPTER XLI.

The New Argonauts

Mrs. van Geist came flustering out to the carriage.

"You and Briggs may get out here, Jarvis. There, that's for you, and that's for Briggs—and thank you both very much!"

"Child, child! what does it mean?"

"Mr. Bines is my husband, Mütterchen, and we're leaving for the West in the morning."

The excitement did not abate for ten minutes or so. "And do say something cheerful, dear," pleaded Avice, at parting.

"You mad child—I was always afraid you might do something like this; but I *will* say I'm not altogether *sure* you've acted foolishly."

"Thank you, you dear old Mütterchen! and you'll come to see us—you shall see how happy I can be with this—this boy—this Lochinvar, Junior—I'm sure Mrs. Lochinvar always lived happily ever after."

Mrs. Van Geist kissed them both.

"Back to Thirty-seventh Street, driver."

"I shall want you at seven-thirty sharp, to-morrow morning," he said, as they alighted. "Will you be here, sure?"

"Sure, boss!"

"You'll make another one of those if you're on time."

The driver faced the bill toward the nearest street-light and scanned it. Then he placed it tenderly in the lining of his hat, and said, fervently:

"I'll *be* here, gent!"

"My trunks," Avice reminded him.

"And, driver, send an express wagon at seven sharp. Do you understand, now?"

"Sure, gent, I'll have it here at seven, and be here at seven-thirty."

They went in.

"You've sent Briggs off, and I've all that packing and unpacking to do."

"You have a husband who is handy at those things."

They went up to her room where two trunks yawned open.

Under her directions and with her help he took out the light summer things and replaced them with heavier gowns, stout shoes, golf-capes, and caps.

"We'll be up on the Bitter Root ranch this summer, and you'll need heavy things," he had told her.

Sometimes he packed clumsily, and she was obliged to do his work over. In these intervals he studied with interest the big old room and her quaint old sampler worked in coloured worsteds that had faded to greys and dull browns: *"La Nuit Porte Conseil."*

"Grandma Loekermann did it at the convent, ages ago," she told him.

"What a cautious young thing she must have been!"

She leaned against his shoulder.

"But she eloped with her true love, young Annekje Van Schoule; left the home in Hickory Street one night, and went far away, away up beyond One Hundred and Twenty-fifth Street, somewhere, and then wrote them about it."

"And left the sampler?"

"She had her husband—she didn't need any old sampler after that—*Le mariage porte conseil, aussi, monsieur.* And now, you've married your wife with her wedding-ring, that came from Holland years and years ago."

It was after midnight when they began to pack. When they finished it was nearly four.

She had laid out a dark dress for the journey, but he insisted that she put it in a suit-case, and wear the one she had on.

"I shouldn't know you in any other—and it's the colour of your eyes. I want that colour all over the place."

"But we shall be travelling."

"In our own car. That car has been described in the public prints as a 'suite of palatial apartments with all modern conveniences.'"

"I forgot."

"We shall be going West like the old '49-ers, seeking adventure and gold."

"Did they go in their private cars?"

"Some of them went in rolling six-horse Concords, and some walked, and some of them pushed their baggage across in little hand-carts, but they had fun at it—and we shall have to work as hard when we get there."

"Dear me! And I'm so tired already. I feel quite done up."

She threw herself on the wide divan, and he fixed pillows under her head.

"You boy! I'm glad it's all over. Let's rest a moment."

He leaned back by her, and drew her head on to his arm.

"I'm glad, too. It's the hardest day's work I ever did. Are you comfortable? Rest."

"It's so good," she murmured, nestling on his shoulder.

"Uncle Peter took his honeymoon in a big wagon drawn by a mule team, two hundred miles over the 'Placerville and Red Dog Trail—over the mountains from California to Nevada. But he says he never had so happy a time."

"He's an old dear! I'll kiss him—how is it you say—'good and plenty.' Did our Uncle Peter elope, too?"

He chuckled.

"Not exactly. It was more like abduction complicated with assault and battery. Uncle Peter is pretty direct in his methods. The young lady's family thought she could do better with a bloated capitalist who owned three-eighths of a saw-mill. But Uncle Peter and she thought she couldn't. So Uncle Peter had to lick her father and two brothers before he could get her away. He would have licked the purse-proud rival, too, but the rival ran into the saw-mill he owned the three-eighths of, and barricaded the whole eight-eighths—the-five-eighths that didn't belong to him at all, you understand—and then he threatened through a chink to shoot somebody if Uncle Peter didn't go off about his business. So Uncle Peter went, not wanting any unnecessary trouble. I've always suspected he was a pretty ready scrapper in those days, but the poor old fellow's getting a bit childish now, with all this trouble about losing the money, and the hard time he had in the snow last winter. By the way, I forgot to ask, and it's almost too late now, but do you like cats?"

"I adore them—aren't kittens the *dearest?*"

"Well—you're healthy—and your nose doesn't really fall below the specifications, though it doesn't promise that you're any *too* sensible,—but if you can make up for it by your infatuation for cats, perhaps it will be all right. Of course I couldn't keep you, you know, if you weren't very fond of cats, because Uncle Peter'd raise a row—"

She was quite still, and he noted from the change in her soft breathing that she slept. With his free hand he carefully shook out a folded steamer rug and drew it over her.

For an hour he watched her, feeling the arm on which she lay growing numb. He reviewed the day and the crowded night. He *could* do something after all. Among other things, now, he would drop a little note to Higbee and add the news of his marriage as a postscript. She was actually his wife. How quickly it had come. His heart was full of a great love for her, but he could not quite repress the pride in his achievement—and Shepler had not been sure until he was poor!

He lost consciousness himself for a little while.

When he awoke the cold light of the morning was stealing in. He was painfully cramped, and chilled from the open window. From outside came the loud chattering of sparrows, and far away he could hear wagons as they rattled across a street of Belgian blocks from asphalt to asphalt. The light had been late in coming, and he could see a sullen grey sky, full of darker clouds.

Above the chiffonier he could see the ancient sampler.

"La Nuit Porte Conseil." It was true.

In the cold, pitiless light of the morning a sudden sickness of doubting seized him. She would awake and reproach him bitterly for coercing her. She had been right, the night before,—it was madness. They had talked afterward so feverishly, as if to forget their situation. Now she would face it coldly after the sleep.

"La Nuit Porte Conseil." Had he not been a fool? And he loved her so. He would have her anyway—no matter what she said, now.

She stirred, and her wide-open eyes were staring up at him—staring with hurt, troubled wonder. The amazement in them grew—she could not understand.

He stopped breathing. His embrace of her relaxed.

And then he saw remembrance—recognition—welcome—and there blazed into her eyes such a look of whole love as makes men thrill to all good; such a look as makes them know they are men, and dare all great deeds to show it. Like a sunrise, it flooded her face with dear, wondrous beauties,— and still she looked, silent, motionless,—in an ecstasy of pure realisation. Then her arms closed about his neck with a swift little rushing, and he—

still half-doubting, still curious—felt himself strained to her. Still more closely she clung, putting out with her intensity all his misgiving.

She sought his lips with her own—eager, pressing.

"Kiss me—kiss me—kiss me! Oh, it's all true—all true! My best-loved dream has come all true! I have rested so in your arms. I never knew rest before. I can't remember when I haven't awakened to doubt, and worry, and heart-sickness. And now it's peace—dear, dear, dearest dear, for ever and ever and ever."

They sat up.

"Now we shall go—get me away quickly."

It was nearly seven. Outside the sky was still all gloom.

In the rush of her reassurance he had forgotten his arm. It hung limp from his shoulder.

"It was cramped."

"And you didn't move it?"

They beat it and kneaded it gaily together, until the fingers were full of the rushing blood and able again to close warmly over her own little hand.

"Now go, and let me get ready. I won't be long."

He went below to the library, and in the dim grey light picked up a book, "The Delights of Delicate Eating." He tried another, "101 Sandwiches." The next was "Famous Epicures of the 17th Century." On the floor was her diary. He placed it on the table. He heard her call him from the stairs:

"Bring me up that ring from the table, please!"

He went up and handed it to her through the narrowly opened door.

As he went down the stairs he heard the bell ring somewhere below, and went to the door.

"Baggage!"

The two trunks were down and out. "They're to go on this car, attached to the Chicago Express." He wrote the directions on one of his cards and paid the man.

At seven-thirty the bell rang again. The cabman was there.

"Seven-thirty, gent!"

"Avice!"

"I'm coming. And there are two bags I wish you'd get from my room." He let her pass him and went up for them.

She went into the library and, taking up the diary, tore out a sheet, marked heavily upon it with a pencil around the passage she had read the evening before, and sealed it in an envelope. She addressed it to her father, and laid it, with a paper-weight on it, upon "The Delights of Delicate Eating," where he would be sure to find it.

The book itself she placed on the wood laid ready in the grate to light, touched a match to the crumpled paper underneath and put up the blower. She stood waiting to see that the fire would burn.

Over the mantel from its yellow canvas looked above her head the humourously benignant eyes of old Annekje Van Schoule, who had once removed from Maspeth Kill on Long Island to New Haarlem on the Island of Manhattan, and carried there, against her father's will, the yellow-haired girl he had loved. His face now seemed to be pretending unconsciousness of the rashly acted scenes he had witnessed—lest, if he betrayed his consciousness, he should be forced, in spite of himself, to disclose his approval—a thing not fitting for an elderly, dignified Dutch burgher to do.

"Avice!"

"Coming!"

She took up a little package she had brought with her and went out to meet him.

"There's one errand to do," she said, as they entered the carriage, "but it's on our way. Have him go up Madison Avenue and deliver this."

She showed him the package addressed: "Mr. Rulon Shepler, Personal."

"And this," she said, giving him an unsealed note. "Read it, please!"

He read:

"DEAR RULON SHEPLER:—I am sure you know women too well to have thought I loved you as a wife should love her husband. And I know your bigness too well to believe you will feel harshly toward me for deciding that I could not marry you. I could of course consistently attribute my change to consideration for you. I should have been very little comfort to you. If I should tell you just the course I had mapped out for myself— just what latitude I proposed to claim—I am certain you would agree with me that I have done you an inestimable favour.

"Yet I have not changed because I do not love you, but because I do love some one else with all my heart; so that I claim no credit except for an entirely consistent selfishness. But do try to believe, at the same time, that my own selfishness has been a kindness to you. I send you a package with this hasty letter, and beg you to believe that I shall remain—and am now for the first time—

"Sincerely yours,

"AVICE MILBREY BINES.

"P.S. I should have preferred to wait and acquaint you with my change of intention before marrying, but my husband's plans were made and he would not let me delay."

He sealed the envelope, placed it securely under the cord that bound the package, and their driver delivered it to the man who opened Shepler's door. As their train emerged from the cut at Spuyten Duyvil and sped to the north along the Hudson, the sun blazed forth.

"There, boy,—I knew the sun must shine to-day."

They had finished their breakfast. One-half of the pink roses were on the table, and one from the other half was in her hair.

"I ordered the sun turned on at just this point," replied her husband, with a large air. "I wanted you to see the last of that town under a cloud, so you might not be homesick so soon."

"You don't know me. You don't know what a good wife I shall be."

"It takes nerve to reach up for a strange support and then kick your environment out from under you—as Doctor von Herzlich would have said if he'd happened to think of it."

"But you shall see how I'll help you with your work; I was capable of it all the time."

"But I had to make you. I had to pick you up just as I did that first time, and again down in the mine—and you were frightened because you knew this time I wouldn't let you go."

"Only half-afraid you wouldn't—the other half I was afraid you would. They got all mixed up—I don't know which was worse."

"Well, I admit I foozled my approach on that copper stock—but I won you—really my winnings in Wall Street are pretty dazzling after all, for a man who didn't know the ropes;—there's a mirror directly back of you, Mrs. Bines, if you wish to look at them—with a pink rose over that kissy place just at their temple."

She turned and looked, pretending to be quite unimpressed.

"I always was capable of it, I tell you,—boy!"

"What hurt me worst that night, it showed you could love *some* one—you did have a heart—but you couldn't love me."

She did not seem to hear at first, nor to comprehend when she went back over his words. Then she stared at him in sudden amazement.

He saw his blunder and looked foolish.

"I see—thank you for saying what you did last night—and you didn't mind—you came to me anyway, in spite of *that*."

She arose, and would have gone around the table to him, but he met her with open arms.

"Oh, you boy! you do love me,—you do!"

"I must buy you one of those nice, shiny black ear-trumpets at the first stop. You can't have been hearing at all well.... See, sweetheart,—out across the river. That's where our big West is, over that way—isn't it fresh and green and beautiful?—and how fast you're going to it—you and your husband. I believe it's going to be a good game... for us both... my love..."